I slipped in [illegible] own fall open sec[illegible] slipped involuntarily to my breasts.

'How about some unbridled passion and rampant sex?' I asked him shakily. Maybe I could do it. Detach the physical from the emotional. Maybe I was strong enough to separate love and lust and play him at his own game.

I kissed him before he could answer, pushing him back into the pillows and sliding my hand into his boxer shorts with the kind of all-in-one manoeuvre that I had only ever seen on TV.

'Wow!' said David when I let him up for air.

'Hmmm, maybe my hands are a little rough. Perhaps I ought to use some lubrication.'

'Lubrication!' sighed David, like it was a new word for fellatio.

I reached into the pocket of my dressing gown.

'Close your eyes,' I murmured seductively.

He obliged quite willingly.

I squirted a big dollop of Hot Stuff Heat Rub into my palm. It took just two firm strokes up and down before he opened his baby blue eyes with a hideous look of recognition that there is a very fine line between pleasure and pain.

Also by Chris Manby

Running Away from Richard
Lizzie Jordan's Secret Life
Second Prize
Flatmates

About the author

Chris Manby grew up in Gloucester and published her first short story in *Just Seventeen* at the age of fourteen. Now in her late twenties, she lives in London and writes full-time.

Deep Heat

Chris Manby

coronet

CORONET BOOKS
Hodder & Stoughton

First published in Great Britain in 1999
by Hodder and Stoughton
First published in Coronet paperback in 1999
by Hodder and Stoughton
A division of Hodder Headline

This Coronet paperback edition 2001

10 9 8 7 6

A CIP catalogue record for this title
is available from the British Library.

ISBN 0 340 71761 0

Printed and bound in Great Britain by
Mackays of Chatham PLC, Chatham, Kent

Hodder and Stoughton
A division of Hodder Headline
338 Euston Road
London NW1 3BH

To Kathryn Arnold

ACKNOWLEDGEMENTS

To the lovely Paul Drummond, for advice and inspiration and feigning interest in stupid questions. To my editor Kate, and to Ant and Natasha for their continued dedication to this cause. To the Lavender Hill Mob: Jane, Wendy, Mark and Jacqui but especially Ripley, for tea and other distractions during the 'fat book days'. To Peter Hamilton, the Delia Smith of science fiction, for friendship, advice and superb roast potatoes. To David Garnett for bringing up the 'L' word whenever I get complacent. To Guy Hazel for being my best friend from Battersea to Bombay. To Mum and Dad for their continued support and patience (I will get a mortgage next year, I promise). And to the rest of my family for the grass roots publicity (room for this one in Hucclecote Library, Uncle Roger?).

This book is dedicated to my sister Kate, who is far nicer than any of the sisters herein!!!

CHAPTER ONE

The week before Christmas just wasn't my week. It started like this. Two days before Christmas Eve, I was meandering down the fruit and veg aisle of Safeway, vaguely thinking that I ought to eat less spicy food, when my appendix burst on me. Pop! Just like a soap bubble. I can't begin to describe the pain. I fell to the floor like a blade of grass before a mower and lay writhing on the obligatory unidentifiable sticky patch you get on supermarket floors for a good ten minutes before someone asked me if anything was wrong. And then only because I was obstructing the avocados.

On the way to hospital I drifted in and out of consciousness. My name escaped me. My address escaped me. My date of birth escaped me. In fact everything escaped me but the fact that I was wearing uncoordinated underwear. (My mother had warned me about that more than once.)

Next thing I knew, I was propped up in a hospital bed, with a new scar on my abdomen and a bunch of yellow chrysanthemums on the bedside table. My mother, my father, my two kid sisters and my gorgeous fiancé David regarded me gravely from behind the white metal grill designed to stop me from falling out onto the floor in my stupor. As they swam into focus before my eyes, they said all the proper things that hospital visitors in television dramas say.

'She's coming round,' said my mother.

'Can you hear us, Ali-baby?'

'It's your father here, Alison. Do you remember me?'

'She's had her appendix out. She hasn't got amnesia,' said my youngest sister, Jo.

'Where am I?' I asked for effect.

'You're in the Brindlesham General Hospital,' said my father. 'You've just had your appendix out.'

I thought that was what Jo had just said.

'The nurse said you can have it in a jar if you like,' Jo added gleefully.

'My appendix? Whaaaa?' I felt a vague aching sensation as I hooked up my nightdress, much to my mother's disgust, and inspected the wound. Well, I inspected the fat wad of cotton wool and surgical tape that was covering it.

'What did they do that for?' I asked. 'And how big is the scar?'

A girl knows her priorities.

'It's all right, darling. The scar will be barely noticeable.'

I recognised that big strong hand on my arm. David, my fiancé, leant in to kiss me on the cheek. 'You had us all very very worried,' he continued. 'For a minute back there I thought I was going to have to get a refund on the engagement ring.'

I laughed. Painfully.

'But you're getting better now,' said my mother,

rearranging my nightdress so that it covered my belly-button once more. 'The doctor says you should be out of here by Christmas Eve. Thank goodness. Not that they don't do their best to make things festive in this hospital, God bless them, but the Christmas decorations in here are terrible.' My mother had recently thrown out a box full of family heirlooms in favour of a tremendously naff fully coordinated tree ensemble in silver and navy blue glitter.

'I brought you these,' said my sister Jane, thrusting a box of Ferrero Rocher in my direction. David looked at them accusingly. I had promised to give up all chocolate (and pretty much everything else that makes life worth living) until I was a comfortable size twelve again. For the wedding, you understand. Still, I figured I must have lost at least a box of chocolates' worth of weight in the shape of my appendix so I accepted the gift with more than good grace.

'Thanks. Can I eat these yet?' I asked the first nurse to pass by.

'I see she's getting better already,' the nurse commented before she added: 'Only two visitors per bed.'

Because they couldn't make their minds up about which two should stay, all my visitors suddenly departed at once. It only really dawned on me then that I was sitting in a hospital. I tried to piece together my journey to this shining white ward in which I found myself. I remembered squeezing a Galia melon. I remembered a feeling deep in my insides like excruciatingly bad wind. The sticky patch. The uncoordinated undies nightmare. No more.

I was wearing one of my own nighties now at least.

* * *

But so much for Mum's promise that I would be out for Christmas Eve. On the afternoon of the twenty-third, my surgeon, the painfully handsome Mr Hedley, decided that he wasn't happy with the way I was healing and prescribed another couple of days in bed, just in case. As the Christmas holiday approached, anyone fit enough to stagger to the hospital door was pointed in that direction, leaving only me and a yellow-haired woman called Marina, who had just had a hysterectomy, in Daffodil Ward for the duration.

Marina's husband visited up to four times a day with their toddling children, Tim and Milly. He looked harassed. The children looked hyperactively delighted in the way that children who are being looked after by their father and have been given free access to additives do. When they had departed for what seemed like the third time in an hour, Marina staggered across to my bed, with her saline drip in tow.

'Bless him,' she began. 'He's only gone and brought me all the same magazines he brought me last week. Do you want them?' She dropped a pile onto my legs and I winced in anticipation, even though she had just about managed to miss my scar.

'Thanks,' I said, flipping through the pages of the top one.

It was called *Complete Woman*. It had a carefully air-brushed thirty-something model on the cover, flinging back her head and laughing to reveal zero fillings (though she probably just had lots of those white ones). The pages inside were packed with ideas for the holiday period ahead. Extra special mince pies (add a couple of cashew nuts and some extra jellied peel). Make your own Christmas crackers (but make sure you buy specially manufactured toilet roll innards for the purpose because you don't want to give your children e-coli). Decorate your tree in this year's most fashionable colours (silver and navy blue – so that's where Mum got it from).

'I've got *Cosmo* over there too,' Marina told me. 'I'd lend you that now but the sex quiz might split your stitches.'

'Thanks,' I said. 'I think *Complete Woman*'s my limit.'

Between lunch and tea-time I learned about rag-rolling and appliqué. Though my usual approach to magazines was to flick through them backwards quickly and read the problem pages first, I was aware that I was surviving on limited resources and so I read every single boring word. Even the whole index. My family wouldn't be visiting that night, since they would all be at Auntie Katherine's Christmas Eve jamboree. David wouldn't be popping in either. He had been in that morning, with a poinsettia for my bedside table. (You know, I really hate those things.)

'I feel terrible about you being stuck in here over Christmas,' David told me as he cleared a space on my bedside table for the miserable-looking pot-plant.

'It's OK,' I said bravely. 'The nurses have been wearing Father Christmas hats today. I'm sure we'll have a wonderful time.'

'Well, if it's any consolation I won't be going to

the party at The Rotunda tonight,' he said gravely. 'I couldn't possibly go along without you.'

The Rotunda was one of our favourite haunts. It was one of those newly refurbished pub/club/sizzling platter-type places with oars, brooms and bicycle wheels, in fact with everything but the kitchen sink, hanging off the walls. (The kitchen sink was hanging from the wall in the ladies.) Anyway, in the absence of anything better to do, The Rotunda was Brindlesham's hottest night-spot and it had sold out of tickets for its extravagant Christmas Eve bash in late September.

'Don't be silly,' I told David. 'You've got to go to The Rotunda. You've been looking forward to tonight for months.'

'I know. But I couldn't possibly enjoy myself. Not with you in hospital. It wouldn't be right.'

'I don't mind,' I said in frustration, hating to seem the party-pooper. 'You go.'

'How can I enjoy myself, thinking of you all alone in this sterile ward?'

'The tickets cost ten pounds each,' I said. 'You go.'

'You're right,' he said suddenly. 'They did cost ten pounds. No point wasting all that money. Perhaps I should go after all.'

My mouth dropped open in surprise. That was wrong. He was meant to hold out until I suggested that he might like to sit in the ward all night with me instead.

'You don't mind, do you?' he checked one last time.

What could I say now? Actually, I do.

'No, I don't mind,' I said wearily, as I picked a dead leaf off the fading Christmas rose. 'You have a good time.'

'I'll sell your ticket to someone else and bring you the money tomorrow. How about that?'

'Thanks.'

What a consolation!

David left with obscene haste.

That night, as it drew close to seven o'clock, the moment when The Rotunda would open its doors for the bacchanalian festivities to begin, I started to find it difficult to concentrate on *Complete Woman*'s suggestions for the best way to serve your Christmas pudding. On the other side of the ward, Marina was already asleep and snoring lightly. I could hear the nightnurses in the corridor, laughing about something or other. Probably my cellulite.

Up until that particular Christmas Eve I had been one of those lucky people who viewed the impending holiday as a happy time, a time for families to be together, a time for loved ones to show each other how much they care with cards and great big presents. Right then, I felt about as happy at the approach of Christmas as the people who lived in the cardboard city underneath the motorway bridge. No, make that slightly less happy. They probably had some booze to hand.

I slipped the hospital radio headphones over my ears and listened to the last of the Christmas dedications. Perhaps David had asked them to play something special for me? But the DJ soon signed off for the evening with that terrible Slade Christmas classic that even your granny headbangs along to. No message from David. No last-minute visit on his way out to the pub. The nightnurse brought me my tablets and switched off the main ward lights.

I couldn't sleep of course. Not while I knew that the world and his whippet were out there having such a good time. I turned on the little light above my bed and buried myself in *Complete Woman*'s five minute fiction slot. I finished that in three minutes. There were only the puzzles left. The puzzles and the 'fantastic annual competition' (their words, not mine).

Are you the United Kingdom's Most Romantic Couple? the headline asked. *If you think that you and your partner are the most romantic couple in Britain, then why not let* Complete Woman *Magazine and Super Sunshine Tours celebrate your wonderful relationship by taking you both on the holiday of a lifetime? The fabulous all-inclusive resort of Santa Bonita on the beautiful island of Antigua awaits your arrival. Seal your love with a kiss on the golden sands of the hotel's own private beach, Royale Bay. Whisper those sweet nothings beneath a fabulous Caribbean sunset. All you have to do is tell us what makes your relationship so special (in less than 500 words).*

I looked at the photograph of the fabulous Santa Bonita resort. I looked wistfully at the glittering white-gold sand and the sparkling blue sea of Royale Bay. I gazed longingly at the charming little wooden huts that nestled right on the beach (each with its own *en suite* bathroom and coffee-making facilities). I thought I could use some of that.

At the bottom of the page was a small photograph of two people locked in a close embrace. *Shandy Evans and her fiancé Tom Devonshire were last year's winners of the* Complete Woman *Most Romantic Couple competition,* read the caption. *They enjoyed a wonderful, two week long, all-inclusive holiday courtesy of Lion King Tours in South Africa. Shandy and Tom were married in Shandy's local parish church in June of this year.*

There followed an extract of the winning entry which had convinced the judges that Shandy and Tom had such a beautiful thing together. 'He makes me a cup of tea every morning without even being asked,' Shandy wrote. 'He fixes my car and puts up shelves and things while I'm stuck doing the ironing. He makes me feel like I am the only woman in the world.'

'Aw, come on, Shandy,' I murmured to myself. 'That's not a good enough reason. He must have a ginormous cock or something as well.'

On the other side of the ward, Marina stirred in her sleep. I continued to read Shandy's testimony but resisted any further urge to comment out loud. But Shandy made no mention of Tom's physical attributes at all if he had any. It seemed that the secret of his romantic success really did lie in his ability to pull his weight in the kitchen. When I had finished reading, I put the article down for a moment and waited until I was sure that I was no longer in danger of gagging on Shandy's sickly sweet words before I dare read the competition rules.

And to think she had won a holiday in South Africa for that piece of unadulterated slush! I could do far better, I thought. Yeah, I could do far far better than that.

Outside, a few icy raindrops pattered against the window. There was no doubt that we were right in the middle of a long hard winter but, ignoring the wind and the freezing rain, I fixed my mind on the idea of two sunny weeks in Antigua, 'the island with a beach for every day of the year', and started to write on the back of a paper bag.

If I couldn't be with David that night, I could at least still think of him. Of his soft brown eyes and his fluffy, curly hair . . . Of his handsome smile and his infectious laugh . . . I could even think of his strong manly arms flexing as he deftly unscrewed the u-bend or nailed up a brand-new shelf for my cuddly toy collection if that was what it would take to win that holiday in the sun. Five hundred words to sing his praises? I needed five thousand! But I would give an edited version my best shot.

'I always thought that love was just something other people sang about, until I met David,' I began.

I made three rough drafts before I dared write out my final version on the official coupon in the magazine. Then, tearing the page out as neatly as I could, I slipped myself painfully out of bed and staggered towards the nightnurse's desk. She had a good supply of envelopes and, amazingly, she also had a single first class stamp in her handbag. I asked her if it was unusual for patients to ask for a stamp in the middle of the night. She told me that a man on the genito-urinary ward had once asked her for a blow-job.

The nurse promised to post the entry for me as soon as she clocked off her shift that night. I climbed back into bed with a couple of sleeping pills and soon forgot all about it.

Next day, Mum and Dad arrived to see me as soon as the hospital was open for business. Apparently Jo and Jane were still sleeping off the Christmas Eve jamboree. Jo had made an idiot of herself at Midnight Mass. Again.

Mum and Dad watched me eagerly as I unwrapped my presents. Three satsumas, slightly squashed. A large box of bath salts in English lavender (good for disguising the smell of kitty litter – but I didn't tell them that). A new nightie (black watch tartan with a black velvet collar and ribbon trim, Mary Queen of Scots might have worn one the night before she lost her head).

'Thought that one you were wearing the other day looked a wee bit see-through,' Mum explained.

And a matching wash-bag.

'How thoughtful!' I exclaimed.

'Now you need never be unprepared when you have to go into hospital again,' said Mum triumphantly, as she plumped up my pillows.

I wasn't exactly planning a return trip anytime soon. But parents always buy you those boring useful presents, don't they? Christmas for me was about the gift that David would bring. (Oh, and the little baby Jesus, naturally.) What would David have bought me, I wondered as I unwrapped three more chocolate oranges from Dad. Jewellery, perfume, a couple of CDs? A totally see-through nightdress perhaps?

On the other side of the ward, Marina was holding up, and actually cooing over, another tartan nightie, identical to mine. It was from her husband. Still, it wasn't as if she was planning to have another kid . . .

'Did David call at all?' I asked, when I had heard

about Jo's drunken Midnight Mass misdemeanours at least four times. (Loud hiccups during the prayers. Falling flat on her face when she went to take communion. The kind of behaviour you'd expect from a teenager who'd been on the Baileys all night.)

'David?' asked Mum. 'Why should he have called us?'

'Well, I thought he might have done. To find out how I'm getting on. He hasn't called me here.'

'I'm sure he'll be in to see you later on,' said Mum. 'He's probably planning a great big surprise.'

But lunchtime soon passed and he still hadn't turned up. I ate just two mouthfuls of the hospital's abridged version of Christmas dinner. The turkey stuffing had obviously been made from shredded medical records.

My hopes were raised briefly at two in the afternoon when Sister Martin drew back the curtain around my bed (I was protecting myself from Marina's kids' new table-tennis-ball guns) and announced that I had a visitor. But it wasn't David. It was my flatmate Emma. My face fell in disappointment.

'What are you doing here?' I asked.

'Well, don't look so pleased to see me,' she said as she arranged herself at the foot of my bed.

'Aren't you supposed to be having lunch with your folks?'

'Do you think I would miss an opportunity to get out of having to stand up for the whole of the Queen's speech?' Emma replied.

'Oh, so your Auntie Mavis made it then?'

'Yep. The orderlies from her funeral home wheeled her through the door as soon as dawn broke this morning. It's all right for her, insisting we stand up for the Queen. She doesn't have to. She sends her love, by the way. And this present. Seeing as how you're an invalid.'

Emma flicked a little square parcel onto the bed. I opened it without any real enthusiasm, knowing it would be monogrammed handkerchiefs. Emma's Auntie Mavis must have had a franchise in the things.

'Aw. What's up?' Emma joked. 'Wrong colour? Never mind. I've got you something much more exciting in here.' She reached into her bag again and this time came out with a long thin parcel that looked altogether much more interesting. I snatched it from her and felt all the way up and down the wrapping paper, trying to guess what it might be.

'Hmm,' I said. 'It's not by any chance that beautiful single rose vase I saw in Liberty is it?'

'Get real,' said Emma. 'Unwrap it for heaven's sake.'

I ripped off the paper and soon wished I hadn't. Marina's youngest, Timmy aged five, had joined us to see me open my presents.

'What is it?' he asked as my mouth dropped open in horror. 'Does it need batteries or can you play with it straightaway?'

Why did I have to have the most embarrassing flatmate in the world?

'What is it for?' he asked again, all innocence, as I tried to rewrap the 'Black Beauty stimulator' in the scraps of paper I had unfortunately torn beyond usefulness. 'Show me what it is,' he pleaded. 'And I'll show you mine.'

'It's for gardening,' said Emma quickly. 'Digging holes. Can I have a look at your gun instead?'

He solemnly handed over the table-tennis-ball firer

while I secreted the big black vibrator beneath my pillow.

'You're dead, Emma Wilson,' I told her.

'Yeah. You're dead!!' mimicked Timmy, snatching back the gun and popping Emma in the eye with a ping pong ball before returning to his mother for a slap.

'What on earth did you buy me that horrible thing for?' I asked her testily as she checked the damage to her contact lens.

'Every girl should have one,' Emma explained.

'But I've got a fiancé.'

'So. Use it to spice things up a little.'

'Things between us are quite spicy enough,' I said, just a little too smugly.

'Well, save it for a rainy day then. What did you get me?'

'I got you what you asked for,' I replied tartly. 'That silver glitter clutch bag you wanted so much is at the bottom of my wardrobe. Didn't have time to wrap it, I'm afraid.'

'Wow, Ali,' said Emma. 'I'll go straight home and get it now. Thanks a million. That's a fantastic present.'

'Yeah. Good job I don't give to receive.'

Emma soon left to retrieve her proper pressie and feed our shared cat, Fattypuss. At four o'clock the nurses brought round Christmas cake. My sisters Jo and Jane, just about recovered from their traditional seasonal hangovers, had smuggled in a piece of Mum's own cake which I ate instead, since I suspected that the hospital cook had his own unorthodox plans for reducing the hospital waiting list.

'What did David get you?' Jo asked excitedly, as she stuffed two chocolate fondant penguins into her mouth at once.

'He hasn't been to see me yet,' I told them, feeling strangely embarrassed by the admission.

'What? The selfish pig. Leaving you all on your own in hospital on Christmas Day. I expect he got totally rat-arsed at The Rotunda last night and he still hasn't woken up. It was a good night by all accounts. The police had to come out three times. And I'll be old enough to go next year,' Jo added proudly.

'I'm sure he's just got family obligations,' said Jane more reasonably.

'Yeah. You're right. The fact that it's Christmas and I'm in hospital isn't going to stop his mother being an old dragon,' I said, forcing a laugh. 'She's probably making him sit at the dinner table until he's finished his cold Brussels sprouts or something equally hideous.'

'OK. So what do you think he's bought you?' Jo persisted. 'You must have some idea.'

'Jewellery, I hope,' I told them. 'Though perfume would be acceptable, since he's so recently splashed out on a ring.' I gave my sparkler an affectionate little polish on the bedspread. 'As long as it's not that new CK stuff though. I hate that. Smells like Jif.'

In actual fact, he bought me a battered box of Milk Tray chocolates from the little 'Friends of Brindlesham General Hospital' shop in the lobby downstairs.

It was half-past-eight when David finally arrived and I had been fighting back tears since my sisters departed at six. As he walked into the ward, I noticed straightaway that he looked different somehow; as if someone had taken my David, sucked out his shining soul and replaced it with something altogether shiftier overnight. He sat down carefully on the edge of my bed, put the chocolates on the table and didn't even look me in the eye.

'Merry Christmas,' I said, pulling myself up painfully so that I could kiss him.

'Merry Christmas,' he replied, as if it was some kind of Resistance password.

'I thought you'd forgotten me,' I said light-heartedly, trying not to show my disappointment at the dreadful gift. 'I'm afraid I haven't got a present to give you, darling. What with the operation and all that, I haven't really had time to do much Christmas shopping.'

'That's OK.' He looked strangely relieved.

'Thanks for the chocolates,' I told him. 'Though I thought I wasn't allowed to eat them, because of . . . you know,' I patted my tummy.

'You can eat whatever you like,' he said.

There was definitely something wrong.

'Did you have a nice time at The Rotunda?' I persisted. 'Did you manage to sell my ticket?'

'Oh. Yeah.' He fumbled in his jacket pocket for his wallet and pulled out a crumpled tenner.

'Thanks. Did you sell it to anyone I know?' I asked.

'Actually,' said David sheepishly. 'I sold it to Lisa Brown.'

'Lisa Brown?'

You know that point in hospital movies where the patient gets a terrible shock and goes reaching for the emergency button? Well, this was one of those.

'Lisa Brown?' I shrieked again.

'Lisa Brown,' he said flatly.

What's the problem with Lisa Brown, you ask?

'Lisa Brown, your ex-fiancée?' I asked.

'Yes,' he said.

'Well,' I tried to take this bad news reasonably. 'At least you're on speaking terms with her again.'

'Yes,' he said.

'Must be very hard for her,' I continued. 'Seeing you again after all these years. After all the heartbreak and embarrassment that must have followed your broken engagement. I'm surprised she didn't just thump you on the nose with her handbag.'

'Yes,' he said. He had dumped Lisa Brown for me.

'Was she with anybody?' I asked, longing to hear that she was with a strapping six-foot-five rugby player and that she was heavily pregnant with their first child.

'No. At least, she wasn't with anybody when she arrived,' said David.

'What do you mean by that?' I asked suspiciously.

'I'm afraid that she came home with me.'

Push the panic button. Push the panic button!

'You gave her a lift?' I asked. Best case scenario.

'Sort of.'

'To her place?'

'To my place.'

'To your place?' It was like a conversation between two people who didn't really understand English.

'Alison,' said David, taking a deep breath. 'I'm afraid I've got to tell you that she stayed the night with me.'

'What?!' I did press the panic button that time.

'She stayed the night?' I shouted. 'With you?! Lisa Brown slept with you in your flat? In your bed? Please, no.' Marina got her husband to prop her up in bed so that she could get a better view of the fight. 'What on earth were you thinking of, David? What on earth will people say?'

'I'm sorry. I don't know what I was thinking of. In fact I still don't know what I am thinking of now. Alison, I think perhaps we need to spend some time apart for a while,' he blurted the ugly words out.

'Spend some time apart? What do you mean? We haven't got time to spend time apart. We're supposed to be getting married in April.'

'Alison, I don't think I can . . .'

The nurse had arrived at the foot of my bed.

'What's the matter?' she asked briskly. 'Are you in pain, Alison? Where does it hurt?'

'Here?' I said, pointing to my head. 'And here.' My heart. 'And here.' My appendix for good measure. As the nurse bustled in to rearrange my pillows, David stood up and started to leave.

'David,' I called after him. 'David, where do you think you're going? You can't just walk away from me like this. Not having said those horrible things. Not while I'm still stuck here in this bed. And it's Christmas. What about that?'

'I'm sorry, Ali. I've got to go,' he told me sadly. 'I left Lisa sitting outside in the car.'

CHAPTER TWO

What a difference a day makes. One day I was a girl with an appendix and a fiancé, the next I was merely a girl without an appendix.

When it finally became clear that David really hadn't been playing some twisted practical joke on me, I got the nurse to call my mother and had her abandon the turkey to come in and sit beside her eldest daughter's bed all night long. I was in far worse shape than I had been when my faulty appendix was actually leaking poison into my body. I cried so much that I was threatened with another saline drip.

'How could he do this to me?' was a pretty much constant refrain of mine over the next two days in that bed.

'I always knew this would happen,' replied Mum wisely. 'Because,' (pick and mix your reasons from the following extensive list) 'he wasn't mature enough for the commitment of marriage, his mother still has too much control over him, he thinks he's too good to be part of the Harris family, he's just like his arrogant father and his eyes are too close together.' I had to take issue on the last part.

Jo, sitting at the bottom of my bed and eating the grapes bought for my convalescence, agreed with Mum.

'No, it's true, Ali. His eyes are way too close together,' she told me. 'And the Chinese physiognomy book I got out of the library last week says that squinty eyes are a tell-tale sign of a selfish mind.'

'Well, thank goodness for that,' I said sarcastically. 'Sounds like I've had a lucky escape.'

How long before it started to feel that way too?

I wasn't feeling too much better when, a week after Christmas, the doctor announced that it was time for me to leave Brindlesham General. Someone much much sicker than I was already on a trolley in the corridor waiting for my bed to become vacant.

When I returned to my little flat, Emma had thoughtfully turned all my framed photographs of David face down on the dressing table so that I wouldn't have to look at him. It wasn't until I dared turn one the right way up three weeks later that I discovered she had also given him devil's horns and a Hitler moustache with thick black felt-tip pen.

My boss, Mr Chivers, very kindly allowed me an extended period of convalescence. I went into self-inflicted purdah for a fortnight, never stepping out of the house or even drawing open my curtains. Luckily all I needed to survive was chocolate, biscuits and fags and Emma was only too happy to oblige. It made her feel as though she was helping my recovery, without meaning that she had to go out of her way to buy vegetables or heavy healthy stuff like that.

I got to know the Teletubbies intimately in that time and, towards the end of the fortnight, even the complicated relationships in *Home and Away* started to make some sense. When I looked in the mirror and saw my sunken cheeks, I started to imagine romantically that I was the Lady of Shallot, doomed to pine until I died. (But no, I didn't turn to Black Beauty, Christmas present from hell.) Every time the telephone or doorbell rang, I would be shot through with a glimmer of hopeless hope that made my desertion all the more difficult to take when the caller turned out to be Mum with an emergency steak and kidney pie to stop me from 'fading away'.

But even a mother's love can only be stretched so far. Just four weeks after the op, and David's terrible announcement that his mother had been right all along – Lisa Brown was better than me – my family and friends adopted a policy of zero tolerance towards tears and self-pity. I was sent back to work. OK, I had been hurt, everyone agreed. And things still looked terrible from where I was sitting. But bills needed to be paid, and I was not an invalid. Physically, at least.

Some people, including my mother, even thought that going back to work might take my mind off the terrible disasters that had befallen me since that fateful trip to Safeway. Easy enough to say, if you've never had the misfortune to work as a floating secretarial assistant at the Hudderston Heavy Engineering Co. (purveyors of fine bits of metal covered in grease). Frankly, I would have given dear old Fattypuss to a fur coat factory if someone could have found me something different to do with my nine-to-five. Unfortunately, interesting jobs in Brindlesham were as rare as hen's teeth.

On the morning of my return to the office, I woke up at four a.m. in a cold sweat and couldn't get back to sleep no matter how much calming camomile I chucked down my neck. It was not unlike the feeling I got the morning I started secondary school. Only this time, my colleagues were a known quantity. Back when I was eleven I at least had the excuse of being justifiably scared by the burly fifth formers I had seen smoking behind the bus station.

'It's OK,' said Emma, over breakfast. 'It will be fine. Everyone will be understanding.' My mother had already taken the rather unwelcome step of calling the Managing Director's secretary, Julie Adams, to explain to her just how badly I had been hit by the whole David affair. And my appendectomy.

'Julie was very sympathetic,' my mother assured me.

I'll bet she was! Had my mother never heard the term 'crocodile tears'? There was no love lost between me and Julie Adams. Though as children, we had almost been best friends.

Julie Adams and I had lived on same road and been in the same year at junior school but at the age of eleven, when some horrific fluke sent me to the local girls' grammar while she went to the secondary modern, our friendship seemed to wane.

Julie quickly acquired the sophisticated patina of a life ill-spent. She would hang about with her new friends in the alley by the corner shop, while I rushed home to do my geography homework. They didn't set much homework at Julie's school after the father of one of the boys brought his Rottweiler in to explain how difficult bloody algebra was for his poor child.

Mum quickly decided that Julie was in with the wrong crowd and that I wasn't to have anything more to do with her. Her opinion was vindicated weekly by tales of smoking and shoplifting from the woman who ran the corner shop.

'She came from such a good family,' my mother would gloatingly lament. Until that dreadful week in my third year when I decided that the wrath of my mother would be infinitely preferable to the sneers and goadings of the Brindlesham Comp schoolgirls when I got off the bus in my shiny-elbowed St Olive's blazer.

Tired of being called a scaredy-cat snob, I rashly told Julie that I wasn't afraid to go shoplifting with her. (In fact I was terrified.) She called my bluff, of course, and, that very afternoon, we went to the notoriously insecure changing rooms in Brindlesham's Top Shop and slipped on bright yellow tube skirts beneath our school skirts (this was the early eighties) with the intention of walking out without paying for them. Julie had done it a dozen times before, she told me. And Top Shop was great for beginners. The bored-looking assistants never counted how many garments you took into the changing rooms and they certainly wouldn't lift your skirt to see how many you were taking out again.

With the tube skirt safely stashed beneath my regulation navy A-line pleated number, I stood alone in my cubicle taking deep, deep breaths. I shouldn't do it, I told myself. If I got caught the agony would be endless. But I had to do it. If I didn't do it, Julie's mates would probably nick my school tie and drape it around the highest point in the bus shelter. With me in it, if I was very unlucky. At the very least I would be going home without my bus money.

'Aren't you ready yet?' hissed Julie through the curtain. 'If you come out now we might make it to the door without seeing any assistants. The manageress is on the phone. Let's leg it.'

It was so carefully planned out. Julie had done it so many times before. Nothing could possibly go wrong. So I picked up my neat little satchel and followed Julie out into the main body of the store. We chucked the things that we weren't going to nick onto the rail by the changing room door and started our escape.

'Nonchalant!' Julie whispered loudly. 'Look nonchalant, Ali. And take your time. Have a gander at the jewellery on your way out or something.'

I took a quick, anguished peek at the price tag on a set of fluorescent plastic bangles. Then a doubly anguished glance in the direction of the till told me that the manageress had put down the phone and was walking towards me. She knew I was nicking something. In actual fact, she probably didn't, but wanted to make sure that I didn't purloin any bangles. I dropped the bangles immediately and scuttled after Julie, who had already made it into the sunshine and was poised to do a Linford Christie all the way home.

'Leg it!' she shouted. Giving the game away immediately. If it hadn't already been blown by the fact that the tube skirt I had chosen was three sizes too large and had suddenly decided to make its way down to my ankles. Tripped by my bounty in quite spectacular style, I ended up crashing down, to land with my chin on an artfully arranged display of cerise kitten-heel slingbacks, right in the middle of the shop's picture window.

Julie and her tough-girl friends looked on in horror from the safety of the record shop on the other side of the road, as I was bodily lifted to my feet and taken to the back of the shop for interrogation. It must have been obvious that I was a first timer, as I cried for my mummy, and then had to beg with the manageress not to call her. She would be so disappointed. I was the first person in our family to get grade three piano.

'And you from the grammar school,' said the manageress, as if that might have made me immune to the two evil forces of fashion and peer pressure.

Unfortunately, my tearful display didn't manage to dissuade her from calling the police. It may well have been my first time, she said, but I had to be made an example of. I sat stiffly on that stool at the back of the shop for a full hour before the local bobby arrived to take me home. As he marched me to his liveried Mini Metro, I hung my head in shame. The entire town seemed to have gathered on the pavement outside Top Shop to watch me being taken away. At the very least, the policeman might have offered me a blanket to cover up my head.

By the time the police car drew up outside our house, Mum was already in hysterics because I had promised to be home by four thirty and it was now getting on for half-past six. She was mortified when the policeman asked if he might have a word about her daughter's delinquent tendencies.

I wasn't charged. I got off with a warning. But in Mum and Dad's eyes I had called down shame upon the Harris name and they wanted to mete out their own punishment. They cancelled my subscription to *Just Seventeen* and took away all my pocket money. Added to that, I wasn't allowed out of the house for six weeks, except to go to school and Mum escorted me both ways to make sure I couldn't get up to anything on that short trip either.

By the time I was allowed out on parole, all my chances of getting in with Julie's hard-nut gang had been blown. They had decided that I had nearly sent them all to Holloway with my pathetic first shoplifting attempt and now called me 'stool pigeon', a reference to the stool at the back of the shop and the Kid Creole song rather than anything clever, amongst the usual barrage of accusations that my navy blue uniform made me a snob. Oh, and a lesbian.

Anyway, Julie left school at sixteen to join the youth training scheme at the Hudderston Heavy Engineering Co. I rather smugly thought myself doing better than her when I left Brindlesham to go to university in Sussex. But six months after graduating with a degree in photography and catering management and with no real prospect of graduate employment on the horizon, I had to go cap in hand to Hudderston Heavy Engineering for a temp job in their typing pool. In the meantime, Julie had worked her way up to the heady heights of secretary to the MD. A position that was accompanied by a decent typing chair, a colour screen on her computer, and all the Karen Millen suits she could wear.

She was wearing her red brocade one when I arrived at work that first morning after my operation. She had done her nails and lipstick to match, of course.

'All right, Ali?' she cooed, slinging a protective arm around my shoulders as she led me to my desk, though I hadn't actually forgotten where it was in the four short weeks I had been away.

'You just take it easy today, darling,' she said, pointing towards my in-tray, which looked as though it was going for the *Guinness Book of Records* biggest pile of crap in an in-tray entry. 'And let me know if it all starts getting too much for you. There's always a friendly ear for you in my office,' she added.

I sat down and flicked aimlessly through the top quarter of my typing pile. Julie had stopped en route to her office to gossip with Irene from accounts.

'Yeah. Well, she'll be better now that she's surrounded by her friends,' I heard her say.

Friends? What friends? I hadn't had any that I knew of at Hudderston Heavy Engineering when it came to the whip-round for my birthday. Two Walnut Whips and a card from the corner shop. Pathetic.

'All right?' said Irene as she too passed me by. Maybe they were just being concerned, I told myself. But I had a sneaky suspicion that a jilted fiancée recovering from a complicated appendectomy was up there with a serious road traffic accident in the entertainment stakes. People like to be reminded that other people are having an even shittier time than themselves, I suppose.

Emma called me halfway through the morning.

'All right?' she asked.

'Please don't ask me if I am all right,' I snapped. 'Because if one more person asks me if I'm all right . . . I shall have to . . . I shall have to . . .' I sniffed loudly. 'Cry!'

Julie was upon me like a vulture, tissue in one hand and big ears at the ready.

'Tell me all about it,' she insisted. 'I might be able to help.'

'Not unless you can hypnotise David Whitworth and convince him to come back to me.'

'Maybe it's for the best. I always say, if it isn't meant to be, it isn't meant to be. There's no point pushing it. David was too good for you,' she said, adding quickly, 'I mean you're far too good for him, Ali.'

I suspected that the former was more than a slip of the tongue. Julie had been on David's case for years, ever since his family moved into the area, bringing David, aged fifteen, and already with a fluffy little moustache staining his top lip, to become the heart-throb of pretty much all the teenage girls in our neighbourhood. The bus stop near our house had been plastered with hastily scrawled notices to the fact that Julie loved him, that they were '4 ever'. As far as I knew, it had never actually happened.

'Time is a great healer,' Julie continued. 'And there are plenty more fish in the sea. A watched pot never boils,' she also added incongruously. 'Perhaps you should come out for a drink with us, after work,' she said. 'It's all too easy to lose touch with your friends when you're in a relationship and then find yourself all alone, but we'll forgive you for that,' smiled Julie. Irene nodded. 'We'll let you back into our gang. Let's go somewhere tonight. There's a new bar opened up by the bus station. It's one of them places with all the pine furniture. Classy. You can get wine if you want it. Chardonnay and everything. What do you say, Ali? We can talk about old times.'

I had a terrible feeling that it was going to be the shoplifting thing all over again.

CHAPTER THREE

I didn't want to go but I figured that I had to. If I didn't, I would continue to be labelled as stand-offish and snobby. And perhaps it wouldn't be so bad, I tried to convince myself. I could have a couple of glasses of wine and race home in time for *EastEnders*. But no such luck. When work finished, Julie announced that we weren't going to be going to the classy winebar after all. We were going to go to 'Top Hat's Discotheque', the one and only discotheque in the area that got passed over in the 1980s flurry of refurbishment that turned most other clubs into half-decent establishments.

I dragged myself along behind Irene and Julie like a toddler being marched around British Home Stores. Once we had struggled through the door and the unnecessarily frisky security men, Julie hustled me straight into the loos. I only just got out of having to have bright silver lips by claiming that I was allergic to the whale fat contained in most lipsticks.

'But it hasn't been tested on animals,' she tried. I shook my head again. 'Pity. 'Cos it's all the rage,' she said, applying a thick layer to her own lips so that she looked as though she had spent a week lying at the bottom of a reservoir. 'You ready for this then, girl?' she asked, fluffing up my hair. 'We'll find you a new man before closing time.'

'I'm not sure that I want one, I mean, not yet.'

'Don't be ridiculous. Every girl needs a man. I know I'm not complete without that warm feeling they give you inside,' she laughed raucously. 'I've got condoms in my bag if you get lucky. Help yourself.'

I blanched at the thought. I hadn't slept with anyone other than David for years. And the boyfriend before him hardly counted, since in his youthful enthusiasm Fred Spencer never really kept at it long enough to make a lasting impression. It struck me then, that one day, and in the not too distant future, I hoped, I might have to take the plunge and sleep with someone else. Oh the agony of finding those incredible positions that disguised my pot belly all over again. Not until I had had time to use up a couple of bottles of Christian Dior's Svelte, I decided. And certainly not that night.

'You looked shocked,' said Julie, misreading the panic signs. 'Listen, I know that carrying condoms makes you look like a bit of a slag, but you've got to be responsible these days. And men, they're so unreliable. But I'm sure you know that.'

Didn't I just.

Irene emerged from the loo then. She had changed out of the tidy little suit she normally wore for work into a black lycra number. 'What do you think?' she asked, twirling for our benefit.

'Sexy,' said Julie.

'You've got a bit of loo paper stuck to your heel,' I said, figuring it was best to be diplomatic.

Irene ripped the trailer off. 'Ready.'

'But you're not,' said Julie, turning her attention to me again. 'At least undo some of the buttons on that shirt of yours.' She yanked the top two open to reveal my grey cotton bra. Well, it was more of a vest really.

'Wonderbras really passed you by, didn't they?' Julie observed. 'Better keep the buttons done up.'

I had downed just two Bacardis for Dutch courage when Julie dragged me out onto the dance floor. Once we had made ourselves a space with our handbags, Irene started a shimmy that had to be interrupted every two minutes so that she could readjust her skirt.

I jigged about unenthusiastically, unable to find the beat with any muscle in my body. Julie waved her arms and pouted her lips. Irene shook her bottom. Halfway through one song, Julie grabbed my hands and made me wave them about a bit.

'Having fun?' she mouthed over the music.

I nodded, gritting my teeth hard together. Beside me, another girl involved in a complicated grinding movement, bashed into me and then gave me a look that suggested she had a shotgun in her handbag, not tampax.

Pretty soon, I had remembered all the reasons why I no longer went to nightclubs. The noise, the heat, the competition. Stick a bunch of women in a nightclub and they are suddenly transformed from allies in the great sisterhood into bitter enemies in a gladiatorial vogueing battle to attract the attention of a bunch of men you wouldn't look at twice in a supermarket.

I had to go. While Julie and Irene were getting down to some fascinating rhythm, I slipped away unnoticed. I hid myself in a toilet cubicle and had a sneaky fag while I pondered making a more permanent escape (I told Julie that I didn't smoke because she never buys her own, know what I mean?). Unfortunately the club the girls had dragged me to was five or six miles from home. I didn't have enough money to get a cab on my own. I would just have to sit the night out until Julie and Irene decided that they were ready to go too.

I sat on the closed loo seat for about half an hour, listening to the comings and goings outside. Every five minutes or so, someone would come in and have a fit of the giggles/burst into tears because so-and-so had just asked them out/chucked them for someone else. Then I heard the familiar dulcet tones of Julie and Irene.

'Well, of course, it was bound to happen. She hardly makes an effort, does she? If I was a man I wouldn't want to marry her.'

'Mmm,' Irene grunted.

'I mean, she never wears any make-up. And the way she dresses? I've seen a sack of potatoes with more sex appeal. Look at that dress she's got on tonight. What is it? A-line? Hardly going to raise any man's temperature in an A-line, are you? Well, I've offered to help her. I said I would help her choose what she wanted to wear tonight but she wouldn't hear of it. Says she's got her "own particular style". What style, I say. Can't imagine she's ever been anywhere near Karen Millen. And her hair?

All those wonderful styling products on the market and she's still going for the natural look. No, you know what her problem is, Irene, she's a snob . . . and it wouldn't surprise me if she was a secret lesbian.'

Oh, how the years fell away when I heard those damning words. I was suddenly back at the bus stop. They could only be talking about me. I didn't know what to do then. Should I walk out of the cubicle, all nonchalant, and pretend I hadn't heard a thing? Or should I stay locked away in there until I died? I opted for the latter. Hidden until death, or at least until I was sure that they were safely out of the way again.

But they were determined to take ages. Julie's shrill voice continued to pierce its way to my ears.

'Went off to do that fancy degree, and then comes back to work with us. Well, she doesn't even know how to use a computer properly. And did I ever tell you about the time she got done for shoplifting?'

By which time I was wondering why she had ever pretended to be my friend.

God, how a minute can feel like a lifetime. I covered my ears and focused on the snag in my tights. Then my attempts at isolation were interrupted by a banging on the door. A fierce hammering, a sign that someone wasn't about to cut their losses and go away.

'Come on, you've been in there for bloody ages. What's the matter? Got diarrhoea or something?' It was Julie.

I tried to disguise my voice.

'I think I need to be in here for a bit longer yet,' I squeaked. 'Can't you use one of the other cubicles?'

'No I can't. One of them's got no seat and the other one's bunged up with loo roll. Get a move on.'

She started up a chorus of 'why are we waiting?' It sounded as though there were fifty girls in the queue for my cubicle. Fifty drunken girls who might just take the measure of kicking the door down if I didn't come out of my own accord soon.

'Alright. I'm coming.' I stood up and flushed the chain. I would walk out there with my head held high. I would look her in the eye and see her blush crimson red at the thought that I had heard all her nasty gossip about me . . .

As it happened, I came out looking at the ground.

'Oh, hiya, Alison. You should have said it was you. She's had an operation,' Julie explained for the benefit of the other waiters. 'I'll just have a slash and then we'll get another drink, yeah? Oh,' she added with a fake coy giggle. 'You didn't hear all that nasty stuff I was saying about Bridget just now, did you?'

Bridget was the other temporary secretary at Hudderston Heavy Engineering. She had never fitted in. She said she liked Vivaldi.

'I won't tell her,' I squeaked. I knew it was a lie, but at that moment, it was a lie that I had to believe in order to be able to walk out of that cubicle on my own two feet.

I should have got a taxi then. It wasn't too late. And I could have got him to wait outside the flat while I begged Emma to put up the fare. But instead, somehow rooted to that club with fear, I found myself back at the bar between Julie and Irene, listening to them adjust my life story so that it appeared to be the story of Bridget. I tried to believe them but as far as I knew, Bridget had never even talked to a man without the supervision of her mother, let alone been engaged to one and lost him because of her penchant for A-line skirts and jersey underwear.

'What about him?' Julie asked later at the bar, nudging me excitedly so that most of the ice-cubes jumped out of my Bacardi and coke.

'Who?' I asked. Squinting in the direction of her pointing and seeing only a man who looked as though he had recently been released from a prison where daily face-bashing with a frying-pan was an integral part of the regime.

'Him,' she said, confirming my worst fears. 'Him in the nice Dolce and Gabbana T-shirt. Do you like them, Ali? They're some of my favourite designers. Do some lovely jeans. Do you want me to call him over for you?' she added seamlessly.

'Er . . .'

But it was a *fait accompli*. Soon Barry had joined us, and was telling Julie, in a peculiar kind of gangsta patois, about his mobile phone.

'He's got a mobile,' she told me excitedly, as if I hadn't heard. I resisted the temptation to respond that even my Dad has a mobile these days, so that Mum can harangue him when he's walking the dog.

'And he's got a car,' she whispered loudly, as one does in a club, while he got in the drinks.

'What kind of car?'

'Mark II Golf. And he says the stereo cost more than the wheels.'

Somehow this only confirmed that he wasn't going to be my kind of man.

'I think he's alright,' Julie continued. 'Do you think he's alright? He's got a nice pair of arms on him.'

True. Though they didn't exactly match up with his legs. Think chimpanzee effect. With a naked lady stencilled on in biro.

'And his hair. I like that.'

True. It was very nice hair. Unfortunately I have a rule of thumb that prevents me from dating men who look as though they spend more on conditioner than I do.

'Ask him for a dance. You can tell what a man will be like in bed from the way he dances.'

David had the disco style of a three-legged llama, I recalled with a faint 'harumph'.

'Go on,' Julie prodded me in Barry's direction. 'Dance with him. Dance with him or I'll tell everyone at work that you're a lesbian,' she added with a cackle.

'That's fair,' I thought. I was about the enter the outer circle of hell.

'Wanna dance?' Barry asked. Julie nodded enthusiastically on my behalf.

'I'll hold your drinks,' she said helpfully. And Barry guided me onto the dance floor by equally helpfully man-handling the cheeks of my bum.

We hadn't exactly chosen the best tune to start dancing to. It was some jungle track that alternated between slow and painful bass beats and frantic riffs that required the dancing skills of a Mexican jumping bean. Barry convulsed before me, his pelvis twitching backwards and forwards within dangerous range of my own. I subtly backed away from him, again and again and again, until I was dancing with my back right against the mirrored wall. The only option then was to sidle along the glass, hoping that Barry would maintain a decent three-inch distance between us.

'All right,' he asked, flooding my face with beery breath.

I nodded, eyes wide like a panicked deer as he leaned forward, lips puckering almost imperceptibly. I couldn't believe his cheek. Trying to grope me when I didn't even know his surname.

Then the music changed. Faster than ever. And this time the lights began to strobe and flash, making everything move in slow motion, like the frames of a film being run too slow through the projector. Barry stumbled backwards a little, his eyes open again. Good, I thought, he's given up on the kissing idea. You can only imagine my horror when he suddenly slumped forward into my arms and began twitching against me with a vengeance.

I was about to make a grab for his balls and twist them from his body when the incredible weight of his body against mine made me realise that he had actually lost consciousness. His grip on my shoulders relaxed as he slid slowly to the floor and lay there in a heap, lips a-quiver and big eyes bulging red.

'Help,' I squeaked. Around us, the crowd continued to dance. It was just like my accident in Safeway. No-one wanted to get involved. Just the occasional snarl when a dancing girl got her stiletto heel caught in Barry's flapping T-shirt.

'Help.'

Barry's face was rapidly turning blue.

With a strength that I could probably never find again even if I wanted to, I managed to haul Barry's inert body to the side of the dance floor and finally, with a sense of perception lacked by the majority of DJs, Mixmaster Mickey Mouse, noticed that something was wrong.

The music came to an ugly halt and all eyes turned on me.

'Help?' I said pathetically. 'Is there a doctor in the house?'

No answer.

'A nurse?'

'Stand back, I'm a vet,' said someone suddenly.

A vet? Well, I know that I had thought Barry a bit of a gorilla, but I couldn't really see how much help a vet would be at that moment.

The vet however, thought otherwise. He got down on his hands and knees next to Barry and quickly started to administer first aid. He rolled him, with some difficulty, into the recovery position, opened his mouth and checked for obstructions. All the time, Barry seemed to be calming down, his body relaxing. Perhaps he wasn't going to die after all.

'Epilepsy,' said the vet decisively, when he was happy with his patient's condition. 'Brought on by the strobe lights, I expect. Didn't you know your boyfriend was an epileptic?' He was directing that question at me.

'He's not my boyfriend,' I said quietly. 'I just met him tonight. I don't really know who he is.'

'Who's he here with then?' The vet scanned the crowd.

'I don't know.'

'He's my brother,' said a girl, with similarly long arms. 'Let me see him.' As she pushed her way to the front of the crowd that had gathered around the little scene, I allowed myself to slip slowly backwards into the sea of faces.

I couldn't see where Julie or Irene had got to. I didn't really want to know. I just wanted to get out of there again. I took one last glance back at Barry where he lay on the floor and caught the vet's eye. I copped a full-on gaze right into his baby blues. He actually seemed to be looking into the crowd after me, concerned perhaps. Disgusted, more likely. But for a moment, I had that delicious shudder you get when you lock eyes with someone that you hope you might one day be locking more with.

Typical for me to encounter him in such a ridiculous circumstance though. He probably thought I was a bitch to run off like that and leave a man while he's down.

I walked home. It was a long way, not helped by the fact that I went the first half mile in completely the wrong direction. Then the rain started. Just spitty spots at first, but soon it was bucketing it down with a vengeance. I didn't care that I was wearing only my deeply unsexy A-line dress and a denim jacket. I wanted to catch pneumonia. I wanted to die there and then. I wanted everyone to be really sorry for me. But then I had a vision of my own funeral. Of Julie weeping at my graveside, telling everyone what a good friend I had been so that they would heap hugs and sympathy on her, and decided that it would be more spiteful to live and exact my revenge at leisure.

'What on earth happened to you?' Emma asked when I staggered into the house. 'Been in a wet T-shirt competition? Julie phoned. She said she was worried about where you had got to. Said you were involved in some kind of medical emergency in a nightclub? You didn't hurt your scar, did you?'

'No, it's fine,' I assured her. 'I went dancing with the girls from work. I guess I just wasn't up to it. Oh, and then this bloke who was chatting me up went and had an epileptic fit on me.'

'How grim,' Emma said, reaching for the restorative kettle. 'Was he good-looking?'

'No.'

'Ah well.'

'The vet who did first aid on him looked alright though.'

'A vet? Oh well, I guess if you can deal with an elephant you can deal with most of the men in Brindlesham. So the vet was gorgeous? Did you ask what his name was?'

'Of course I didn't. It was hardly the right time. But it's no good anyway, Emma. I just can't do it. I just can't go out there and meet people yet. David is too much on my mind. No-one can ever match up to him. I'm doomed to be single forever.'

'Give yourself some time,' said Emma sensibly, as she gave me a consolatory hug. 'And don't leave the match-making up to Julie Adams. Unless you're into primates, of course. But believe me, things will get better.'

Perhaps she was right. Certainly, my operation scar was no longer wrapped up with a duvet's worth of wadding. It was just a bit pink. If I didn't poke it, I couldn't even feel that it was there.

I decided that I'd just have to apply the same theory to David.

CHAPTER FOUR

January the 30th. David had been gone from my life for a whole calendar month and five days. I was just congratulating myself for not having thought about him for at least twenty-four hours (telling myself that I wasn't thinking about him didn't count as thinking of him, you understand) when the postman arrived. Three envelopes tumbled onto the mat. Two were brown and addressed to Emma. The third was white and addressed, in neat typescript, to me.

Now this was unusual. I didn't get letters. I got credit card bills and final demands for the council tax. Maybe it was *Reader's Digest* writing to let me know that I really had won something in one of their fantastic prize draws. A cheque for a whole pound perhaps? One of those infinitesimally small cheques that I must be the only person in Britain sad enough to actually cash in.

But it wasn't from *Reader's Digest*.

It was from *Complete Woman* magazine. The modern woman's Bible. Otherwise known as the magazine for girls who like to pretend they are really doing something rather interesting with their lives other than simply waiting for Mr Right to come along and take them away from it all. Looking at the address at the top of that letter, for a moment I couldn't even remember ever having picked the magazine up.

Dear Miss Harris, the letter began. *We are delighted to inform you that you have won a holiday for two at the fabulous Santa Bonita all-inclusive resort in Antigua.*

Oh my God! A holiday! My heart leapt for joy at the word. I'd won a holiday in the sunshine and, believe me, a holiday was exactly what I needed after that miserable month without David Whitworth. I started to shake with excitement.

But the letter continued . . . *The whole* Complete Woman *office was touched by your heart-rending account of your fiancé's devotion to you throughout your terrible illness. There can be no doubt in our minds that you and David Whitworth are the* United Kingdom's Most Romantic Couple! *A member of staff will be contacting you shortly to arrange a convenient time for a photo shoot of you and your fiancé to accompany an article about your successful relationship for our magazine.*

'Pah!' I spat. Now I remembered *Complete Woman* magazine only too well.

May we congratulate you once again on being the United Kingdom's Most Romantic Couple 1998, the letter ended.

'Ha!'

I tore the letter in two and threw it onto the carpet.

I had won a holiday in the Caribbean and, thanks to that scumbag ex-boyfriend of mine running out on me, I couldn't even take it.

Emma sauntered downstairs just then to catch me in the throes of my impression of a soloist in *Riverdance*.

'Telephone bill?' she guessed insightfully as she rubbed the sleep from her eyes.

'No. Holiday for two in Antigua,' I replied.

'Bloody hell,' she was suddenly very much awake again. 'What are you doing then?' Emma made a dangerous dive to retrieve the now tatty scrap of paper from beneath my feet.

'What are you doing?' she asked again, as she smoothed out the paper until it was almost readable.

'I've won a holiday for two in Antigua. First prize in *Complete Woman*'s Most Romantic Couple competition.'

'You're kidding?' Emma quickly read the letter and confirmed that I was not having one of my sarcastic moments and merely pretending that I was not stomping on the telephone bill.

'You're not kidding. Most Romantic Couple? Fuck me, Ali. You're right,' she said.

'I wish I was fucking you,' I said blithely. 'Then we could go together.'

'They want to do a photo shoot of you and your fiancé,' Emma read.

'That's right.'

'Oh, Ali,' said Emma. 'Bad luck.'

So much for not thinking about David. The news that I had won the *Complete Woman* romance competition brought it all flooding back. Spending Christmas Eve alone in the hospital, writing out a thousand reasons why I loved David Whitworth more than anyone or anything else in the world, while he was out giving my Christmas Eve dance ticket and his wicked fickle heart to the girl he had promised he would never see again.

How could she have done it? How could Lisa Brown have taken advantage of the fact that I was languishing in hospital? Never mind that I had spirited David out of his commitment to her while she was on a mercy mission to Bosnia as part of her employer's personnel personal improvement course.

I hadn't seen David since Christmas Day but my sister Jo had gleefully reported that David and Lisa had been seen hovering with intent outside Ratners. When I asked her why she had to be so spiteful, Jo claimed that she was only trying to do me a favour by reminding me what a rat he was.

I still had my own engagement ring, though it no longer lived on my finger. Now the tasteful little diamond solitaire sat forlornly on my dressing table in a ceramic heart-shaped box with flowers on the lid that David had bought me on our first Valentine's Day together. I had thought about marching round to his flat and hurling the ring at him, or down a drain in front of him, but Emma said that would be undignified. Why didn't I just take it to a pawn shop instead? I could buy a flight to Rio with the proceeds. And take her too, of course. Have a good time. That would be true revenge. But perhaps I didn't take her advice because, even after hearing that David had been window-shopping at the jeweller's with Lisa, I was still harbouring the foolish notion that this was a nightmare from which I would soon wake up. (In any case, if I did try to pawn the ring, I had a terrible feeling that it would turn out to be cubic zirconia anyway.)

'What are you going to do about this holiday?'

Emma interrupted my downward spiral of thought as I moped over toast and marmalade.

'I suppose I'll just have to ring the people at *Complete Woman* and tell them that they picked the wrong couple.'

'Perhaps they'll feel sorry for you and say that you can still have the holiday regardless. You could take me with you instead,' she said optimistically.

'I can't see that happening,' I moaned. 'They're planning to make a big feature of their most romantic couple. They don't want to have to tell their readers that the winners of their Most Romantic Couple competition have sadly separated but "here are some pictures of Ali Harris and her flatmate in their spinster pad with a cat instead".' I mimicked a *Complete Woman*-type voice.

'Try it,' Emma insisted. 'You never know. Like I said, they might feel sorry for you.'

'I don't want people to feel sorry for me,' I snarled in frustration. 'No, Emma, I'm going to come clean and suggest that they award my prize to the people who came second instead.'

'Your altruism makes me puke,' said Emma as she left for work.

By the time I got into the office, the news that I had left some poor bloke dying on the dance floor had already been distributed on the ultra-efficient Hudderston grapevine. Julie and Irene regarded me judgementally as I slunk to my desk.

'I wonder if he's alright,' said Julie loudly, then she came across and leaned on my desk. 'We were worried about you,' she said, full of *faux* concern for me all of a sudden. 'Going off like that without saying goodbye. What were we supposed to think?'

'I had to get some air.'

'We could have looked after you. That guy that saved Barry wanted to know where you'd gone as well. He said he thought from the look of you that you might have gone into shock.'

'Really?'

'Yeah. Said he would have given you a lift to the accident unit to get checked out. As it was, he gave us a lift home instead. He was really nice. A vet. I've never been out with a vet myself,' she mused. 'But I suppose it must be like going out with a doctor without having to worry that he spends all day ogling other women's tits. Anyway, I told him you'd just split up with your fiancé and had your appendix out, so that was probably the real reason why you looked so pale.'

'Thanks.'

'You look awful this morning too,' she added. Just to really cheer me up.

Later that day, I must have looked even paler as I dialled the number of *Complete Woman* with shaking fingers and asked for Amanda the editorial assistant.

'Speaking,' she said, taking me by surprise.

'I, er . . . I . . .' I whispered, wanting to get this thing over with without attracting Julie's attention.

'Yes?'

'I, er . . . I won the competition.'

'Which competition, darling? We've got lots of competitions going on here at *Complete Woman*,' she told me chirpily.

'Er, Most Romantic Couple.'

'Most Romantic Couple! Fantastic. Then you must be Ali Harris. My goodness, how lovely to hear from you!' I could almost hear her beaming. 'Oh, Ali. We were all so moved by your story. It was absolutely heart-rending. I swear I was nearly in tears by the time I finished reading it. Are you completely better now, my love?'

'Yes,' I said guiltily. 'I'm much better now.'

'I bet you're really looking forward to your holiday then. It'll help you recuperate from your operation and be such a nice rest for David after the way he single-handedly nursed you through your pain.'

'Mmm,' I said. (I suppose I ought to warn you at this point that I had exaggerated my appendicitis into something a little more long-term and life-threatening. Artistic licence, I thought at the time. I guess that what I had experienced since then might well have been divine retribution.)

'Have you decided when you're going to take the trip?' Amanda continued. 'February is simply gorgeous in the Caribbean. With a bit of luck you might even be able to be on the island for Valentine's Day. Wouldn't that be great?'

'Er . . .'

'But listen to me waffling on. You go when you want to of course, Ali. It's your special holiday after all. All we at *Complete Woman* ask is that we get to see the holiday snaps when you return. Naughty ones edited out of course. Ha ha!!'

'Amanda, I . . . I . . .' I had to tell her that I wouldn't be going before she exploded with enthusiasm.

'Yes, Ali. What is it? Do you want to arrange a date for the preliminary photo shoot now? I know that the fashion department are just itching to get their hands on you for a reader makeover. You know – how to look good in a bikini without being embarrassed about nasty operation scars – that kind of thing. And the features department will definitely want a few juicy quotes for a piece they're putting together on the secrets of maintaining that perfect love affair. Do you have your diary open in front of you now?'

'Actually, Amanda . . . I . . .'

'You can come in to the studio, or we can send someone round to your home, if you prefer. I quite understand if you don't want to travel long distances in your fragile condition.'

Rubbish, I would happily have travelled a very very long way away right then. I had to put her straight. Or at the very least put her off before she booked me in with Lord Lichfield.

'Amanda,' I said in the most measured tone I could muster. 'As you can probably imagine, all this has come as rather a surprise to me. I mean to us, to David and I. I'm not looking my best after the operation. I wonder if you could be kind enough to postpone the photo shoot for a week or so? Until I'm feeling more in the pink, as it were.'

'Ali,' said Amanda smoothly. 'It really is no problem at all. Though the make-up girl we've got here at *Complete Woman* can make anyone look in the full flush of health. She trained as a mortuary assistant. Ha ha ha. Only joking. Can't I persuade you, darling?

You won't believe the difference some of those new mascaras can make.'

'Amanda, I'll call you tomorrow,' I told her. Julie was striding across the office in my direction.

'OK. Think it over for as long as you like. As long as you can give me a decision within twenty-four hours that is! Ha ha! Mwah, mwah. Please give our regards to that darling little man of yours. We're all simply dying to meet him.'

I put down the phone and felt a hot and cold flush race over my body leaving me covered in freezing sweat.

'Are you sure you're OK, Ali?' Julie asked, as she plopped a pile of typing into my in-tray. 'You were looking rather stressed out on the phone just now. It wasn't you-know-who by any chance?'

'Who?' I asked in genuine confusion.

'The D-word?' Julie mouthed. 'I know it's hard, Ali, but it really is best not to call him, you know. The harder you chase him, the faster he'll run away.'

'It wasn't David,' I put her straight. 'Whatever you think of me, Julie, I'm big and brave enough not to have to phone my ex-fiancé begging him to come back,' I added snappily.

'Fine,' said Julie. 'But in my capacity as secretary to the MD, I suppose I ought to remind you that personal phone calls are strictly forbidden in any case. Except emergencies.'

Then she left me to have an emergency telephone conversation with her friend Stella about the outfits they were going to wear when they hit the town that night.

My own emergency telephone conversation with

Amanda at *Complete Woman* had not been what I could have described as a success and now I felt doubly bad because I had accepted Amanda's praise for the fantastic state of my currently non-existent love life. This was going to be far harder than I thought. But by the time I called her again the next day, I resolved, I would be a big enough person to come clean.

I'd get some moral support from my friends. Marvin Naylor, my best friend but one, was having a dinner party that night.

CHAPTER FIVE

The only reason why Marvin actually invited women to his dinner parties at all was so that they could cook all the food for him. I swear that he used to tell us girls to arrive an hour earlier than the men, and then, when we arrived, we would find Marvin sobbing in the kitchen, with flour all over his forehead and every pan in his usually pristine kitchen, dirty and piled up in the sink.

'Ali, I just don't know what to do,' he would whimper pathetically. 'I wanted so much to impress you all tonight. I thought I'd make a soufflé. No one told me it would be this hard.'

Upon which, we girls, granting him major brownie points for having even decided to attempt something more complicated and glamorous than spag bol in the first place, would step in and cook the whole bloody lot for him. We did this several times, until one day Emma pointed out that all the dishes in Marvin's sink bore the remains of cornflakes and baked beans, and that there was no evidence of soufflé-making whatsoever, however abortive. We decided that sneaky old Marvin might just have rubbed flour into his hairline for effect as we arrived and resolved never to help him out by turning up early again.

Besides, this particular evening, I didn't have time to turn up early and help out in the kitchen. My embryonic friendship with Julie had obviously hit the skids already and she spitefully had me stay behind in the office till seven typing out some awful report.

By the time I had finished at work, I just wanted to go home and flop out on the sofa until retirement age. Marvin only enticed me away from my regime of biscuits and soap operas at all by guaranteeing me at least one single and attentive young man if I went to his party. A single and attentive young man without tattoos, a mobile phone or a tendency to pass out in my arms at inopportune moments. Oh, and not a gay one either.

With Marvin's promise in mind, I needed to dress to impress. Incredibly, despite my haphazard chocolate digestive, Wagon Wheel and Camel lights diet, I had actually lost a little weight since Christmas. How this happened, I wasn't sure, though my mother had a theory that you could cry out fat with tears. Anyway, as a result, none of my dresses fitted me properly any more. Emma walked in on me as I was gathering in the waist of my all-time favourite dress with the bit of fancy rope that normally tied back the curtains in my bedroom.

'Are you really wearing that?' she asked in the voice that she also used for saying 'Are you really eating that?' when I ordered a tuna pizza with extra anchovies.

I nodded. 'Think I need a belt with it though.'

'It always looked like it needed a belt,' she told me. 'That dress is horrible, Ali. It looks like a flippin' sack.'

'It was David's favourite,' I whined.

'Exactly. Don't you know he only made you wear it so that no other man would look at you twice?'

'Really?'

That came as news to me.

'Really. And these days you need a man to look at you twice. You're not going out like that. Try this.' She threw in my direction a little red dress that looked as though it had a day job as a tubi-grip.

'I'll look like a slapper,' I protested.

'Perfect,' said Emma. 'Because Marvin tells me that a slapper is exactly what the spare man at his dinner party wants in his life.'

'And that's supposed to encourage me? Great. I don't want to be somebody else's consolation prize.'

'Oh, live a little,' said Emma as she started to vigorously back-comb my hair, giving me a painful flashback to the nightclub ladies' toilets. 'One night stands are good for the soul. There,' she said, when my hitherto sleek and sensible hair had started to resemble candyfloss. 'You look better already.'

I sat down at the dressing table and surveyed my new look critically. Fattypuss, our ageing tabby, leapt onto my lap to offer some encouragement and put a big hole in my tights.

But a constant stream of encouraging words from Emma just about helped me make it to Marvin's house. When he opened the door, he was covered from head to foot in flour.

'Where on earth have you bad girls been?' he asked

distractedly with one eye still on something that was boiling over in the kitchen. 'It's half-past-eight. I thought I said six thirty.'

'Yes,' said Emma sweetly. 'You did. But we always seem to arrive while you're still up to your elbows in the kitchen. We didn't want to get under your feet again. What are we having tonight, Marvin?'

'Spaghetti bolognese,' he snarled.

'Who's here?' asked Emma cheerfully as we wound our way down the dark corridor towards the dining room.

'Fred, Tiffany, Andrew and Peta.'

'Is Peter the mystery man?' Emma asked.

'No, Peta's a girl. The mystery man has yet to arrive,' he smiled.

We emerged into the light of the dining room. Marvin looked me up and down. 'Oh, Ali,' he said, taking in my red tube dress properly. 'You look nice. Different. Though you should maybe try some finer tights with that dress.'

Thanks, Fattypuss, I thought.

'Sexy.' Andrew gave a low wolf whistle that boosted my self-esteem stock by twelve points. Marvin kissed the tips of his fingers before returning to the nightmare in the kitchen.

'Guess what Marvin's making,' Tiffany whispered.

'I know,' said Emma. 'Spaghetti bolognese. Did you turn up late too?'

'You bet I did. Those deep fried zucchini he took so much praise for last time we ate here made an absolute disaster zone of my Nicole Farhi shift dress. He didn't even provide me with an apron.'

'I just got so sick of him shouting at me,' said Peta.

'Last time I was here he had me dicing up onions the second I stepped through the door and then he had the bloody cheek to shout at me for not doing it thinly enough. I felt like one of those underlings in a Marco Pierre White restaurant. And my mascara was all over the place. I don't know why he insists on such complicated menus. Hasn't he heard of Marks and Spencer? I noticed they've increased their range of vol-au-vents the other day.'

'Marvin's dinner parties are legendary,' Andrew piped up.

'Yes. But not because of the food,' said Peta. 'It doesn't matter what's served up as long as the wine keeps flowing and you're surrounded by good company. He should know that.'

'Hope you still feel the same when you taste his spag bol,' said Emma into her glass.

'Is everybody here now?' asked Tiffany.

'Just one more to come,' said Emma. 'A mystery man for Ali here.'

All eyes turned to me and I coloured to match my dress. 'Don't say that kind of thing, Emma,' I protested. 'You make me sound like some Indian spinster that's got to be married off tonight or else burned to a crisp on my father's funeral pyre. Besides, I'm not the only single girl in this room.'

'That's true enough.' Emma was single too, but as far as social gatherings went, she and Marvin were almost what you could call an item. They had met each other on an art foundation course at the local sixth form college. Emma had developed an immediate and intensely deep crush on Marvin, who had seemed so creative and different from the other boys in his purple velvet tail coat and his Cuban-heeled suede boots. Sadly, it soon turned out that he was different from the other boys in more than just his attire.

The crush came to a climax one terrible evening when Emma tried to seduce Marvin at one of those 'two items of clothing parties' thrown by the students' union, where you get free drink all night if one of the items you're wearing is a hat. Faced by Emma in a leopard-print negligee Marvin had broken down and flung himself headlong out of the closet. Emma didn't speak to him for three days. After that, they made it up and strangely seemed closer than ever. They declared themselves to be 'platonically in love' and Emma took on the honorary mantle of Marvin's 'stunt girlfriend' for those tricky formal occasions when a boyfriend dressed like Carmen Miranda just won't do.

Emma swore that her crush on Marvin had ended on that terrible night, but I wasn't so sure. She had had boyfriends since then. Lots of them. Handsome but thick ones. Ugly but artistic types. Rich bastards. Poor diamond geezers. None of them stayed around for long, though some of them continued to phone up and cry on my shoulder for years after Emma lost interest. For a while I tried dressing and wearing my hair like Emma in the hope that some of her cast-offs might find a bit more physical solace with me than just blubbing. But I grew so used to rejection that it took me six months to notice when someone was taking a real interest in me, not just using me as a medium to get a message of love across to Emma.

'David Whitworth really fancies you.'

I can remember so clearly the time that Emma first said it. We were standing at the bar of The Rotunda –

The Rotunda as it was before the trendy, new brewery image bods got hold of it. This was back in the days when you could stand at the bar without risking having your eye poked out by a combine harvester hanging artistically from the shelf where they used to keep the pint glasses. In fact, I was peeling a big piece of that lovely fleecy red wallpaper off the wall when Emma dropped the bombshell.

'David Whitworth,' I said in surprise. 'But he's got a fiancée, hasn't he?'

'So?'

So indeed. Emma beckoned David over and started the chat off by asking him about his souped-up Escort GTI. Then she said something truly awful like, 'Ooh, this cystitis of mine is killing me. I've got to go to the bogs,' and left me alone with him.

'How's your fiancée?' I asked straightaway, glad that Emma wasn't around to kick me for opening up with such a conversation-stopper.

David then told me, 'She's not my fiancée any more.'

That wasn't strictly true. In fact Lisa Brown was still his fiancée until David and I had our first passionate encounter on the grey velvet sofa in the flat he actually shared with her. She was a police switchboard operator. Her shift wasn't meant to finish until eleven. Unfortunately she got off early because a punter who rang up shouting rude things about 'Pigs' had put her under 'unnecessary stress'. Not as much stress as she was about to be put under at home.

Lisa Brown really did cease to be David's fiancée that night and I must admit that I didn't think about the horrors I had put her through very much at all.

Emma was actually impressed by my wicked achievement and insisted on calling me Homewrecker-Harris for about a month. But I was almost sorry now that I knew what it was like to have your intended whipped away from under your nose, which was why I was at Marvin's dinner party, eagerly, but not without trepidation, awaiting the arrival of a single man.

'Ali, are you listening to me?' Emma dragged me back into the conversation. 'I was just saying to Tiffany that our landlord has refused point blank to mend the leaky ceiling in our bathroom. I've phoned the letting agents but they're completely bloody useless. What do they think their job is, eh? They're more than happy to take a share of the tenants' money but they act like you're the scum of the earth when you ring up and ask if it would be possible to have a roof over your head for the money you're paying.'

With a sigh I thought of the week before Christmas, the calm before the storm, when the bathroom leak saga had begun. I hadn't taken much notice of the problem then, figuring that I would be moving into a brand new place with David after our wedding in April anyway. Now, however, Emma and I had just signed a lease on our grotty little flat above the kebab shop for another six months. It was a symbolic act for me, underlining my status as a girl without a man and no hope of biblical style co-habitation in the immediate future.

'Renting is a nightmare,' Tiffany agreed. 'But you can't possibly hope to buy a place on your own these days. Andrew and I couldn't have managed without each other.' She gave Andrew a smug little smile with that. It made me feel quite sick.

'Perhaps Ali and I will have to go in on a place together one day,' said Emma. 'What do you think Ali? A spinster pad of our very own. We could get another cat.'

Marvin emerged from the kitchen just then. 'Ladies and gentlemen,' he sighed, rubbing a flour-covered arm across his forehead. 'Dinner will be ready in just a short while. In the meantime, to whet your appetite for the main course, I've made some delicious canapés.'

He dumped a plate in front of us. The canapés looked suspiciously like little triangles of toast covered in fish paste and Marmite to me.

'Thank you, Marvin,' said Emma as he retreated to finish stirring the spag bol. 'Do you need a hand out there?' she teased. 'No? Of course you don't. I'm sure you've got it all under control, you clever lad.'

Andrew gingerly tried one of the canapés. I guessed then that I had been right about the ingredients since he quickly replaced the bitten triangle at the bottom of the pile and refilled his glass with something to wash the taste away.

'Andrew, take it easy on the booze,' whined Tiffany. 'You've already had far too much to drive me home. Now I shall have to be on water for the rest of the night, you selfish little man.'

'Makes you glad to be single, doesn't it?' whispered Emma to me.

Almost, I thought. But I'd make my mind up about that when I finally met the mystery guest. Meanwhile, I was matching Andrew on the booze front, glass for glass. Dutch courage. I had enough for a football team.

The doorbell rang three times in quick succession,

interrupting an intense discussion about the real meaning of *Captain Pugwash*.

'That'll be Marvin's mysterious friend,' said Tiffany. 'I don't have any idea who it is? Do you?'

'Marvin's been acting like we're awaiting the appearance of Mick Jagger. It's probably one of his terrible drug-dealer friends,' said Peta.

I felt the butterflies rise in my stomach and hit their heads against the walls. Sod butterflies. There were bats in there too. I hoped the stranger would like me. I hoped that I would like him. I decided that I would like him, even if he was short with a beard and thick glasses. Even if he wore grey slip-on shoes and white socks. Even if he had a speech impediment that made him pronounce my surname 'Hawwis'. Sad to say, in case you hadn't guessed, I was desperate for even a scrap of male attention from someone with a measurable IQ.

'Hello!! How are you!!!' we heard Marvin trill. 'You're just in time. I've been slaving away in the kitchen since lunchtime. Everyone else is just lazing about in the dining room. As per usual.'

The mystery guest muffled something in reply. Still no clues as to who he was. The assembled group in the dining room went silent in anticipation. I knew that if I opened my mouth the nerve bats would escape so I just sat there too and gulped down my fear in huge mouthfuls. We could hear Marvin bringing the guest up the long dark corridor towards us. He was chattering away about the burnt sienna paint he was going to use on the walls when the plastering had been done. How long could it possibly take them to walk up that bloody hall, I wondered?

The door opened. I sucked in my stomach automatically.

Marvin entered, followed by . . .

'Oh my god, Marvin. How could you?' Emma started shrieking. 'How could you do this to us? You utter, utter creep.'

To us? Do this to us? As Emma quickly shuffled me from the dining room into the bathroom and locked the door behind us, I got the vague impression that Marvin's mystery guest was in fact my ex-fiancé.

CHAPTER SIX

'There, there,' said Emma, dabbing at my eyes with a piece of rolled up loo paper before I had even got around to crying. 'We don't have to stay here a moment longer if you don't want to, Ali. I can't think what Marvin was playing at, inviting that stupid bastard along.'

'It was David, wasn't it?' I asked. I wasn't quite sure. Emma had whisked me out of the way so quickly my head was still spinning.

'Yes, it was David. The smug bastard. If he had even a hint of decency about him, he wouldn't have agreed to come here at all.'

'Perhaps he didn't know that I was going to be here?' I reasoned.

'But he knows that we're always here whenever Marvin has a dinner party. Who else does he think would do the washing up? We're practically Marvin's live-in geisha girls.'

That much was true.

'I'm going to go out there and give Marvin a piece of my mind. He did it deliberately, the spiteful little worm. How could he do such a thing to his friends? We've stood by him all these years . . . I practically wiped his bum for him when he had that bad turn after splitting up with Marco.' (Marco had been a holiday romance.)

'Emma,' I restrained her first with a hand on her shoulder, but later more bodily when it was clear that a hand wasn't going to be enough. 'Emma, perhaps Marvin meant well. Perhaps he thought he could hurl me and David back together tonight. Men don't understand about relationships and the etiquette of keeping exes apart for a given time like women do.'

'Of course Marvin understands about relationships,' Emma protested. 'He's gay. And right now I'm going to kill him.'

'Emma,' I held her tight against my chest so that she couldn't possibly escape. 'Please don't make a scene about this. I'm begging you. For my sake.'

'Scene? Scene?' she shrieked. 'I'm going to make a whole bloody opera out of this.'

'But don't you see, that's exactly what everyone wants. Supposing, just supposing, that Marvin really is nasty enough to want to see me squirm in the face of my ex-intended, if you go out there shouting the odds, he will have got exactly what he wanted, won't he? If, however, we carry on as if nothing has happened, as if David and I are just two old friends who simply haven't seen each other in a while, Marvin will be robbed of his drama and I might just about make it home with my self-esteem intact.'

'You don't understand,' Emma shrieked, as she wriggled to be free.

'No. You don't understand,' I told her fiercely. 'It's

my relationship, Emma. Rather, it was my relationship and as such, I think it is my right to choose how we're going to handle this little scenario.'

Emma's struggling grew a little less frantic. I released her to sit on the loo seat with her head in her hands while she calmed down.

'It's so embarrassing,' she whined. 'He doesn't know how much this hurts.'

'Emma,' I reminded her, a little less patiently this time. 'Which one of us was actually dumped by that bastard out there? You or me?' Emma looked at me and I could have sworn her eyes were blinking back tears. 'It was me, right? And I'm still standing even though David Whitworth is just on the other side of that wall. What do you say we go back out there, with our heads held high, and watch the bastard choke on Marvin's bolognese?'

Emma sniffed up a little smile.

'You're right,' she told me. 'You're so right.'

I hustled her back into the dining room before I stopped feeling it.

'Everything OK?' asked Marvin ingenuously when we emerged.

'Yes, thanks,' I said, as nicely as I could. 'Hope we're not holding dinner up. Emma got something stuck in her eye.'

I sat back down in my seat and noticed to my horror that I had been seated right opposite my ex-fiancé. David smiled an unsure smile.

'Oh. Hello, David,' I said shakily. 'Long time, no see.'

'How's your appendix?' he asked.

'Don't know. I haven't got it anymore,' I replied.

I sensed that the eyes of the whole table were upon us as we made our first faltering attempt to have a civil conversation.

'That's a lovely dress,' he said suddenly.

I looked down at my cleavage involuntarily. 'Thanks,' I replied. 'It's Emma's.'

'Right,' said Marvin, breaking the tension at last. Everyone in the room seemed to breathe a sigh of relief. 'Dinner is served. Everyone for spaghetti? You'll have to serve yourselves. I'm exhausted.' He plonked two saucepans down in the middle of the table. One was full of spaghetti. Not drained. The other was full of red stuff with floaty black bits in it. The black bits later turned out to be burnt scrapings from the bottom of the pan.

'Can I get you some of this sauce stuff?' David asked me, when I had managed to pull three strands of spaghetti safely from the knot Marvin had presented us with. I passed my plate across the centre of the table and for a second, I had one of those big budget movie moments, when the conversation around the heroine is faded out and all you can hear is her heartbeat as the hero uses the excuse of taking her plate to touch her hand.

Dream moment was rudely interrupted however when Tiffany bumped David as she reached for some burnt garlic bread, and my hard-won spaghetti ended up on the floor. I came round to notice Emma staring daggers at me. 'He was touching your hand,' she hissed.

'I know,' I mouthed back.

Fortunately, I didn't want to eat much anyway.

Seeing David again for the first time was not at all as I had imagined it. I had imagined a sordid rendezvous in the supermarket car park where we would swap back the items of each other's property we had gathered over the years. There would be an argument over who owned the programme from that matinee performance of *Grease* we saw on our first proper date. It was signed by all the cast. He would let me have it, of course, because when it came down to it, he didn't have such a big thing about Shane Ritchie as I did. But then David would drive off to meet Lisa from her late shift and I would tear the programme up anyway and let the pieces scatter across the wet ground. Symbolically.

Instead, David and I were sitting across a table at Marvin's house, of all places. There were no bitter recriminations. He wasn't even paying too much attention to me in the way that people do when they know they've done you wrong. He was discussing engine sizes with Andrew. Just like old times. Then, suddenly, David turned and looked at me. He actually smiled at me in the special way he had smiled at me during dozens of these dinner parties over the time that we were together. It was a smile that said, this guy is boring me rigid, can't wait to rip these morons apart with you on the journey home. Can't wait to rip your clothes off when we get home, was what it usually also meant.

I blushed and pretended that I was really interested in the pattern on my plate. Only the plate was actually plain white. When I looked up again, David was still looking at me. When I looked down again, his left foot, minus a shoe, was in my lap.

My mouth dropped open. What did this mean? It was what he always used to do at parties. He would wriggle his toes in my crotch until I was barely able to speak for excitement. But that was back then. In the good old days. Now, in the context of our new status as ex-lovers, it was surely a wholly inappropriate thing to do. I gave him a 'what do you think you're doing?' kind of look.

He gave me an innocent 'am I doing something wrong?' kind of look back.

Emma leaned across to ask me to pass the salt. I quickly covered David's foot with my napkin before she could see what was going on.

'Are you OK?' she asked, seeing the surprised and perturbed look that I just couldn't keep off my face. 'You look a bit weird, Al.'

'It's hot in here,' I said hurriedly. 'Aren't you hot too?'

'No.' Emma put some salt on her inedible pasta and thankfully returned to that interminable conversation about the benefits of a mortgage over renting with Tiffany.

As I tried to force down a piece of rock-hard garlic bread, David's toes began to move. It was almost imperceptible at first, but pretty soon, I was sure that everyone in the room must have been able to see the napkin jumping up and down in my lap. I forced myself further back in my chair in an attempt to make myself out of his range. David, while continuing to talk house prices with Andrew, abandoned his food altogether and slid lower in his chair to better help him get to me. I gestured at him to stop, wildly flashing my eyes, but David wasn't even looking at me so that he could get the signs.

Finally, I had no choice. This had to stop. David Whitworth no longer had the right to try to turn me on.

So I stabbed him with a fork.

'Fuck!'

Andrew fell off his chair and began to roll about on the floor, clutching desperately at his newly perforated ankle.

CHAPTER SEVEN

'Fuck! Fuck! Fuck!'

'Andrew, what's wrong?'

Tiffany leapt up from her seat and went to his rescue.

'What's wrong, darling? What's wrong? What on earth has happened to you?'

'Must have been stung by a bloody wasp or something,' Andrew muttered. 'Underneath the table.'

Everyone peered beneath the tablecloth in horror.

A wasp? In January? That was a good one. I made a swift beeline myself for the bathroom. Safely locked inside, I listened to the commotion continuing downstairs. Tiffany was getting hysterical.

'But I can't find the sting!' she shouted. 'It must have gone in really deep. We'll have to get him to hospital. He's bleeding so much. Might be an allergic reaction. Call an ambulance. Help me somebody. Quick!'

Poor Andrew, I thought as I made myself comfortable on the loo seat and lit up a fag. If I had known it was him, I wouldn't have been quite so vicious. Just a little pinch would have been enough for him. But hell,

I told myself, men who go around putting their toes in ladies' private places deserve to be stung by the occasional wasp. No wonder David had been looking at me as if I had gone mad when I thought that it was him who was toying with my affections.

I was just stubbing my fag out in Marvin's soapdish when I heard a knock at the bathroom door.

'Nearly finished,' I said out of habit.

'Ali, it's David. Can I come in?'

I opened the door just a crack.

'David? I don't think you can pee in front of me now that we're no longer engaged,' I warned him.

'I don't want to pee. I just want to talk.'

Beyond David, the house was suspiciously quiet.

'What's everybody else doing?' I asked.

'They've all gone to the hospital, of course.'

'What? All of them?'

'Yes. Andrew because he was "stung" (heavy sarcasm on that word). Fred because he had to drive. Tiffany was too shocked to drive but she had to go to give Andrew moral support and Peta won't go anywhere without Fred or let him go anywhere without her. Emma and Marvin just went along to ogle young doctors in the Accident Unit.'

'Incorrigible pair,' I laughed.

'So we're all alone,' David concluded. 'You can even come out of the bathroom now if you like.'

'I'm not sure how much I like the idea of being alone with you anymore,' I told him as I emerged, lighting up another precautionary fag to help him keep his distance. David had always hated me smoking.

'I see you're smoking again,' he said.

'Yes, I know. Does it annoy you?' I asked innocently.

'You know it does. It annoys me when anyone smokes in my presence. But I don't suppose I have much right to complain about your disgusting habits anymore, do I?'

'No. I don't suppose you do.'

We sat down together on the top stair.

'You really do look fantastic in that dress by the way,' he told me.

I flicked my hair backwards over my shoulder seductively. 'Really?'

'Wonderful. Red suits you. Don't know why you don't wear it more often. It brings out the highlights in your hair.' He wrapped a strand of the said hair around his fingers. I pulled my head away.

'You can stop buttering me up now, David,' I warned. 'I thought you wanted to talk seriously with me, not be a creep about my hairdo.'

'I do want to talk seriously. Listen, Ali,' David began. 'I suppose that the first thing I should do is apologise to you for the way I've behaved.'

'It's certainly a start.'

'I know I've been really out of order over this whole thing. It was really shitty of me to tell you that it was all over between us on Christmas Day, while you were still in hospital recovering from your operation and everything.'

I nodded. But there had to be more or I would push him down the stairs.

'We always had a great time together and we were more than just lovers . . . You and I were best friends, Ali. I owed you a decent ending because of that more than anything else. But I ran off like a real coward. I didn't know what to do. My emotions were whirling like a maelstrom.'

'Nice choice of word,' I said flippantly.

'Seriously,' said David, annoyed that I was interrupting the deep bit. 'They were. My mind was all over the place. I didn't know where to turn. I was like a ship adrift on the ocean. I suppose I should have just kept it all inside until you were better. Thought about the consequences more instead of steaming ahead. That would have been the decent thing to do.'

I stubbed out my cigarette on the carpet. Then I remembered that though I was talking to David I wasn't actually at his place and I had to make a desperate attempt to cover up the burn hole I had made so symbolically.

'I've been meaning to call you for a long time, Ali,' he said.

I nodded in the cynical way we girls reserve for such statements as that.

'I have. I really have,' David protested. 'But it's so hard to know where to start. I don't think you know how difficult all of this is for me.'

Talk about red rag to a bull. I think I may actually have snorted with disgust.

'What? Is it as difficult as taking a wedding dress back to the shop and asking for a refund?' I asked. 'Is it as difficult as uninviting 150 guests to a reception you've just lost a thousand pound deposit on, perhaps? Is it as difficult as cancelling a five-star honeymoon in Barbados?'

David looked downcast. 'I'm saving up to pay you back for all that, Ali. Really, I am.'

'It doesn't matter,' I told him quietly. 'I'd hate to think that all this boils down to is how far I am out of pocket. The money's inconsequential.'

David suddenly reached into my lap and took hold of both my hands.

'You know, I knew that you would take it like this. You're so composed, Ali. A lot of women wouldn't be in this situation. Lisa certainly wasn't when I ended things with her.'

'There's no need to use the L-word with me,' I said.

'When I see you being this brave, this big and forgiving, it makes me think what a fool I must have been to ever let you go.'

I squeezed his hands then let them fall back into his lap. So much for my bloody composure, it was slipping away by the minute. 'Don't say things like that,' I told him. 'It only makes it worse.'

'Ali,' said David, taking my chin in his hand and twisting my face towards his. 'You know that you will always be very special to me, don't you? That deep down, whatever happens, I will always have loved you. Do still love you, in fact. Even now. Even though we're apart.'

'David,' I whined. 'How can you say that to me now?' At which point my composure fell to the ground and was swiftly trodden underfoot by a dozen other things fleeing my body, like common sense, and dignity, and that last little bit of self-esteem. 'How can you leave me this way?'

He answered me with a kiss. A kiss that sucked out the last vestiges of the big, brave woman I thought I had become since he called off the engagement. Before

I could remind myself that this was the man I was going to spit on if I ever saw him again, we were rolling around like a pair of teenagers on Marvin's landing. David's hand was beneath the hem of the little red dress that Emma had loaned me so that I could look marvellous for the mystery man and I was doomed, suckered like a chocaholic faced with the world's last remaining Twix.

We broke off from rolling about for just long enough to call a cab to take us back to David's place. Then we snogged in the hallway until the mini-cab driver rang the door bell. As we canoodled in the back of the taxi, I swear he took us four times around the city walls and bumped our fare up by a tenner.

'David, we shouldn't,' I protested half-heartedly as he struggled to get his key into the door without taking his lips from my face.

'But it feels so natural, Ali. So right.'

So it should have done. We had had enough practice at the business over the last three years.

Reason made one last stab at saving my dignity as I popped into the bathroom to empty my bladder. I couldn't have missed the gaudy pair of gold earrings that sat on the shelf by the sink. A pair of earrings that certainly hadn't been left behind when I last cleaned my teeth in that bathroom.

'He's with Lisa now, you idiot,' screamed Ms Reason from deep inside me. 'There's the solid evidence. What more do you need? Get out, get out, get out!!!'

But then David appeared at the bathroom door, wearing nothing but his silky boxer shorts and smiling that disarming smile. 'What's taking you so long?' he asked. 'I'm getting cold out here without you.'

I quickly took out my own earrings and flipped the mystery pair haphazardly into the bin. With my cubic zirconia sparklers in their place, I felt triumphant. Lisa, Schmisa, I thought as I trotted eagerly into the bedroom. Lisa Brown was just a blip in the smooth history of our relationship. I had wrestled David Whitworth from her terrible clutches once before and I was about to do it all over again.

Waking up the next morning was a surreal experience. Everything looked strangely normal. Exactly the same as it had done every other morning for the past two years. And yet it was not normal. I was in David's bed, but we were no longer engaged to be married. As far as I knew he was still, strictly speaking, another woman's man and thus together we had committed an infidelity.

David wasn't awake. He was snoring. Something which he had always done while we were together and something which told me that he was going to be asleep for a fair while yet.

Gingerly I put a toe out onto the carpet. When David and I were engaged and spending every other night together at his house, I had kept a spare pair of slippers in his room. Not slippers exactly, but some tatty blue cotton espadrilles that were no longer smart enough to be taken on holiday. Instinctively, I looked under the bed to see if they were still there.

They weren't.

And neither was my special Snoopy toothbrush, I discovered to my horror when I made a proper foray around the bathroom. My heart sank fifty feet as

I surveyed the new contents of David's bathroom cabinet. Lady's razors for sensitive skin in germoline pink, and a tube of contraceptive jelly.

As if I was hoping that it would morph into a tube of Savlon, I picked the contraceptive jelly up and looked at it. Who did that belong to? As if I didn't know. But, against all rationality, I told myself that at least the cupboard was bereft of evidence to suggest that she had really moved herself in. No mascara, no foundation, no lipstick, and I knew that Lisa Brown was the kind of major shareholder in Max Factor who couldn't let the cat out unless she was wearing her 'face'.

Added to this was the fact that David had brought me back there at all, which he wouldn't have done if he was actually living with her, surely. Hang on a minute, cried a deep buried memory, what about the time that he . . .

OK, OK, I acknowledged that particle of brain. So he had taken me back to the flat that he shared with Lisa before they split up for the first time. But the majority of my grey cells were still bathed in a dangerous soup of optimism and denial as I dressed myself that morning. She doesn't seem to have taken root, they said. No problem to get rid of every last trace of her if she hasn't really taken root yet.

I scrubbed at my teeth triumphantly with David's toothbrush. Forget rampant shagging and the swapping of bodily fluids, everyone knows that sharing a toothbrush is the ultimate gesture of intimacy. Then I squirted beneath my arms with his manly deodorant. I had often done that while we were together, then later on, while I was at work, every time I lifted my arms up to do something like fetch down a file or draw a blind, a waft of the stuff would remind me of David and my luck in being with him.

Returning to the bedroom, I shook David gently by the arm.

He woke up and gave a little start, which disappointed me, until the surprise on his face was replaced by a contented smile.

'Ali,' he murmured softly.

'That's me. Listen, David, I've got to go to work. Will I see you later on?' I asked.

In answer David wrapped his big arms around my waist and tried to pull me back under the covers.

'No. Don't start that,' I said, happily wriggling free from his embrace. 'We can do it all again later on.'

'Yes, later on,' he murmured.

'What time?' I asked. I had to pin him down again. 'What time? When are you working today?' The employees in his insurance company office did shifts for customer convenience.

'I'm not working at all today,' he told me. 'I've got a day due in flexi-time. I'm taking it off.'

'Oh.' I hovered between getting up and sitting back down again. Maybe I should take the day off as well. We could spend the whole of it together. In bed. Cementing things. Putting our relationship back together for good. I could tell Julie that my appendix was giving me pain again. But I decided against it. One thing I had promised myself in the long month since we were last together is that, if David ever did come crawling back to me, he would find me slightly changed. More independent. Much less likely to drop everything for him when he gave the nod.

'Have the day off too,' he said.

The fact that he wanted me to was all that I needed right then.

'No,' I said, firmly but affectionately. 'I have a job to go to. I had to have a long time off work because of my appendix, remember?'

'Your appendix.' He traced the place where I had a scar. 'It doesn't hurt you anymore, does it, Ali?'

'No, it doesn't hurt,' I said, pushing him back down into the pillows. 'Listen, you just behave yourself today and I'll see you later on.'

'Come round as soon as you've finished work,' he told me.

'I'll see what I can do,' I said as nonchalantly as I could manage.

I knew I'd be there like a shot.

CHAPTER EIGHT

In the excitement of my reunion with David, I had almost forgotten about the terrible dilemma that was the *Complete Woman* Most Romantic Couple competition. But just as I was about to leave the office at five on the dot to rejoin David in bed, the telephone on my desk rang out accusingly.

I could tell it was an external call because of the ringing tone. I didn't normally get external calls. All my calls were from my boss, Mr Chivers, asking why I was still such an appalling typist after three years of promising to change and a fortune spent on computer courses.

'Ali Harris's desk,' I said officially.

'Is Ali there?'

'Speaking,' I said, wondering briefly why I had referred to myself as a desk.

'Hi, Ali. It's Amanda here. You said you were going to call me today, you naughty girl. Remember? About the photo shoot? For *Complete Woman*?'

'Ah, Amanda, yes,' I said, sitting down again so that my thinking muscles wouldn't be overstretched by having to keep me upright as well as sensible. 'I did promise to call you, didn't I? I'm sorry. I've been ever so busy at the office today. I'm sure you know how it is.' In fact I had spent most of the day in the seedy little smoking room, mulling over the details of my sudden reunion with David with Kim from the reprographics department. Julie, surprisingly, hadn't wanted to know apart from telling me that it would all end in disaster.

'Well?' asked Amanda.

'What?' said I.

'Well, have you decided when we're going to do these blasted photos? I know it's a bit of a bore darling, but frankly it's a small price to pay for a fortnight at Santa Bonita, don't you think? All inclusive. I went there myself last year. It's fabulous. Really luxurious. You will love it, love it, love it.'

A vision of the hot sand and the blue sea wafted briefly through my imagination. I would love it. Yes please. But how on earth could I take the Most Romantic prize up now that I no longer had a fiancé?

'Have you spoken to your other half about days which would be suitable for him?'

'Er . . . er?' I fumbled. Then suddenly it hit me. I almost had an other half again, didn't I? And I was supposed to be on my way to see him at that very moment. Surely it was just a matter of time before that ring was back on my finger. I didn't have to turn the holiday down anymore. I just had to ask David to come with me.

'Amanda,' I said happily. 'You know what? I'm supposed to be meeting David in just ten minutes time. I'll run some dates past him tonight and call you first thing tomorrow morning. OK?'

'Promise me, Ali,' said Amanda gravely. 'I'm on a tight deadline, you know. Will you really call tomorrow?'

'I will,' I promised.

I put the phone down and allowed myself a moment of smug reflection on my luck before heading over to David's. However, just as I was about to close the office door behind me, the phone rang again. External.

I bit my lip. Should I answer it, or should I just leave it ringing? It was probably just a pesky customer. But what if it was David, frantic with worry that I hadn't arrived home yet? Or calling to ask if I wanted to be picked up in his nice new car? I picked up the phone to talk to him.

'I hate you,' said the caller.

'Oh,' I said. Fear spread through my body like ice forming on the surface of a puddle. Was it Lisa Brown? Did she know about last night already?

'What happened to you last night, you whore?'

No. I sighed with relief. It was only Emma.

'When we got back from the hospital you were gone. I was really worried about you, Ali Harris. Until Marvin pointed out that David had left a note on the kitchen table to say that he had "scored".'

'He did what?' I asked. The scumbag, I thought. Must have been while I was fetching my coat.

'He said that he had "scored". Am I right to assume that the unlucky woman was you? No, don't tell me . . . The real story is, you didn't get off with David. You called for a taxi home and ended up spending the night in the back of a Ford sierra with a delicious mini-cab driver instead? Since we both know there's no such thing as a delicious mini-cab driver, as I said when I first called up – I hate you, Alison Harris.'

'Why?'

'For letting me down again.'

'Letting you down?' I repeated incredulously.

'Yes. How long did you make him grovel for this time, Ali? Ten minutes? Five minutes? Two minutes? Or did you grovel to him perchance while we were all down at the hospital tending to poor sick Andrew?'

'I did not grovel to David.'

'You do know what he's after, don't you?' she asked.

'He said that he's missed me since we split up. He thinks he wants us to get back together.'

'Pah!' Emma spat. 'He just wants to go to Antigua.'

The words seemed to sting.

'How can he?' I protested. 'He doesn't even know about that! I only told you.'

'Yeah. And I told Marvin. And Marvin, as you must have guessed, told everybody else at the party while we were having that panic in the loo. It's obvious, Ali. David simply thinks that if he gets in with you now, he's got a chance of a two week all-inclusive holiday in the sun. Gratis.'

'It's not like that. Don't be so cynical. He's asked me to go straight round to his place after work. Why would he do that if he wasn't serious about getting back together with me? Lisa might come round at any minute.'

'Unlikely. Lisa Brown is on a three week self-assertiveness course in Hastings,' said Emma smugly. 'Marvin told me. He knows her sister.'

'Well, she won't walk in on us then,' I replied frostily.

'But I'm not stupid, Emma. I know when someone's just taking advantage of me for sex. And David isn't. David's serious about getting back together. I could tell it from the way he kissed me last night.'

'Oh please. David's a schmuck.'

'We'll see about that. I'll ask him straight out about him and Lisa and about whether he's only interested in me for the holiday. How about that? I know what he'll say to me, Emma. I'll tell you the good news later on.'

'If you come home,' Emma snorted.

'Well, you could try to be optimistic for me. You're supposed to be my best friend.'

'If I wasn't your best friend I'd be delighted that you're getting your oats. As it is, I don't want you to get hurt all over again. Look, just don't do anything I wouldn't do tonight, OK? And by that I mean don't go inviting any slimy ex-boyfriends of yours to Antigua . . .'

[illegible] stupid [illegible] when [illegible]
[illegible] And Lloyd [illegible]
[illegible] that [illegible]
talk from the way he behaved [illegible] night.
[illegible]
We [illegible] about that [illegible] straight out again
[illegible] and Lisa and asked whether [illegible] interested
in [illegible] the holiday. [illegible] know [illegible]
[illegible] I'll [illegible] you [illegible]
later on.
[illegible]
[illegible]
supposed to be [illegible] friends.
[illegible]
[illegible]
[illegible]
[illegible]
[illegible]
[illegible]

CHAPTER NINE

'David,' I said, almost as soon as he opened the door to me. 'Do you want to come to Antigua?'

'Antigua?' he asked disingenuously. 'Where's that then, Ali? What's happening there?'

'It's in the West Indies, silly,' I told him. 'I've won this fantastic fortnight-long holiday for two in a magazine competition. It's going to be all-inclusive. Do you want to come?'

'Does the Pope have a smoking handbag?' David replied excitedly. 'When do we go?'

'Well, two weeks next Thursday provisionally. But I can change the dates if you'd prefer.'

David made a mental calculation and nodded. 'No. Two weeks next Thursday sounds perfect to me. How did you win this trip, you clever girl?'

'Oh, I just had to answer a couple of questions and finish a tie-breaker,' I lied. 'You know the kind of thing.' No point in telling him the truth just yet, I figured. I didn't want to frighten him off again by putting him under the pressure of being one half of the alleged happiest couple in the world.

'I had no idea you could do that kind of thing,' David marvelled.

'I had a lot of spare time while my appendix scar was healing up.'

'But are you sure you want to take me?' David asked suddenly. 'I mean, I haven't exactly been the best of friends to you since then.' He stroked the base of my neck, fishing for forgiveness. 'You could take Emma instead.'

'I know. But I want to take you,' I assured him. 'I don't want to have to share two weeks on a paradise isle with Emma. She snores. And I can't say I really fancy her all that much.'

'A paradise isle,' David mused. 'This is just what we need, Ali. To put our relationship back on the right track. Two weeks away from all the trials and pressures of everyday life.'

We both lay back on the sofa and dreamed about feeling the sun beating down on our hot bodies as we lay on the golden sand.

'All-inclusive, you said?' David asked suddenly. 'Does that mean booze as well?'

'Local drinks, it said in the brochure they sent me. I think that just means rum. But I'm sure you can buy lager there, if you want it.'

'It's a small price to pay, I guess, for two weeks in the sun with my dream woman.' He pulled me close to him and kissed me on the top of my head. 'You're such a clever girl, Ali. What did you say the tie-breaker was?'

'I didn't. But it was to do with suntan lotion, I think,' I added quickly for authenticity.

'Aw, come on, Ali. Stop trying to pretend you can't remember what you wrote. You must do. Tell me. You should be proud of your slogan. It's taking us away on holiday after all. Tell me, Ali. Please.'

'No, it's really very silly,' I protested.

'Tell me, Ali.' He grabbed my left ankle and I knew he meant business. If I didn't tell him a slogan, he would tickle me to within an inch of my life.

'Er. It was "Make sure you slap me on, before you go and sit in the sun",' I blurted before he could start tickling. 'Do you get it?'

'I think so. And that was it? Doesn't even rhyme properly,' David commented as he dropped my foot.

'Guess the others must have been even worse,' I said.

'Guess they must have been. Ah well, who cares? We won!'

He started to sing 'Viva Espana!'

'We're going to the Caribbean,' I reminded him. 'Not Spain.'

'Don't know any songs for that,' he replied. 'Now, are you sure I don't owe you anything for this trip?'

'Well,' I said as I wriggled into a prone position on the sofa. 'Perhaps you could give me something in kind.'

I was happier than a pig in shit as I fell asleep that night. David was curled up like a puppy dog beside me, his big hand resting gently on my waist, just near my scar. I looked across at him, at that familiar handsome profile, and suddenly it was as if the sun had started to shine on my life again. The terrible revelations of Christmas Day seemed like something I had just imagined in the aftermath of my operation. We were back together again. And stronger for the time we had spent apart.

'I'll never let you go again, David Whitworth,' I whispered into his sweet-smelling hair. 'You mean more to me than anyone in the whole wide world and I really, really love you.'

'I love you too, Lisa,' he said.

I sprang upright against the pillows and stared at him. But he was still fast asleep, oblivious to his little cock-up. It was an easy mistake to make, I decided. He had spent a lot of time with her recently. But by the time we got back from Antigua, Lisa Brown would be totally forgotten. If he said her name then, though, I'd throttle him with my bare hands.

'Can I use your phone?' David asked the next morning.

I had insisted that we go back to my place because I wanted to parade David in front of Emma at the breakfast table to show her how wrong she had been about our reunion. As it was, Emma didn't have the decency to be home when I wanted to gloat. She later let me know that she had decided to stay with Marvin to give me some privacy while I came to the right decision. Instead, the only member of the flat team to witness the historic moment was Fattypuss. She was unimpressed, since she had been sleeping on my bed since David's departure and felt usurped by his sudden return.

'Who do you want to call?' I asked him innocently.

'Well, I've got to call my boss as soon as possible.'

'It's Saturday morning.'

'He'll be in the office. Almost lives there. I've got to call him right away because I need to get two weeks worth of holiday all of a sudden. Remember?'

'Of course,' I smiled coyly. I gestured to the Mickey Mouse phone which stood on my bedside table.

'Er, haven't you got another phone?' David asked.

'It works,' I reassured him. 'You just dial the numbers on the back of Mickey's ear.'

'I don't think I can talk to my boss on that phone,' David said firmly.

'You've done it before,' I protested.

'Yes, but not when I have had to think this hard and this seriously about something. I've got to come up with a really good reason why I want to take two weeks off in the middle of the busiest period of the business year, Ali. February's a boom time for burst pipes and floods. I need to be able to think straight. Come up with a foolproof excuse.'

He looked stern.

'You can use the one in the living room,' I conceded.

He jumped up and headed for the door, closing it carefully behind him. I lay back in bed for thirty seconds, revelling in the smell of his aftershave on my pillow before the curiosity bug bit me. I wondered what kind of tale of woe he was making up to convince his boss that he should have two weeks off work. I hoped he wasn't using the old 'got to go to a funeral' trick. That always seemed too much like tempting fate to me.

Mickey the phone smiled at me vacantly from the side of my bed. If I picked the receiver up I would be able to hear exactly what David was saying downstairs.

No, that would be underhand, I chided myself. He would tell me what he had said himself when he came back to bed.

But then again, I wanted to hear his boss's voice, to see

if he was really convinced by the excuse. David would never know that I had listened in. I had practised the art of picking the receiver up noiselessly during the brief paranoid period when I had thought that Emma might be flirting with my man. She hadn't been, of course. But it's hard to believe that your Mars Bar of a man could be someone else's fish paste sandwich. Emma only had eyes for her hopeless case Marvin.

'Fattypuss, don't you tell a soul what I am about to do,' I warned the rotund tabby peril as I picked the receiver up. She merely continued to clean her paws haughtily. My secret would be safe with her.

'. . . so you see, I'm going to be away for two whole weeks. You'll be able to manage without me for that long won't you?' said David on the other line.

Wow, perhaps he was simply telling his boss the truth, I thought. Now that would be a novelty.

'Oh, David. I don't know if I can,' said his boss.

Hang on a minute, I said to myself. I thought David's boss was a man.

'But it's my big chance for promotion,' David continued. 'You always knew that to get ahead with my work I would have to travel abroad. It's just two weeks, honey-pie. Two liccle-iccle weeks. I'm doing it for us, honestly, my sweet.'

'Do you mean that, Twinky-winky?'

Twinky-winky? It suddenly hit me right between the eyes that David wasn't talking to his boss at all.

'I really mean that, my little angel,' David continued. 'And I'll bring you back a lovely present.'

I put the Mickey receiver back noiselessly and surprised myself by managing not to scream out in pain. It was another three minutes before David came back to bed. I guess he must have called his boss for real after hanging up on Lisa bloody bitch-face Brown.

'Hello again,' I said, aware that my voice was shaking. 'Do you think you got away with it?'

'Scot-free,' said David proudly as he slid beneath the duvet and put his hand straight up my tartan nightie. 'No-one knows anything. I could do with a cup of tea to calm my nerves down again though. You going anywhere near the kitchen, Twinky-winky?'

'Twinky-winky?' I repeated accusingly.

'That's my new name for you,' he said hurriedly. 'Suits you, don't you think?'

'I'm not sure,' I replied. I got to my feet unsteadily. David had never used a pet-name for me before. In fact, he had once actually said that people only used pet-names when they were frightened of being caught out by saying the wrong real one at an inconvenient moment.

'I'll make that cup of tea,' I said, knowing that if I didn't get out of that bedroom pretty damn quickly there was going to be blood on the duvet and it wouldn't be mine.

'Tea. Milk. Two sugars, my Caribbean Queen,' David murmured, holding me back for a moment and kissing each of my fingers in turn before letting go of my hands. 'Though I'm sure you haven't forgotten how I like my cuppa.'

'Tea, milk, two sugars,' I murmured in reply as I stood at the door to my bedroom and looked back at David settling himself back under the sheets. I walked to the kitchen about as steadily as someone who had just received a hard blow to the head.

* * *

I put the kettle on and felt the steam rising in me as the water in the kettle boiled. This was not working out as I had intended. The evidence presented to me by my sneaky snooping suggested unequivocally that David had no intention of telling Lisa that things were over between them yet. In fact, it seemed he was planning to go straight to see her as soon as our plane touched the ground.

I should tell him where to go, I thought.

On the other hand, I could hardly have expected him to break the news of our reunion to Lisa over the phone, could I? Not while she was on her self-assertiveness course in Hastings. He was probably intending to tell her the truth when we got back. Or perhaps he was going to write her a 'Dear John' letter to read while we were away in the sun.

I should go ahead with the trip as planned, I thought.

But why on earth would David Whitworth be bothering to be so bloody tactful? So, Lisa Brown was on a self-assertiveness course? I had been recovering from a serious operation on Christmas Day when he pulled the plug on me!!!

I should tell David exactly where to stick his bucket and spade.

He was obviously intending to use this period while Lisa was out of town and I had two tickets to the sun to help him choose between us. But I didn't want him to have to make his mind up. I wanted him to know that he wanted me right now. I couldn't go to Antigua with David while there was still the vague chance that he would run straight into Lisa's longing arms upon our return. It would turn the whole dream holiday into a nightmare. I didn't want to feel like I had to perform all the time in order to hang on to him. Worse still was the nagging doubt that he had already chosen and the winner was Lisa. I was getting the booby prize. Two weeks of togetherness in lieu of forever.

The kettle finished boiling and I slopped the hot water onto two tea bags in the mugs. David had a thing about his tea. No mugs and definitely no tea bags. Strictly bone china and leaves for him. But right then I wasn't sure he deserved such close attention to his whims.

Maybe I hadn't made my mind up about him either, I told myself as I slopped in the milk (slightly curdled). Maybe I should look upon this two weeks in Antigua as an opportunity for unbridled sex that I could leave behind with my flip-flops at the end of the fortnight. Maybe I could use him too.

No way, I was telling myself by the time I stirred in two sugars. I was way too emotionally involved to use someone. I had never had a one night stand and walked away in the morning leaving the wrong phone number on the poor sucker's pillow as Emma seemed to do on a weekly basis. And I had read far too many magazine articles about the dangers of trying to have unbridled passion with an ex. It is never unbridled. Never. Never. Never.

I slumped onto a stool and sat staring at the tube of Hot Stuff Heat Rub Emma had bought for her dodgy stiff knee while I waited for sanity to return in full.

'That tea ready yet?' David shouted from the bedroom.

'Nearly,' I called like the girl I used to be, before Lisa Brown and before the loss of my appendix, while squashing the tube of Hot Stuff Heat Rub hard in the middle to keep the anger out of my voice.

'Bring it up here then, will you? I'm gasping.'

Dutifully, I loaded a tray with the two mugs of tea and a packet of chocolate biscuits and began the climb up the stairs. As I handed him his mug, David's nose wrinkled in just the slightest hint of disdain at the presentation.

'Lovely,' he said. 'You always did make a good cup of tea.'

'Thank you.'

'Now,' he said. 'Hop in here next to me. I've been getting cold in bed without you.'

David turfed Fattypuss off the bed unceremoniously to make a space for me. I slipped in under the covers with him and let my dressing gown fall open seductively. David's eyes slipped involuntarily to my breasts.

'How about some unbridled passion and rampant sex?' I asked him shakily. Maybe I could do it. Detach the physical from the emotional. Maybe I was strong enough to separate love and lust and play him at his own game.

I kissed him before he could answer, pushing him back into the pillows and sliding my hand into his boxer shorts with the kind of all-in-one manoeuvre that I had only ever seen on TV.

'Wow!!' said David when I let him up for air.

'Thought I would give you a little help in choosing between me and Lisa Brown, since I know that's what you're doing, David Whitworth,' I told him ominously as I reached for his cock. 'Hmmm, maybe my hands are a little rough,' I said. 'Perhaps I ought to use some lubrication.'

'Lubrication!' sighed David, like it was a new word for fellatio.

I reached into the pocket of my dressing gown.

'Close your eyes,' I murmured seductively.

He obliged quite willingly.

I squirted a big dollop of Hot Stuff Heat Rub into my palm and made a grab for his willy. It took just two firm strokes up and down before he opened his baby blue eyes with a hideous look of recognition that there is a very fine line between pleasure and pain.

'Hells-fucking-bells.' He slapped my hands away and leapt to his feet. 'What the fuck, Ali? My balls, my balls! What have you done to me? I'm burning up! I'm dying.'

He raced to the bathroom and I soon heard the cold tap being turned on full.

'Bugger! Fuck!' he shouted.

I guess it must have been stinging pretty badly.

'Call an ambulance for crying out loud, Ali. Fuck! You've finished me!'

I meandered to the bathroom door and leaned nonchalantly against the door frame.

'What's wrong? Are you hurt, my dear?'

'What the fuck did you put on me, you bitch?'

'Nothing. I mean, just something I thought would make things a little more exciting for you.' I brought the tube of Hot Stuff out of my pocket again and looked at it as if I didn't know what it really was supposed to be used for.

'You put Heat Rub on me!' he screamed. 'You're a bloody psycho!'

'What did I do wrong?'

David turned away from the sink then and ran back to the bedroom still clutching his balls. He then redressed with obscene haste.

'What's wrong with you, you nutter? What do you think? Were you trying to hurt me deliberately?'

'Were you trying to hurt me deliberately?' I countered. 'I just listened to you telling Lisa Brown that you're going to be away from town on business for two weeks. You weren't going to tell her about me and the holiday at all, were you, you scumbag?'

'Eh?'

'I used Mickey Mouse while you were on the phone downstairs,' I explained. 'I can't do it, David. I can't go to Antigua with you knowing that you're going to go straight back to her when we get home. You have to choose between us right now. Me or Lisa Brown? Make your choice.'

'Oh, I've bloody chosen all right,' said David, still cupping his balls like they were made of solid gold. 'I don't need a holiday this much. You can go on your own for all I care. You're a nutter, Ali Harris. A nutter and a psycho. You ought to be locked up for good!'

'And you're scum, David Whitworth,' I screamed from my bedroom window as he ran quickly from the flat to his car like a Bosnian escaping sniper fire. 'You're two steps down from plankton. No, make that three steps! And one day Lisa Brown will realise that too.' He fired up his engine. 'Why would I have wanted to lie on a beach next to you anyway, you big fat lump of lard?' Unfortunately I don't think he heard that particularly inspired remark.

David's car disappeared around the corner. I closed the window when I noticed that the man across the road was looking in at me in my untied dressing gown.

Bugger, bugger, bugger.

David had gone again.

Why did Emma always have to be right?

CHAPTER TEN

As if to rub my nose in it, the day that David chose to exit from my life again was the day that my parents celebrated their thirtieth wedding anniversary. When I called Mum to say that the bottom had fallen out of my life again and what possible choice did I have but to fling myself headlong from a high window onto a spiky wrought iron fence, she was too stressed out by her vol-au-vents to care.

'I'm sure they're supposed to have puffed up by now, but they're not even slightly bigger,' she wailed. 'This is going to be a disaster. We should have got a professional caterer in, but oh no, your father said that it was too expensive. Said that they would only charge us a fortune to put some Marks and Spencers titbits in the microwave. We could do that ourselves and save loads of money, he said. He's always been the same. Ever since I met him. Tight as a tick, he is. Always coming up with some money-saving plan that turns out to be a disaster that costs us twice as much as getting a professional in would have cost in the first place. Thirty years we've been together. It's a wonder we lasted thirty minutes.'

'Mum,' I said, attempting to interrupt while she drew breath. 'Mum, I don't think I can come to your party tonight.'

'Whaaattt!?!'

'I said, I don't think I can come to your party tonight. You know, David suddenly calling things off again has laid me pretty low. If I come to your party I'll only spoil things by standing around looking miserable all night.'

'John! You'll never believe what your eldest daughter is saying to me now,' she shrieked to my father. Strange how I was always his daughter when I was pissing her off. 'John, come in here and talk to her at once.'

With that, my mother put the receiver down. Not down so that I got cut off. Just down on the hall table while she went to fetch my Dad. I could hear her shrieking even when she was out in the garage, where Dad would probably be hiding on the pretence of tidying up some old deckchairs so that they could be brought into the house for the anniversary bash. I knew my family so well.

When my mother really started to raise her voice, Berkeley the family dog would always join in too. I could hear him barking now. It was five minutes before the receiver was picked up again. It wasn't Dad though. It was my sister Jo.

'Listen Ali, you'll be in deep shit for the rest of your life if you don't come to this party tonight,' she warned me. 'How could you even suggest that you're not going to come? Dad is getting it in the neck something chronic because of you.'

'Put him on,' I begged her, thinking that he, of all the people in that house of insensitive ball-breakers, might understand the plight of the recently broken-hearted.

'I can't. Mum hasn't finished with him yet. And I'm going to have to put the phone down on you now anyway. I'm waiting for a call.'

'A man?' I asked.

'Of course,' she said. 'I'll see you later. Don't be late.'

My little sister put the phone down on me. I stared at the receiver for a while. Then I picked it up and tried to call home again. I thought I would disguise my voice and make sure that I got Dad by pretending to be calling from a garage or something. But when I called back the phone was engaged. I imagined Jo sitting at the bottom of the stairs, twisting the phone cable round and round her elegant fingers as she listened to some poor sap telling her how beautiful and talented she was. Pretty much the entire upper sixth form of the local boys' grammar school had failed their mock A levels because of our Jo.

Then I thought of Dad in the garage, faced by Mum and the dog, and with nothing to look forward to but a night with his mother-in-law and her cronies, and suddenly there was no doubt that I would be at that anniversary party after all.

I went upstairs to my bedroom and studied my bedraggled-looking face in the dressing-table mirror. My hair hung about my cheeks like two lank curtains of seaweed. My eyes were barely visible for the big puffy bags that surrounded them. I looked like the kind of hideous mess that not even Clarins Beauty Flash could deal with. And what on earth was I going to wear? What did one wear to one's parents' anniversary party? Most of my wardrobe sent my mother running for her old Doctor Spock manual to see where she had gone wrong.

Emma would know. But of course she wasn't in. Where was she when I needed her?

You know how it is at these moments in your life. Things seem interminably black. You can feel your canoe scraping along the bottom of life's river. You've got a hole in your boat and you can't bail out fast enough. You're rapidly sinking, but from somewhere deep inside you a little voice calls out: 'We've done this all before, remember? When the canoe hits the bottom, you can let it sink and swim for it instead!!' And then you start the long hard metaphorical swim back to happiness. Well, I was having exactly that thought when the phone rang and my canoe went over a waterfall, with me still pathetically trapped inside.

'Ali!' trilled a voice which had become all too familiar to me. 'Ali darling, it's Amanda from *Complete Woman*. We've still got to sort out that photo shoot haven't we, you naughty little Miss Camera-shy you. Listen, I know it's Saturday, and you're probably up to your eyeballs in the ironing, but I've got a photographer in your part of town right now. Is your better half available to do the photographs at your place tonight?'

'Tonight?' Suddenly what to wear to the anniversary party was the least of my worries. 'Tonight, tonight?'

'Yes. Tonight. Well, about six o'clock to be precise. That's not too late is it? Doesn't interfere with any plans you might have?'

'Well, actually,' I began, thanking heaven for my latest excuse. 'It might do. You see, tonight is my Mum and Dad's thirtieth wedding anniversary party. I promised to help. You know how it is. I've got to be there at five to help cook the vol-au-vents.'

'Mmm, interesting,' said Amanda. 'Where do they live?'

'Brindlesham,' I said. But probably nowhere near me or Amanda's convenient photographer, I added hastily.

'Farehurst Street? Why, fabulous. That's just round the corner from the photographer's first call. Did you know there's a woman who does really accurate horoscopes for pets in your town centre?'

I certainly didn't.

'Listen, Ali,' Amanda persisted. 'I've just had the most fantastic idea. Why don't we take the photos of you and David at your parents' anniversary party? It'll make a great feature. Really interesting. I can see the headline now: *Britain's most romantic couple celebrate their everlasting love with the older generation*. I love it.'

'Er, er. I don't know how Mum and Dad will feel about that,' I blustered. 'I mean, it is their party and I wouldn't want to upstage them.'

'Nonsense. They'll be delighted,' said Amanda with unshakeable certainty. 'Believe me. Think of what a fabulous souvenir it will be for them. Their thirtieth wedding anniversary celebrated in the glossy pages of *Complete Woman*. There aren't many couples who can say they've had such an honour.'

I collapsed onto the stool beside the telephone table and clutched up a handful of my hair, ready to pull it out.

'OK,' Amanda continued regardless of my reservations. 'What time will things kick off in earnest? When will David arrive at their house?'

'Actually, that's the problem.'

Was I about to tell her the truth?

'What's the problem, Ali?'

'David won't be there,' I said very slowly.

Peculiar silence on the other end of the line.

'David won't be there?' Amanda asked eventually. 'But it's your parents' thirtieth anniversary party. How could he possibly not be there for you? What are you talking about, sweetheart?'

'David and I,' I began. 'David and I have decided that it's for the best.'

'Ali, what are you trying to tell me?'

'It's for the best that he isn't there.'

The longer this took, the further away from me my courage was running. It was at the front door already, taking off the chain and fiddling at the latch.

'It's for the best that he isn't there because some of the old ladies present at the party might be susceptible to shingles.'

What? I thought even as I said it.

'What?' said Amanda.

I took a deep breath. 'You see, David has just come down with chickenpox. He missed it as a child, but he has it now and, as you must know, chickenpox can have terrible complications in the elderly. We thought that it wouldn't be fair to expose them to that risk. Not while he's still contagious. And of course, the spots are another reason why David isn't terribly keen to have his photograph taken just yet. I don't know why I didn't tell you earlier, Amanda. I suppose I just thought that you wouldn't believe me.'

'Oh, Ali.' I could tell immediately that I had her hook, line and sinker. 'How could you have thought that of little old me? Of course I believe you. Of course I understand. Chickenpox is such a nightmare! I didn't have it until my teens, you know. I tried ever so hard not to pick at the spots but I still managed to end up with some terrible scars. Have you had it yourself?'

'Fortunately yes.'

'Oh, thank goodness for that. Because the last thing a bride needs on her big day is to have to cover up chickenpox scars. Well, I suppose we're just going to have to put that photo shoot on hold till he's better. I'm so terribly sorry to hear he's unwell. I wouldn't have hassled you half so much if I had known the truth. I thought you were just being shy. Anyway, I'm sure you've got calamine lotion to dab. Please pass on the very best wishes of *Complete Woman* to your poor dear man.'

'I will,' I said. 'And I'm sure he'll appreciate it. Better go. I think I can see David scratching right now.' I looked in the direction of my empty bedroom. 'Oh, hang on. There's something I've been meaning to ask you. Amanda, I was wondering, what would you wear to an anniversary party?'

'Oooh, now there's a conundrum,' she muttered. 'How about a little white trouser suit with flat gold loafers and a pistachio silk blouse?'

Yeah, how about that, I thought. 'Thanks, Amanda. I'll call you as soon as the spots have gone.' I put down the phone and clutched my head in my hands.

CHAPTER ELEVEN

In the end I went to Mum and Dad's anniversary party dressed in the navy blue suit I kept for job interviews and a mustard coloured blouse that I pinched from Emma's extensive wardrobe. When I arrived, Mum seemed to have forgiven me for the shock I had given her that morning, but she still disapproved of the outfit.

She herself was dressed from head to toe in baby pink Frank Usher with enough sequins on the bodice for a whole episode of *Come Dancing*. My sisters were in matching stretchy velvet mini-dresses of the kind that I would have thought were vetoed in front of my miserable old Auntie Eileen.

'This is supposed to be a party, Ali,' Mum told me when she saw what I was wearing. 'You look like you've come to do an audit.'

Feeling thoroughly dowdy, I was summoned straight into the kitchen where a veritable production line of vol-au-vents and sausage-on-stick-type things was in operation. Jane was laying the vol-au-vents out on baking trays and Jo was slopping milk from a jug onto the little pastry cases to make them shine. There were already enough completed canapés to feed the five thousand balancing precariously on top of the microwave.

'Who is coming tonight?' I asked, as I filched some cheese and pineapple. 'Billy Bunter and his family?'

'We've had fifty-seven RSVPs,' said my mother proudly.

'Wow. I didn't think we knew that many people. Who?'

'Auntie Eileen, Auntie Maureen, Auntie Gwendoline, Auntie . . .'

'OK. Stop right there,' I said. 'All the maiden aunts, of course. They'll go anywhere for a free sausage. But who else?'

'The people who used to live next door,' said Jo with a wicked smile on her face. 'The Baxters. Do you remember them from when we lived in Saintbridge Road?'

'The Baxters?'

'Yes,' said Jo. 'And Jeremy.'

'Jeremy Baxter?'

'Jeremy Baxter,' said Jo.

'But . . .'

'Mum invited him for you,' my little sister said, exploding with laughter at the thought.

'Mum!!!' I whined. 'How could you?'

You see, Jeremy Baxter was the first boy I ever kissed. As you've probably gathered, he and his family lived next door to my family in the house where I spent my early and most formative years. Jeremy Baxter was a year older than me, which made him a good catch in those days of skipping ropes and Bubblicious. And because my sisters and I weren't allowed to play any further away from our house than the end of the road, I didn't really have much to compare him with. But when I got to junior school and heard him referred to as a dweeb, I quickly stopped trying to make him kiss me behind the greenhouse. By the time I was twelve and he was thirteen, Jeremy had been struck by acne and I never really spoke to him again. The fact that Mum had invited him to this party was obviously divine retribution for the time that I had refused to invite him to my thirteenth birthday party because he had big red pustules on his neck.

'Wonder what he looks like now?' said Jane wistfully.

'I know! I know!' shrieked Jo. 'He's probably spent the past ten years glued to a computer screen. He will be wearing glasses this thick,' she picked up a couple of whisky tumblers to demonstrate. 'And his skin will be like the skin of one of those translucent fishy things that lives at the bottom of the sea and never sees the light of day. He will either be a pathetic weed or he will make Jabba the Hutt look like the latest winner of Weightwatcher of the Year.'

'Don't be so cruel,' warned my mother.

'But I'm probably right, Mum! You know I am,' Jo protested. 'I bet he's still got those disgusting boils on the back of his neck as well.'

'I wonder if he's hairy,' asked Jane. 'His dad was horribly hairy. He had to shave right down to the top of his T-shirt.'

Both my sisters gave an involuntary shudder at the thought.

'Ah well,' said Jo. 'Who cares? It's Ali that's got to look after him if he is a wart hog. Not us.'

'I have not got to look after Jeremy Baxter. I'm not going anywhere near him,' I protested. 'Tell them, Mum.'

'You will not ignore any of my guests,' Mum suddenly exploded. 'You girls may all be almost adults now, but under my roof, you will abide by my rules. And my rules say that you will all be nice to Jeremy Baxter, no matter what he looks like. And you won't make fun of his stutter.'

Oh yes. His stutter. I had forgotten about that.

'I would never m-m-make f-f-fun of s-someone with a st-st-stutter,' said Jo.

Mum twatted her around the head with a tea towel.

Fortunately any further violence was curtailed by the return of our Dad from his first taxi trip to the OAP's home to fetch the pensioners who had been slightly spritlier guests at their wedding thirty years before. My own maternal grandmother was among the first load from The Daisy Lawns Senior Citizens Complex, otherwise known as God's waiting room. When I went outside to help Dad wheel Gran up the garden path in her souped up turbo wheelchair, I noticed to my horror that she was wearing exactly the same dress as Mum beneath her tartan travel blanket. Only Gran had accessorised the chiffon ensemble with a hat. A hat that looked as though it had been made from the tissue paper the dress had been wrapped up in.

'Dad,' I hissed, as we positioned Gran by the fire, but not too close in case the synthetic extravaganza on her head went up in flames. 'She's wearing the same dress as Mum.'

'So?' he said.

Men never understand these things do they?

'So, Mum will be really upset,' I explained. 'She wants to be the belle of the ball. It's her special party. She can't stand out from the crowd if her mother is dressed in exactly the same outfit as her.'

'What are you whispering about?' Grandma asked.

I know you're supposed to love your Granny and all that, but our Grandma Wilson was a cantankerous old bat with ears to match. She could hone in on gossip from 150 yards. And grab the wrong end of any stick you were offering at the same time.

'We were just saying how lovely you look in that dress, Grandma,' I lied. She fluffed out her skirt like a strutting pea-hen. 'Dad,' I whispered even more quietly then. 'Who's going to tell Mum?'

'Where's Josephine?' asked Grandma. 'Where's my daughter? Why isn't she here to greet me like a proper hostess?'

'She's in the kitchen, Gran,' I said loudly. 'She's putting finishing touches to the food.'

'Well, tell her to come out here and make her guests feel at home. I'll have a gin and tonic for a start.'

I could hear Mum coming through to the lounge already. I raced towards the kitchen and blocked her path.

'What's the matter with you?' she asked, as I ushered her backwards down the hall.

'Mum, I don't know how to say this,' I began. Then I decided on the direct approach that would probably get me, the messenger, shot. 'It's Gran,' I blurted. 'It's her dress. She's wearing the same dress as you.'

'What!'

'The exact same dress, Mum. With the matching chiffon scarf and everything.'

'In pink? Or in the blue? They had it in blue too,' my mother said desperately.

'In pink,' I admitted.

'Oh, how could she?'

'She looks just like Barbara Cartland if it's any consolation.'

It was no consolation whatsoever. Mum slumped against the refrigerator with her head in her hands.

Jo burst in. 'Shit, everybody. Have you see what Grandma's wearing . . . It's exactly the same as . . .'

'We've all heard, thank you very much,' said Mum, straightening up and setting her face to 'hard'. 'Well, she'll just have to go home and change into something else, won't she?'

'Mum,' I protested. 'She can't. That means that Dad will have to drive her all the way back to the home. Then one of the nurses there will have to dress her again. You know how long that will take. If she agrees to change at all. You know what she's like. She'll probably take offence and won't come back again after that.'

'You're right,' said Mum sadly. 'Oh, I can't believe it. How could she even afford a dress like this on her pension?'

'She sold that shepherdess figurine you liked so much,' said Jo helpfully. 'She just told me.'

'I don't know why you think that's so funny,' Mum replied. 'She's frittering away your inheritance too.'

Jo clamped a hand across her mouth to muffle the sound of her giggles. Jane had wandered back into the kitchen too.

'The blancmange wants a gin and tonic,' Jane said.

'Ooh, I'll give her bloody gin and tonic,' spat Mum. 'Does she want arsenic in that too?'

'Mum,' I said, in a voice intended to be calming. 'Perhaps it doesn't really matter. Perhaps you can get away with wearing the same dress.'

'What? And have her pretending that we're twin sisters all night? No thank you. She's done this to me one too many times. When I was first seeing your father, she turned up at a dance we were at wearing exactly the same Biba dress as me. I was eighteen. She was forty-two. She kept fishing for compliments about her legs all night long and for about six months afterwards people kept asking me when I was going to bring my big sister out again.'

'Go Gran,' said Jo. I shot her a 'shut-up' look.

'Come on, Ali,' said Mum despondently. 'I suppose you'll have to help me choose something different to wear. I'll just have to take that dress back to the shop on Monday morning and use the money to buy a new Hoover.'

'Never mind, Mum. You'll have a good twenty years to wear whatever you like after she's dead,' said Jo.

'Jo-anna,' said my mother sharply. 'Go and make sure your Gran doesn't choke on the peanuts.'

So my mother's Frank Usher fantasy was consigned to a plastic hanging bag and half an hour later, Mum re-emerged wearing her best navy blue suit. To be honest, I thought she looked much much better. Pink frills had never appeared in *Complete Woman*'s list of fashion musts for the fuller figure.

Mum kissed Gran hello, then returned to the kitchen to fume while my sisters and I were subjected to the usual round of grandparental inquisition.

'Got a new boyfriend yet?' Gran asked me predictably once we had established that Jo's new shoes would probably give her corns.

'Not yet, Gran,' I replied.

'Hardly surprising,' she said, momentarily dislodging her false teeth and pushing them forward so that she looked just like the dog. 'Wearing that horrible outfit. You look just like your mother. If only you'd both inherited my sartorial good taste.'

'If only,' I replied.

CHAPTER TWELVE

The Baxters arrived shortly after the last bus load of toxic grannies from God's waiting room. That is the Baxters minus their youngest son Jeremy. Their older daughter, Jennifer, who had seemed so cool during the early eighties in her ankle length pink tube skirt with her spiked up hair, was very much toned down. Turned out that the teenage rebel had gotten herself mixed up in Marks and Spencer management traineeism and it was all downhill from there. Now she looked like the kind of daughter my Mum had always wished for. Albeit unmarried. Which was a surprise that cheered me up immensely in my sorry position.

'Where's Jeremy?' asked my sister Jo, before even saying hello to the rest of the Baxter family. Seeing Jennifer Baxter looking like a Stepford creation was pretty gratifying but not half as interesting as seeing how the real geek in the family had turned out would be.

'Jeremy will be along later,' said his father. 'He didn't get up terribly early this morning. Looks like he's got a bit of a hangover.'

Hangover? Jo and I exchanged a look of surprise. Later in the kitchen she said, 'Cider. That'll be it. It's what all those computer geeks drink.'

'Still living at home though,' I said smugly.

'Actually,' interrupted Jane, the only one of we three sisters who was actually polite enough to listen long enough to catch the real truth behind the gossip. 'Actually he isn't living at home anymore at all. He's been living in Poland for the past twelve months.'

'Poland? What's he want to live there for?' asked Jo. 'It's cold the whole time.'

'Something to do with his computer job.'

'Oh,' said Jo. 'For a minute I thought he was about to get all exciting. Like turn out to be a spy or something.'

'Ex-pats get a lot of leave apparently,' Jane continued. 'He's back in England for a whole month. Staying with his family.'

'At least now the skinny geek stroke fatty lard bucket question is solved,' Jo interrupted. 'He'll be a fatty lard bucket for sure. This girl from the year above me at school had to go to Poland as part of her language degree. She said there was nothing to eat but potatoes and pork scratchings – or whatever their Polish equivalent is. She came back weighing fifteen stone.'

'If you're talking about Samantha Leeson, she went out there weighing fourteen and a half stone,' said Jane. 'The fact that Jeremy has been living in Poland for a year proves nothing.'

'OK. Let's take bets,' said Jo. 'I'll put a fiver on him being Mr Wobble-bottom.'

'And I'll put a fiver on him still looking thin as a string bean,' retorted Jane.

'What about you, Ali?' asked Jo.

'There isn't an option left for me to bet on, is there?'

'Yes there is,' said Jane, thinking quickly. 'You can bet on him being completely normal.'

'But the odds on that are ridiculous! Do we mean normal, normal? Or do we mean "normal" in the weird sense of the word?' I asked.

'Normal as in you wouldn't kick him out of bed for farting. If he had just paid your credit card bills,' Jo added as a proviso.

'I wouldn't kick a man out of bed for being an axe-murderer if he had just paid my credit card bills,' I told Jo. 'OK. You've got my fiver.'

Jo pocketed all three bills. 'Right, the winner gets all fifteen pounds. Which is just enough to cover the cost of that new *Squeaking Fieldmice* album I've been after.'

'Dream on,' said Jane. 'It's going towards my new Birkenstocks.'

The doorbell rang out again.

'The moment of reckoning is nigh, methinks,' said Jo with a smug smile.

We practically fought each other for the opportunity to open the door then, not to Jeremy, but to the man who lives next door to my parents now. He stepped back in delighted surprise at the sight of three young girls fighting to get a look at him.

'Well, well, well,' he said, smoothing back the three strands of hair that still clung grimly to his shiny head and grinning widely. 'This is quite a welcoming committee. Three lovely young ladies just for me.'

Jo and Jane disappeared instantly, leaving me to deal with old Mr Griffiths' coat and his absurdly continental way of kissing me hello. While his chilly lips were locked to my cheek, I caught sight of another guest meandering up the garden path. Though at first sight, I thought that he couldn't possibly be a guest at my parents' anniversary party. Perhaps something else, something far more hip and happening, was going on further down the street.

The handsome young man was carrying a vast bouquet of roses that by rights only ought to go to the kind of girl who wears Impulse and nothing else. He was dressed in a beautifully cut blue suit, that had a Nehru collar, with a white collarless shirt beneath. No tie. No ridiculous witty cartoon-character printed waistcoat to mark him out as someone who didn't normally dress up for any occasion but snooker tournaments like most of the men in our little town. He was tall, but not gawky. He looked comfortable with his height. He had sun-kissed blond hair that fell into his eyes, just asking to be brushed gently out of the way by a loving hand . . . In short, he was gorgeous.

And he was coming up our garden path!

'Yes?' I asked the stranger, simultaneously pushing Mr Griffiths away politely but firmly and directing him in the direction of the other geriatrics. 'Can I help you? Are you lost?'

'I don't think so,' said Mr Unfeasibly Gorgeous. 'I spotted my Mum and Dad's car parked just down the road there. This is the Harris family's house, right?'

'Right?' I said. I wondered who of the guests already assembled he could possibly belong to.

'Then can I come in? I've brought these roses for Josephine.'

'For Josephine. You mean, for my mother?'

'She's your mother?' he asked in surprise.

I didn't know whether to be offended or relieved that he didn't make an immediate connection.

'Yes, she is.'

'Then that must make you Jo, the little one.'

'Oh no,' I laughed. 'I'm not the little one. I'm Ali. The big one, in fact. In age, I mean.'

'Ali?' Did I see his eyes narrow at my name? 'Ali Harris? My God, you've changed.'

'So have you,' I told him. 'I mean, I don't wish to be rude or anything, but who exactly are you? Are you my mother's toy-boy, come to break the party up by declaring your love for her in front of my father?'

'You don't recognise me?' he laughed. 'I don't believe it. I haven't changed so much surely.'

He certainly had. Whoever he was. I had never known anybody so gorgeous, or with even the seeds of such rampant gorgeousness waiting to sprout after puberty.

'You really don't recognise me, do you, Ali?'

''Fraid not.'

'Well, I'll put you out of your misery. It's Jeremy, Jeremy Baxter.' He thrust out his hand.

OK, OK, I thought as we shook. And the next person to walk up the garden path would be Jeremy Beadle . . .

'But you can't be,' I said. I looked back up the hallway to see if Jo and Jane were sniggering at the top of the stairs, having summoned one of their good-looking mates to pop round and make me think that I had won the Jeremy Baxter bet.

'Do you need to see some ID? Or can I come in anyway? It's not exactly hot out here in the street, you know.'

I stood aside to let him pass.

'Wow,' I said banally. 'You've really changed.'

'You're not exactly the Ali Harris I remember, yourself. What happened to the pigtails?'

'Disastrous perm at the beginning of my third year in senior school. What happened to your glasses?'

'Never heard of contact lenses?'

'What happened to your hair?'

'The miracle of Sun-in. Hey, you used that once, didn't you, and it made your fringe go orange. That was hilarious.'

'Huh. For everyone else,' I laughed. 'What about the time you tried gluing back your ears?'

'Three days in hospital. Thanks for reminding me. And they still stick out, look.' He lifted up a flap of hair.

'My God,' I said, realising how rude I had been. 'I didn't mean to say that. I mean, about your ears . . . It was like we were twelve again for a moment there. I can't believe it. It really is you.'

Jo and Jane had appeared now, and were hovering a couple of feet behind us waiting to be introduced.

'Who is this?' asked Jo worriedly. 'Is he here to deliver those flowers?'

'Don't be so rude,' I said triumphantly. 'Jo and Jane, this is Jeremy Baxter.'

'Ohmigod. It can't be,' said Jo.

But before Jeremy could show her his passport, my mother appeared to rescue him. She took the flowers with a beam.

'Oh, Jeremy, so glad you could make it at last,' she simpered.

'That's a lovely outfit, Josephine,' Jeremy said as she led him through into the sitting room.

'Thank you,' she said. 'One tries so hard not to be mutton dressed as lamb,' she added, shooting a look at her own mother.

'What's wrong with her?' said Jo, as we followed Mum and Jeremy through into the party. 'She's batting her eyelashes at him for heaven's sake.'

'Well, wouldn't you bat your eyelashes at him,' said Jane. 'He's gorgeous.'

'That's a bit of an exaggeration, surely,' Jo protested. 'What do you think of him, Ali?'

I shrugged my shoulders in a non-committal way. 'Well, he's definitely normal. In the normal sense of the word. Where's my money, Jo?'

'Hang on. We don't know that he's completely normal,' Jo protested. 'I haven't heard him speak yet.'

'I thought we were going on physical appearance alone,' I reminded her. 'Anyway, I have heard him speak. And he didn't stutter once.'

'Unbelievable,' said Jane. 'Do you think he's been having some kind of speech therapy?'

'Can't be him,' insisted Jo. 'You must be mistaken.'

'Pay up, Joanna.'

Jo pulled the crumpled fivers out of her pocket reluctantly.

'Great,' I said, folding them into my own purse. 'I might just treat myself to some new underwear.'

'New underwear? What do you need that for?' Jo asked me.

'Perhaps she fancies her chances with Jeremy,' said Jane.

'Jeremy? You've got to be joking. Besides, looking like that, he's probably got a girlfriend already.'

'Or a boyfriend,' said Jo. 'I mean, have you seen what he's wearing. He's definitely gay.'

At that point Jeremy briefly looked up from the conversation he was having with Grandma and shot we three witches by the kitchen a dazzling smile.

'He must have heard that,' said Jane.

'Well,' I found myself saying. 'I hope Jo is wrong.'

With all the guests finally present, the party really started to kick off. If you can imagine a room full of people over the age of fifty doing such a thing as 'kicking off'. Dad had brought the record player out of the attic, to where it had been consigned just six months before, when he finally went CD-crazy, and the old biddies went gaga over his collection of 45s from the fifties and sixties (and 78s too. Have you ever even seen one of those?).

Despite his colostomy bag, Uncle Harry led the dancing as usual. The maiden aunts lined up in a row behind him to do can-can style high kicks, with Jo and Jeremy on one end and Jane and I on the other end of the line to provide some stability. Why is it that the older women get, the higher they seem to want to throw their legs, eh? The room was soon a flurry of beige pop-socks and waist-high knickers. Then one of the biddies fell over of course and the festivities were toned down to a nice game of charades, while Mum busied herself with picking vol-au-vents out of the carpet.

'*Upstairs, Downstairs*?' asked my sister Jo, when Auntie Alice had finally finished a protracted mime that was very nearly the death of her. 'What on earth was that about?'

'Beats me,' said Jane. 'Must have been on at the same time as that "*Z-cars*" thing Uncle Harry was trying to do.'

'Well, I can't guess any of these,' Jo complained. Then Uncle Harry announced that it was her turn to mime and the rest of the room spent three quarters of an hour struggling with a lesser known track by Oasis.

By this time the excitement was way too much for me, so I elected to start tidying up the remains of the buffet. It was a great trick that I had learned over many a family Christmas. When the going gets excruciating, get going into the kitchen. That way, I got out of having to make a complete idiot of myself with a mime of *One Flew Over the Cuckoo's Nest* or, worse still, *The Poseidon Adventure*, while simultaneously winning hundreds of 'good daughter' brownie points because people actually thought that I was sacrificing my own enjoyment to do the hard work. Jo and Jane had never cottoned on, not quite believing that washing-up could ever be preferable to Harris family party games. But that evening I discovered that someone had beaten me to it. Someone was already donning the Marigolds. It was Jeremy Baxter.

'You don't have to do that,' I told him. 'It's my parents' party. Get out there and enjoy yourself with the other guests.'

'What?' he looked horrified. 'No, please, Ali. Let me help you out here. They're still playing charades and I hate that game. I can never think of anything to act out.'

'Ah, so the truth will out,' I said. 'In that case, I don't know if I should excuse you.'

Jeremy got down on his knees with the tea towel clasped between his hands.

'Oh, OK then,' I conceded. 'Just this once. Especially

as I feel exactly the same way. It's the worst game ever, isn't it?'

'I thought that old lady doing *Upstairs, Downstairs* was going to have a heart attack.'

'Don't joke,' I warned him. 'She had a funny turn at the Church barbecue last year. They were playing Pass the Parcel at the time.'

'Pass the Parcel?'

'The stakes were high,' I explained to him. 'The prize was a packet of Maltesers.'

'Now I have heard everything. Listen, do you have any idea how much longer this party is going to go on for? I mean, don't the old dears have to be back in their retirement homes before a certain curfew?'

'Unfortunately, I think they all have late passes tonight. But surely you don't mean to say you're getting bored by all this?'

'It's not that, Ali. It's just that I've been out of the country for a while. I've only got a month here in Brindlesham and there are lots of people I'd really like to catch up with before I go back. Places I'd like to visit. I'd kill for a pint at The Rotunda . . .'

The Rotunda. I winced. After David's fatal infidelity had been revealed I hadn't been able to bring myself to go back to the place where the end of my engagement started. In fact, I couldn't even walk past it these days without needing to burst into tears.

'Is it still the same old place?' Jeremy asked me.

'I'm not sure,' I told him, hoping we could quickly change the subject. 'Last time I went there they had a variety of farming instruments for decoration but now I hear they might be turning it into an underwater-themed bar with topless mermaid barmaids.'

'No kidding.'

'No. I was kidding. I'm sure it hasn't changed at all since you were last there. It's just that I haven't been near the place since December.'

'Oh, found a better place to go?'

'I wish.'

'I take it that Fifth Avenue is still the only club round here then?'

'Not since someone was fatally wounded with a flick-knife there last weekend.'

'Then this party is probably as good as the local nightlife is going to get?'

'Oh, it'll get better. Can you hear that?' I cupped my ear, as if listening for the sound of distant drums. 'They're striking up the conga!'

'Well, what do you say to you and I escaping all this hilarity and going for a coffee somewhere?'

'Me and you?'

I thought that he then smiled a twinkly, flirtatious kind of smile. But I shrugged it off. I had been at the Bacardi and coke all evening, so it was far more likely that he was giving me a simple friendly smile, transformed in my mind into something more by some serious wishful thinking.

'Where could we go?' I asked, ready to bring out the dampeners. 'It's already half-past ten. The only place you can get coffee at this time of night is at Keith's Korn-Fried Chicken, which serves the only cup of coffee I've ever seen that actually has grease swimming on top of it. Besides, I can't leave my mother to deal with all this cleaning up. She'll go spare.'

'You've got to get back home at some point though, haven't you?' Jeremy persisted.

'I was planning to stay overnight.' I continued to shoot myself in the foot.

'Say you've changed your mind. Say I've offered to give you a lift home, but we have to leave immediately.'

I chewed my lip. 'To do what?'

'We'll go to Keith's FC. I can stand the grease and you can fill me in on all the gossip.'

'I'm not sure that Mum will appreciate that. I've got to stay.'

Jeremy shrugged. 'Well, if I really can't persuade you . . . I'm not the kind of guy who asks twice. I'll see you around, yeah?'

With that, Jeremy folded up the tea towel and went to take his leave of my mother. He kissed me lightly on the cheek, making sure that his aftershave would stay in my mind to make me regret being such a chicken for at least the next hour. There was much kissing in the sitting room too. A result of far too much sherry on my Mum's part.

'Ooh, I always knew you'd grow up to be a handsome bugger,' my mother shouted as Jeremy tried to make his way through the groping grannies to the door with his dignity still intact.

'I wish she'd told us that,' said my sister Jane as she joined me at the kitchen window to watch his car drive by. 'He's a dreamboat.'

'Ugh. He's such a creep,' said Jo. 'It was disgusting in there. All those crusty old grannies slobbering over a piece of young flesh. He's only after a spot in their last will and testaments.'

'He seemed genuinely nice to me,' I mused.

'Handsome,' murmured Jane once more.

'Oh, cut it out, you two,' Jo interrupted. 'Mum says she wants one of us to make sure Mr Griffiths gets home in one piece. He's been hoovering up the Babycham all evening. Either of you two girls want to volunteer or shall we just say that the loser is the girl with the most fivers in her possession tonight?'

That was me of course.

'Oh, this takes me back,' said Mr Griffiths as I used every last ounce of strength in my body to heave him over his front step and into his hallway. 'Are you going to help me get into bed now too?'

I settled him on the bottom step of his staircase and found a rather hairy blanket from his grumpy Jack Russell's basket with which to cover him up.

'No, I'm not going to help you get into bed,' I told Mr Griffiths firmly as he grasped hold of my ankle when I made to leave. 'You'll be perfectly fine there.' I'd get Dad to check that he wasn't dead in the morning.

As I walked back up Mum and Dad's garden path to see Grandma flashing her knickers with an impromptu impression of the Follies Bergères, I began to wonder exactly where it was written that the elderly deserve our respect. If only I hadn't been such a good daughter, I mused. Right then, I might have been gazing at a handsome man over coffee at Keith's FC. Though maybe I wouldn't have had the guts. Something about Jeremy Baxter made me feel quite shy.

I rejoined my sisters in the kitchen and we set about washing up. Rather Jane and I set about washing up. Jo just flicked washing-up bubbles at the dog, while she regaled us with an improbable tale about a boy at the local grammar school who had tattooed her name on his arm with a compass and a biro. (She still wouldn't snog him, poor fool.) Then Jane twisted up a tea towel into a painful looking knot as she told us hopefully about the new guy who had just started at her office.

At the bottom of the garden, just about visible from the kitchen window, Dad lit up a well-earned cigar. Mum soon stalked down the path after him, but, for once, instead of berating him, she simply wrapped her arms around him and gave him a kiss. Quite a passionate one for a pair of oldies.

'There's someone for everyone,' said Jane wistfully, as she drew down the blind on this happy little scene.

And then I was hit with a crippling vision of my special someone with someone else.

CHAPTER THIRTEEN

'You need to get out more often,' said Emma later that week, as she cleared a space for herself on the sofa amongst the detritus of too many TV dinners.

'I get out every day,' I assured her.

'You drag yourself into work looking like someone who should be en route to the out-patients department,' she corrected.

'I went to my parents' anniversary party on Saturday.'

'Family occasions do not count as "getting out". When I say "getting out" I mean, you need to start rebuilding your social life. Your single social life. As a single woman.'

'I'll do it in my own time.'

'That really isn't good enough, Ali. If you wait until you think you're ready to get out on the town again, my grandchildren will be coming round to help you get into your wheelchair. Why don't you come out with me tonight?'

'What? To The Rotunda? To face the humiliation of everyone in that place knowing that David has gone back to Lisa Brown again? Or to watch you getting chatted up by life-forms slightly further down the evolutionary scale than amoebas? I'd rather stay in and watch *You've Been Framed* thanks all the same.'

'Has it never occurred to you that there might be more to my life than the eternal search for Mr Right?' she reprimanded.

I had to admit that it hadn't. Men were Emma's *raison d'être*, surely. Just as they were the *raison d'être* of every woman I knew. Except for the two lesbians I had encountered in my media class at college, and they were just as sad about the search for eternal companionship in their own special way.

'I've got myself a hobby,' Emma said proudly. 'So that when the time comes, I can at least say to myself that whatever else happens I got something out of my life other than a lifetime's worth of tips about man-catching mascara that only works for girls who are supermodels already.'

'A hobby?' What was one of those? I seemed to vaguely remember having one at school. For the purposes of French conversation class, at least.

'What is your hobby?' I asked sarcastically. 'Stamp collecting? Train-spotting? Or best-friend baiting?'

'It's first aid, actually.'

'First aid? That's not a hobby, Emma. That's something you have to do to get a senior job at McDonalds.'

'Actually, it is a hobby. Probably the most noble hobby at all, since one day, it might actually come in useful. You'll be laughing on the other side of your face when I save you from choking to death,' Emma added.

'What? On my own disbelief?'

'OK. You just lie there and scoff, Ali Harris. And

scoff,' she added, referring to the bag of tortillas I had just opened. (My second that afternoon.) 'Believe me, the feeling of satisfaction I get from tonight will last far longer than the feeling you get from that junk food. Though your waistline might taunt you with the memory of your choice of pastime for years to come.'

That was it. Emma knew that the best way to scare me into action was the 'lingering evidence' threat. I folded over the top of the tortilla bag to keep them fresh and then put them out of reach on the coffee table.

'So are you coming?' she asked.

'Well, first aid doesn't exactly burn calories, does it?' I reasoned. 'I'll be all right if I just watch soaps and don't touch the tortillas.'

'But you'll be better than all right if you walk to and from the health centre and spend half an hour or so puffing into a pair of plastic lungs.'

'Yuk,' I said, remembering the horrible wax-faced doll we had been forced to practise artificial resuscitation on at Brownies. I always seemed to have to go after the girl with a cold sore.

'The male to female ratio is going to be two to one,' Emma continued. 'Since tonight is training night for the sea-scouts.'

The sea-scouts? What a temptation! Little did Emma know that she was making it much easier for me to resist. A pair of plastic lips to kiss in front of a bunch of spotty sea-scouts? It was bad enough that she was expecting me to get up from the chair I was sitting in, let alone put make-up on. Because I would have to put make-up on if there were going to be members of the opposite sex present.

'It's too much effort!' I wailed.

'Anything worth anything in this life requires a certain amount of effort!' Emma replied. 'Please come with me.'

'You'll have more fun on your own.'

'I won't,' she whined, and I had a sense that the truth was about to be outed. 'I need you there. I can't go on my own, please come with me.'

'Take Marvin.'

'I can't. I have to take a girlfriend. If I take Marvin, the situation will be too . . . too ambiguous.'

'And why should that matter?'

'I need to make it clear that I'm single.'

'To do first aid?'

'No,' Emma finally cracked and owned up to it. 'If I'm going to get off with the instructor.'

Turned out that Emma had taken a fancy to one of the doctors at the accident unit on the night of Marvin's dinner party and had recently discovered that he also gave first aid classes. She'd heard him discussing the fact with another doctor and then used all her powers of research and deduction to find out the 'when' and the 'where'. After that, it was easy to join up. But then her courage deserted her, which was where I came in. As moral support stroke straight man to her glittering wit. (She'd just been reading an article about men who like funny women.) There was also the fact that, in my post-David state, I would make her look like Cameron Diaz even if I dressed up in Gucci stilettos and a ballgown to her jeans.

Emma was pathetically grateful when I agreed to accompany her after just another hour of haranguing.

So grateful in fact that I managed to secure a promise that if I ever had a date again in my life, it would be while wearing her favourite silk Armani jacket.

Before we left the house, Emma slapped up. Lipstick, eye-liner, foundation, the works. I just combed my hair, figuring that if, by some fluky chance, I met the sea-scout of my life, he would probably appreciate my fresh-faceness as a sign that I would be happy to get wet in a catamaran with him.

'Jeans or leather skirt?' Emma asked for a fourth time as I waited for her in the hallway.

'Whichever you feel most comfortable in,' I said, again for the fourth time. I was wearing my jeans.

'I'll wear the leather,' she said. Hardly the most comfortable garment in her wardrobe. It took two of us to zip the thing up.

When we finally got to the hall where the class was being held, with Emma changed once more into some sensible trousers, Emma then stopped me from charging inside while she said her mantra. Not a high-brow Buddhist mantra, you understand, but 'You are irresistible', for what seemed like three hundred times.

'Am I glowing yet?' she asked when she had finished.

'No. But you are going mad. Do you think that chanting business really works?'

'Well, I did it before I went into the corner shop last Friday and the assistant winked at me when he gave me my change,' she told me.

'He always winks,' I said, hoping I wouldn't disappoint her too much. 'He's got a lazy eye.'

'Christ! Just blow my confidence to pieces why don't you?' she snapped. 'Now I'll have to do the other chant to compose myself again.' Cue, 'I am a warm and wonderful human being, ad infinitum'. In the old days she would simply have had a fag.

'Are we ready yet?' I asked while she finished off her chanting with a nice long 'ohm'. It wasn't exactly warm standing where we were in the car park. The sea-scouts had already arrived in a minibus and filed inside with regimental precision. Then the instructor arrived, in his dashing little blue Metro, and started to unload huge crates of equipment from the tiny boot.

'There he is! It's Doctor Martin!' Emma swooned.

'Like the boot?' I asked.

'Don't you dare make that joke.'

'Well, do you think we should help him?' I asked, seeing him buckle beneath the weight of a box of bandages. 'That'd earn you some brownie points.'

'Good idea,' Emma agreed. And we were about to offer our services when someone beat us to it. Someone who looked incongruously, for our little town, like an extra from *Baywatch*.

'Who's that?' asked Emma as she pulled me into hiding behind a wall.

'I don't know.'

'God. I knew it. I bet it's his girlfriend. I knew he had to have a girlfriend. It just wasn't possible that someone as gorgeous and wonderful as he is could be single and just waiting for me to come along. Let's go home.'

'Now hang on a minute,' I said. I had come round to the idea of learning how to do bandages again and was quite looking forward to it. 'Let's not jump to conclusions. She didn't arrive in the same car as him.'

'You're right,' said Emma, face brightening.

'So she obviously doesn't live with him. And if she was his girlfriend, don't you think she would have thrown her arms around him dramatically as soon as she saw him?'

'She kissed him,' said Emma gloomily.

'On the cheek. That means nothing. It was a social kiss. Marvin kisses everyone.'

'You're right. She's probably a lesbian.'

'Well, I wouldn't have gone that far, but I think it's pretty safe to say that all is not lost at this stage. Let's get in there.'

As if on cue, the *Baywatch* babe, bid the doctor farewell and headed off in the opposite direction. The change in Emma's facial expression was like the sun coming out after a weekend of rain.

'He's dreamy, isn't he?' Emma sighed as we watched the brave doctor carry the artificial resuscitation dummy inside alone. 'I just wish I was that doll.' We walked into the hall behind him and settled ourselves at the back of the class.

'OK, everybody,' said Dr Martin in his loud instructor's voice. 'It's time for you to partner up and practise your bandaging skills on each other. If there's anyone left without a partner, they can come up here and practise on me.'

Emma made a lighting fast calculation of the number of people in the room. There was an odd number of sea-scouts and before I knew it, she was pushing me in the direction of a gangling looking lad with a spot of germoline hovering like a jellyfish over his top lip.

'I think it's a good idea to mix with people you don't know at these things, don't you?' she said by way of an explanation, then she proceeded to battle off all-comers who wanted to partner her, until she was left standing alone, and looking faintly forlorn, in the middle of the room.

'I seem to have missed out in the rush for partners,' she said sweetly.

Dr Martin waved her towards him and bade her take a chair on the platform. She wiggled her way up to it and gave me a wink.

'Now, I'm going to demonstrate the sling just one more time,' he told the class. Emma looked ecstatic as he bound her arm to her chest. Then Spotty Lip started on me and managed to stick a safety pin right into my funny bone.

'Want me to kiss it better?' he asked.

'I wouldn't bother if I were you,' I said primly. 'I've got impetigo.'

'Last new trick of the day,' Dr Martin announced when I had managed to bind Spotty Lips roving hands safely behind his back in the strangest sling I've ever come across. 'Now the thing that most people are most interested in when they come to a first aid class is arguably artificial resuscitation. Otherwise known as "the kiss of life",' he added, raising a ripple of titters from the sea-scouts.

'Do we need to stay with our partners for this?' Emma asked hopefully.

'No, because if you practise on a normally breathing human being, you might do them an injury.'

'Can't you just pretend to blow?'

'That wouldn't be very good practice, would it? Now, ladies and gentlemen, if you'd like to form a circle around me and Dolly here, I'll show you how it's done.'

Emma was sidelined for the wax-faced doll and joined me at the back of the group.

'Lucky bloody dummy,' she muttered. 'Did you see me up there, Ali? How do you think I did? And how did he look when he was bandaging up my ankle? I knew I should have worn a skirt instead of these stupid trousers.'

'If everyone would be quiet, perhaps I'll only need to explain this once,' said Dr Martin suddenly. Emma snapped to attention.

'Perhaps I should feign a faint,' she said a moment later, when the authority of his command had worn off. 'Then he'd have to give me the kiss of life, wouldn't he?'

'He might make one of the sea-scouts do it instead,' I warned.

'I suppose you're right. And it could be that one with the cold sore.'

'You mean the one you left me in the capable hands of just now? I tell you what, I'm getting in front of him in the queue for the blow-up doll,' I told her.

'Me too. Yuck. Think I'll just put on a protective layer of lipstick to fight off the nasties.' She began to apply a carmine coating to her pout. In the meantime, we had missed all of Dr Martin's instructions and Emma didn't have a clue what she was supposed to be doing when Dr Martin said: 'Emma, perhaps you'd like to come up here and have first go?'

The sea-scouts parted to let her through, and suddenly Emma was face to face with Dolly.

'Haven't you got a male one?' she joked.

'I'm afraid that first aid situations aren't exactly gender specific,' Dr Martin said humourlessly. 'Off you go.'

'OK,' said Emma. 'As long as she doesn't use her tongue.' Then Emma went straight to it. She put her lips, tightly closed together, against the dummy's lips and stayed there, locked in a chilly embrace, for what seemed like a couple of minutes. When she pulled away, smiling broadly, the room exploded into laughter.

'Now that was a great demonstration of a real lip smacker,' said Doctor Martin, as he wiped Emma's bright red lipstick off the dummy with just the faintest hint of disdain, 'but rather than the kiss of life, that would have been a kiss goodbye. Why?' He pointed to a sea-scout for an answer.

'Because she didn't tilt the dummy's head back,' said the first.

'Because she didn't check that the dummy's airways were clear,' said the next.

'And because she didn't actually blow,' said Dr Martin. 'Remind me not to drown in your garden fishpond,' he added as she tried to fade back into the ranks.

'Why didn't you tell me what to do?' Emma snarled at me.

'I didn't know either. I couldn't hear what he was saying because you were so busy yacking.'

'Quiet at the back,' said the sea-scout master, obviously thinking that the muttering was coming from two of his charges. 'The harder you concentrate, the more quickly we can be out of here and back to the hut.'

'Well, I'm going now,' said Emma.

'You can't,' I protested. 'Everyone will notice.'

'So? I'm never coming back here again. I've never been more humiliated in my life.'

'But this is your hobby, Emma.'

'Was my hobby.'

'Just hang on till the end,' I persuaded her. 'When he was bandaging your ankle, I really did think I noticed a flicker of interest.'

'You did?'

'Yeah.'

'Really? Well, maybe I should stay until this bit is over.'

In fact, we stayed for an hour after class. Emma used the excuse of her poor technique to have Dr Martin explain the finer points of artificial resuscitation at least eleven times. But when I thought I'd try to help her out by reminding her that wc had an appointment at the pub – thereby giving her the perfect excuse to ask him to join us, I thought – Dr Martin made his excuses. He was going to be on call, he said, all night long.

'He's so selfless,' Emma swooned as we waited for thc bus to take us home. 'Making sick people well all day, then teaching us first aid in the evenings and helping the sick again all night long. I would never have believed that anyone could be so altruistic.'

I nodded.

But then her face fell. 'Because nobody could possibly be that altruistic, could they? Do you think he was just fobbing me off with that "on call" business?'

I shrugged.

'Oh, God. I'm going to die,' she whined. 'Why does this always happen to me? Why do I always throw myself headlong at men who aren't interested in me? Why, Ali? Why?'

'I don't know. I mean, if I knew, I probably wouldn't keep doing exactly the same thing myself. Look, he probably was on call. I just shrugged because my own love life has made me feel so pessimistic about romance.'

Emma hugged me. 'I'm sorry. I was forgetting all about what you've had to go through these past few weeks. How are you feeling right now?'

'Much better actually,' I had to admit. 'You know, it was a really good idea of yours to drag me out. I was almost enjoying myself when I got that ankle bandage right.'

'Good. Then we'll go to the class again next week.'

'I don't know about that,' I said warily.

'But you said you enjoyed yourself.'

'I did. It's just that there's not much opportunity to pull at a first aid class, is there? I mean, you've got the instructor to work on, but I've just got the sea-scouts. I was thinking we might have a proper girls' night out instead. No bandages. No plastic dummies. Just lots of margaritas and a place where we can find men over the age of consent.'

Emma grinned. 'I know just the place.'

'Great. Because I think it's about time that Ali Harris faced the world again. Properly.' I got to my feet dramatically and waved my arms about in the air in an approximation of a dance. 'Lock up your sons, Ali Harris is back!!'

But before Emma had time to give me three cheers, someone opened that trapdoor beneath me again and I was plunged back into misery. Crossing the road and scuttling to get out of my sight as quickly as they could, was a painfully familiar couple. My arms dropped weakly to my sides as I recognised David's car and watched him open the passenger door for her. My successor. Lisa Brown.

'Don't look,' said Emma, covering my eyes with her hands.

'It's too late. I've already seen them,' I squeaked.

Where had they been? I wondered. The only place around there worth visiting, if you didn't have to go to the hospital, was the wonderful Chinese restaurant that David and I had discovered after I picked him up from the accident unit on the day when he nearly killed himself by attempting to mend the photocopier with wet hands. Unless Lisa Brown had had a terrible accident (and I promise that I tried to stop myself from wishing it) David must have been taking her to our special restaurant. The restaurant where the proprietor knew me by name and had taught me how not to use my chopsticks like a peasant. (I had to hold them right at the ends apparently, preventing me from picking up even the smallest mouthful – no wonder Chinese women are so short.)

'He's been taking her to our special places,' I sobbed.

Emma, in her inimitably tactless way told me, 'They were probably her special places too before you came along.'

I stared after David's brakelights until his car disappeared round the corner. It was too late. I was filled with melancholy once more. The good work that Emma had done by taking me out was all but negated by the terrible reminder that my fiancé was not mine anymore. He was getting on with his life with someone else. The pinnacle of my recent social life had been an evening practising life-saving snogs on a dummy.

When we got home, I crawled beneath my duvet on the sofa and had Emma bring me cups of tea and listen to my rantings about David until the Open University came on.

'We will both find true love yet,' Emma insisted. 'We're young.'

'I'm twenty-six.'

'We're attractive.'

'That's a matter for debate.'

'We are positive-thinking women.'

'I'll let you know in the morning,' I said.

And so another week crawled by in an agony of trying not to think about David and avoiding calls from Amanda at *Complete Woman* who was eager to know whether his spots had cleared up. On the Thursday evening, I was summoned to supper at the family home so that my mother could convince herself that I wasn't starving/drinking/working myself to death in my misery. Jo, having unravelled herself from the clutches of someone who looked not unlike my dreaded sea-scout at the bottom of the driveway, came into the house full of news.

'I just saw Jeremy Baxter,' she said.

'So he's still in town,' Jane sighed.

'For another four weeks. He said he's decided that he's missing England so much that he got an extension on his leave.'

'He's probably got a girlfriend over here,' said Jane wistfully.

'He wasn't out with her, if he has,' Jo explained. 'He was in The Rotunda with a couple of other lads. No girls.'

'In the where?' called my mother from the kitchen.

'The Rotunda,' said Jo innocently before she could stop herself. Realising too late what she had just let slip, her face had all but drained of blood when Mum stormed into the sitting room to shout, 'I thought I told you never to go near that place again. You're not eighteen years old yet, Joanna Harris. Do you want to bring the police round here to have you up for underage drinking? And it's a school night. You're out of control, you are. You all were. I don't know where I went wrong with you girls. I'll never forget the shame of the Top Shop incident.'

I groaned at the memory.

'But I was never in trouble with the police,' said goody-goody Jane.

'Only because they didn't catch you,' replied our mother. 'You look like you're on drugs, wearing those horrible black clothes all the time. Come here,' she said to Jo. 'Open your mouth. Let me see if you've been drinking.'

CHAPTER FOURTEEN

I left my mother smelling my sister's breath and went home to the flat, where Emma was reading a first aid manual.

'Got to get to the head of the class,' she explained.

When I had tested Emma on the ABCs of artificial resuscitation (don't quote me on that), we set the next Saturday evening as the date for our girls' night out. It was going to be a big one, we decided. Epic. Lock up your sons and all that. So naturally we would have to go shopping that Saturday afternoon for the kind of dresses that would make us feel like man-eaters and look like supermodels. As opposed to feeling like men and looking like super-noodles, which was the usual scenario.

Three o'clock, Saturday afternoon. We were just walking out of Miss Selfridge with our bags of swag when Emma spotted him.

'There he is,' she shrieked, digging her fingers into my sleeve.

'Who?' I asked, squinting into the crowd. I really needed to get my eyes tested.

'Doctor Martin. He's over there. Just coming out of Marks and Spencers. Is he on his own, Ali? My God, please tell me he is on his own. I can't bear to look.' She covered her eyes with her fingers.

I hadn't even managed to locate Dr Martin yet.

'He's in the navy blue puffa jacket,' said Emma impatiently. 'He's got aviator-frame sunglasses on and he's carrying three shopping bags. Two from M & S and one La Senza.'

I was just taking in the fact that Emma had managed to memorise such a lot about her hero's appearance in such a short space of time when the gravity of her words hit her like a skip full of bricks. 'La Senza!' she groaned. 'That's an underwear shop. Who's he buying underwear for?'

'Himself?' I said helpfully.

'From La Senza? Not likely.'

'They do boxer shorts.'

'Yeah. But they wrap them up in all that smelly tissue-paper stuff. No man in his right mind would go in that shop unless he had to. Unless he had to buy a present for his girlfriend,' she intoned ominously.

'Now we don't know that,' I began.

'We do. We do know that. It was that girl in the car park after all. They are an item. Oh, God. He's crossing the road now. He's coming this way. What shall I do?'

'How about saying hello to him?' I suggested.

'No way,' she said, looking at me as if I were the mad one. 'Let's hide.'

With that, she dragged me backwards by my shirt collar into Dixons and had me duck down behind the stereo equipment. It was probably not the best place in town to hide out from a man, I thought, and sure enough pretty soon Dr Martin had walked into the shop and was strolling nonchalantly straight towards us.

'You're going to have to say hello now,' I told Emma. 'My knees are killing me, crouching down like this.'

'You should take more exercise. Stay hidden.'

'Well, if I only had my love life to worry about, I wouldn't be doing all this squatting down behind shelves business in the first place,' I complained. 'I'm getting up.'

But by this time, Dr Martin had drawn level with us and I could actually see his feet. He was wearing a rather nice pair of brown lace-up shoes. Such a nice change, I thought, from the smelly old trainers that David had been so attached to.

'Look at his shoes,' Emma hissed. 'Handmade I reckon. Real leather soles. Must have cost a fortune. You can tell a lot about a man from his shoes, you know. Big feet, don't you think?' she added.

But then, to our horror, the nice brown brogues were joined by a very different pair of feet. A pair of feet in the kind of sky-scraper platform heels that I could only fantasise about wearing with my arches.

'Ashley,' someone purred. 'Fancy seeing you here.'

There were some kissing sounds. Emma covered her ears. I felt I had to listen. It was my duty as her best friend to find out all the gory details.

'Hi, Lou,' he said back. 'You look fantastic today.'

'Oh, Ashley,' she shivered. 'You're making me blush, you old fibber.'

'I never say things I don't mean.'

Emma made eye signals that I figured meant, 'can I uncover my ears yet?' I made signals that said, 'best not'.

'Mmmm, La Senza,' the shoe-hussy observed. 'Been buying presents for someone special?'

'I suppose you could say that.'

I clamped my own hands over Emma's ears as well. This could be disastrous.

'It's a bit embarrassing really,' Dr Martin continued. 'I had to get a bra and suspender set for the med school rag. We're putting on a performance of *The Rocky Horror Show* for the end of term.'

'You could have asked me. I would have lent you some of mine.'

'Thanks, Lou. But I'd never have filled them out like you do.'

She made a disgusting kitteny noise then. Like a purr. Right there in the middle of Dixons. The trollop.

'Well, don't be a stranger,' she said at last. 'You know what my number is, don't you?'

'How could I forget?'

And with that she was gone. I took my hands from Emma's ears and quickly filled her in. 'You're in the clear. It's for a med school party,' I told her. 'He was buying the underwear for himself. *Rocky Horror Show*.

'Thank God for that. But who was she? Did you get a look at her face?'

'How could I? I was down on the floor next to you the whole time.'

'Can I help you two ladies?' We had been joined on the floor by one of the shop assistants. No doubt he was worried that we were two of those 'mystery customers' sent to check out the cleanliness of his carpets.

'Er, no,' said Emma, automatically standing up, and, in an effort to look nonchalant, leaning against the shelf in such a manner that she sent a couple of hundred pounds worth of stereo equipment flying. Straight off the shelf and into Dr Martin.

'My God! What are you doing here?' Emma squeaked as the poor man tried to defend himself from falling hi-fi pieces.

'Shopping,' he said flatly. 'What are you doing here? Trying to create a first aid emergency?'

Emma gave a single hysterical snort of laughter, then the three of us smiled stiffly. Meanwhile, assistants scuttled around us, picking up their stock and trying to assess the damage.

'Are you hurt?' asked Emma hopefully. 'I know how to do bandages.'

'No. I'm not hurt. But . . . er . . . I've got to go now or I'll be late for work. Will I see you girls on Thursday night?'

Emma gave the thumbs-up sign. 'You bet. Wouldn't miss it for the world.'

Then Dr Martin nodded, in a worried way, I thought, and scurried out of the shop like a cockroach out of the kitchen when you turn on the lights.

'In a hurry to get to the hospital,' Emma explained to the shop assistant, whose face had gone from helpful to thunderous in the space of her blunder. 'He's a doctor, you know. Everything OK?'

'Actually, no,' said the assistant. 'And I'm afraid you'll have to pay for the damage.'

So, we ended up going home without the drop-dead outfits we had searched so long for to pay instead for a brand new stereo. Albeit a brand new stereo without a door on the tape deck, and whose CD player would only work properly if the whole thing was set on a slope. But Emma didn't seem to mind that she had just inflicted four hundred pounds worth of damage on her already heaving credit cards.

'He asked if he'd be seeing us on Thursday,' she muttered again and again like a mantra. 'That must mean he wants to see me.'

I wasn't going to burst her bubble.

But so much for our girls' night out. Emma tried to cry off a big session for financial reasons, then we got home to a message on the answer-machine from Marvin, saying that he had been stood up by a dishy German bloke he met at the local Turkish Baths and so we had agreed to let him join us for dinner. When he finally turned up, an hour later (owing to a problem with getting his highlights to take or something), there followed a bitter squabble about whether it should be Indian or Italian. Garlic in both, which would not be good for our pulling power on a Saturday night, but Marvin insisted that the garlic in Indian food seems to linger longer. So Italian it was. You never can tell when your ship is going to come in, said Marvin, flicking his fringe.

Between us, we polished off two bottles of red wine while we picked at our pasta (Emma in love, Marvin on a diet, me simply too depressed to stuff myself that night), but we didn't feel the effects of our overindulgence while we sat around the checker-clothed table. We were too serious to get giggly anymore, having got to that stage in our lives where conversations about who we fancied quickly became heart to hearts about whether we should start going for older men who, due to the dual forces of receding hair and expanding waistlines, might be inclined to settle down before we girls started to need HRT.

'He's a doctor. And they tend to settle down more quickly than, say, lawyers or men who work in the City,' theorised Marvin on Emma's Dr Martin. 'It's all that death and disease they encounter. Makes them realise that life is short and you need to seize the moment with both hands. If you catch him, Emma, I reckon you could be engaged by Christmas.'

'Do you really think so?' she purred delightedly.

'I'd place a bet on it. So when are you seeing him next?'

'Thursday night. At the first aid class.'

'Then you need to formulate an action plan right now. What are you going to be wearing?'

'My black jeans, I thought. With that stretchy lace top. The red one.'

'Jeans?' said Marvin, pulling a face. 'What about that leather mini-skirt you bought? Much sexier.'

'I know. But we have to spend a lot of time on our knees, dealing with that stupid artificial resuscitation dummy,' she explained. 'I'd have a load of sea-scouts looking at my bum.'

'What a delightful thought,' sighed Marvin. 'But where's your problem with that anyway? You go out in a short skirt to a club don't you.'

'That's different. I don't have to bend down and look proficient in a club.'

'Perhaps you should. You might get more offers.'

And so it went on. Marvin and Emma bickering about the best way to catch a man, with me staring wistfully through the steamed-up window onto the rain-swept street outside. I was having one of those 'this time last year' moments that are particularly dangerous in the newly single.

This time last year, I thought, David and I had been on a ski-ing trip to Andorra. Neither of us had ever skied before, but David had been invited on the trip by his boss and was keen to ingratiate himself by going along. Unfortunately (or fortunately in my case), he had sprained his wrist first time out on the slope and we didn't have to reveal the extent of our ski-ing ignorance. David and I spent the rest of the week sight-seeing. And it was on that trip that we decided that our next big holiday, our honeymoon, would be somewhere fabulously hot. Barbados was the first choice. We were neither of us snow bunnies.

Of course, that particular train of thought brought me crashing back to earth with the reminder that I was currently the holder of a ridiculous title and a fabulous prize holiday in the blazing sun. Amanda still needed to know the truth. A week after the Hot Stuff Heat Rub incident, David had only called to leave a message on my answer-machine requesting the swift and safe return of his Fun Lovin' Criminals CD. We weren't about to get back together any time soon.

'Ali,' Marvin said, bringing me back from the land of the loveless. 'How much was your starter?'

We split the bill precisely. As we always did. We used to do the straight three-way thing but Marvin and Emma would always end up rowing over who had drunk the most expensive brandy. With the bill paid, the waiter helped Emma and me on with our coats and Marvin looked extremely disappointed when the waiter merely handed him his.

'I thought I was in there,' Marvin explained as he sneakily took back one of the four pound coins we had left as a tip.

'He wasn't gay,' said Emma flatly.

'What? With that haircut? Darling, the boy was as camp as a row of tents.'

'That haircut was camp? Looked perfectly normal to me.'

'No no no. It was parted in a special way,' Marvin explained as we meandered to the bus stop. 'It's something we gay men are attuned to. One of those little signals that lets you know when you're of a similar mind. Now, you see that tall guy getting out of the blue car over there?' He pointed to a man locking up a smart Mini metro.

'If you tell me he's gay, I will kill you,' said Emma suddenly. Then she grabbed my arm as she started swooning. 'It's him. It's Dr Martin. He's the one I've just been telling you about.'

We froze on the pavement to watch Dr Martin checking that he had locked up his boot.

'Oh my God. He's gorgeous,' said Marvin.

'But is he gay?' asked Emma.

'One can only hope.'

Emma swiped at him with her handbag. 'Marvin. Stop messing me about. Is he gay or not? Bear in mind it could be the end of me if he is.'

'OK,' Marvin sighed. 'I don't think he is. Though his hair is a bit on the tidy side for a straight guy.'

'Has to be tidy for work,' I said, hoping to avoid a fatal argument between my two favourite people.

'So, aren't you going to introduce us?' Marvin asked Emma. Dr Martin had finished checking his car security and was starting to walk away. He hadn't even spotted us, I hoped.

'I can't introduce you,' Emma wailed. 'It'll be too embarrassing. My mouth goes dry. I get all tongue-tied. I just can't talk to him like I would to any other normal person. He's like a demi-god or something. I need an excuse to go up to him.'

'An excuse? Right, let's sort this out once and for all,' said Marvin firmly. 'Emma Wilson, prepare to be a heroine.'

Emma and I shared a split-second worried glance before Marvin went into his world-beating impression of a man in terrible pain.

'Aaagh! Aaaagh! My ankle!' he shrieked. 'These high heels! I should never have worn them. My ankle! I think I've just broken my ankle! Can anybody help?'

Marvin staggered realistically from one side of the pavement to the other, then, as if some terrible fate had been tempted, he staggered straight off the pavement and into the path of an oncoming car.

'Screeech! Crash!!! Aaaagh!!'

Only this time it was for real. Dr Martin was on the spot in a second. I half expected him to strip off his anorak to reveal a white coat beneath. Emma meanwhile was frozen where she stood in shock. Marvin had always claimed that he would do anything for her, but this . . . This was truly ridiculous.

'Is he dead? Is he dead?' was all Emma could ask as she peeped at me through her hands.

'He's not dead,' said Dr Martin reassuringly. Marvin swooned on the pavement beneath the doctor's healing hands. 'But he does need to go to the hospital for a check-up and so, by the looks of it, do you. I think you might be suffering from shock.' He put his arm around Emma's shoulders in a gesture of concern and she nodded in a distant kind of way. She was so shocked in fact, that she had completely forgotten how to simper.

'How's the driver of the car?' I asked. 'Is he all right too?' I couldn't bear the thought that our stupidity might have been the cause of an innocent stranger's injury. The driver of the bright yellow Megane had been sitting behind his wheel all along. Too afraid to move, I supposed.

'He's fine,' said Dr Martin, after administering a quick health check through the driver's window. 'He's a little shocked, understandably. But thankfully, he was just reversing his car into a parking space, so he was going pretty slowly and hasn't suffered any whiplash. What was it that made your friend stumble into the road anyway?'

Emma declined to answer. Instead, she limped in the direction of the newly arrived ambulance (her own 'fuck-me' boots were killing her) and I followed. Then, while I was sitting on the tailgate of the ambulance, watching Marvin being loaded onto a stretcher, the driver finally got out of his car and suddenly Emma wasn't the only one suffering from shock.

'Alison Harris, we meet again,' he said. 'Didn't think it would be because I knocked one of your pals over, though! Sorry!'

'Who's this?' asked Emma brusquely.

'Emma, this is Jeremy Baxter.'

So, that night at the accident unit was a bit of a result

for both of us. Emma got to be bandaged lovingly by her hero. (The boots had rubbed her heel quite raw.) And I got to meet Jeremy Baxter again, without having to contrive some terrible reason to get his phone number from my mother. Fortunately, Dr Martin had been right and Jeremy had come away from the catastrophe without a scratch. Marvin hadn't been quite so lucky. He really had hurt his ankle, having managed to get his big fat foot stuck firm beneath the back wheel of Jeremy's car. And as for his new suede boots? Well, they were a total write-off.

'One hundred and twenty quid, he says they cost,' moaned Emma later. 'And he expects me to pay for them.'

'Why?' Jeremy asked innocently.

'Emma spilt spaghetti sauce on them in the restaurant,' I said quickly, thinking it was probably best not to go into the real details of that evening's events.

'Yeah, well. I suppose it was worth it,' Emma conceded. 'Since he's agreed to go for a coffee with me.' She grabbed my arm excitedly. 'Dr Martin. Tonight. When he finishes his shift. God, I hope no one else has a car accident tonight.'

Lovely Emma. Always so concerned about others.

'I guess I'm going home on my own then,' I said, since Marvin was being kept in overnight for observation. He didn't mind too much, since he rather fancied the hunky male staff nurse who would be giving him a sponge bath in the morning. 'Hope the buses are still running.' I added.

'I could give you a lift,' Jeremy said suddenly.

'But your car . . .'

'Is fine. Only evidence that anything happened to it

at all is a bit of leopard-print suede snagged on one of the wheelnuts.'

'Go for it!' Emma mouthed to me from behind his back.

'Is it on your way?' I asked him.

'I think I can make a little detour for you.'

Emma gave me a wild thumbs-up sign.

'Come on.'

I gathered up my bag. 'I'll see you later,' I told Emma.

'Not if I can help it,' she replied.

So I left Emma flicking through the pages of *Woman's Own* and followed Jeremy Baxter out to his car. It was a spotless, brand new Renault Megane in bright yellow with body-coloured bumpers.

'Everyone's got to have one little indulgence,' Jeremy told me as he pulled on his leather driving gloves. 'Where will it be, Cinderella?'

'Nowhere much to go at this time of night,' I shrugged. 'How about The Trout? That sometimes has a late licence.'

'Sounds perfect,' said Jeremy. And we sped off into the night. Carefully observing the highway code as we went, I noticed.

CHAPTER FIFTEEN

So it was that I found myself in The Trout on a Saturday night.

The Trout was what we girls called an old man's pub, full of regulars who had their own tankards hanging from the shelves behind the bar and their own special chairs that only the truly stupid would dare to sit in uninvited. Having said that, The Trout had once been quite a hot spot for Brindlesham youth. That was for all of two weeks in 1989, when our regular den of iniquity was under serious surveillance from the police for suspected underage drinking. It was easy to convince the one-eyed barman at The Trout that our sixth-form college library cards were in fact the official over-eighteen ID cards that the local Council had tried so hard to push.

'I used to come in here quite often,' said Jeremy, as we settled ourselves in a seat by the fire that had recently become vacant through the sudden death of some old git. 'I never quite felt at home in The Rotunda,' Jeremy continued. 'Never quite fitted in with the cool crowd. All the misfits came in here.'

'Well,' I told him. 'We girls from the "cool crowd"

didn't dare come in here because of all the Goths and Heavy Metal freaks. They looked so hard. Especially the girls.'

'That's the irony, you see,' Jeremy laughed. 'You can pretty much guarantee that someone who has a penchant for black leather and skull and crossbones earrings is a vegetarian, or a librarian, or both. It's camouflage. Self-defence. So many people are not quite what they appear to be.'

'That's deep,' I sighed.

'I remember seeing you in here once though,' Jeremy continued. 'You were wearing a short green dress, with some kind of scoop neck.'

'I remember that dress,' I laughed. 'I kept having to pull it down to cover my knickers. I can't believe you remember me in it though.'

'How could I forget? You looked fantastic that night. I thought about walking up to you and introducing myself. But I was afraid that you wouldn't remember who I was, let alone actually want to talk to me. Besides, you were with that ugly bloke you used to go out with.'

'Ugly? Oh, you must mean Stu Chivers.'

'That's the one. Whatever did you see in him?'

It was hard to remember. But I tried to find an explanation. 'I'm not sure really. I suppose it just seemed glamorous at the time. He was older. He had a Vauxhall Chevette when every other bloke I knew had a BMX bicycle. And he was always saying that he was going to get a tattoo.'

'Did he?'

'You've got to be kidding. He cried whenever he had to pull a sticking plaster off.'

'I've got a tattoo,' Jeremy whispered, leaning in close.

'Now that I find very hard to believe.' I murmured, as I wondered if he could feel the heat from my burning cheeks as he crossed that strange interpersonal space line from friendly to 'with intent'.

'You'll just have to ask me if you can see it later on. Shall we go?'

'Go?' I looked at my watch reflexively. 'Where to?' I felt a nervous rumble deep in my stomach. Was Jeremy Baxter propositioning me?

'Your carriage awaits, madam. It's not quite a Vauxhall Chevette but how about we just get in my Renault and go where the mood takes us?'

As it was, the mood, and the late hour, took us to Keith's Korn-Fried Chicken.

'I'm so sorry about the way we acted when you first showed up at my parents' party the other evening. We were so rude,' I said between picking the last of a chicken supreme out of my back teeth.

'It doesn't matter,' said Jeremy. 'In some ways, it's comforting to know just how much I have changed. I was a total geek when we last met. There's no denying that. The way people react when they see me is recognition of a long time in surgery.'

'Plastic surgery?' I squeaked.

'No, not really. Just a long time in the gym.'

'Must have been a very long time,' I said before I could stop myself. 'I mean, I wish I had your dedication.'

'By the look of you, I thought you already did.'

I felt a blush spread across my cheeks. 'You don't mean that.'

'I do. You've changed a great deal too, Ali. I never

imagined that the skinny little tomboy who lived next door would grow up to be such a fabulous, beautiful woman. So, er . . . curvy.' He made a little demonstration of my figure with his hands that had me going magenta.

'Oh, Jeremy,' I squeaked.

'I like a curvy girl. Women these days are so concerned with being thin they diet away all the bits that men are actually interested in. But not you. You're perfect.'

Boy, was I glad it was dark in that car. I fanned my neck with my collar.

'Jeremy,' I said. 'If I hadn't known you since we both started primary school, I might think that you've been flirting with me all night.'

'Thank God, I thought you'd never notice.'

'You mean, you have been flirting with me?' I said in astonishment.

'I've been flirting with you since we met on the doorstep of your parents' house last Saturday evening. I prayed that fate would hurl us back together before I had to leave England for Warsaw again.'

'Jeremy . . . I . . .'

'What is it, Ali? Listen, before you start to get all heavy-hearted and introspective about things, I know you've just split up from your fiancé and I know that you're probably still feeling a little raw about that, but if it's OK with you, I'd really like to see you again before I go back to Poland.'

I didn't know what to say. I was still trying to digest the fact that someone had already briefed him on my sex life. (Rather my non-existent sex life.) The culprit was my mother undoubtedly. Then I started to wonder whether she had offered up the information unsolicited or whether he had actually been interested enough to ask.

'Just for a coffee or something?' Jeremy persisted.

Was he really asking me out? On a proper date? Or a sympathy one?

'In fact, if you don't think I'm being too forward, I could use a coffee right now.'

'But we've just had one,' I said.

'Bit small weren't they? Why don't you make me a bigger one at your place? You can ask me to go whenever you like.'

Go? I didn't want him to go. Ever. Instinctively, I looked up at the windows of my flat in an attempt to guess whether Emma was in and up. The flat was dark. She was still at the accident unit.

'OK,' I said. 'Come in.'

'This is a beautiful flat,' said Jeremy as I guided him into the sitting room, which was frankly rather tatty.

'Don't say that,' I warned him. 'It might make me think that everything you've said so far has been a lie. Tea or coffee?'

'Coffee. Tea is for grandmas.'

'Well, I'm having tea. Camomile tea in fact.'

'Why? It'll make you go to sleep.'

'Which is what I need to do. I've got to go to Mum and Dad's for lunch tomorrow.'

'Your parents won't mind if they think you're late for a good reason.'

'Such as . . .'

'Such as catching up with your childhood sweetheart.'

'Childhood sweetheart?' I exclaimed. 'Since when were we childhood sweethearts, Jeremy Baxter?'

'Since you promised yourself to me, Valentine's Day 1979. Don't you remember? At the time I think I may have churlishly turned the generous offer down, but since then I've definitely changed my mind.'

I remembered now the Valentine's card that I had slipped under the garden fence at the point where Jeremy and I would sometimes sneakily exchange pieces of chewing gum. This was long before the days when smoking was the worst thing I could do in my parents' eyes. I had never been allowed chewing or bubble gum as a child for fear that I would swallow it and clog up my lungs with the goo. Jeremy's lax parents actually bought him cola flavoured Bubblicious.

'You broke my heart then,' I told him jokily. 'I don't know if you get a second chance.'

'But I was young,' he protested. 'Besides, when we went to secondary school, I seem to remember that it was you who broke off all channels of communication because I just wasn't cool enough for your new found friends, like Stacey Mitchell and Darren Applefield. By the way, what happened to them?'

'Darren's warehouse manager at Safeway and Stacey is married with two point three kids and a labrador. At least she was married when I last saw her. Apparently since then she's been passed over for the barmaid in her husband's local.'

Jeremy tried to suppress a smug smile. He didn't manage it.

'Still think Darren's cooler than I am?' he asked me.

'That's not fair,' I replied. 'I haven't seen him for years. Besides, you are a computer geek.'

'I'm a computer geek with the whole of Eastern Europe in the palm of my hand,' he corrected. 'Don't knock it.'

He took hold of my hand then and pulled me down onto the sofa beside him.

'I claim my prize,' he murmured. 'February 14th 1979.'

'Jeremy!!!'

Before I could protest, he had fastened his mouth onto mine and was fast working his tongue in between my teeth. As his hand crept up the back of that disgusting mustard shirt of Emma's, I finally managed to forget the Jeremy Baxter who had once shown me his collection of worms and let myself relax into his embrace.

Soon, his feet were no longer proprietorially on the floor and we were both fully prone on the sofa. He had my skirt up round my waist and my knickers halfway down my thighs. My bra was undone and he was tweaking my nipples into erection. All this without taking his mouth away from mine for even one breath. He was amazing.

'Wow.' In the end it was me who pushed him away before I suffocated. 'Wow! Jeremy!'

But I was looking into the eyes of someone different. No longer Jeremy Baxter, but Jezzie B. The intelligent, charismatic, if somewhat arrogant, computer genius stroke businessman with the whole of Eastern Europe at his feet. And he wanted me. I could tell. He was drooling.

'I want you so much,' he said, confirming my suspicions. 'I want to sink my teeth into the firm white flesh of your glorious breasts.'

It sounded painful but I guessed that it was meant to be romantic so I nodded.

'I want to drink deeply from the cup of your hidden desire.'

Was that something to do with oral sex, I wondered? I wasn't overly familiar with the concept, let alone the metaphors. I nodded again.

'I want to give you a night of passion that neither of us will ever forget, when you are alone again here in Brindlesham, and I am in my lonely cell in the never-ending winter of Warsaw.'

'Oh, Jeremy.' I was just too flustered to be poetic back.

'Let me take you, Alison. Let me take you to places where you have never been. Let me awaken parts of your body that didn't even know they were still alive. Let me take you to the doors of passion and lead you further inside the dark warm corridor of love.'

Oooh, sounded good to me. And all the time he was keeping up the physical persuasion. I hate to say it, but I was starting to feel like the heroine in the trashy novel that Emma kept under her bed for fallow periods in her love life. My breasts were growing rosy with the first flush of desire. I was wetter than a haddock's bathing costume. (OK, so the author of Musical Affairs might have put it better than that.)

'Er, Jeremy,' I said, when he flung my purple knickers across the room to hang rakishly from a standard lamp. 'Do you think we might go into the bedroom before we start?' I was convinced that someone would walk in on us.

'I will go with you to the ends of the earth, my princess,' he replied smoothly. And with that, he scooped me up and carried me through to the bedroom as though I was light as a feather and not nudging ten and a half stone. He carried me all the way to the bed that I had last shared with David Whitworth. And somehow, slipping between the covers that I had not even changed since David left in such a hurry was the biggest thrill of all.

CHAPTER SIXTEEN

Well, they say that the best sex is the kind you can laugh about afterwards. No sooner had Jeremy jumped into my bed than he jumped straight back out again.

'Aaa-choo!!!' He sneezed so hard that he had to check his contact lenses hadn't flown out. 'Aaa-choo! Aaa-choo! Aaa-choo!'

He staggered backwards against the dressing table and rubbed violently at his eyes.

'What's wrong?' I cried clutching the duvet protectively to my chest.

'You've got a cat, haven't you?' he said accusingly.

'Yes,' I told him. 'Fattypuss. Are you allergic to them or something?'

'If I get into contact with the hair it brings me out in blotches,' he confirmed.

'Oh.'

'It must have been on your bed,' he said, looking at the duvet as though it was covered in fleas.

'Well, yes,' I said. 'She always sleeps in here during the day. I'll shake the duvet out, if you like.'

'That won't make a difference, Ali. I can't get in there with you again. My throat might swell up and suffocate me in the night. It's happening already.'

'You're suffocating? But that's terrible! What can we do?'

Jeremy opened the window and hung his head outside to get some air.

'Well, we can't go back to my place,' he said. 'I don't think Mum would approve of me bringing a girl home, even now I am twenty-six and a half.'

I clutched the duvet more tightly around my body. With Jeremy standing on the other side of the room, I was rapidly going cold again. Just my luck to find a man with an allergy to girl's best friend.

'The cat isn't in the room now,' I tried. 'Won't you start to get used to it in a minute?'

'Get used to it? No,' he wheezed. 'I'll be dead first. I've got to get out of here, Ali. I'm sorry. I've got to go.'

'You were OK in the other room,' I reasoned. This was not going as planned.

'I did feel a bit sniffly even then. Isn't there a room in the house where the damn cat hasn't been?'

'Well, she won't go in the bathroom after Emma got her with the shower hose one morning,' I tried.

'We can't do it in the bathroom. What if one of us slips on the tiles?' he said sensibly.

'Oh,' I said, disappointed. I'd always wanted to try it in the shower. But then I had a sudden flash of inspiration. 'Hey. She doesn't go in Emma's room at all,' I told him. 'Fattypuss and Emma don't get on that well, you see.'

'Great. Let's go into Emma's room.'

'But . . . but what if she comes home?' I asked, suddenly thinking better of the whole idea.

'I don't care. Emma can sleep in here. We'll leave her a note. Nothing is going to stand in the way of my desire tonight. I have to have you, wherever we are.'

'Oh, Jeremy,' I sighed.

He risked asphyxiation to pick me up from the bed – a little less manfully this time – and as he carried me through the door he sneezed and knocked my head against the doorframe. But I was so excited I barely felt the bump.

Next hurdle was finding a pen that worked to leave a note for Emma. The last thing we wanted was for her to burst in on us when we finally got going. The three ancient biros in the pot on the window-ledge had long since run out. In the end, I resorted to using my electric blue eye-liner pencil, snapping it in half as I scrawled, 'In your room. Use mine.'

'Fantastic, fantastic,' Jeremy muttered as he shuffled me quickly into Emma's bedroom. I tactfully flicked her fancy frilly knickers off the bed into a dingy corner and closed the door behind us, much to the disgust of a doleful Fattypuss who had thought she might try to follow.

'Sorry, Fattypuss,' I told her in my head. 'But there are some nights in a girl's life when she needs more than a flatulent old tabby.'

And so, at last, I was about to do it. I was about to do it with a man who wasn't David. I was momentarily exhilarated by the thought. Then it hit me that I was about to do it with a man who didn't know and love my lumps and bumps. (Actually, there was little evidence that David had loved my lumps and bumps either.)

And I was terrified. Perhaps I should try to put it off, I thought, wrapping the duvet more tightly around me. Until I could afford that Dior Svelte. I could fob Jeremy off with a tale about not being ready to dive into a sexual relationship again, the usual thing. The wait would probably drive him wild. Only problem was, the wait was driving me wild too. Without wishing to be too descriptive, I had started to feel stirrings deep inside even during that disgusting meal at the chicken shack. I couldn't wait until my thighs were in shape before we did it. That could mean waiting forever.

Instead, I did the next best thing to exercising for six months before embarking upon a new affair, I casually rolled over Jeremy and made a grab for the bedside light switch, intending to black the room out. But instead of pulling the light-switch, I managed to pull the whole thing off the table, and Emma's beautiful antique tiffany lamp-stand was soon a mess of smashed ceramic on the floor.

'Shit,' I said, jumping up to clear away the mess.

'Forget it,' Jeremy thundered, hauling me back onto the bed. 'We'll buy her another one.'

'There isn't another one, that lamp was unique.'

'And so am I,' said Jeremy testily. 'So have me now, or you won't have me at all.'

As it was, it all happened rather quickly after that. At least we were in the dark.

'What's this?' Jeremy asked me afterwards as he ran a gentle finger over my bright pink scar.

'I had my appendix out for Christmas. Didn't sew me up again very tidily, did they?' I added, trying to defuse the situation with a joke.

'I think it's beautiful,' he murmured, as he planted a row of kisses along its length.

'You don't really mean that,' I said, pushing his head away and rearranging the duvet so that I was covered right up to my neck.

'I do mean it. Every inch of you is beautiful, Ali. Even the bits that are damaged,' he pulled the duvet down again.

'It's a scar,' I said flatly.

'Yes. But it's our scars that make us interesting, don't you think?'

'I've never thought about it like that before.'

'Well, you must, Ali,' said Jeremy, kissing his way up to my belly button. 'A scar shows that you're a woman of experience. I could see that in your face too. In the way your eyes are slightly crinkled at the corners. Laughter lines.'

My hands flew up to check automatically. Crows' feet. Damn. I was only twenty-six.

'You've lived life to the full,' Jeremy continued. 'You've known happiness, but you've also known tears.'

You can say that again, I thought, making a mental note to buy some more miracle-working eye gel.

'Physical perfection betrays a lack of those emotions that make a human being wonderful.'

'Do you really think so?' Funny how physical perfection was still what most of us went after.

'I really do,' he promised.

CHAPTER SEVENTEEN

But when I woke up the next morning the bed was empty. I should have known that all that stuff about scars and personality was just so much flannel, I berated myself. It was just a wicked way to get into my pants. One that I hadn't met before, granted, having hitherto only been out with the kind of seductive Neanderthals who relied on the pulling power of their souped-up cars. I was just about to call the Samaritans and ask whether being deserted twice in just over a week was some kind of miserable record when the bedroom door creaked open and there stood Jeremy, with breakfast laid out on a tray. And not just breakfast. He had used an empty Perrier bottle to make a vase for a single red rose. Albeit a plastic one, nicked from the naff bouquet on the bathroom windowsill.

'Good morning, Sleeping Beauty,' he said. 'Hope these are your cornflakes.'

'Jeremy, you're still here,' I exclaimed.

'Of course I'm still here.'

'I know but . . .' Get a grip on yourself Ali, said a voice deep inside me. Acting like you're always being deserted is a sure way to put the idea of running away into a man's mind. 'But I thought you might have rushed home to be with your parents today,' I continued. 'What with you only having a month left in the country and all that.'

'I still feel like I have a lot more catching up to do with you.' He set the tray down on the floor beside the bed and slid his hands beneath the covers to caress my thighs. I wriggled in a mixture of excitement and discomfort. The night before it had been pretty dark and I had been quite pissed. Now, in the cold light of day, things might suddenly be quite different. I figured that Jeremy Baxter wasn't one of those rare men who hadn't heard about cellulite and didn't recognise it when they jiggled it.

Jeremy slipped off his shoes and slid under the covers beside me.

'Well,' he asked. 'Aren't you going to help me take my clothes back off?'

I didn't get a chance. Before I even had Jeremy's belt buckle undone, we were rudely interrupted. Emma had obviously come straight from the front door to her room without reading my note. She hadn't been home all night.

She was halfway through taking her dress off when she noticed that she wasn't alone.

'Ali! What are you doing in here?'

'I needed to borrow your room.'

'Well, you can get right out again. I didn't get a wink of sleep last night. I had to wait in the accident unit until half past two for Ashley to finish work. That's his name, Doctor Ashley Martin. Wonderful isn't it? Anyway, he got tied up in stitching up some idiot guy who'd been in a pub brawl. If they're going to fight, let them bleed, I say. But when Ashley finally got free he more than made up for it. He took me to this special doctor's cafe place. It's open all night long . . . So they can get pissed whatever time their shift finishes.'

She obviously hadn't noticed that Jeremy was sticking out from both ends of the duvet.

'So we got completely trolleyed,' Emma continued, as she turned her back on me and unhooked her bra. 'Then we went back to his room in the medic's quarters and he spent the rest of the night explaining the finer points of female anatomy to me. I tell you, it was fantastic.'

'Emma,' I squeaked. 'Keep your knickers on.'

'What do you mean, keep your knickers on? I'm only telling you what happened with Ashley. I'm not in a bad mood even if you are hogging my bed.'

'No, Emma,' I said more slowly. 'I mean, keep your knickers on. Literally. And your dressing gown. I can't wait to hear the rest of the gory details of your night with the doctor, but do you remember how I didn't go home alone last night? How I met up with an old friend who offered to give me a lift?'

'Oh yeah,' said Emma with a disgraceful leer. 'What happened there? You're a bit of a dark horse aren't you, Ali Harris? Where did he take you? Was it worth a ride in a Renault Megane? I saw you getting into it from the accident unit window. Did he choose it himself? Or is he some kind of travelling salesman?' She pulled a face of thinly veiled disgust. 'Weird dress sense too,' she added.

At which point Jeremy poked his head cautiously out of the duvet and said, 'Hello.'

Emma shrieked and clutched her dressing gown to her chest.

'You've got a man in there!'

'Yes, I've got a man in here. That's what I've been trying to tell you since you walked in. I left you a note on the kitchen table.'

'Well, that's a great place to leave me a note. How was I supposed to find that?'

'You usually go into the kitchen when you come home,' I protested.

'Yeah. But this time, I didn't. God, how embarrassing.' She snatched up her sweatshirt. 'What are you doing in my bed with a man anyway? Do you get some kind of weird kick out of doing it under other people's duvets?'

I made a throat cutting gesture at her then, as I saw Jeremy's hand appear from beneath the duvet and grope about on the floor for his socks. While I argued with Emma, I could tell that he was pulling them on.

'Uh-hm,' he coughed politely while Emma spouted on about the best place to leave a note for her if I ever needed to take liberties with her property again. And would I mind washing the sheets when I'd finished? And what on earth had happened to her lamp?

'I think I should go,' said Jeremy, slipping from my side, gathering his remaining clothes and fleeing before I could protest.

'I'll call you later, Ali!' he shouted as he slammed the front door behind him.

Emma shut up for long enough to look surprised.

'What's up with him?' she asked innocently.

'Perhaps he didn't feel welcome,' I snorted. 'Look,

Emma, I'm sorry I used your bed without asking, but you did the same the night that you got hideously drunk and wet yours. We couldn't stay in my bed because Jeremy is allergic to cats and Fattypuss had been sleeping all over my duvet again. And I'm really sorry about your lamp. But couldn't you have made yourself scarce for half an hour? Couldn't you see that I was in the middle of something?'

'I don't want to think about that,' she quipped.

'Emma!' I flew at her like an angry cat, claws out. 'You scared him away with your horrible comments about his car.'

'I did not. You heard him. He said he'd call you.'

But suddenly, a wave of doubt washed me out into an ocean of despair. 'He can't call,' I told her pitifully. 'He doesn't have my number.'

'Idiot! I didn't know that.' We both flew to the bedroom window to see if we could catch his attention.

Emma shouted after him, 'I didn't mean to be rude about the Megane. I was just jealous. I've never been out with a man who had anything more than a bicycle. And I'm not really angry about the lamp.' But Jeremy either didn't hear her, or he had chosen to ignore us, and moments later, his beautiful yellow Renault was sailing around the corner and out of my life. I was desperate. 'How could you do this to me?' I asked my former best friend.

'It's not the end of the world,' she promised me. 'He does know where you live, after all.'

'Yeah, but . . . But he can't just come round, can he? That's like, way too formal. He'll never do it.'

'He will if he wants you. You know he will.'

'Perhaps he doesn't want me. If he did, he would

have made sure he had my number before he left, right? Oh, Emma. Why did you have to be so rude about him?'

'If his skin's that thin, I've probably done you a favour,' she said, as she ran an inspecting eye over her duvet cover and started to pick up the remains of her lamp.

'This is so unfair,' I whined, then I flopped down onto her bed again and began to plough my way through a rainforest's worth of tissues.

'Honestly, Ali. By the time he gets home he'll have forgotten about my snide remarks. Philip Allard went out with me for two years after I called him "Radar" because of his ears.'

'You were only twelve at the time. And he's since committed suicide.'

'OK. So I've really cocked up again, haven't I?' Emma asked. 'Still, look on the bright side. At least my intervention has forced you to ration yourself. It's given him something to look forward to. To make him come back.'

'If you think that really works, then you should have been around last night,' I told her miserably.

'You mean, you've already done it with him?'

I nodded

'Bloody hell, Ali. That was a bit quick, wasn't it?'

'He is an old friend.'

Emma's eyes narrowed. 'Hang on a minute. That Jeremy, wasn't *the* Jeremy we were talking about last night? At the restaurant.'

'Jeremy Baxter? Yeah. It was him.'

Suddenly Emma exploded with laughter. 'Oh my God, Ali. Talk about scraping the barrel. Jeremy Baxter!

I didn't even recognise him. Did he have those awful boils of his on his you-know-what?'

'No,' I said flatly. 'He didn't.'

'I can't believe it. Old Boily Baxter. Just wait till I tell Shona about this.'

'What is there to tell her? He's changed. You saw him.'

'Yes, but not without his clothes on. They could be hiding a multitude of sins. You'd never let on, would you?'

'I assure you they weren't. Anyway, what does it matter. You've ruined everything, Emma. You've finished it all before it even started. I'll probably never see him again.'

She pulled a comically guilty face. 'I've probably done you a favour.'

'Well,' I said, getting out of bed and wrapping myself in my tatty towelling dressing gown. 'I wish you hadn't. I'm having a bath now.'

I locked myself in the bathroom and tried to steam out my rage. But I was just sinking into the warm soup of bubbles and bath oils when the telephone rang. Instinctively, I tried to struggle out again, just in case, by some fluke of flukes, it was for me. I twisted my ankle on the bathmat in my hurry.

'Oh hello, how are you?' Emma trilled in her flirtatious voice. Might have known it would be for her, I thought miserably. I had one foot back in the delicious bath when she called out mischievously, 'Ali, it's a man for you!!'

My heart beat a path to my mouth. He had got my number. Already. Somehow Jeremy Baxter had tracked me down. It wouldn't have been that hard, of course, since there was such a thing as directory inquiries and I had taken the precaution of being listed therein for just such an incredible occasion.

'Hello,' I said breathlessly into the receiver. Keen but cool, I hoped.

'Oh, hello, love,' said my Dad, sounding a little surprised at my keenness. My heart plummeted back into my boots. 'Your mother told me to call. Wants me to remind you that you're expected over here for Sunday dinner.'

'What?' I said, unnecessarily snappily. 'Did I really say I'd be over today?' I knew I had, but I still was hoping that I could get out of death by lunch by pleading ignorance.

'I think so. At least that's what your mother says, and she usually knows. Your grandmother's coming too. Shall I pick you up on the way back from fetching her from the home? That'll give you another hour to get ready.'

My shoulders sank. My heart sank. My so recently hopeful spirit suddenly resembled the *Titanic*. That day had started off with the promise of a romantic twenty-four-hour bedathon, now it was rapidly turning into the kind of Sunday that Morrisey used to write miserable songs about. Sunday lunch with Gran. Hang out the flags.

'I'll be ready in an hour, Dad,' I told him.

At least I wouldn't be able to sit and stare at the phone if I wasn't at home. But by the time I had hung up on Dad, Emma was already in my bath-water.

'Thought you would be ages on the phone,' she explained as she rinsed my new deep conditioner out of her hair. 'You don't mind, do you, Ali. Only Ashley doesn't have to work this afternoon and he's taking me out to lunch.'

He would be. Funny how there's such a thin line between your best friend and the person you hate most of all in the world sometimes.

'I'm having lunch with my Grandma,' I said, despondently.

'Ah well, chin up,' said Emma. 'Can't be too much longer until you see the will now.'

'That's no consolation,' I told her. 'As far as I can tell, the front-runner for her fast-dwindling fortune is still the family dog.'

CHAPTER EIGHTEEN

In fact, the dog was sitting in the front passenger seat of Dad's car when he arrived to pick me up (Fattypuss spat her disdain from the safety of my bedroom window). Gran was in the back of the car, wearing another Barbara Cartland rip-off with matching hat and handbag.

'Couldn't resist it,' she explained to me, as she ran a shaking hand over the beaded bodice. 'Pink goes so well with my colouring. So I thought, what the hell. I've always hated that bloody shepherd boy ornament your grandfather bought me. May as well flog it and wear the proceeds instead.'

'Which shepherd boy?' I mouthed to Dad.

'The Meissen,' said Dad, somewhat desperately.

'And there was just enough money left over for me to buy a lovely present for my favourite grandchild.'

Which one of us was that, I wondered for a foolish second. Jane, Jo or Ali? The answer was, of course, the dog.

'Don't you think it looks wonderful with Berkeley's fur?' Gran continued. Berkeley obliged me with a closer look at his new collar as he slobbered half my foundation off with his big pink tongue. The tag was engraved. And it was silver. Tiffany silver. I quickly estimated that that stinking mongrel was wearing a choke chain that had probably cost more than my old engagement ring.

'It's lovely, Gran,' I said with all the good grace I could muster. I could tell that Dad was already plotting to pawn it as soon as he had taken her home again. We could say that it had slipped off over Berkeley's pea-brained head while he was out on an extra long walk.

So, as you can imagine, from the very start I knew that Sunday lunch was going to be a nightmare. Mum's tight-lipped smile when Gran pointed out Berkeley's new collar reached new heights in the 'barely containing a scream' stakes. Jo was in a sulk because Dad was refusing to lend her the money to buy a motorbike. Jane was in a panic because her insurance company exams were less than a week away.

Only Berkeley seemed truly at ease that Sunday lunchtime. He sat at Grandma's feet, occasionally poking his nose out from beneath the table for a scrap. Berkeley would even eat Brussels sprouts if Gran was offering them. Such a fickle dog that one.

'Gran, you will lend me the money to buy a motorbike, won't you?' Jo said when the conversation found another one of those natural pauses that never seem to end.

'What's that, dear?'

Gran was selectively deaf and, right then, she wanted Jo to repeat her request to better enrage my mother.

'A motorbike, Gran,' Jo obliged.

'Don't be ridiculous, Jo,' interrupted my mother. 'You know what your father and I think about that.'

'I'm not asking you and Dad,' said Jo. 'I'm asking my Gran.'

'Well, your gran doesn't want to be bothered with things like that. She hasn't got money to burn, you know. Not living on her pension.'

'Who's she?' said Gran. 'The cat's mother? I may have entered the third age, Josephine, but I am not finished yet. I can hear perfectly well. And I've got plenty of things left to sell to raise money. What kind of motorbike do you want, my darling?'

Jo grinned in triumph. 'Just a small one. To start with. I only need about five hundred pounds.'

'That's not fair,' Jane piped up suddenly. 'I needed five hundred pounds to retake my insurance exams. No one would lend any money to me then.'

'Let's stop all this talk about money,' said Dad bravely. 'It's Sunday. God's day. There's no place for money talk today.'

'What's he on about?' Gran asked my mother loudly. 'God's day? He's a religious bloody nutter, he is. I always knew you should have married that other one. You know, what was he called?'

Mum went slightly red and a little vein began to pulse on Dad's temple.

'Marvin Shinshanker,' Jo obliged. 'The man from America.'

'Yes, the one from America. Now he was always going to make something of himself. You wouldn't be stuck here today if you'd married that Marvin Shinshanker. Your poor old mother wouldn't have to worry about giving her granddaughter five hundred pounds if you'd married Marvin Shinshanker.'

'You wouldn't have any granddaughters at all if I'd married Marvin Shinshanker,' Mum pointed out. 'He was as queer as a nine-bob note.'

Jane and Dad both smirked.

But Gran hadn't finished.

'Didn't seem all that queer when he came to see me.'

'Mother, you didn't.'

'Well, someone had to console him after you decided to throw away your life on this bloody loser. What have you done to these sprouts, Josephine?' she added seamlessly. 'Taste like bullets.'

'If only they were,' said Dad.

Gran fixed him with her good eye. 'I beg your pardon, young man?' And we waited for all hell to break loose.

Then the phone rang. You should have seen us. We were like five greyhounds. Me, my sisters, my Mum and Dad all raced to answer the phone, praying that we would be the lucky one. Praying that the caller would give us an excuse to escape the wrath of Gran.

Jo got it. She had the youngest legs after all.

'Hello?' she said breathlessly. Then, with a look of disbelief on her face she exclaimed, 'My God, Ali. It's for you. And it's a man.'

I took the receiver from her hand and the world seemed to go into slow motion as my family drifted back to face their fate in the dining room. I held my hand over the receiver as Gran squawked 'What are we having for dessert?' and thanked God for the gradual decline of short-term memory with age. A disaster had been averted by senility.

Who would it be? David? Marvin calling from the

hospital to say that he needed picking up since he couldn't walk on his jippy foot?

'Hello?' squeaked the receiver.

I had almost forgotten that there was actually someone waiting for me on the other end of the line.

'Oh, hello. Who is it?'

'You don't recognise me, Ali? Crikey, it's only been half a day since we were in bed together.'

'Jeremy?'

He must have called as soon as the last mouthful of his mother's torturous Sunday lunch passed his lips.

'Jeremy, I didn't expect it to be you. How did you know where to find me?'

'It didn't take that much detective work, Ali. Though I didn't actually expect to find you on this number. I thought I'd get your home number off your mum. You didn't let me have it, did you? And if the truth be known I feel a bit of an idiot now. I suppose you didn't give me your number because you didn't really want me to ring you.'

'Oh, no, no, no,' I protested, a little too keenly in all probability. 'I . . . er . . . (I wanted to tell him I'd been thinking of nothing else since he left but that would have been sad . . . and my family were listening). I'm glad you caught me here,' I said instead. 'I was going to track you down myself.'

'Good. Because I am missing you so much already,' he said seductively. 'I thought about you all through lunch. Every time I lifted a glass to my lips, I could smell the rich warm smell of your body on my hands.'

I squirmed very slightly at the thought.

'When Mum brought out her famous raspberry pavlova, all I could think about was that pavlova, your beautiful flat stomach and not having to use a spoon. I want you, Ali. I've been wanting you all day and I don't know how much longer I can stand to be without you. It makes me hard just thinking about seeing you again.'

'Jeremy,' I murmured, fanning my neck with my collar. 'I'm at my parents' house.' And the dining room had gone silent while my family strained to hear my private conversation.

'I know. I'm sorry. I'm being a naughty boy. But it's just so difficult for me to keep these feelings under control. I've never met anyone quite like you, Ali Harris. You stir me deep inside. You really do. I just think of your beautiful body and I need to explode.'

'Oh.' I put my hand up to my burning cheek instinctively. This was getting a bit embarrassing.

'Don't keep me in suspense, my darling,' Jeremy continued. 'Can we meet again tonight?'

I glanced across at my family. Five interested faces peered out from behind the slightly open dining room door.

'Yes,' I said. 'Yes. I guess we can.'

'How about we go out for dinner?' he asked. 'Most of what I had at lunchtime ended up in the dog. I couldn't eat for thinking about you.'

'Where can we go? It isn't exactly Egon Ronay central round here.'

'How about The Aspidistra?' he asked. 'I hear that's pretty good.'

'So do I,' I gasped. 'If you're a Rockerfeller. It's so expensive, Jeremy. I don't know . . .' The Aspidistra was so posh it had even been visited by Michael Winner! Not so posh that it had turned him away again, though.

'Stop right there. Forget the money. I'm the man in

charge of Eastern Europe, remember? And before you say it, Ali, we're not going halves. After what you gave me last night, I think I'm going to be owing you dinner for the rest of your life.'

'Really?'

'Really. Alison, you were like a tigress. A tigress that hasn't been fed in weeks.'

'Make that years,' I said, suddenly viewing the whole of my relationship with David as an emotional famine compared to that one night of bounty with Jeremy.

'Well, I'll be round to fetch you from your place at eight-thirty. Make yourself look special, my darling. Shouldn't take you more than thirty seconds.'

I put the phone down and floated across to the dining room.

'Who was that?' my sisters asked.

'I'm going out for dinner with Jeremy,' I told them.

'What? Jeremy? Jeremy Boil-face Baxter?' Jo asked.

'The very same.'

'Urgh. I don't believe it! He's disgusting. He's got warts and boils all over him.'

'Not anymore, he hasn't.'

'Ooh,' said my mother. 'This is a nice surprise. He's a lovely young man, Ali. Very eligible. You go and have a good time.'

'Just make sure you don't blow it by dressing like a bloody nun again,' said Gran.

Emma was in again when I went home to change. Her lunch with Ashley had been cut short by some inconsiderate buggers staging a motorway pile-up that had him bleeped into ER halfway through dessert.

'I'm sorry about this morning,' she said, looking sheepish.

'You're forgiven,' I breezed. 'He called me.'

'He called you? Where?'

'At Mum and Dad's house. We're going out tonight. To The Aspidistra.'

'My God. Better make yourself beautiful then,' Emma said. 'You look like you've been sleeping on a bed of nails.'

'Do I?' I sat down on the sofa and ran my fingers through my hair distractedly. 'I feel fabulous. He's so romantic, Emma. He already calls me "darling". Isn't that just fantastic?'

Emma put the tub of ice-cream she had been eating from straight down on the newly polished coffee-table.

'He calls you "darling"?' she repeated.

'Yes. And Sugar-lump and Sweetie-pie.'

'Well, just make sure that he's not calling you those names so that he doesn't have to remember your real one before you invite him to Antigua.'

I'd almost forgotten about that.

CHAPTER NINETEEN

'I'd like you to come to Antigua with me.'

Jeremy's eyes grew to the size of saucers in seconds.

'Antigua?' he repeated incredulously. 'You mean the Antigua? In the West Indies?'

'Yes. The very same. I've won a two week holiday there. All-inclusive,' I gabbled. 'It was first prize in a writing competition held by a women's magazine called *Complete Woman*. I'm meant to be leaving on Thursday morning, but the person I was supposed to be going with has dropped out.' That was putting it nicely.

'Dropped out? Of two weeks all expenses paid in Antigua? That other person must be completely mad,' said Jeremy.

'Yes, well. He had his reasons,' I said, thinking it best that they were glossed over right then. 'Would you like to come instead?'

'Like to come? I'd love to come. I can't believe you're really asking me. But shouldn't you be taking Emma? She is your best friend, after all.'

'I know,' I sighed. 'But the person I take has to be

a man. You see, there are a couple of complications, Jeremy. To do with the competition. If you want to come with me, I'm afraid that I'll have to ask you to do me a little bit of a favour first.'

'Fire away,' he said, settling back into the armchair as if I couldn't really ask him for too much right then. We had had a wonderful meal at The Aspidistra (which went on his company credit card) and had talked like friends who had known each other forever. We had, of course, known each other for almost ever, but what I really mean is that it was as though we had liked each other for all that time too. Now he probably thought I was going to ask him if he could find somebody to look after my cat Fattypuss while we were away.

'You'll have to do a photo shoot with me,' I told him. 'A kind of makeover thingy, for the magazine.'

'A makeover? You mean with stylists and stuff? No problem,' he said, laughing and smoothing down an eyebrow. 'In fact, I've always fancied myself as a bit of a model. Is that it? Is that the favour?'

I smiled nervously. 'I'm afraid it's not. The difficult bit comes next.' I sat on the arm of the chair he had chosen and twisted a lock of his hair in my fingers in an attempt to be especially appealing. 'Jeremy, if you want to come on this holiday with me, you're going to have to pretend to be my fiancé.'

There, I'd said it. Now for the fireworks. And the point blank refusal to cooperate with my hairbrain scheme.

'Your fiancé?' he repeated slowly and his face grew slightly pale. 'Alison, we've only really known each other for a couple of days. I mean properly known each other, not counting when we were kids, of course.'

'I know, Jeremy. But I'm not asking you to actually be my fiancé,' I elaborated. 'I'm just asking you to pretend you are until we get to Antigua. You see, the competition I won was to find Britain's Most Romantic Couple. I entered it while I still thought that David and I fitted the bill. The prize was intended for me and him. If the people at *Complete Woman* find out that David and I are no longer together, I'm pretty sure I won't be allowed to take the prize up on my own.'

'But I'm not David, Ali. What if they don't let you take me instead?'

'But they won't have to know that you're not David, don't you see? They've never met him. They don't have a clue what he looks like. Oh, except that I think I did mention he had brown hair in my winning piece about our doomed relationship,' I sighed. 'Never mind. We can always say that you've dyed your hair since then. I just need a male body for the photo shoot.' I clapped my hand to my mouth. 'Shit, I didn't mean to say that. I don't mean to imply that just any male body would do, you understand. I need you, you specifically. Can you imagine anything better than two weeks in the Caribbean?'

'I have to say that the idea of two weeks in the sunshine before I have to go back to Warsaw sounds very, very tempting indeed.'

'It's only a teensy-weensy little white lie I'm asking you for.'

'You're asking me to pretend we're getting married, Ali! What if my Mum finds out?'

'How? I can't imagine that she'd be the type to read *Complete Woman*,' I lied. In fact, she was exactly the type of woman who would be attracted to its unique blend of expert gardening advice and healthy relationship tips.

'I'll do it,' Jeremy said suddenly, throwing his hands up in the air in a gesture of playful defeat. 'I'll do it. Of course I will. What possible harm can it do? I would lie about anything to spend two weeks in the sun with you.'

'Would you really?'

'Anything. Take me to the photographic studio at once.'

'Oh, Jez,' I squealed, jumping up from my seat and flinging my arms around his neck. 'You can't begin to know how much this means to me. You're so kind to do this.'

'Kind? Pah! It's not difficult to be kind when you're faced with the reward I've just landed. Two whole weeks in the Caribbean. Can you show me a picture of the place we're going to?'

I delved eagerly into the wastepaper basket to retrieve the Santa Bonita brochure which had been consigned there after David's last departure. I squeezed into Jeremy's armchair beside him and pointed out all the beautiful details. The air-conditioned cabanas with front doors that opened straight onto the pure white sand. The glittering blue sea. The watersports. The twenty-four-hour seafood buffet. The swim-up poolside bar. I nearly wet myself with excitement.

'Wow,' said Jeremy. 'I would even pretend to be married to you if I had to for two weeks of this. You've got no idea how much I love water-skiing, Ali. Don't get much opportunity to practise in Warsaw.'

'It's going to be fantastic,' I murmured into his ear, while simultaneously nibbling at his lobe.

'Mmmm.' Jeremy grasped my hand and pressed it to the front of his trousers where a hard-on was already beginning to bulge. 'I can't wait. I'm going to have you in one of those cabanas, then on the white sand, then in the glittering blue sea, and then on top of the sea-food buffet. If I've still got the energy.'

'I've got to phone Amanda and arrange the photo shoot first,' I protested as Jeremy slipped his hand under my blouse.

'Later,' he murmured. 'Call her later on.'

Next time I saw the outside of my bedroom (I had exiled Fattypuss for the time being and changed the sheets), it was tomorrow.

CHAPTER TWENTY

'At last! Thank goodness you've called,' said Amanda in a most disgruntled tone of voice when I called her first thing the next morning. 'I have left about a hundred messages on your answerphone, Alison Harris,' she spat. 'The deadline for copy for next month's issue is this afternoon, you know. You've given me a very, very big headache about all this indeed.'

'Well, I'm calling with good news,' I told her reassuringly. 'David's chickenpox finally seems to have cleared up. He thinks that he's spot-free enough to do the photos now. In fact, we're both free to do the photo shoot this morning if you like.'

'This morning? Hmmm.' I could hear Amanda flicking through her diary. 'Can you get into London for eleven o'clock? Don't you dare try to cancel this time.'

'Eleven o'clock sounds fine. Where?' She reeled off the name and address of a photographic studio which I quickly scribbled down.

Jeremy and I were at that central London address at

eleven on the dot. I had to take another sickie from work to do it. Complications with my appendectomy scar was the reason I gave Julie. She didn't question it for a minute, she was too keen to tell me the latest gossip about Bridget and the new assistant in accounts. Naughty goings on in the stationery cupboard. I listened for ten minutes then faked a spasm of pain. We'd never have got out of the house and to London otherwise.

Upstairs in the photographer's studio, which was basically a dusty attic room in a draughty old warehouse, Amanda was already knee deep in the bright and beautiful clothes that she and the fashion editor had chosen for the shoot. Amanda wasn't at all as I had expected. I had imagined her to be all Lycra and highlights. Instead, she looked not unlike a home counties mum in her neat jumper and knee length skirt and when she saw us, her eyes lit up to match her gap-toothed smile.

'Deedee, I told you,' she said to the fashion ed, who really was all lycra and highlights. 'Perfect size twelve.'

'Bordering a fourteen,' said the fashion ed, without even saying hello.

Amanda got up from the little nest she had made out of party dresses and slingbacks to welcome us to the world of *Complete Woman*. She shook my hand warmly enough but I noticed that she lingered a little longer over her handshake with Jeremy.

'You must be David,' she purred. Inappropriately seductively I thought, considering he and I were meant to be engaged to be married. 'David?' she repeated when he looked at her somewhat blankly. I pulled a desperate look at Jeremy until he remembered that he was indeed that man.

'That's right,' he said smoothly, pulling Amanda into an unexpected continental kiss situation which I hoped would take her mind off the unnatural pause while Jeremy remembered his name. 'And you must be Amanda. Ali has been telling me all about you. I'm sorry it's taken so long for us to get around to doing this photo thing. You know how it is with such a high-pressured job as mine.'

'And your chickenpox, of course,' added Amanda kindly, as she fiddled with the single string of glossy pearls around her ecru cashmere polo neck. Jeremy looked confused. As Amanda conferred with the photographer on the subject of backdrops, I had to fill Jeremy in on the situation using sign language.

'What on earth's the matter with you?' Jeremy hissed as I mimed out the scratching. 'Have you been bitten by another cat flea or something? Bloody unhygienic animals, cats. You should have it neutered.'

Before I could protest that Fattypuss was a girl anyway, or explain about the chickenpox, Amanda returned to whisk Jeremy away to the changing room where he was transformed from gorgeous to bloody gorgeous in the poof of a powder puff.

'No scars,' the make-up artist commented, referring of course to the chickenpox. 'You must have been really lucky, David. I had loads of scars and I swear I didn't pick a single one.'

'Me too,' sighed Amanda. 'I've got a really big one just here,' she added, giving him a flash of her midriff, which, as far as I could see, was pretty damn flawless. 'Would you mind trying some of these bits and bobs on for me,' she added, passing him a couple of beautifully cut suits. I noticed that she didn't bother to offer to leave the changing room as he did.

'Perfect,' she murmured, before Jeremy even had the silky Armani trousers past his knees. 'What do you think, Ali? The green or the blue? You know him best. Perhaps he should try the blue again.'

Another excuse to see his pants, I thought. Though I couldn't really blame her. He was gorgeous in his stretchy cotton Calvins.

Next, it was my turn. I had been dreading the makeover moment, thinking that Amanda would have me made up like all the other women I had seen in her mag – or worse, like her – that is, looking like I was going to ladies' night at the local golf club. But my fears were unfounded. To my eternal relief Amanda picked out a beautiful little blue shift dress that perfectly complemented the suit she had finally chosen for Jeremy after making him dress and undress at least five times. With my hair bouffed out by the hairdresser to give it the kind of body that no shampoo on earth could achieve, no matter how much I spent on it, and all my facial flaws covered in slap, I took my place beside Jeremy in front of the camera.

'Gorgeous,' Amanda murmured. I guessed she was referring to Jeremy again. Then she added. 'You two look as though you were made for each other. Lovely. Really lovely.'

I couldn't help grinning like a fool at the thought. Made for each other. Oh, how I hoped we were. I gazed at Jeremy through rose-tinted contacts. Jeremy however, had gone straight into supermodel mode and wasn't looking at me at all. He stared directly into the long lens of the camera and licked his plump, smooth lips. If he had had long hair, he probably would have flicked it back.

'Fantastic,' said the photographer, another woman, called Running Star or something like that. I just remember that she had a Red Indian name though her accent was pure scouse. 'That's great, David. Just keep giving me that face. Ali, could you turn to the left a little,' she said to me. 'Full face really isn't your best angle.'

'Oh. OK. Thanks,' I said. What else could I say to that? I angled myself so that I wouldn't crack the lens.

'Right. That's brilliant,' the photographer continued. 'Wow, David. You're really smouldering over there. Have you ever thought about being a model? You know, professionally?'

Jeremy placed a hand on his chest in a gesture that reminded me of being in the chorus line of a junior school production of Hans Christian Andersen's *Ugly Duckling*. It came at the point when the duckling said, 'Me? A swan?' Anyway, I'm sure you know what I mean.

'She's right,' I simpered, while the stylist adjusted the bulldog clips at the back of my dress so that they wouldn't be in shot. I had just ruined half a film by turning so that they were in view. 'You're really good at this modelling thing.'

'I have to say I'm quite enjoying myself,' he replied. 'Thanks to you.'

'Ali, keep your chin up, darling. I keep thinking I've got double vision,' said the photographer, crushing our intimate moment beneath the hot studio lights. Not to mention my self-esteem.

Amanda and her assistant pored over a Polaroid at the back of the room. 'David, you look fab,' Amanda announced with a thumbs up. 'But Ali, you just look worried.'

'Yeah,' said the photographer. 'Unclench your jaw, sweetheart. You look like you're doing pelvic floor exercises.'

The magazine crew fell about laughing.

'Either that or holding back a fart,' added Amanda.

I almost began to regret all those times I had scoffed when supermodels said in interviews that having your photo taken for a living is really hard work. Then, as if I couldn't feel any worse, the photographer's assistant, a girl called Jo who didn't smile – ever, since it might just give her wrinkles – opened the studio window and I was hit by a blast of cold air. It was alright for Jeremy. He was wearing a jacket. I asked if I might have one too.

'Not now we've got the line right, Ali,' sighed Amanda. 'Only another roll and a half to go. Stiff upper lip!'

I gritted my teeth (but not too hard), tried to contain one of my chins and to think myself warm. But by the end of the shoot I felt as though they had been testing my face in a Rover car factory wind-tunnel. I could barely move. That last smile was more of a rictus.

With the shoot over and the photographer busy dismantling the set they had built around us, Amanda helped Jeremy to undress. It was necessary, she assured me, to make sure that the delicate Paul Smith suit she had chosen didn't end up in a crumpled heap on the floor. It seemed that I, on the other hand, could fling my Armani about exactly as I wished.

'What a gorgeous man,' Amanda sighed as the make-up artist helped Jeremy take his war-paint off. 'You're ever so lucky, Ali. When we read your competition entry we all knew that David was going to be a gem, but we really had no idea that he was going to be so . . . well, so bloody good-looking. Makes a single girl quite sick.'

I beamed with pride, as if she were complimenting me.

'If I didn't think you'd been through such a lot together,' Amanda confided with a smirk. 'I might have tried to steal him for myself.'

'Well, thanks for being so restrained,' I told her.

Jeremy had finished cleaning up now. He walked across the studio with a lollop carefully designed to put magazine editors in mind of a catwalk king. He kissed Amanda on both cheeks.

'Thank you so much, Amanda. We've had a wonderful day,' he said.

I nodded. The feeling was just about returning to my wind-frozen arms.

'Oh,' Amanda sighed theatrically. 'You lovely man. Take him away before I faint, Ali. But wait, before you go, I've got something for you. David, take this.' She handed him her card. 'Just in case you ever decide to give up that boring old insurance job of yours.'

'Insurance?' Jeremy asked. For a moment, Jeremy had completely forgotten who he was supposed to be.

'Ha. Isn't he funny?' I covered. 'Pretending that a day being a model has made him forget what he really does for a living. Let's go.' I dragged him down the stairs before things could get any worse.

'Don't go signing up with any model agency without

speaking to me first,' Amanda called after us. 'Mwah! Mwah! Safe journey, darlings!'

'What was she on about? Insurance?' Jeremy asked me when we were out on the street again.

'It's what David does, stupid. You nearly dropped us in it. Come on, let's get out of here. I need a drink. My hands are shaking.'

'You should have filled me in properly before we came out,' Jeremy complained.

'I did. You must have forgotten everything I told you while you were busy being the male equivalent of Cindy Crawford. Still, it doesn't matter now. I think we pulled it off, don't you?'

'Hold on a minute!'

We were halfway up the street and almost out of sight of the studio's dusty windows when Amanda caught up with us. 'You thought you could get away with it, didn't you?' she shouted.

I felt my blood temperature drop ten degrees. What had happened? How had she found out? Had Jeremy dropped his credit cards, plastered all over with his real name, on the way out of the studio? Or had she heard our revealing conversation on the stairs? We stood guiltily still as Amanda drew up alongside us. But when she did, she was grinning.

'Well, we've done the pictures,' she said breathlessly. 'But you naughty children haven't given me any decent quotes for the accompanying article. I was so caught up in the excitement of our session that I didn't write down a word either of you said.'

She brought a Dictaphone out of her handbag and held it in front of our noses.

'OK. Let's have some sound-bites from you two

young lovers,' she giggled. 'David, can you tell me in just one short sentence, what you believe to be the secret of your romantic success?'

Jeremy looked at me and bit his lip, thinking hard. Then he turned back to Amanda with a beam. 'Let's just say, the secret of my romantic success is that I happened to meet and fall in love with the most wonderful woman in the world.'

Amanda recorded the platitude, then turned her Dictaphone off and sighed.

'Oh, David, that's perfect. You are such an angel. Ali, I may have to kill you and steal your man after all,' she added with a disarming smile. 'I know you've been through a lot together, but all's fair . . .'

'Wonderful,' I replied.

'Only joking. And you, Ali?' she continued. 'What do you think your secret has been?'

'Oh, there's no secret,' I told her. 'It's easy to be romantic when you wake up every morning next to the most beautiful man in the world.'

Jeremy and I locked eyes and smiled beatifically.

'Lovely,' said Amanda. 'Well, that should just about do it. I'll make the rest up, if you don't mind.'

'Not at all,' Jeremy and I assured her. I had heard that's the professional way after all.

'Ah,' Amanda sighed again, hugging her Dictaphone to her chest. 'Seeing you two looking so happy together in that studio reaffirms my faith in romance. There really is someone for everyone, isn't there?'

We nodded. Amanda put her Dictaphone back in her handbag and kissed us both goodbye. Mwah! Mwah! Mwah! Jeremy got two.

'Now, you two make sure that you have the best

holiday of your lives. I'll be thinking of you both. Jealously!'

Then she re-adjusted her velvet Alice band, turned and went back to the studio, leaving Jeremy and me just about ready to crack up with the tension of it all.

'My God, they take their romance seriously at *Complete Woman*,' said Jeremy as we got back into his car for the drive home to Brindlesham.

'Yeah, makes me feel a bit guilty to tell you the truth, telling her all those lies.'

'Rubbish. People like her deserve to have the wool pulled over their eyes from time to time. Someone for everyone? She'll be lucky. I'd run a mile if a girl like her came over to me and started gushing all that crap about true romance.'

I made a mental note: 'I must remember not to gush crap.'

CHAPTER TWENTY-ONE

So at last I had my escort for the holiday of a lifetime and the photos had been taken to prove it. The only hurdles remaining were how on earth I would manage to get yet another two weeks off work without losing my job altogether and how to tell my mother what was going on. Work was relatively easy. I simply put a handkerchief over the receiver and called Julie.

'Feeling worse,' I croaked. 'Septicaemia probably. Seeing the doctor this afternoon.'

'Well, you just stay home until you start to feel better again,' she said, all mother hen (though I had been at Hudderston's for long enough to know that the second she was off the phone she would be taking my name in vain around the office). I remembered when Bridget the other temp had a throat infection so bad that they thought they might have to amputate her head. A temperature of 104 degrees, yet as soon as Julie let Bridget go home, Julie was on the edge of my desk complaining about skivers. (The same rules didn't apply when she had to get her ingrowing toenail seen to during office hours, of course.)

'Call me this afternoon to let me know what the doctor says though,' she said, just when I thought I was in the clear.

Mum was going to be altogether more difficult. I had yet to even tell her about winning the competition because I hadn't wanted to go through another round of 'told you sos' about the end of my relationship with David, but now I had no choice. Not least because I was going to be out of the country on February the 14th.

February the 14th? Valentine's Day? So what, you ask. So February the 14th is my maternal grandmother's birthday and nobody in our family has ever got out of the torturous celebratory tea-party that usually marks the occasion. At least not for as long as I can remember. In fact, attendance had been made far stricter over the past couple of years, since every time dear old Granny sneezed over the pepper she would try to convince us that it was a herald of the beginning of the end, and we had all better be a lot nicer to her in future if we wanted to see any of her vast collection of figurines when she was gone. (Only Saddam Hussein could have commanded more obedience from his family.)

'It only takes one of you not to be there and that's the whole lot of us out of the will,' my mother had told Jo only last year, when Jo tried to get a special dispensation by pleading that she had a starring role in the school play. School plays happen every year, said Mum adamantly. But so did Gran's birthday, and I was pretty sure that Gran's birthday would still be an annual event long after Jo had finished her A-levels and had kids of her own. My previous attempts to get Valentine's Night off for a romantic dinner with David had been met with the emotional equivalent of a United Nations air-strike.

Anyway, I drove round to Mum and Dad's and started to improve the chances that I would not be disinherited by helping Mum to clear out the kitchen cupboards. She was having one of her spring clean binges. Complicated this year by the fact that she had been watching some programme about Feng Shui and wanted all her tin labels facing east. God, was it dusty in those cupboards. There were packets of blancmange in there for heaven's sake and I'm pretty certain that no-one under the age of twenty-three has even heard of the stuff.

'What are you being so helpful for?'

With her powers of maternal deduction, my mum had me sussed as soon as I donned an apron.

'Er, nothing,' I began. I would keep up the 'nothing' line until I really had to cave in and confess. That was my usual modus operandi.

'Rubbish. I can tell when you're up to something, Alison Harris. I'm not your mother for nothing, you know.'

'Well, I might as well tell you the truth . . .' I sighed, straightening up from scrubbing at a particularly persistent puddle of molasses.

'You're pregnant, aren't you?' she sighed dramatically. 'Good God, whatever will the neighbours think? Me, a grandmother at forty-three?'

(And the rest.) She seemed to have forgotten that she'd just celebrated her thirtieth wedding anniversary. Was I suddenly supposed to believe that she had married at thirteen?

'No,' I protested. 'No, Mum, I'm not pregnant.'

'Oh. You need a bigger pair of trousers then.'

'Thanks a lot.' After that morning's photo shoot my self-esteem was already at an all-time low.

'Do you need a loan?'

'No.'

'You scratched your father's car on the way into the driveway?'

'No.'

'You're off to join the Moonies?'

'No.'

'Then what is it? I've been through all the obvious things.'

Moonies? Obvious? Perhaps if she had been talking to my hippie sister Jane.

I decided to take my life in my hands. 'I'm going to be away for Grandma's birthday.'

'You what?' My mother let the dishcloth plop into the washing-up bowl, splashing bubbles all over her newly cleaned work surfaces.

'I'm not going to be at Grandma's birthday party.'

'Why not?'

'I'm going to be in Antigua.'

My mother leaned against the sink and looked at me cleaning out the cupboards through narrowed eyes.

'And what's that? Some posh new club opened up in town, I'll bet. You mean to tell me that you're going to go out with your friends to some gin palace on your grandmother's birthday? Which, incidentally, could be her last.'

'Mum, you know as well as I do that Gran will outlive the Queen Mother and the Queen Mother will outlive just about everyone else on this planet. So I'm going to miss her birthday tea on this one solitary occasion to go to Antigua the country,' I tried to explain. 'It's in the Caribbean. I've won a competition, Mum. I won a holiday. I'm flying out tomorrow.'

'Tomorrow? That's a bit bloody sudden. And when exactly did you win this competition?'

'About two weeks ago.'

'Two weeks ago! And you didn't warn me that you were thinking of going away as soon as you heard?'

'I didn't bother telling you because I didn't think I would be going. And I didn't plan to go over Grandma's birthday either, it just sort of happened like that.'

'Well, can't you change it to some other week?'

'No. I can't.'

'And who are you taking on this jolly jamboree?'

'No-one. Just me.'

'Rubbish. The prizes in those competitions are always for two.'

'Not this one,' I lied. 'It's just me. On a beach. On my own. Recovering from my annus horribilis.'

Mum pursed her lips cynically. 'You can cut out the Latin when you're talking to me. I bet you're taking that floosy Emma. It's your Grandma's birthday and you're jetting off to the sun with that no-good flatmate of yours. She's a bad influence on you, she is. Hardly ever sees her family.'

'She's not coming with me.'

'Then you can take your Gran.'

'What?'

'If you're not going to be in England on her birthday, then she can bloody well be in the Caribbean with you. Might take her mind off selling any more of the family silver. She flogged the little violet seller figurine on

Thursday night and bought herself a Sega Megadrive with the proceeds.'

'Good for her,' said Jo, who had wandered in for a biscuit.

'She hasn't got a flippin' television to watch it on,' said Mum. 'No, Alison, you've got to take her with you to try and stop this madness. If she sells the Staffordshire Pottery King Charles Spaniels I don't know what I'll do.'

'Mum!'

'What about the family, Ali? This could be your grandmother's last chance to see some of the world. She never gets to go on holiday.'

'She went to Scarborough in November,' Jo pointed out.

'Oh, that hardly counts. If you take her to the Caribbean, she might finally stop going on about how your Auntie June's family has always loved her more than us. Auntie June can afford to take your Gran on fancy trips because she lives two hundred miles away and doesn't have to put up with her every bloody weekend. I should have followed her out of Brindlesham when I still had the chance. Brains, that's what my sister's got. Great big bloody brains.' Mum was almost sobbing.

'I can't take Gran, Mum,' I said in desperation. 'I'm taking someone else.'

'Who?' asked Jo. 'You haven't got any friends except Emma and David's still going out with that Lisa Brown girl.'

'You don't need to remind me of that,' I warned her, riding the stab to my heart with considerable poise, I thought. 'I'm taking Jeremy Baxter.'

The room fell silent. Even Jo stopped chewing on her Wagon Wheel to stare at me in wonder.

'What did you say?' said my mother finally.

'I said, I'm taking Jeremy Baxter to Antigua.'

Another minute's silence.

'But you hardly know him,' Mum protested.

'I've known him all my life,' I said.

'You'd have slapped me if I said that,' said Jo.

'Shut up you,' Mum told my little sister. 'Shouldn't you be doing some revision?'

'Oh, I've finished for today. It's only Further Maths mock tomorrow and I'm not expecting to pass that anyway.'

'Jo-anna,' thundered Mum, pointing her towards the door.

Jo shrugged. 'OK. But Alison might want a witness here if you're about to kill her.'

Mum turned her ocular destruction lasers on Jo and sent her scurrying up the stairs. I put my coat on, ready for a quick escape.

'There's a name for girls like you, going off on holiday with men they've only just met,' she began.

'Young women on the verge of the twenty-first century?' I tried.

'Don't get saucy with me. You'll just have to tell him that the holiday's off. You've got family obligations.'

'It's too late. His name's on the ticket. In any case, I've got to take a man.'

'Then take your father,' Mum said. 'I could do without him under my feet for a fortnight. Your Grandma won't miss him. She'll probably be pleased he's gone.'

'I can't take Dad. I've got to take a young man. I've got to take a man who's supposed to be my fiancé.'

'You've got engaged?' Mum shrieked then, hearing half of the message. 'You've gone and got engaged again without telling us. Haven't you learnt your lesson after that David Whitworth? You needn't think your aunts are going to be happy to go buying you engagement presents again. Auntie Eileen has already asked for her British Home Stores saucepan set back.'

'Don't panic. I'm not engaged, Mum. I'm just pretending to be. Jeremy is pretending to be David.'

'Why?'

'For the competition. I won it for me and David, but I can't take him now, can I? Not now that he's gone back to her.'

'You should have tried harder to keep your hands on him when he started messing around with that Lisa.'

'Perhaps he should have tried harder to keep his hands off her. Look, Mum. The bottom line is, I'm going away tomorrow and I'm going with Jeremy Baxter. I don't care if I am telling a big porky to get this holiday. There's going to be no more Miss Nice Guy from me. I'm always getting walked on but I'm going to go out and get what I want from now on.'

'Well, my dear. You go ahead and do exactly as you want,' my mother sighed as though her heart was breaking. 'Heaven knows you always have done before. But mark my words, Alison Harris. No good ever came of telling lies.'

'This time it will,' I assured her.

'And even less good ever came from answering back.'

Terrific. A chance for real happiness in my life at last and my mother refused to give me her blessing. I couldn't see Jeremy that afternoon, since he was under obligation to visit some relatives in the country before he disappeared again, so I decided on a spot of retail therapy to cheer myself up. I had a lot of pre-holiday shopping to do. First stop was Brindlesham's solitary big department store for a bikini. I knew that Hays and Sons had an all-year-round 'cruise-wear' collection and rather fancied myself in a gold lamé two-piece. Credit card in hand, I was ready to spend whatever it would take to turn me into Bridget Bardot. Bridget Bardot in the sixties, that is. I could already do a pretty good impression of Bridget Bardot the dotty animal lover. Unfortunately, the swimwear buyers at Hays and Sons obviously assumed that no-one under the age of fifty ever went on holiday outside August and I came away empty handed after trying on a ruched bottle-green one-piece that reached down to my knees.

Toiletries next. One of the most important things on my list was sun-screen. I had a bottle of it at home, but it had been bought eight years earlier for my post-A-levels trip to Majorca and if it was still any use at all, I couldn't get it out of the bottle.

'Going on holiday at this time of year?' asked the cashier in Boots as she swiped my Ambre Solaire and a packet of bikini line wax through her EPOS. The cashier's name was Lorna. I knew her vaguely. She had been going out with David's best friend's brother or some spurious connection like that and we'd swapped platitudes a couple of times over rum and coke in The Rotunda.

'I am actually,' I told her smugly.

'Anywhere nice?'

'Antigua. It's in the Caribbean.'

'You're kidding me? The Caribbean,' she sighed. 'I've always wanted to go there. Fred says we might make it out there for our honeymoon but only if he has a really really good year with his carpet cleaning business. Who are you going with, if you don't mind me asking? I mean, I know that you and David Whitworth aren't together any more. Heard it on the grapevine,' she said with a sympathetic smile. 'Very sorry to hear that news. I never did much like Lisa.'

'It's OK. You don't have to say that.' I knew damn well that she and Lisa were as thick as thieves. 'Besides I've got a new man now,' I told her triumphantly, secretly hoping that it would get straight back to David's ears. 'His name is Jeremy Baxter and he's in charge of the whole of the Eastern European market for this huge computer company. You probably won't have heard of them.'

'Wow,' said Lorna. 'Head of Eastern Europe. He must have a bob or two to take you to the Caribbean and so quickly after getting together. And over Valentine's Day. He must be a romantic.'

'Actually,' I said, slipping the suntan lotion and wax into my bag, 'I'm taking him.' Lorna's mouth dropped open.

'I'll pop round when I'm back and show you my tan.'

Then back home to call in to Hudderston's one more time before the great escape. I did my bikini line simultaneously for that authentic hint of anguish to my voice. I got through to Irene first but Julie insisted on taking the call herself.

'Feeling any better?' she asked. 'I don't mean to put the pressure on you, Ali, but your in-tray isn't looking terribly tidy.'

I coughed into the receiver, then pulled a sticky, warm wax strip from my pubic bone and the tears flooded into my eyes. 'Well, if you're really really pushed, I'll drag myself in. But the doctor said that because my scar's gone septic again, I really shouldn't try to move out of bed at all. In case it bursts and I get blood poisoning. Which can be fatal, you understand,' I added with another rattling breath.

'Oh, is it catching?' Julie asked.

'Septicaemia? Certainly sounds it,' I replied, ripping off another strip. I sucked in a breath in genuine agony.

'Alison, you sound terrible.'

'I'm fine,' I said bravely, pressing down on my freshly plucked skin in an attempt to dull the painful stinging. 'I mean, I'm not fine, but I will get through this. I just need some more time. About another two weeks, the doctor says.'

We decided that I should probably stay off work for as long as I needed to for the sake of the rest of the workforce who had children and wives.

Emma had listened to me make the call.

'Was I convincing?'

'Terrifying. I was scared to sit too close to you,' she muttered as she peeled one of the discarded wax strips from where it had landed on the wall beside the telephone.

CHAPTER TWENTY-TWO

Before I knew it it was two o'clock in the morning. In less than twelve hours I would be in the air. I had just finished packing and was preparing myself for some serious beauty sleep, complete with a pair of soggy tea bags taped to my eyes, when Emma appeared at my bedroom door with a very weary look upon her face.

'Ali,' she said. 'It's David. He says he wants to talk to you. Desperately.'

'Well, tell him I'll call him when I get back from my holiday,' I told her, without even bothering to uncover my eyes.

'He's not on the phone,' she sighed. 'He's here. In the house.' And before I could make myself look presentable she had let him into my bedroom. David Whitworth stood at the bottom of my bed like an apparition of Valentine's Eve past, pale-faced and with a huge bouquet of white roses held tight in his clammy little hands. Emma slipped out as he came in.

'Ali,' he said. 'Ali, are you awake?'

'I am now, you idiot,' I snarled, taking off my tea bags

and putting them into the ashtray on my bedside table. 'What do you want?'

'I want to talk to you,' he told me feebly.

'About what?'

'About us.'

'There is no "us" anymore, David,' I spat at him, as I pulled my pyjama top tighter around my neck. 'There's only you and Lisa Brown and me and my new man.'

'Your new man. I heard all about him. Fred's girlfriend Lorna said you were in Boots today crowing your head off about him.'

'Hardly crowing. I was just answering her nosy questions.'

'She said he was some Eastern European diplomat or something. Where the hell did you meet someone like him, Ali?'

'Not down The Rotunda, that's for sure.'

'And how long has it been going on?' he asked accusingly.

'Well, if that cloth-eared bimbo had listened properly she would have been able to tell you that my new man is not actually a diplomat, he's the head of the Eastern European branch of a multi-national computer conglomerate, and it's been going on since about twelve hours after I found out that you were seeing Lisa Brown again. It is allowed, you know. I am single again, remember? Or do I have to go into a convent until you decide that you want me back once more?'

'Who is he?' asked David with an anguished look upon his creepy mug.

'No-one you know. At least, I don't think you know him.'

'Just tell me his name,' said David passionately.

'His name's Jeremy Baxter. He used to live in Saintbridge Road.'

'Not the Jeremy Baxter,' David asked, a sudden glimmer of joy crossing his deliberately downcast eyes. 'Jeremy Baxter with the boils? You're joking?'

Why would no-one let that single unhappy incident lie? The boils had only lasted for two weeks.

'That's the one,' I said coolly. 'But he doesn't have boils any more, thank you very much. He's grown up a great deal since junior school. Changed. Matured. Become a real man. You know, like people are supposed to do as they get older?'

'But I've changed too,' David protested.

'What? Since the Saturday before last? Now come on,' I warned him. 'I seem to remember hearing this little speech back then too. Evolution happens over millennia, David, not weekends. It'll be a long time before I even consider your species to be part of the human race again.'

'Ali, will you just cut the wisecracks and listen to me?' He flung the roses down upon my bed to underline his frustration. 'It's no wonder that things have got so bad between us lately. Every single time I try to apologise to you for the way I've been behaving, you just start making stupid digs at me and before I know it, I'm storming out on you again.'

'You limped out last time,' I reminded him.

'Yeah. And if I wasn't such a nice guy, you could be talking to my solicitor right now, not me. You did me some damage with that stuff.'

'Huh. I could get my solicitor to talk to you about forcing your way into people's houses in the middle of the night.'

'Emma let me in. I didn't force anything. But I'd appreciate a little bit more respect from you, Alison Harris. Because I could still be tempted to press charges for grievous bodily harm, you know.'

'Is there permanent scarring to poor Mister Stiffy then?' I asked hopefully.

'No.'

'Shame.'

'But it still hurts when I pee,' he said pathetically. 'I might never be able to have children, you realise.'

'Oh, don't be ridiculous. It won't come to that. I'm sure I read in one of your lad's magazines that Hot Stuff Heat Rub is a great aid to foreplay.'

'You're thinking of Vaseline,' said David dryly. 'Whatever, I don't want to talk about that right now. Just thinking about that Saturday morning brings tears to my eyes. I haven't been able to get an erection since I left this house.'

'So? Hasn't affected me much,' I shrugged. Then it clicked. 'Oh, are you using this as an obscure way to tell me that you haven't been porking Lisa since you left me in the lurch? That you've been almost faithful to me by default? No, I forgot. Lisa hasn't been in town. Are you telling me you've been trying to get a hard-on with some other old slag instead?'

'Ali. Why do you have to talk like a fishwife all of a sudden?'

'If I was still going to be your wife I might take some notice of that comment.'

'OK. Point taken.' He sat down on the end of the bed then and put his hand on my knee beneath the sheets.

'Out of bounds,' I told him, not least because it was

still stinging from the leg wax I had given myself that afternoon.

He took his hand away.

'Look, Ali,' he whined. 'This is all going wrong. Let me start again. I've come here tonight to tell you that I've been thinking about you non-stop all week. I can't help myself. I miss you. Really miss you. I miss the things we used to do together. I think I'm going to miss them for the rest of my life. Unless you can do something about that now.'

'You miss things like what?' I probed.

'Like the way you used to laugh at my jokes. The way you smile. The dimples in your cheeks when you giggle. That funny squinty look you get when you're reading your stars on Teletext.'

'Do I squint?' I asked in horror.

'Only a bit. But I miss it. Like I miss the way you push your hair back from your face.'

'I thought you said that irritated you?'

'It used to but . . . oh, just shut up for a minute will you, Ali? I'm trying to tell you something really important here.'

'Oh, my lips are sealed if it's something really important,' I said sarcastically.

'It is. It is. I'm trying to tell you that I've been a fool. Again. I'm trying to tell you that I can't live without you, Ali. And I just can't bear to think of a future without you beside me. I don't want to be with anyone else. Not even Lisa Brown. And I'm prepared to forget all about the Hot Stuff Heat Rub incident if you tell me that you'll be my wife.'

'This isn't happening,' I murmured to myself. 'I'm supposed to be getting my beauty sleep, ready for a fortnight in Antigua with my handsome new lover, but instead I'm listening to an apparition in the shape of David Whitworth muttering on about my charming dimples. I know he must be an apparition because he's just asked me to be his wife.'

David moved up the bed to grasp my hands in a pleading kind of way.

'Stop messing around. I'm serious, Ali,' he told me. 'Deadly serious.'

'Well, I'm glad. Because I wouldn't want to be woken up in the middle of the night by someone who wasn't deadly serious.'

'What do you say, Ali? Marry me. I'll forget all about that Saturday morning. I'll wipe the slate clean. You'll call off going to Antigua with that boil-faced boyfriend of yours and we'll go out there together in a week or so and be a proper couple again instead. Like we used to be. It could even be our honeymoon. I'm sure we could fit in a quickie ceremony at the registry office. Ali and David Whitworth, we'd be. Together forever.' He puckered up his lips and started to move in for a kiss.

'Now hang on,' I said, darting out of range. 'I think you'll find that the dirt on your side of the slate goes back way beyond last Saturday.'

He looked confused.

'Lisa?' I reminded him.

'That's over. I've told you.'

'But have you told her?'

David squirmed. 'Er . . . Not yet. She's at the training group in Hastings again. Some course or other. Information technology, I think. I didn't like to upset her before she went.'

'Ha!' I spat. 'So when exactly were you proposing to do the deed?'

'When she gets back. On Saturday night. I'll call her from Antigua if you want me to.'

I shook my head and laughed bitterly. 'Too late, David. I can't give up a fantastic holiday that starts tomorrow on the off-chance that you'll get round to chucking Lisa Brown in four days time. Tell you what, why don't I go to Antigua with Jeremy as I've planned and we can discuss all this again when I return? In the day-time perhaps next time. It's only two weeks. You can wait that long, can't you?'

'No way!' David exploded. 'If you go away with him tomorrow you can kiss goodbye to me forever, Alison Harris. Forever. I really mean that.'

I blew him a kiss and rolled over to hide my face in the pillow so that he couldn't see me sniggering. 'Bye-bye then, David. You know your way to the door.'

David stood shaking in the middle of my bedroom floor for a minute longer, as if he didn't know the way to the door at all. Then he picked up the roses and shook them at me in a vaguely threatening fashion.

'You'll be sorry.'

'I'll let you know,' I told him. 'Now if you don't mind, I really must get some beauty sleep.'

David stood there for a moment longer, opening and closing his mouth like a grounded fish as he struggled to find a reply. Then, giving up as suddenly as he had arrived, he turned on his heels and began his grand exit. As David made a grab for the handle and yanked the door open however, Emma tumbled onto her back on the landing and nearly tripped him up. She had been listening at the keyhole, quite unprepared for the discussion's sudden end.

'You've had it now,' David warned me from the doorway. 'I'm going to sue you. I swear. You could go down for a long long time you know.'

'Just because I didn't?' I laughed, surprised by the cleverness of my own impromptu joke.

'I'm serious, Alison Harris. It's no laughing matter. When the men of this town find out what a psycho bitch you are, you won't ever see the inside of a man's bedroom again.'

'Promises, promises.'

'You're finished. You wait. When you get back from your wonderful romantic holiday in Antigua, you'll find a letter from my lawyer waiting on your doormat.'

'I'm shaking in my boots,' I said.

Then he raced down the hallway shouting obscenities to do with my thighs in a bikini and slammed the front door shut behind him. Emma and I waited until we heard the engine of his little Fiat Uno firing up before we burst out laughing.

'Jesus Christ, Ali,' Emma exclaimed. 'Did you really Hot Stuff Heat Rub him on the you know what?'

'Only a little bit.'

'Excellent. That must have hurt like hell. Not that he didn't deserve it after all he's done to you. But you could have really done him some serious damage, couldn't you?'

'Absolutely not. He's pretending.'

'He was limping a bit when he left just now.'

'That's because of his ingrowing toenail,' I assured her.

'Yuk. There is no bigger passion killer than an ingrowing toenail. Hot Stuff Heat Rub, eh?' she mused again. 'You're my heroine, Ali. So clever. I would never have thought of that.'

'It was your Hot Stuff Heat Rub,' I told her.

'Wow! Thanks,' she said sincerely. 'I feel like I was part of it now. When I get into college tomorrow morning I think I'm going to set up a new Web-site in your honour – Alison Harris is The New Lorena Bobbitt. Women can write in for handy revenge tips. Got any more up your sleeve?'

'How about taking a studmuffin to Antigua for two whole weeks?'

CHAPTER TWENTY-THREE

But so much for beauty sleep. I could barely sleep at all for the rest of that night. If the truth be told, I think I might even have been feeling just a little bit guilty about David. The ugly thought nagged at the back of my mind that he might have been genuine when he asked if we could get back together and I had well and truly slammed the proverbial door in his face. Did I care? I wasn't sure.

By going away with Jeremy I would be sealing that part of my life I had once shared with David into a tomb. We girls may be soft enough to have men back time and time again when they've been dip-sticking all over the neighbourhood, but I know how different it is for men. They prize their pride well above their emotional well-being and I knew that David would never have me back if he thought I had slept with Jeremy. As I was obviously going to do on this trip. Several times if I was lucky.

Anyway, I was up at seven, checking and re-checking my baggage, moving my passport from one pocket of my jacket to the next until I had decided which of them would be simultaneously easily accessible to me and utterly inaccessible to passport snatchers.

The plane tickets lay in a prominent position on the kitchen table. Hard to believe that those little pieces of paper would soon be transformed into two weeks of utter joy. Jeremy was due to arrive at my house at ten past ten so that we could catch a taxi to the airport together. (I had suggested that we took the Megane but he told me there was no way he was leaving his precious baby in an airport car park.) By five past ten, I was getting twitchy. At eleven minutes past ten, I was almost in tears.

'He'll be here,' Emma comforted me. 'He's not going to drop out of this trip is he?'

'Why not?' I said tragically. 'David did. And what if Jeremy hasn't dropped out? What if he's had an accident?'

Emma swiped me around the head with my passport. She had slipped it out of my ultra-safe pocket while I was blubbing on her shoulder.

'If he turns up at the accident unit, Ashley will call to let you know. Look Ali, I'll sympathise with you when he still hasn't rolled up at half-past eleven. Right now it is ten past ten and fifty seconds. He isn't even a minute late, which in my opinion isn't late at all.'

'He is two whole minutes late,' I wailed, pointing at the dial on my ancient Sekonda. 'Besides, I only said ten past ten as an approximate time. I expected him to get here a bit early, just in case. Surely he would have been here early if he was as excited as I am.'

'He will be here,' said Emma impatiently, as she walked to the window to scan the streets with me again. 'Look, there he is.' She grabbed my head by the ears and turned it in the direction of a very distant figure.

'How do you know it's him? I can't see him properly from here.'

'I'm making an educated guess. Look. It's definitely a man with a suitcase and this isn't exactly the type of area where people fly to the Caribbean on a whim at this time of year, is it? He's heading in this direction, therefore, it stands to reason that it's got to be Jeremy.'

I held my breath until I could be certain.

'It is him! Thank God,' I sighed, when I could finally make out his glasses. (He said that flying interfered with his contact lenses.) 'Now where's the bloody taxi? The taxi was supposed to be here at ten past ten as well. Oh, bloody hell! I knew everything would go wrong for me . . .'

'Stop panicking before I cave your head in and steal your place. Taxi drivers are always late. It's part of their job description.'

'I know. I'm sorry. It's just that, after the way things have been going for me lately, I can't quite believe that I'm really going to pull this trip off. Something always goes wrong for me. If I have any luck at all, I usually end up paying double for it.'

'Sit down for a minute and listen to the voice of reason.' Emma dragged me away from the window and forced me to sit down at the kitchen table. 'The way I see it, Ali, you've more than paid for this holiday in advance. In the last two months you've lost an appendix and a fiancé. Don't you think that each of those disasters adds up to at least a week in the Caribbean in the big scheme of things? Nothing will go wrong.'

'Do you really think that?'

'If you're still not convinced, I could take your place.'

'No,' I protested, just as the doorbell rang. 'You are right. I do deserve this holiday, don't I? Everything will be perfect, won't it? How do I look?'

'You look as though you've been up all night arguing with an ex-boyfriend and spent the morning in tears.' I made a grab for my vanity case. 'Only joking,' said Emma. 'You look fine. Shall I let him in?'

'I suppose you'd better.'

Jeremy really looked the part. Though outside the grey February sky was threatening drizzle, Jeremy was dressed in readiness for the blazing sun and an azure sea. He was wearing a cream linen jacket over his faded blue jeans. On his head was the kind of Panama hat that can be rolled up into a tube to pack away when the holiday's done. He took it off when the door opened and swept it in front of him as he bowed.

'Wow,' I said involuntarily.

'Ready for the off?' he asked.

'Have you got the camels ready for all her baggage?' asked Emma sarcastically.

'Luckily I passed a taxi downstairs. He says he's waiting for us. Ali darling, you say goodbye to your friend while I lug this lot down to the car. Don't be long.' He left dragging my vanity case behind him with some difficulty. (I needed a lot of sun protection, you understand. There's ginger in my genes.)

'Oh, Emma, this will be OK won't it?' I asked.

'It will be like a dream,' she told me once more. 'Just get out there and enjoy yourself. Once you're on the plane, not even the True Romance Police from *Complete Woman* will be able to get you anymore. Now, hurry up and get in that taxi. It's very hard for me to keep consoling you on your amazing luck, you know. Especially when I'm just going to be stuck here with Fattypuss, waiting for Ashley to finish stitching up builders and pulling children's heads out of saucepans.'

'And you know what to do if anyone from work calls?' I persisted.

'I'll tell them that you're in bed and you're not allowed visitors. Doctor's orders,' she said. 'Rest assured, I'll fend them off for you.' With a little bit of arm twisting, she was certain that she could persuade Ashley to write me a sick note on my return.

'Emma, you're a star,' I told her. 'You're the very best friend a girl could have.'

'Just remember that when you're buying me a present.'

Jeremy had left nothing behind for me to carry but the little string rucksack that contained my most important worldly goods. My wallet, my passport, and of course, our tickets. I gathered that little lot up and kissing Emma three times for luck, I finally made it through the door.

But I couldn't truly relax until we had got through passport control and onto the plane. I was utterly convinced that Amanda the editorial assistant would pop up at Heathrow, just to wish us a happy holiday from the *Complete Woman* gang, and our cover would be blown when she playfully asked to see David's passport photo and saw that he was really called Jeremy Baxter.

But she wasn't there. She was probably busy interviewing some B-list celeb about the close relationship she had grown to have with her horses since parts in *The Bill* had dried up. Instead, we were met by a smiling air stewardess who plucked us out of the queue waiting to check in.

'You're in first class, silly,' she told me. 'No need to queue with this rowdy bunch.' She whisked us straight into a private lounge and the formalities were over in seconds. I couldn't believe it. We were flying first class. It was fantastic enough just to be in the first class departure lounge sipping chilled champagne and not fighting for a coffee at a Burger King concession with the hoi polloi. That didn't stop me from shredding a drinks mat with nerves however.

'It's OK,' said Jeremy, quickly relaxing into the atmosphere as if he had been born to it. 'No-one can get us now. We're going to Antigua, Ali. Please don't spoil the whole flight by worrying.'

'I'm sorry. I just don't know when I'm going to realise that this is for real. I'm absolutely convinced that I'm going to wake up in my bed at home any second. I probably haven't even come round from the anaesthetic they gave me for my appendectomy yet. Or perhaps I really died on the operating table and all this is just the afterlife.'

Jeremy laughed. 'No, it's definitely not the afterlife, because with the disgraceful thoughts I've been having ever since I met you, I certainly won't be able to get into heaven if I die now.'

'What thoughts?' I probed.

'Bad ones. Hey,' he leaned in close. 'Do you fancy joining the Mile High Club this afternoon?'

'Oh no,' I said hurriedly. 'What if there's an emergency or something? I'd never live it down if they had to drag us out of the loo while we were, you know, entangled.'

'You worry too much about what people might think,' Jeremy told me. 'You should be like me, Ali. A free spirit. Unrestrained by social convention.'

'Mmmm. I don't know how you do it,' I said admiringly. 'I always worry what the neighbours might think.'

'You can be sure that they'll be thinking the worst anyway, so my philosophy is, you might as well prove them right.'

Though in the end, we didn't bother with the Mile High Club after all. We were too busy drinking the complimentary champagne and eating canapés. Added to that was the fact that the minor soap opera star sitting in front of us hogged the loo with her Italian-looking boyfriend from ten minutes outside Heathrow to at least halfway over the Atlantic, forcing the rest of the first class passengers to cross their legs or, worse, cross the class barrier and use the economy loos. I didn't like to ask for her autograph after that.

Ten hours later, jelly-legged with jet lag (not to mention the free booze that I had been more than making the most of), Jeremy and I stumbled into the arrivals lounge of the tiny airport at St John's in Antigua, pushing our cases on a predictably errant trolley.

CHAPTER TWENTY-FOUR

'Do you think we should get ourselves a cab?' I asked as we ambled out into the sunshine, but before I could spot a free taxi, Jeremy had spotted a smartly dressed man with a board that bore the name of our hotel. The man was wearing a proper chauffeur's uniform complete with hat and gold braiding and he smiled widely at everyone just in case: he obviously didn't know who he was actually waiting for.

Jeremy strode up to him. 'Hello, I think we're staying at your hotel. Santa Bonita?'

'What your name, please?' asked the man.

I could see that Jeremy was scanning down the list written on the driver's clipboard. 'Whitworth,' Jeremy announced finally. 'Mr and Mrs Whitworth. That's us.' The driver smilingly relieved Jeremy of our cases and ushered us into the back of his waiting car. But it wasn't any ordinary car. It was a white limo, specially polished for the occasion and finished off with a pink satin ribbon on the bonnet.

'You are the Most Romantic Couple in the United Kingdom?' the man asked. I was too dazed by the opulence of the limo to even manage a nod. 'Antigua salutes you,' said the chauffeur. He clicked his heels together and doffed his cap in a bizarre military parody.

'Ohmigod,' I muttered into Jeremy's shoulder, as we sank into the white leather seats of the car. 'Antigua salutes us. I feel such a fraud.' I daren't even look out of the frosted windows in case a welcoming party had been assembled to wave us into town.

'Ali,' murmured Jeremy comfortingly. 'Relax, will you? We'll be at the hotel in ten minutes and then we'll finally be on our own.'

'It is a very great honour to drive you to Santa Bonita,' the driver was telling us as he sped along the sparsely surfaced road. 'I have had many famous people in my car. Princess Margaret, Joan Collins and now you.'

'Not quite in the same league,' I said nervously.

'My car is the one that they always use whenever anyone really famous is in town,' the driver continued regardless.

'Jeremy,' I squeaked. 'I don't think I can stand much more of this.'

But he was already popping open the half bottle of champagne which had been so thoughtfully provided in the limo's minibar. He handed me a glass, then used the electric controls to wind down the windows on both sides of us.

'Smell the ocean,' he told me. 'Look at the sunshine and the palm trees out there. Is this paradise or what?'

Children playing in the dust at the side of the road looked up as the huge car passed them. They waved happily to us. But all I could think was, if only they knew. If only they knew the truth. No-one would be happy for us then.

But soon we were at the hotel. The driver leapt out of the car to help me out too. Liveried porters were already waiting on the bright marble steps to whisk our luggage away. The smiling manager shook Jeremy warmly by the hand and planted a wet kiss on mine.

'We are very honoured to have you both here,' the platitudes started again. 'We have reserved you the very best room.'

But first there was the register signing to get over. I was sure I must be visibly shaking as we stood at the check-in desk, just waiting for those dreaded words. 'Please may we see your passports?'

'Mr Whitworth, your passport please,' asked the manager.

He handed over both his passport and mine with a big smile on his face.

'Jeremy, what are you doing?' I thought as I dug my nails into his hand. The manager opened up the little red booklet that bore Jeremy's real name and his eyebrows knotted together in confusion.

'Jeremy Baxter?' he said very slowly. 'Mister Jeremy Baxter.' Perhaps he would think that Jeremy had somehow had his passport switched in customs, I prayed. But no, the face was right.

'Jeremy Baxter?' Jeremy repeated as if the revelation had confused him too. 'Let me see that.'

He took the passport back and studied it with a frown that soon blossomed into a wide, wide smile.

'Ha! I don't believe it. I am David Whitworth, I promise you!' He turned to me. 'Darling, can you believe I must have picked up my twin brother's passport by mistake again. I can't believe we managed to get through customs at Heathrow. Still, doesn't really matter, does it?' he winked at the manager, while simultaneously slipping him a fifty dollar note. 'We're the same in every respect apart from our names. Except that I'm the more romantic twin, of course. When our parents divorced, Jeremy took our father's name but I sided with my mother.'

The manager nodded warily.

'If you could just sign the register,' he said.

Jeremy signed David's name with a flourish. David himself had only just been able to manage a signature in joined-up writing.

'Thanks for being so understanding,' Jeremy continued. 'I'll pop down to the British Embassy first thing in the morning to see if I can't sort this dreadful mess out.'

At last the porter picked our bags up again and led us to our room.

Our room, rather our hut, was incredible. The bath in the *en-suite* was easily as big as the swimming pool at the last hotel I had stayed at. And when I opened the minibar, I found another complimentary bottle of champagne inside.

'Open it up then,' said Jeremy.

'No. We should save it for a special occasion.'

'But this is a very special occasion,' he reminded me. 'You and me, alone at last, in our fabulously well-appointed beach hut in Antigua.' He wrested the champagne bottle from my grip and proceeded to unwrap the foil. Pop! The cork exploded out of the bottle and ricocheted against the lampshade.

'Get the glasses, then,' Jeremy laughed.

I hadn't thought of that. And I couldn't find them quickly enough, so in the end we had to drink champagne out of the tooth mugs I found on the bathroom shelf. I didn't mind too much. It seemed more romantic somehow.

'I can't wait to have a dip in the sea,' I told Jeremy as I gazed dreamily at the rolling waves, sitting on our balcony, sipping champagne from a plastic cup.

Jeremy nodded. 'Neither can I. But I think we should test out the bed first. And I know exactly what I'm going to do with the rest of this champagne . . .'

Funny how those Jackie Collins' books forgot to mention that it just gets really sticky.

CHAPTER TWENTY-FIVE

So we didn't get to paddle that afternoon and that evening at dinner we were in for a bit of a surprise. Instead of being ushered towards a small secluded table on our own, we found ourselves being directed towards a huge round table laid for eight.

'Er, we are the UK's Most Romantic Couple,' Jeremy hinted.

'That's right,' said the Maître d'. 'Follow me please. We have a place for you right here.'

Jeremy shrugged and we followed the Maître d' to the big table.

'Here.' He pulled out my golden chair for me. At the head of my place setting was a little white card adorned with scrawly pink writing. 'Most Romantic Couple (UK) Woman' it said.

'Have you got one of these?' I asked Jeremy, showing him my little card. 'Not very romantic, is it? Most Romantic UK Woman. Hang on a minute.' I noticed another. 'Who's sitting next to you?'

'Most Romantic Couple (Aus) Man.'

'I don't believe it. I've got Most Romantic Couple

(USA) Woman on one side and Most Romantic Couple (Can) Woman on the other.'

'They've obviously got a job lot of us in.'

'Amanda didn't mention this,' I protested.

'No,' said Jeremy. 'I'll bet she didn't. But never mind. We can insist on a table of our own tomorrow night. I'm sure the rest of the romantic world will feel exactly the same way about wanting some time alone. Especially on Valentine's Day. It could be a bit of fun to meet them though. I wonder what they'll be like.'

'I wonder,' I murmured, as I saw a couple who looked as though they might be about our age walk into the dining room. He was wearing a white Western-style suit with a rhinestone covered waistcoat and a matching Stetson. She was wearing an Elizabeth Walton-style Sunday best dress in pink chiffon and sequins. Jeremy turned to see who I was gawping at.

'Are you thinking what I'm thinking?' he asked with a grimace as he too copped an eyeful of the All American nightmare.

'Oh my, what a simply darling little restaurant,' the girl trilled as, naturally, she and her other half were led across the floor to join us. When they finally got to the table, having admired every place setting and table arrangement along the way, Mr Romantic USA and the Maître d' had a small battle over who should pull Ms Romantic USA's chair out for her. As it was, Mr Romantic USA won and jerked the seat back so suddenly that his missus nearly ended up on the floor. Not that she'd have felt a thing through the myriad layers of that skirt. In my stretchy little black number from Miss Selfridge, I suddenly felt rather underdressed by comparison.

'Hi y'all,' drawled Ms Romantic USA while she straightened herself up and tried to fix her tiara back in place. Yes, now that she was up close I could see that beneath her bright blonde candyfloss hair there really nestled a small, glittering tiara! 'I'm Shelly Adamson and this is my fiancé Luke Connolly. Did you guys win the *Complete Woman* Most Romantic Couple competition too?'

I nodded.

'Isn't that sweet? Don't you think that's sweet, Luke? They've put all of us here together tonight. I see that I'm going to be sitting next to Mr Romantic (Aus). Where's that, honey? Is that somewhere near Arkansas?'

'I think they're from Australia, actually,' said Jeremy helpfully.

'Oh, my God,' Shelly exclaimed. 'Did you hear his accent, honey? Say something again. Are you guys from England?'

'Yes, we are,' said Jeremy, giving it the full Roger Moore as 007 treatment this time. 'I'm David Whitworth and this is my other half, Alison Harris.'

'Where exactly are you from?' Shelly asked me.

'Somewhere near London,' I said, knowing that Brindlesham would probably mean less than nothing to her.

'Wow. London. Do you know Hugh Grant by any chance?'

I had to bite down hard on my tongue to stop myself laughing when Jeremy told her that we did indeed know both Hugh and Liz, though Liz and I hadn't been too friendly since she borrowed my best Versace dress to go to a party and managed to drop red wine all over it.

'Didn't even offer to pay for the dry-cleaning,' Jeremy continued. Shelly's jaw was on the table. I gave Jeremy a kick beneath it.

'That's a lovely tiara,' I said to change the subject.

Shelly touched it affectionately. 'Why thank you. I won this in the Most Romantic Couple heats in Tucson, Arizona. We were up against three hundred other couples that night. All of them lovely people, just like you. But I have to say we were far and away the most romantic. Some of them didn't even hold hands. Luke here won a tie pin.' He showed up the tie pin, which was stuck in his waistcoat, since it wouldn't have looked right on the bootlace tie. I couldn't actually see it. Jeremy later claimed it was a little rhinestone heart with a cupid's arrow. There were so many rhinestones on Luke's ensemble, I thought he must have mugged the Follies Bergères.

'Didn't you get a tiara?' Shelly asked me next.

'I told you you should have brought yours, darling,' said Jeremy. 'It's similar to yours, Shelly. But bigger. And I think Alison's may have had rubies.'

I delivered a warning shot to Jeremy's foot with the heel of my new Pied A Terre sandals.

Thankfully, the most romantic people in Canada and Australia turned up before Jeremy could go any further. Chad and Penny Spencer from Ontario were pretty sweet. Like Luke and Shelly slightly watered down. But Mark from Australia was simply gorgeous. Unfortunately so was his half-Italian fiancée, Marguerite, and they only had eyes for each other. Not that I would really have strayed from Jeremy's side anyway.

'Alison knows Hugh Grant,' said Shelly reverently when the introductions had been made.

I smiled stiffly. Jeremy was just too good at this lying lark. And I told him so later that evening, when the Maître d' rather embarrassingly called us all up onto the dancefloor to start the evening's dancing with an anniversary waltz. Whirling round out of time in Jeremy's arms, I said, 'You really are being cruel to her you know.'

'So what,' he said. 'Shelly will go back to Little Hole, Nebraska or wherever it is they come from and dine out for years on the story. "We met some people who know Hugh Grant," ' he mimicked. 'She loves it.'

'I think you're being patronising.'

'No I'm not. She'll never know otherwise, believe me. I'm just giving her a little piece of a dream. That's all. Just a little piece of a dream.'

I smiled. It did seem pretty harmless then.

But when the band had packed up for the night, Shelly was still raring to go, pressing me for more details of my falling out with Liz. When it was clear that I wasn't going to come up with any more juicy titbits – I simply didn't have the imagination for it – Shelly said, 'It's so sweet that you're being so discreet about her even after the way she took such a liberty with your Versace.'

I allowed myself to bask guiltily in her high opinion of me.

'I have an idea,' she said then. 'We have champagne in our room.'

'We've finished ours,' said everybody else.

'Well, Luke and I wanted to save ours for a special occasion and I think that this is it. Right now. Here we are, the eight most romantic people in the world altogether in Antigua. Isn't it wonderful? I say that we go back to our room and read each other the elegies that got us where we are today.'

Jeremy and I shared a tortured glance. I had been under the impression that elegies were for the dead.

'Come on,' Shelly said, mustering us with her best cheerleading powers. 'I want to hear them. I need to know what we're up against this week.'

'Up against?' I asked.

'Yes,' she said. 'In the grand final. The competition to find the most romantic couple in the world. I hope you've all been practising.'

'For what? What do we have to do?'

We seemed to be the only couple who hadn't heard about this little development.

'We have to prove the strength of our love of course,' Shelly explained patiently. 'Aw, you're kidding me aren't you, Alison? You do know what we have to do really?'

Jeremy's face went slightly paler.

'We have to answer questions about each other's preferences and then talk about the things which keep our love going strong through the bad times. If you get an answer wrong. For example, if you say that his favourite kind of jelly is blackcurrant when it's really loganberry, then you're out. No second chances. Not that any one of us girls here would make a mistake that fundamental, of course.'

'Of course we wouldn't,' I agreed. But I didn't even know Jeremy's phone number off by heart yet, let alone his favourite kind of jam.

'Oh, it's going to be such a lot of fun,' Shelly clapped her hands together.

'Sounds like a bloody stupid idea to me,' said Mark from Brisbane.

'Now, don't you be such an old sourpuss,' said Shelly. 'Come on. I want to hear what you girls all wrote about your men. I'll start.'

I heaved a sigh of relief. With a bit of luck, the American version of the competition wouldn't have had a word limit on entries and we'd all be dead before I had to read mine out. Not that I could anyway. I hadn't exactly kept a copy.

'I knew from the moment I first set eyes on Luke,' Shelly began, 'that one day we would grow old together and find ourselves at fifty on the front porch of life . . .'

Jeremy yawned ostentatiously. So ostentatiously that Shelly paused.

'Jet lag,' I explained.

Shelly nodded and continued. 'No challenge in my working life could possibly give me the same satisfaction as making sandwiches for my fiancé to take to work . . .'

Marguerite nodded.

'No public honour could be so great as the right to wear his engagement ring on my left hand.'

Penny gave a hearty sigh.

'Are these girls from Planet Stepford?' Jeremy whispered in my ear.

'Looks like it. Have you got a gippy tummy yet?'

He looked at me in confusion. But he wasn't the only one who could make up a good story in times of utter desperation.

'Shelly,' I interrupted. 'We'd really love to hear the rest of your elegy but I think that David's suffering . . .'

All eyes turned to discover what from.

'No, no, no. Of course he's not bored,' I reassured them. 'It's just the heat and the rich food. Interferes with his natural functions. You know how men are.'

Shelly covered her mouth with her hand in case he was infectious. 'Then you had better go and take some rest,' she told Jeremy through her fingers. 'You don't want to spoil the whole holiday. Missing you already,' she added with a hand-covered smile.

Jeremy nodded bravely and as we left, I was sure I heard Shelly say, 'Those Englishmen. Always suffering in silence. It's those stiff upper lips they have, isn't it?'

So ended our first night at the lovely resort of Santa Bonita. Jeremy and I lay on our ocean-wide bed, staring up at the fan that slowly chopped the air above us to keep us cool.

'Recovered from your tummy upset yet?' I asked him as I rolled across to kiss him goodnight.

'Certainly have,' he said as he wrapped me in his arms and began to kiss me all over and I mean all over, though there was no champagne to lick off this time. An hour later, panting with exertion, we rolled apart once more.

'You were a lioness tonight,' Jeremy told me.

I roared obligingly. Then wished that I hadn't. The walls of that hut must have been really thin, because I was sure I heard Shelly wishing goodnight to her man.

'Goodnight, Luke.'

'Goodnight, Shelly.'

We were staying next door to the Waltons.

CHAPTER TWENTY-SIX

The second day of our holiday was of course February the 14th. Though in the excitement and panic of going to Antigua I had completely lost track of the passing time. When I woke up on the morning of the sunniest Valentine's Day I had ever seen, Jeremy wasn't in the bed beside me. Instead, a small envelope lay on the pillow with my name written upon it in swirly writing.

I sat up suddenly. No-one had ever left a note on my pillow before. In fact, no-one had ever left me a note anywhere before, apart from my boss at Hudderston's, to tell me that I needed to order more staples. My stomach lurched up into my mouth as, barely awake, I opened what could only be a 'Dear John'.

'I know it's twenty years later, but I'd like to say yes to being your Valentine.'

I began to laugh with relief at the reference to the card I had sent Jeremy in 1979. At that moment he walked back into the hut, dripping from an early dip in the sea, and carrying a pink conch shell that covered half my face when Jeremy held it to my ear so that I could hear the waves.

'Happy Valentine's Day,' he said, as he kissed me good morning.

I couldn't help crying then, as I always do when something really wonderful happened. Just a little sob. I'm a sap like that. I'm afraid I just can't help thinking forward to a time when the happy moment will be but a distant memory. I also miss people in advance, sulking about them going away for a week before they leave then hardly noticing the difference when they've actually gone.

'I haven't got you anything,' I told him, wiping the tears from my eyes. 'I'd completely forgotten in my hurry to get ready for this trip.'

Jeremy put the conch shell into my hands and smiled handsomely. 'I don't need presents. I've got you.'

It was perfect. So perfect. I thought I was going to explode with happiness.

Meanwhile, in the hut next door, Shelly and Luke had obviously woken up. We heard Shelly shriek with delight and when we next saw the United States' most romantic couple at breakfast, she was dressed from head to toe in hearts. Pink heart-shaped earrings. A red heart-printed dress. There were even fluffy hearts on the tops of her little white socks.

'Isn't this outfit just the sweetest?' she asked me. 'Luke chose it all himself. I'm so lucky to have a man with such amazing taste.'

Amazing was the word for it, but I just smiled. It was hard to be sarcastic when faced with such blind faith in romance. Besides, if Jeremy had turned up that morning with a pair of heart-patterned pedal-pushers instead of the conch shell, I probably would have put them on too.

I wrote my postcards on the second day, because there's nothing worse than beating your postcards home, especially if you're sending one to your housemate so that you actually see it arrive while you're picking off the last of your tan over breakfast.

Anyway, even though I had been on the island for less than twenty-four hours, it wasn't as if I didn't have anything to write about. I could have written a whole book on the beauty of the place. I kept looking at the sparkling sea, then rubbing my eyes, as if it just wasn't possible that water could be so blue. Or the sky. Not a cloud. Not a whisper of wind to spoil the day.

'Dear Emma,' I wrote. 'Life just couldn't get any better. Jeremy woke me up this morning, Valentine's Day, with the gift of a perfect conch shell he had found on the beach for me. I feel as though I am living in a dream-world. Please give my love to Fattypuss.'

I stuck to the usual platitudes when writing home, including 'Wish you were here' on the card I sent to my parents. My mother would have been upset if I hadn't made some pretence at missing her. I wondered how Grandma's birthday party was going. But not for too long.

When I had licked the last of the stamps I needed I found that I had one card and one stamp left over.

'Got anyone you need to write to?' I asked Jeremy. He was stretched out on a sun-lounger with his new paperback novel protecting his beautiful nose from burning up.

'No,' he told me. 'I don't even want to think about anyone back home, let alone write to them.'

It seemed a shame to waste the postcard though, particularly as I had already licked the stamp.

I don't know quite what came over me then, but I decided that I would send the spare card to David. It wasn't to gloat, you understand. At least that's what I told myself. I was simply sending him a card to suggest that there were no hard feelings on my part and that perhaps when I did get back from Antigua we really might start to think about becoming friends again. If he was especially nice to me.

'Dear David,' I wrote. 'Well, here I am on the sun-drenched island of Antigua. It's eighty degrees in the shade, really hot stuff! The only thing I have to worry about is where my next *cock*-tail is coming from. See you soon. Love, Ali.' At first I didn't put any kisses at the bottom, but then I added two. It seemed petty not to.

I took the postcards to the lobby and handed them to the duty receptionist to post. Then, chores done, I stripped down to my borrowed pink bikini (Emma had come to the rescue) and flopped into the pool with a triumphant whoop of joy. I flopped so triumphantly that the water splashed out of the pool and all over Jeremy's paperback.

'Do you have to be quite so exuberant?' he asked.

I did. I was having the time of my life. If you can't be exuberant while you're sitting in the sunshine, I asked him, when everyone back home is fighting to work through gales, when can you be? If you can't be exuberant when you only have to click your fingers for a pina colada to arrive at your side, you may as well holiday in a morgue.

Sensing defeat, Jeremy put down his book and joined me in the pool. I managed just one and a half lengths before I felt the urge to swim up and wrap my arms around him. He kissed me on the nose and I felt like I was floating on something far more magical than water.

'Are you glad you came?' I asked him prettily.

'Ask me again in half an hour,' he said, hauling me back out of the pool and dragging me off in the direction of our beach hut.

Our second night. We made our way down to dinner and were about to take our places at the big round table when the Maître d' came over with an apologetic mutter and told us that the sea view table had been promised to someone else that night. Now, I would have gone quietly, happy to be in a corner with Jeremy, alone. But Mr and Miss Romantic America were outraged.

'Someone else,' Shelly shrieked. 'Whaddya mean? We're the most romantic couple in America. Who deserves this view more than we do?'

'Candida Bianca,' said the Maître d' quietly. I didn't even catch what he had said first time, but I guessed it must have been pretty impressive when Shelly's mouth dropped open so that she looked like one of the shoal of grouper I had seen on that afternoon's snorkelling trip.

'The Candida Bianca?' she asked.

Then my mouth dropped open too. And Luke's and Jeremy's and the mouths of anyone else close enough to eavesdrop on this incredible revelation.

'She's staying here? In this hotel? You're kidding me? The Candida Bianca?' asked Luke, with the kind of reverence my mother reserved for talking about the Pope.

'She stays here every year, and I'm afraid that this is her favourite table in the dining room,' explained the man in charge.

'That's fine,' said Shelly, throwing her hands up in defeat. 'You tell her she can sit on my fiancé's knee if she wants to. She is such a great actress. I don't believe she's really here. Please give her our very fondest regards.'

'Yes, and mine,' said Jeremy, his eyes still glistening with that look that children get in the run-up to Christmas. Then he brought out a scrap of paper from his pocket and thrust it at the Maître d' asking if he would be so kind as to ask Miss Bianca to sign it, to Jeremy, if she had a moment. Or the inclination.

'I heard she never signs autographs,' said Shelly in warning. 'Not since that guy threatened to kill himself and President Clinton if she wouldn't marry him.'

'That was terrible,' I said, remembering the newspaper reports of the incident well. She had been walking out of a smart Hollywood restaurant with Kevin Costner. Some madman had asked for her autograph, thrusting a piece of paper in front of her nose. On it, he had written his demands: 'Marry me or the president dies.' In green ink, a true sign of madness. Then he flashed open his jacket to reveal enough semtex to blow up the whole of Los Angeles strapped to his body with gaffer tape.

'I don't know how she carried on after that,' said Shelly in awe.

'She was just born to act,' said Luke. 'She is the most incredible actress since . . . er, since . . . since the most incredible actresses you can think of really.'

'Have you seen *The Twelve Days of Christmas* yet?' asked Shelly. It had been released in England at the end of November. Candida Bianca played an angel, setting the world to rights, reforming muggers and bringing broken families back together for the holidays. I had insisted on seeing the film with a rather reluctant David in tow. I wondered briefly if things would have been different had I let him see the Jean Claude Van Damme blood-fest instead.

'I liked her best in *Terminator Seven*,' said Jeremy.

'No, no, no. She definitely gave her best performance in the screen version of Sir Cliff Richard's *Wuthering Heights*,' Shelly protested.

But the discussion was cut short when we were ushered to the table next to the kitchen door, as at the other end of the room, and even as we sat down, the beaded curtain was lifted aside for the guest of honour. The room went silent, even cutlery stopped clinking against porcelain when Candida Bianca walked in. The star of last summer's three hottest movies. Hollywood's highest paid female star of the moment. She was so stratospherically successful that she made Julia Roberts look like the office junior of the movie world.

'She is so beautiful,' murmured Shelly.

'She's shorter than I expected,' I said, but no-one seemed to hear.

The room continued to stand still as everyone watched their heroine glide across the carpet in a pair of impossibly high-heeled iridescent gold shoes, to go with the sparkling beaded dress she wore. It was actually less a dress than a second skin, clinging tightly to her pneumatic curves; it was the perfect accompaniment to the honey-gold tan that made her teeth look even whiter than Hollywood white. Her long black hair, worn loose for her role as a Latino temptress in *August Moon*, was tied up in a graceful, glossy chignon, as it had been for her latest role as a hot-shot lawyer. She had been dubbed La Chameleon, for her ability to look perfectly cast whether she was playing white trash or a Jewish princess. Whatever she was playing, she always looked beautiful.

But most surprising of all was that she entered the restaurant alone. She sat alone at her table, back to the room, facing the sea, ordered with a whisper and then proceeded to watch the twinkling lights on the bay until her meal came.

Everyone at my table could watch only Candida Bianca.

'Want to swap sides?' Jeremy asked me after our first course. 'You might get a stiff neck from sitting in the draught from that window.' I swapped gratefully, not thinking for a moment that Jeremy could have such a dastardly ulterior motive as wanting a better view of Candida Bianca.

As she neared the end of her meal, we watched on tenterhooks as the Maître d' asked Candida whether she would sign Jeremy's scrap of paper. Her forehead crumpled into a frown as she took the scrap, then the Maître d' pointed in Jeremy's direction and Candida looked up, caught his eye and actually smiled. She smiled straight at my boyfriend. Then she scribbled something onto the paper and left the dining room with a little wave in his direction.

Jeremy was jumpy as a cat with fleas as he waited for the Maître d' to bring the scrap of paper back to us. When he did, we crowded round to see what she had written. Shelly said that she had done a graphology course and would be happy to analyse the signature for us.

'What colour has she written in?' Shelly asked.

'Red,' said Jeremy.

'Oooh, that's very passionate. Red represents sensuality. A good sign.'

'She just took the pen that the Maître d' handed her,' I protested.

'What does it actually say?' asked Mark, Mr Romantic Australia by name but ever the practical sheep farmer at heart.

'Er, just her name,' Jeremy said, looking somewhat unnaturally flustered as we others fought to have a look at the sacred superstar signature.

'And her room number!' Mark suddenly boomed. 'Way-hey! You're in there, mate.'

'Excuse me,' said his girlfriend, Marguerite, speaking up on my behalf. 'Aren't you forgetting someone?'

'Er, sorry, Alison,' said Mark.

'Is it really her room number?' I asked Jeremy as I struggled to keep the jealousy from my voice.

'No,' said Jeremy. 'Of course it isn't. She's just written the date under her signature, that's all. See, 14th of the 6.'

'But it's February now,' said Shelly.

'Did she write 6?' Jeremy blushed. 'She must have meant a 2.'

Well, I was convinced. After all, gorgeous as Jeremy was to me, I didn't really think I needed to protect my interests from the clutches of a woman who could have had Brad Pitt for breakfast. What would she want with a lowly computer programmer from England? Even if he did hold the whole of Eastern Europe in his hands . . .

'Well, she seems pretty friendly. I'm going to ask for her autograph tomorrow night,' Luke decided.

'No, you're not,' said Shelly adamantly. 'You're going to leave her alone. I'm sure she just wants her privacy.'

'Hear, hear,' said Marguerite, Penny and I.

CHAPTER TWENTY-SEVEN

'Hi.'

Next morning, I was sitting by the pool, feeling rather proud of my budding tan, and the fact that my belly was looking more gently rolling tundra than hillock at the moment, when I was joined by Candida Bianca.

'Mind if I join you?' she asked.

It was a difficult one. Of course I didn't mind being joined by a celebrity, but at the same time, I knew my satisfaction with my newly, reasonably decent body was going to be pretty short-lived once she slipped off her robe and revealed whatever dental floss piece of bikini she had chosen for that morning.

'Where's your boyfriend?' she asked me as she untied her sandals.

'Scuba diving,' I told her.

'And you're not joining him?'

'I don't like to get my hair wet,' I joked, but she seemed to have taken me seriously so I added, 'Makes me feel a bit claustrophobic actually. I did try to learn once, in a swimming pool, but I just know that if I ever came face to face with a shark or something horrible like that I would shoot up to the surface too quickly and get the bends.'

'The bends? What's that?' Candida Bianca asked.

'Nitrogen in your brain I think,' I bluffed. 'Makes you feel like you're pissed apparently.'

'What? Angry?'

'No, pissed in the English sense. Drunk.'

'Sounds like fun.'

'It can kill you.'

'I'd like to learn to dive anyway,' she said, unpacking her beach bag to reveal a Harvey Nichols' beauty department's worth of expensive unguents. 'Do you think your boyfriend would teach me?'

'Well, I don't think he knows that much about it himself. He's just learning too.'

'Pity,' she said, shrugging off her robe. Iridescent pink dental floss this time, with bra cups the size of Dairylea triangles, on breasts the size of generous Edams.

'You two been together long?' she asked.

'Not really,' I said. 'About a week if I'm truthful.'

'A week!' she shrieked. 'And he's brought you to the Caribbean already? That's really something. Though Brad Pitt did fly me to Rio for our second date, I suppose. Whatever does your boyfriend do, to enable him to make such incredible gestures?'

'Actually, it was my gesture. I brought him.'

'Wow. Then what do you do?' she asked, rolling onto her elbow to look at me while she heard my reply.

'I'm a . . .' I hesitated. Candida Bianca wouldn't want to talk to a lowly secretary who'd won a poxy competition. 'I'm an engineer,' I said instead. It was almost true. I had worked with several in my time. And lying was becoming so natural . . .

'Wow,' Candida cooed. 'That's so . . . so noble of you. I really admire women who are prepared to throw off feminine convention and get their hands dirty for a change. Have you invented anything I might know? Or are you one of those brave people who work in a nuclear power station or something like that?'

'I deal with pipes mostly,' I said nonchalantly. 'Hydraulics. Tubes and stuff.'

'Oh.' She visibly wilted at the thought of having to listen to any further explanation. 'That's nice. And what about your boyfriend?'

'Computers. In the eastern bloc. He's actually based in Warsaw.'

'Oh, Germany? How lovely.'

'It's Poland, actually.'

'Wow,' she said again. 'You guys really are brains and beauty. I mean to say that you're the beauty of course,' she added just a little unconvincingly.

'Well, thank you. But I have to say that I don't feel particularly beautiful next to you, Miss Bianca.'

'Oh, call me Candida,' she purred. 'And don't ever let me hear you say that silly thing about not feeling beautiful again. It isn't a skin deep thing. Real beauty comes from the inside. Sometimes I feel like a dog myself. You just have to think positive and you'll glow with something far greater than superficial beauty.'

'Try explaining that to any man I've ever met,' I snorted.

'But don't you see that your boyfriend already knows

it? I wouldn't care if all my hair fell out tomorrow if I could have just an hour of the happiness you two so obviously have together.'

'Really?' I was incredulous. 'But you've dated Brad Pitt and all those other famous stars. Every girl in the universe envies you.'

'Empty experiences, darling. Mostly set up by my agent for PR purposes. There's always some up and coming male star in Hollywood who needs to avoid a sudden gay relationship scandal. No, you don't know how lucky you are to be normal, Alison. Real, honest, decent men are just too afraid to approach me half the time. They'd have a surprise if they did. I get asked out on a proper date so rarely that I'd say yes to the pizza delivery man if he asked me.'

'I don't believe it,' I said. 'I'd love to be famous.'

'Be careful what you wish for,' said Candida. 'In case it just happens to come true.'

It was very difficult to concentrate on sunbathing next to the world's most beautiful woman. Every thirty seconds or so I would think that a cloud was passing over the sun as every man, woman and child staying at the Santa Bonita resort made some spurious excuse to saunter over to our side of the pool and linger, casting a shadow over Candida and me, as she tanned and I blushed at the thought of them making unflattering comparisons. Inner beauty isn't immediately obvious in a bikini.

I couldn't wait to write more postcards. I spent a good deal of the afternoon imagining Marvin's stunned and disbelieving face when I told him that I had actually sunbathed next to a living, breathing movie star, and, more importantly, that she had told me that she actually envied my simple, uncomplicated life. She was so nice. She let me share her Estée Lauder sun-cream. It's always a surprise when famous people are nice, isn't it? You can't help imagining that anyone who's ever been on TV becomes a monster as soon as the camera is off, swiping at little children with manicured claws if they dare ask for an autograph.

Despite her terrible experiences with the President Clinton nut, Candida seemed happy to sign anything for anyone that afternoon. At one point, she even had the good grace to sign some disgusting Italian man's left buttock. He said that he was going to get her signature tattooed over so that he could remember the moment forever.

'Pervert,' Candida commented in a whisper as he swaggered back to show his mates the biro scrawl.

'Do you think he'll really get a tattoo?' I asked her.

'Well, if all the men that said they were going to did, my name would be more popular than "Mum" in the tattoo world. I don't think so. This week I'm their favourite star, they say they've watched all of my films . . . next week they'll be telling Danny Devito exactly the same.'

'I don't think anyone would ask him to sign a buttock.'

'You'd be surprised. Anyway, when is that boyfriend of yours coming back? Aren't you worried that he might have been eaten by sharks?'

'He said he'd be a couple of hours.'

'It's been that long already, surely,' she said, checking the time on the Cartier watch she had taken off and placed on the floor beneath her lounger so that the strap mark didn't interfere with her perfect tan.

'You seem more worried about him than I am,' I laughed, nervously.

'Oh no,' she said, slipping her sunglasses over her eyes so that she was inscrutable once more. 'I'm just interested to hear about this diving.'

Well, Candida certainly asked questions about diving when Jeremy finally came back from the sea with a big red mark on his nose where the snorkel mask had been. Unfortunately Jeremy was too gob-smacked to tell her much, but he agreed readily when she asked if she could be his partner on a dive the next morning.

'You'll look after me, won't you?' she asked, patting him on the arm.

'Nnngh,' said Jeremy.

It was only when we got back to our room that the magnitude of that conversation by the pool seemed to sink in.

'She wants me to look after her on a dive,' said Jeremy.

'Yes,' I said, somewhat jealous. If only I hadn't had that irrational fear of man-eating sharks, I could have gone along to chaperone.

'She wants me to look after her on a dive,' he said again.

'You just said that,' I replied.

'You don't mind, do you, Ali?' Jeremy asked. 'No, of course you don't,' he continued before I could form an answer. 'Imagine the amazing stories we're going to have to tell people when we get back home to England.'

'Yes, imagine,' I said. Though I would have been happy enough just to say that Candida Bianca and I had shared a bottle of Factor 8.

From next door, Shelly and Luke's room, there suddenly came the sound of voices being raised.

'You will not ask her!' Shelly was shrieking. 'You're here to celebrate our romance, not chase some silver-screen tart. You're ruining my Valentine's Day.'

Jeremy and I shared an amused glance as we listened to Luke trying to make amends.

'I won't ask her for her autograph, Shelly, I promise I won't. I don't know why I even dared think about it.'

'You're lucky I'm not Shelly,' I told Jeremy then. 'Sounds like she would string you up by your air hose.'

'Yes, I'm lucky to be with you,' he said, wrapping his arms around me. 'If it were any other girl, Alison, you know that I wouldn't have said yes to taking her diving. I'm meant to be here for you. But Candida Bianca . . . It's such a rare opportunity. You have to understand . . .'

'You don't have to say it,' I said, shaking him off and heading for the shower. I tried in vain to wash out my jealousy with two whole sachets of hotel shower gel.

'It's all right,' I told myself as I scrubbed furiously at the rough skin on my heels. 'They're just going diving together. If Brad Pitt were diving here too, she would definitely go with him instead.'

But I couldn't fight that stab of pain when I came out of the bathroom to catch Jeremy at the mirror, checking his reflection in a snorkel mask.

CHAPTER TWENTY-EIGHT

That night was Limbo Night at the resort's own Beach Bar. I wasn't desperately keen to join in, since I was barely flexible enough to touch my own knees let alone shimmy through a six-inch gap, but Jeremy was insistent. He wanted to see everything, and make the most of this all-inclusive business by trying every cocktail on the menu. We joined Luke and Shelly at a table reserved specially for the world's most romantic lovers. Ms Canada had sunstroke and Australia's Mark had wimped out having made the most of the free cocktails since breakfast.

'I had heard that Australians like their alcohol,' said Shelly primly. 'But I've always tried to resist classing people by racial stereotypes. Still, if he keeps it up, it'll be less competition for us on the night of the grand finale,' she added with a smile. 'You're looking very brown, Alison. I didn't think the English tanned.'

'I spent the afternoon by the pool, with Candida.'

'Candida Bianca? You mean she was by the pool as well.'

'Yes, right next to me.'

'But not with you, surely,' Shelly probed.

'She let me borrow some of her sun-cream.'

Before Shelly could articulate her surprise, the place fell into the usual silence that heralded the arrival of Candida in that evening's fabulous dress.

This time it was red. A silken slip of a thing, with a diagonal hem, that fluttered like a flame around her perfect legs. She shook her head when the Maître d' offered her her usual table and made a bee-line for us, instead.

'Oh my God, she's coming over here,' Shelly muttered into her napkin as Candida walked through a crowd that parted like the Red Sea around her and took what would have been Marguerite's place were she not nursing Mark through a bout of alcohol poisoning.

'I hope you don't mind me joining you,' the megastar said sweetly. As if anybody ever did. Shelly just gulped air like a frog.

The cocktails flowed like water all night that night. Every time I put an empty glass down on the table, Jeremy reminded me that we were on an all-inclusive deal and it was my duty to make the most of it. So the cocktails kept on coming. Blue ones, pink ones, green ones. Fruity, fiery and creamy ones. Tall ones and short ones, all with a variety of cocktail stirrers and paper umbrellas, until the surface of the table started to look slightly wobbly and I knew that whatever I did, I mustn't stand up.

'Come to the bathroom with me,' Shelly said suddenly, hauling me to my feet and dragging me behind her to the ladies.

'It's OK! It's OK!' I protested, as the room swirled around me. 'I'm not really drunk at all.'

'What?' said Shelly as she positioned herself in the best place at the mirror and started to reapply her lipstick.

'I said I'm not drunk,' I mumbled.

'You surely are,' said Shelly flatly. 'But that is your business. Now, what do you think she's up to?'

'Who?' I asked.

'That Candida woman, of course. What is she doing, joining us for dinner when she could have had the best table in the place to herself?'

'She said she wanted company.'

'Huh. And I think I know exactly whose company she wants. She can't take her eyes off him. She's been undressing him in her mind ever since she sat down at the table with us. Well, I'll tell you what, she's going to have to quit messing around because I don't care how much her nose-job cost, I'm going to flatten that pretty little ski-jump right to her face if she does it once more.'

'Eh?'

'She's been making eyes at my Luke, Ali. All night. I was starting to feel like I was the gooseberry out there. She's driving me crazy. What should I do about it? You've got to help me out.'

'She wasn't making eyes at him,' I tried, hoping that I might be able to calm her down. 'You must have been imagining things. What would she want with someone like Luke, anyway?'

'What do you mean? What would she want with someone like Luke? Are you joking with me? He's the most romantic man in America. Officially. And I know when a woman wants my fiancé. My imagination is perfectly under control and I know what I saw with my very own eyes. You've got to help me, Ali. You've got to suggest that we all move places around the table so that we can better talk to the people we haven't spoken to so far, then you've got to sit right between her and Luke, so that she can't start playing footsie or putting her hand in his lap. I can trust you to do that can't I, Ali?'

She shook me so that the ceiling seemed to lurch dangerously towards my head.

'Well, there's no way I'll be playing footsie with Luke,' I said when the room stopped moving.

'Good. Now, do you want to sort yourself out before we go back into the restaurant. I'll hold your hair back while you puke if you like.'

'No, I'm fine, really.'

'You look a little bilious. I'm quite happy to help you, Ali. I've been bringing on my vomit since high school. How else can one keep slim and yet still pretend to have a sensual appetite?'

I felt sick at the thought. I had never actually brought a chunder on. Instead, I refused her kind offer and staggered back out into the restaurant with my alcohol quota still very much intact. But so much for Shelly's seating-plan plan. Only Jeremy remained at our table. Candida had already spirited Luke onto the dance floor to join her in a particularly filthy looking merengue.

'Why didn't you stop him?' Shelly shrieked when she spotted her beau.

'Stop him what?' asked Jeremy.

'From dancing with her.'

'Why don't you just go and interrupt them yourself?' he asked.

'I will,' said Shelly, setting her jaw. 'You know what. I will.'

'Got to see this,' said Jeremy, as Shelly flounced onto

the dance floor. 'Come on.' He hauled me to my feet and manhandled me out there after her, to stagger around the fight in an approximation of a waltz.

'Excuse me,' said Shelly, baring her teeth like an irritated Jack Russell. 'If it's OK with you, Miss Bianca, I'd like to dance with my fiancé.' She injected the word with such venom you might have thought she was using a different f-word altogether.

Candida stepped away with her hands up. 'Feel free, I was just about to sit down anyway. My feet are killing me in these shoes.'

'Hope they give you bunions,' said Shelly to the star's retreating back.

Jeremy and I did two more spins around the dance floor but my head was in such a bad way that when Jeremy told me that he thought he should ask Candida to dance, since she was starting to look lonely after two minutes off the floor, I was almost pleased at the prospect of a nice quiet sit-down. Jeremy escorted me back to the table and settled me safely in a chair.

'One more for the road, I suppose,' I agreed when a cocktail waitress asked me if I wanted a Brain Haemorrhage. I downed the disgusting Baileys and grenadine concoction in one, then I put my head down on my folded arms as Jeremy led Candida out onto the dance floor and was asleep before they'd made one trip around the room.

The music still played inside my head. I dreamed of a swirling room. Of concerned faces crowding round me as I started to spin myself. I was spinning, spinning, out of control. Then:

'Oh, my God! Will somebody deal with this woman?' Shelly was shouting.

I was vomiting all over my bare arms and onto the floor.

Thank goodness someone in that room had trained as a nurse. She quickly pushed all others aside to clear my air passages and had her boyfriend help Jeremy carry me back to our room.

'What happens now?' I heard Jeremy ask as if he were a long way off into the distance.

'You just have to leave her until she sleeps through it. If she's in this position, she can't do herself an injury if she vomits.'

'Is it OK if I go back to the party?' Jeremy asked.

'You go. I'll look in on her later on,' the nurse kindly said.

Then everything went black and fuzzy.

CHAPTER TWENTY-NINE

When I next woke up it was fairly late in the day. I rolled over to face Jeremy in bed, except he wasn't there. His pillow looked undented.

I sat up suddenly, but was quickly pinned back down again by the mother of all headaches. I couldn't exactly remember what had happened but all the evidence pointed to one shandy too many. Dried sick stained the front of my Jean Paul Gaultier sundress (another acquisition from Emma's trendy wardrobe).

'Uugh.'

I crept into the bathroom and started to spruce myself up. My watch, which somebody had kindly placed on the washstand, told me that it was eleven o'clock. I had slept right through breakfast. I decided that the housekeeper must have been in to make up Jeremy's side of the bed while I dreamed my drunkenness off.

Grateful for my shades to cut out the light, I made my way down to the pool. When my entrance seemed to inspire almost as much awe as the magical nightly appearance of Candida Bianca in evening dress, I knew that whatever I had done the night before, I must have done it in spectacular style.

'Why is everybody staring at me today?' I asked Shelly.

'They are probably just concerned,' she assured me. 'You overdid it just a little at the beach barbecue.'

'I guessed as much. What happened after I left?'

'Well, Candida was up to her usual tricks. She did a couple of turns around the floor with David, then she set her sights on Chad. Like dancing with an octopus, he said it was. I don't know why she can't go for the single men. There are plenty of them around here.'

I stole a glance at the Italian Stallions, playing with a beach ball, hairy chests rippling like cornfields in the breeze. 'Maybe she isn't actually looking for anything more than a dance,' I suggested. 'If she dances with the men who are already attached, then nothing more can happen, can it?'

'Well, whatever you think, I will be keeping Luke under close observation from now on,' said Shelly, scanning the pool for her puppy dog. 'That woman is dangerous, Ali. I'm telling you. She's poison.'

Then Miss Poison herself sat down next to us.

'Oh, hi Candida,' Shelly trilled. 'Can I just say what a fantastic dress you were wearing last evening?'

'Why thank you. Would you like to have it?'

'What? Moi?' Shelly clutched her hand to her heart. 'Are you serious? Me have your dress?'

'Sure. I can never wear the same dress twice. Imagine what the press would say.'

'Imagine,' I sighed.

'What about you, Ali? You'd look fantastic in that

pink dress I wore on Tuesday. Would you like to have that? It's vintage Versace.'

'Wow,' I couldn't help myself. 'But it's OK, you keep it,' I told her. 'I'd need to get shoes to go with it . . .'

'Have mine,' said Candida generously. 'I'd say we're about the same size.' She stretched out her leg alongside mine so that we could compare the size of our feet. I quickly tucked mine beneath me. My crusty toenails were no match for her pedicure in the latest cult colour by Chanel.

'Come round and fetch them from my room whenever you like.'

'That's so generous,' said Shelly. 'So very kind.'

'Think nothing of it. You girls want a drink, I'm going to the bar?'

'Make mine a margarita,' said Shelly.

'Coke,' said I.

As soon as Candida was out of earshot, Shelly started again. 'And what do you think that is all about?' she asked. 'Offering us her cast-offs as some kind of consolation prize for trying to steal our men.'

'We didn't have to accept.'

'Are you kidding? That red dress she wore last night wasn't off the peg at Nordstrom, you know. No, I'll take the dress, but I'm not dropping my guard for one moment. I've heard about these Hollywood women. She probably expects us to turn a blind eye to her escapades if we accept her presents. Probably expects us to treat it as a honour that she wants to sleep with what's ours.'

'Perhaps she's just a generous soul.'

* * *

We were certainly making the most of our holiday. Every day, from dawn till dusk, was like a scene from a Hollywood movie. Breakfast in bed. Cocktails by the pool. The sun beating down on the sea as Jeremy and Candida scuba dived and I snorkelled in the shallows, trying to pet the big, rainbow-bright fish which swam fearlessly around me, until it was time to go back to the restaurant and eat some of their less fortunate cousins.

I felt like a princess. No, better than a princess, since I wasn't having to fight off the waistline criticising paparazzi while I lounged on the sand.

Our fellow romantic winners seemed to be having an equally good time, but in their own special way. Mark and Marguerite started every morning with a jog along the beach. (They might have been the World's Fittest Couple too.) Chad and Penny did a spot of bird-watching. And Shelly kept Luke well occupied. After breakfast, they would go straight down to the pool. He would oil her all over with factor twenty-five sunscreen, then he would spend the morning moving the parasol which shaded her every five minutes so that her face was never fully in the sun.

'Keep young and beautiful,' she warned me once while I slathered on the factor nil cooking oil I had bought at the airport. Hell, I wasn't likely to get another holiday like this in a hurry, I reassured myself. I was going to go home with a tan even if it was my last.

CHAPTER THIRTY

Then suddenly we had just two days left to go. The first layer of my tan was already flaking off so I planned to spend my last 48 hours baking. Jeremy wanted to get in as much diving as he could, with Candida of course. I had trained myself not to mind, since she spent every evening with us talking about Hollywood men she had big crushes on, and my wardrobe now boasted a Versace.

But Candida wasn't alone by the pool and ready to go diving that last but one morning. Squinting through my sleep-bleary eyes as we walked across the empty garden to the restaurant, I thought at first that she was sitting on one of the loungers with a man. The youngish looking chap had a clipboard, and he was ticking things off while Candida lounged and lolled and looked terribly bored by it all. Her face changed dramatically when she spotted me with Jeremy. She waved a long brown arm in our direction and beckoned us over. I just about managed to hide my surprise when she introduced us to Loretta, her personal assistant. A girl.

Loretta grunted hello, rearranged the straps on her

short denim dungarees and dragged a hand through her bleached crew-cut hair in a masculine fashion.

'I can't come diving today,' she told a horribly disappointed Jeremy. 'Loretta has flown out here to harangue me. She doesn't think I should have been diving at all. Says it isn't covered by my life insurance. Honestly, Alison, you have no idea what a drag it is to be a successful actress. I can't be away from work for five minutes. Can I?' She looked at Loretta accusingly.

'Jerry says that we have to sort this French contract out by tonight or you'll lose it altogether,' Loretta complained.

'Maybe I don't want to do his crumby little film anyway,' Candida spat. 'Well, would you want to spend a month in Paris shooting the life story of Coco Chanel, Ali? I'm only playing her until she starts to get all middle-aged and doggy. Demi Moore's doing the rest.' She smiled her disarming smile, as though she was unaware of how bitchy her comment had sounded. 'Besides, Paris is in Europe. What is there to do in Europe for heaven's sake? I don't have any friends there. And the food? They don't have Granola, you know. It's all snails and horse-meat. Yuk.'

'You have us in Europe,' Jeremy piped up suddenly. Candida turned on the full beam again.

'Why yes, I do. How far is London from Paris?' she asked suddenly.

'Three hours by Eurostar,' I said helpfully.

'And you'll be in London?' she asked us.

'Well, not exactly. Brindlesham is on the outskirts. And David will be in Warsaw again.'

Candida's face fell. 'But that's in Germany, isn't it?' she asked hopefully.

'No. Poland. But it's just a short flight away from Paris,' Jeremy said soothingly. 'I could show you around.'

I could see Candida's brain working as she hovered with a biro over the dotted line on her contract to play fashion's greatest doyenne.

'What was that other job?' she asked Loretta suddenly. 'The cold one.'

'The one in Warsaw?' said Loretta with a look of surprise. 'The last days of the Tsars. I thought you weren't interested in all that "highbrow stuff",' she added mockingly.

'I never said that,' said Candida. 'Does it clash with the Coco Chanel business?'

'Absolutely. They start shooting on the exact same day.'

'Then send my apologies to Jerry, but tell him that I want to make something arthouse instead. Tell him I want to make sure I'm not typecast as a fashion bimbo.'

'Coco Chanel was hardly a fashion bimbo,' I said in surprise.

'She was hardly Versace either,' Candida replied. 'Loretta, send Vadim my tape again and tell him that you turned the part of Anastasia down on my behalf by mistake. I'd love to play the Tsarina. Tell him I've fired you as well while you're at it.'

Loretta took the notes down dutifully.

'I meant that last bit,' said Candida, when she caught a hint of a smile on her PA's face. 'I can't abide incompetence. You guys had breakfast yet?' she asked me and Jeremy cheerfully. Then she linked her arm through Jeremy's and Loretta and I followed them inside.

For someone who had just been fired, Loretta seemed to get an awful lot of errands to run over that breakfast. There were letters to write, contracts to chase and the right suntan lotion to source. I wondered what Loretta was doing working for a woman like Candida. With her funky, ethnic nose-ring and her bleached, cropped hair, Loretta looked as though she would be more at home giving a reading of the latest in anarchic poetry in some basement bar rather than running about looking for the right lipstick for a woman who was only one step up the intellectual evolutionary chain from a toy poodle. But Loretta took the gibes Candida rained on her like a mother ignoring the bleatings of a spoilt child. I longed to get Loretta on her own and ask for the real gossip about her boss. Shelly would be delighted with any dirt I could share.

Later that day, I had my opportunity. Jeremy took Candida diving again, and after I had cursed my fear of being twenty feet below the surface of the sea with an unfriendly underwater native one more time, I took up my position by the pool again. Loretta was sitting beneath a sun umbrella, with her nose covered by a bright stripe of zinc block, despatching letters and instructions to every part of the civilised world with the help of her laptop, mobile and modem.

'Hi,' she smiled widely when she saw me. 'Thanks so much for persuading your man to take her off my hands for a while.'

'Oh, he didn't need persuading,' I said, a little ruefully. 'Have you been working for her long?'

'Too long. It started out as a short term thing. While I waited for someone to be wowed into submission by my first screenplay. But that didn't exactly happen and now

I seem to have landed myself with a life-long sentence and no chance of parole.'

'How did you get a job as assistant to a film star?'

'By looking like a dyke,' she said flatly. 'Her Majesty Candida had a dozen applications from people who would have made better assistants than me, but she didn't want someone who would show her up. I guess I'm like the coalface for her sparkling diamond.'

'Don't put yourself down. Even Candida says that beauty comes from the inside.'

'She says that to every ugly person she meets.'

'Oh.'

'But don't worry about me, Ali. I used to get something from this fucked up working relationship too. I fancied her like mad before I actually started working for her.'

'You fancied her?' the shock must have registered on my face.

'Yeah. I know she's a terrible bimbo and all that, but I've always been a sucker for a pretty face,' she smiled.

'Me too. On boys though.'

Loretta laughed.

'Everybody loves Candida, don't they? She really does have it all, doesn't she?' I said, as I settled back onto my sunbed.

'Including athlete's foot,' said Loretta, punching yet another number into her mobile. 'Excuse me for a moment, Ali. I have to call the only pharmacist on this godforsaken island and find out if he has any fungicide.'

He didn't. Loretta clicked off her mobile and flung it onto the sunbed on her other side.

'Well, that's me fired. Again.'

'I thought she fired you this morning.'

'She reinstated me after breakfast when she couldn't work out how to send an e-mail herself.'

'Does she fire you often?'

'Every other day. I just can't wait until I'm in a position to accept one of my enforced resignations.'

'I find it really hard to believe that she's such a difficult person. I mean, she's been lovely to us, and we're only ordinary people.'

Loretta snorted.

'She's flesh and blood, too, Ali. She never does anything out of niceness. And if I were you I would watch her around that boyfriend of yours.'

I raised my eyebrows. 'My boyfriend? But she's dated Brad Pitt.'

'Just because a girl gets to eat caviar from time to time, doesn't mean she stops liking roast chicken.'

I was rather offended by the chicken part of that. But I guessed that Loretta meant well.

'Drink?' she asked me then.

'Why not?' They were free after all.

Like a magical genie, a waiter soon appeared at our side with a tray loaded down with candy-coloured cocktails and a bowl heaped high with peanuts. Loretta dived straight into the nuts, tipping a huge handful into her mouth and talking while she chewed.

'Oh, yeah,' she assured me as she downed another cocktail and warmed to her theme. 'Hollywood is simply crawling with queers. Name a sex symbol and I'll name you his boyfriend. Go on. Go on. Anyone at all,' she dared me.

'I don't think I want to know. You'll shatter my illusions.'

'Illusions were made to be shattered. It's much more fun when you know what really goes on beneath the make-up and the bright lights. Listen, I've got to tell you this story about Candida. It's quite ironic really, when you know that Candida is the Latin name for thru . . .'

Suddenly, Loretta's eyes widened in horror. Then she began to cough. Nasty, pent-up little coughs that told me she was choking on a half-chewed nut. I waited politely for her to get over it and continue with her story. But after thirty seconds or so, I realised that she wasn't about to finish.

'Want some water?' I asked her, handing her my glass. Loretta was still hacking violently, her face growing red with the exertion. She took the glass and attempted to take a sip, but could only spurt the water straight back out again. I gave her a stiff whack between the shoulder blades but she simply fell forward and began choking in doggy position on the floor instead.

'Help? Somebody? Is there a doctor round here?' I called. I had a nasty feeling of *déjà vu* and hoped that it might extend to the arrival of a helpful vet. But while a circle of people had already gathered around us, it was clear that they knew far less about the business of saving someone's life than I did.

Yes. I had almost forgotten how much I actually knew. The Heimlich manoeuvre. We had been shown how to do it at Ashley's first aid class. Thank goodness Emma had forced me to attend. The sea-scout practising on me that day had almost squeezed my lungs out through my nose but I had quickly absorbed the principle.

Knowing that if I got it wrong I was going to look like

a prat but realising that if I didn't even try, I was almost certainly going to have a corpse on my hands, I got behind Loretta, pulled her into a semi-upright position and brought my fists together just beneath her breast bone. Then, one quick hard hoik and a half-chewed peanut sailed through the air at an impressive velocity to land in the suntanned cleavage of a horrified Italian beach-babe.

Loretta stopped choking and started gasping in an altogether more manageable manner. She rolled onto her back and looked up at me with blinking, disbelieving eyes.

'You just saved my life,' she murmured.

I shrugged my shoulders and sneaked an embarrassed glance at the Italian woman inviting her boyfriend to fish out Loretta's projectile.

'I don't know how I can ever, ever repay you.'

I shrugged again. 'I'm sure you'll think of something.'

'Alison, you're amazing. So modest. You know that if we were American Indians my life would now belong to you. You could do anything you wanted with me.'

'That's quite alright.' I wondered if this was a roundabout way of asking me to kiss her. But before I could find out, Candida and Jeremy returned from their dive. Everyone had been so absorbed in my life-saving antics that they didn't notice the diva striding across to us, Bond-girl style, complete with diving knife strapped to her thigh. Parting the crowd, Candida stood over her PA and dripped sea water from her gorgeous long hair into the poor girl's face.

'Uugh. What happened to you?' she asked. 'You look all green about the face.'

'I was choking on a nut,' Loretta explained breathlessly. 'Ali here saved my life.' She gave me a puppy-eyed gaze.

'Did you get the stuff I asked for?' Candida asked, without missing a beat. I noticed that she was not mentioning in front of Jeremy what exactly it was she had asked for.

Loretta shook her head. 'The chemist didn't have any. He offered to make up a herbal solution, though.'

'Herbal solution? Do I look like I'm interested in witch doctor crap?'

'No,' said Loretta in a small voice.

'Then Ali really needn't have wasted her time bringing you back to life. You're fired, Loretta.'

'Does that mean I can fly back to LA now?' Loretta asked hopefully.

Candida looked about to boil over. 'No. You're still on a week's notice. Make sure you get that stuff flown in.'

Then Candida flounced off in the direction of her beach hut, with Loretta following behind like a scolded puppy.

'It must be a nightmare, working for Candida,' I commented when they were out of earshot.

'It must be very difficult to find staff who don't try to take advantage of a woman in her position,' Jeremy replied. 'Candida told me that girls usually only want to work for her as a way to meet Brad Pitt. That's why she hired Loretta. She's a lesbian.'

'That doesn't give Candida an excuse to treat her so badly.'

'She doesn't. Loretta gets a private health plan and three weeks paid holiday a year.'

'Well it's better than being a child slave in India, I

suppose,' I said sarcastically. 'But I wouldn't put up with the way Candida behaves for that.'

'She has a very stressful lifestyle.'

'Yeah. Swimming pool, diving, beautician.'

'When she's on set,' Jeremy corrected. It was clear that he wasn't going to join me in a bitch-fest so I gave up. 'I hope she gets that Warsaw job. She's really excited about playing such a meaty part.'

I put my sunglasses on and pretended to read my bonkbuster.

Jeremy was obviously star-struck, but I had seen a different side of Candida and, in my opinion, it didn't matter how many times she had to reshoot a love scene with Brad Pitt, there was no excuse for being such a cow. I scanned the pool for Shelly and Luke. They had been going to spend the day exploring some of Antigua's other three hundred and sixty five beaches. Luke was interested in seeing some of the red-breasted booby birds that lived along the shore apparently. Shelly was only really interested in shopping, but, she assured me, it was important to let Luke do exactly what he wanted to every so often. Give and take, she said. It was the secret of a great relationship.

I sneaked a sidelong glance at Jeremy's gorgeous profile. He hadn't even attempted to speak to me since I picked up my book. Putting it down again, I reached a hand across to his sunbed and gently caressed his bronzed arm. But he brushed my hand away.

'Little bit burnt,' he explained. It didn't look all that red to me, but I decided that I had better leave him alone for a while in any case. Shelly had told me something about men needing to be allowed to sit alone in their 'caves' from time to time, revelling in their solitude.

This was probably one of those times. But I couldn't help hating Candida for being the cause of the first angry-ish words that ever passed between us.

Thankfully, an hour later, the cloud seemed to have passed. Instead of complaining that he didn't want me to touch his burned arm, Jeremy suggested that I rub in some aftersun. I did so joyfully, taking extra special care to do it lovingly when Candida and Loretta re-emerged and wandered across to join us.

'I got it,' Candida announced. 'I got the job in Warsaw.'

Jeremy's eyes widened. Loretta shot me a knowing glancc.

'Vadim said that he couldn't really have contemplated having anyone else in the part. He's giving Gwyneth her marching orders tomorrow. I'm sure she'll just be relieved that she doesn't have to dye her hair. And I'll be in Warsaw at the end of the month. Do I need to have any vaccinations for going that far?'

'This is fabulous news,' said Jeremy, throwing his arms around Candida and swinging her round.

'I'm very, very sorry,' said Loretta to me.

CHAPTER THIRTY-ONE

I had fallen asleep with a paperback over my eyes when somebody asked, 'Can I buy you a margarita?'

It was Luke.

'No,' I told him. 'You can't.'

Luke recoiled slightly, before I reminded him. 'It's all inclusive here, remember.'

Luke guffawed and shovelled a handful of peanuts into his mouth.

'That'll make you thirsty,' I said.

Luke nodded. He raised a finger to summon the barman, but had to point to the drink he wanted because if he'd opened his mouth he would have sprayed us all with shrapnel.

'Where's Shelly this afternoon?' I asked him.

'Oh.' He gulped a slug of his beer. 'She's in the beach hut. She's getting some sleep for tomorrow night.'

'Really. What's so special about tomorrow?' I yawned.

'It's the competition,' said Luke, as if I was an idiot.

'Oh yes, the competition.' I had been suppressing

that thought and almost completely succeeded in blocking it from my mind.

'I don't know what she'll do if we don't win,' Luke continued. 'I mean, she's set her heart on us being the most romantic couple in the world and all.'

'I'm sure you are,' I reassured him.

'I don't know,' Luke muttered, then: 'Ali, do you think you and I might go somewhere and talk for a while?'

'What?'

'It's just that you seem like you're a really nice person and right now a nice person is what I really need.'

'Oh.' I smiled awkwardly. 'That's sweet. I suppose I could spare you ten minutes in my busy schedule of laying about. Where do you want to go?'

'Down on the beach, perhaps. We could walk up to the sunbeds and back. No, hang on. I'm forgetting myself. Where's David?'

'Scuba diving. I think he's becoming a fish. I can give you a few minutes.'

'That's real kind of you.'

He was quite sweet. In fact there was something about Luke that reminded me of the real David. Maybe it was the way he could put away more peanuts than the average elephant without seeming to need to swallow between huge handfuls.

I gathered up my beach towel and wrapped it around my waist as a makeshift sarong. We headed down towards the edge of the water, where the sunbeds lay in strangely regimented order for such a laid-back kind of place.

'What do you want to tell me?' I asked, to get

the ball rolling. He probably wanted to know what fantastic going-home gift he should buy for his future bride, or something sick-making like that. Luke took off his baseball cap and started to wring it between his hands.

'Ali, me and Shelly can't be the world's most romantic couple any more,' he began. 'Because I think I'm falling in love with you.'

I choked on thin air.

'I tried to stop myself, but I can't,' Luke continued. 'Every time I see you I get that thump, thump, thump feeling inside my chest. I haven't had that with Shelly in years now. Shelly only ever wants to talk about how the wedding's gonna be and when we're gonna start having a family, but you, you're not like that. You're wonderful, Ali. You're just so full of life. So exciting.'

He lunged towards me, lips puckered.

'Luke,' I held him back. 'You don't know what you're doing.'

'I do,' he protested. 'I've made my decision. It's better to live one day as a sheep than a lifetime as a tiger.'

'I don't think you mean that,' I said. But I didn't bother to point out his mistake. 'Listen Luke, Shelly will make hamburger of you if she finds out about this.'

'I don't care. I can't go on living this lie any longer.'

'Please do,' I asked him. 'At least until this holiday is over. It's one thing deciding that you don't love Shelly any more, but it's quite another to lay her open to the ridicule of the whole world while you're at it. After all, you're supposed to be entering a worldwide competition as America's most successful love match tomorrow night.'

'So you want me to keep quiet until tomorrow night?' Luke asked. 'Then can we be together? I've got this aunt in Reno. She has a caravan there, where we could hide out until things between me and Shelly are properly settled. It's empty. We could move in straightaway.'

'Er. I don't think so,' I said, still having to push him away.

'Don't you like the idea of a caravan? I know you English girls. Home is your castle and all that.'

'It's not the caravan part,' I assured him. 'There's David as well, remember. I still love him.'

'Ali, you know that's a lie.'

'What?'

'I feel real bad telling you this, but it's been obvious to the rest of us from the start that you and David don't really even know each other. He doesn't love you. I can tell by the way he looks at you. He may love the idea of being here with you but he doesn't have that softness in his eyes that says it will work out back home. Forget him, Ali. I can show you what real love is all about.'

'Luke,' I said, giving him one last shove that landed him bum-first on the sand. 'You are really talking rubbish. Now why don't you just go back to Shelly and give her some of your soft-eyed crap. I love David and he loves me. But I will never, never love you.'

'You don't mean that. I know you're saying that because I've taken you by surprise . . .' Luke called after me as I made a slow exit in the foot-sucking sand. 'David doesn't love you, Ali. He's been getting it on with Candida.'

I stopped in my tracks. 'What? You're just saying that to get a reaction. Forget it, Luke. I'm a one man woman.'

Poor Shelly, I thought, lying in the beach hut, getting her beauty sleep. She had no idea. As I passed the hut she shared with her hopeless fiancé, she emerged, face covered in an avocado-green pack.

'Hi, Ali. You getting ready for tomorrow night? You know, I couldn't find a drugstore on the whole of this goddamn island. I had to get the guys in the kitchen to give me some real avocado for this mask. You want some? I got plenty left.'

'No thanks. I've already eaten,' I told her.

'For your face, dufus!' she laughed. 'You should try it. Luke is always telling me that one of the things he loves most about me is the softness of my skin.'

I forced myself to smile.

'Hey, I hope we didn't keep you guys up last night,' she continued. 'We were playing cards with Mark and Marguerite until well past eleven and the walls of these places are awful thin.'

'Oh, you didn't keep us up,' I reassured her. If she was worried that we might have heard them playing cards, then surely she would have heard that Jeremy and I weren't asleep at all.

'You know,' she said to change the subject, 'avocados aren't the only miracle product in nature's beauty cabinet.' Shelly was poised to impart some more of her all-American wisdom but we were suddenly interrupted by Luke, red-faced from racing up the beach, no doubt terrified that I had gone straight to Shelly to tell her what I thought of the rat that he had revealed himself to be.

'Hi, honey,' Shelly beamed, instantly putting his mind at rest. 'I was just telling Alison about my avocado face pack. But hell, I shouldn't be letting you see me like this,' she added, pushing him away playfully. 'Seeing your fiancée all covered in a face pack hardly makes you want to be the world's most romantic man does it?'

She laughed her tinkling chandelier laugh and disappeared back into the cool darkness of the hut. Luke went to say something to me, but I stopped him by raising my hand.

'Let's forget it ever happened,' I whispered.

'But it's true what I said about Candida.'

'I'm especially forgetting you said that.'

Luke nodded in resignation and turned to follow Shelly. In the past, when anyone had given me the all-men-are-bastards line I had thought that they were overreacting, but seeing Luke, America's Most Romantic Man, lighting up Shelly's face again just moments after telling me that he loved me, I felt pretty sure that the all-men-are-bastards generalisation could be applied to about 80% of the species. Jeremy wasn't among them of course. The bit about Candida had been made up. Just over lunch she had said she had a crush on the director she would be working with in Warsaw.

I told Jeremy about the incident as soon as he came back from scuba diving.

'Ha,' he laughed. 'I could have told you that about Luke days ago. I could tell by the way he looked at you.'

'What do you mean? I thought you guys couldn't read emotions anyway.'

'That's a clever myth,' Jeremy explained. 'Gives us an excuse when we go trampling all over a woman's.'

'And the Candida thing? Is that true?'

'Don't be crazy, Ali. What would she want with me? She's in love with that hot-shot director.'

Exactly, I thought. Jeremy and Candida? It just wasn't a possibility. Luke Connolly was mad.

'Did you see any good fish today?' I asked to change the subject.

'One or two,' he said. 'Thought we might have seen a shark but it was quite far in the distance.'

'How big?' I gasped, eyes widening.

Jeremy stretched his arms out as far as they could go.

'Candida remained quite calm.'

'Only because she was with you. You're so brave,' I cooed. 'All you need to do now to make you the most perfect man in the world is learn my preferences on the jelly flavour front.'

'Shit. The big competition. I'd forgotten all about that.'

'We don't have to enter if you don't want to,' I told him. 'We can be indisposed.'

'No way,' Jeremy protested, as he searched the drawers next to the bed for a pad and pencil. 'You better start telling me what I need to know about you. There's ten thousand pounds at stake, you know.'

'Yes. But how can we possibly win it anyway? We're up against three couples who have known each other for ever. Shelly probably even knows exactly how many hairs Luke has on his head. We've got no chance against the likes of them.'

'Ali, let's not waste time thinking about whether we've got a chance or not. What's your favourite colour?'

'Blue,' I suppose.

'Great, that's mine too. I won't forget that one. What's your favourite animal?'

'Cats.'

'I like dogs.'

'Dogs. Really? I never had you down as a dog person.'

'Much better than flea-ridden felines,' he snapped. 'What's your favourite TV soap?'

'Hang on a second,' I said, slipping myself onto the bed beside him. 'I'm just trying to get over the fact that you prefer dogs to cats. Can't we think about this later?'

I ran my hand gently over his shoulders.

'Ali,' Jeremy protested. 'Not now. If we put our minds to it, this could be the easiest ten thousand pounds we have ever earned in our lives. And I need the money to . . . er, never mind.'

I sat up again disappointedly. 'OK,' I said. 'But to be honest, I don't think they're going to want to know this stuff. This is so basic and we're taking part in the grand final. I think they're going to want something more juicy. We need to make up some stories. The history of our grand affair. How we met. Passionate arguments we've had.'

'Arguments? But we're meant to be the most romantic couple.'

'I know,' I said. 'But don't you think it's romantic to have fights sometimes too? All that kissing and making up. How about this for one? You were struggling to come to terms with the depth of your feelings for me. You thought that you would be overcome by love, swept up by it and eventually dashed against the jagged rocks of abandonment. We were apart for a whole week before you realised that you didn't care if you would end up being hurt one day. To have loved so wholly just once was all that mattered.' I was pretty moved by the idea.

'That's great,' said Jeremy, scribbling the basic points down. 'Now what about if we had one when you borrowed my car and smashed into another car while you were parking.'

'Oh, thanks a lot. Do you think I can't park?'

'Well, it's more realistic than your tale. Women crash cars all the time.'

'How about the row we had over the fact that you sometimes act just a little too much like a male chauvinist pig?'

'You'll ruin my image.'

'Oh, this is mad, isn't it,' I told him. 'Let's just pretend we've never had a row in our lives.'

'Well, that's sort of true.'

'What do you mean, sort of?'

'You seemed a bit tetchy with me when I came back from diving this morning.'

'Only because you went straight back out to dive again in the afternoon. You spend so much time in the water that you're starting to look like a prune. And you spend so much time with Candida that people are telling me to watch my back. I think I had every right to get a bit tetchy.'

'Oh, Ali,' Jeremy enfolded me in his arms. 'I didn't mean to upset you. I just got carried away with having a famous friend. We'll spend the rest of our holiday together.'

'Huh,' I snorted. 'All twenty-four hours.'

'Candida won't be diving tomorrow. That director, Vadim, is flying out here tonight.'

'Good,' I said, 'then you won't have to worry about her being lonely.'

Jeremy shook his head (and if I had been less love-struck I might have noticed he shook it sadly). 'No,' he said. 'I suppose I won't.'

CHAPTER THIRTY-TWO

The big day dawned. The Grand Final of *Complete Woman International*'s search to find the most romantic couple in the world was just eight hours away.

As an extra special treat, an internationally renowned hairdresser had been flown in from Florida to make us all look our best for the photos. Or at least, to make the girls look their best. I think Jeremy was quite disappointed to be left out. Mark from Australia wouldn't even let shampoo near his ultra-manly hair, let alone other less necessary styling products.

Shelly and I sat side by side under the kind of hairdryers that had been banned in the rest of the world since the sixties. She was excited. No hint at all that things weren't all well between her and her beau. I guessed Luke must have taken my advice.

'It's been so interesting meeting you lovely guys,' she told me warmly, with the air of someone who thought that she had already won the race. 'So many of our friends back home, the couples that we know, they don't take their relationships so seriously. They don't respect each other like Luke and I do. Meeting you guys has reaffirmed my faith in romance.'

'Thanks,' I muttered. I didn't really feel like getting into a conversation, but luckily Shelly was the kind of girl who could easily be set off on a soliloquy. 'So,' I couldn't resist it. 'What do you think your secret is?'

'Well,' she began, popping out from beneath her drier so that she could address me head-on like a missionary. 'Have you heard of positive imaging?'

I shrugged.

'It's like this, Alison. What you want, you can have. You can have anything at all. But you have to want it hard enough. You have to want it so hard that you are able to visualise it. Almost touch it in your mind's eye. I first got to hear about it on the television. There was a guru. She was talking about her new book and she said that she knew she was going to be able to finish it as soon as she could picture the cover in her mind. After that, she set about imagining the covers of all her books before she even started to write them. She made them real in her mind first. Now she's a millionairess. Do you follow me so far?'

I nodded.

'Well, when I saw what positive imaging could do for her, I decided to try it for myself. I didn't know Luke at all in those days. I had just seen him working in the body shop of his father's garage. I thought, wow, he's cute. But I never imagined that he could be mine. I swear, girls all over my town suddenly lost the ability to drive around lampposts when Luke became a mechanic. I know you probably can't imagine it now, seeing us looking so right together, but I had so much competition I thought the game was lost.'

'Really?'

'Yeah. So I started to try this positive imaging thing. At first, it was for a bit of fun. I imagined myself walking into the garage to ask about getting my car serviced. I imagined Luke looking back at me with a spark of recognition in his eyes that I could be the girl of his dreams. Two weeks after our first proper date I imagined us getting married and three years later, he proposed.'

'So it doesn't have instant results, this method of yours?'

'Love isn't instant, Ali.'

Unless it's true love, I thought, thinking of the moment it had hit me that Jeremy was the man of my dreams. It had been at my parents' party, when we were standing at the sink together. I hadn't known at the time, but now I knew clearly that what I thought had been wind caused by undercooked vol-au-vents, had in fact been the first rumblings of desire.

'Good luck tonight,' said Shelly, as she was allowed out from beneath her drier and went to mug up on Luke's personal habits.

'Good luck,' I replied. But I meant it.

Alone under my drier I turned Shelly's words over in my mind. Positive imaging, eh? It sounded too good to be true. But it wouldn't cost anything to try it, I figured. And if it didn't work, no-one need know, so I closed my eyes and tried it for myself.

I imagined the final of the Most Romantic Couple

Competition. I imagined a pedestal, like you see at the Olympics, with different levels for the couples who came first, second and third. I imagined Chad and Penny in third place. Luke and Shelly taking the silver. And right on the top . . . Well, you can guess it wasn't Marguerite and Mark.

I imagined the feeling of ten thousand pounds in my pocket and Jeremy's hand in my own. I imagined him whispering something in my ear. 'Let's do it for real,' he was saying. 'Let's really tie the knot.'

'Yuck. Just full of knots.'

I was rudely awoken by the hairdresser. 'You really haven't been taking care of your hair in the sun,' he complained. 'Have you never thought about wearing a sun hat?'

'Not much call for a sun hat in England,' I shrugged.

'No, I suppose not. But you know, if you took a little more care you could almost have tresses like Candida Bianca. Now she's got the most beautiful tresses in the world.'

'What would it take to have a body like hers too?' I wondered out loud.

'Settle for the hair, dearie,' the hairdresser said bitchily as his comb tugged painfully at my scalp. 'You can cover a multitude of sins with Lycra.'

The hotel's fabulous Sea View dining room had been totally rearranged for the final of *Complete Woman International*'s Most Romantic Couple competition. The tables had been cleared away from an area in front of the wide, panoramic window where stood just one solitary chair. The hot seat. The walls had been covered with swags of red velvet, dotted with gold-painted hearts so that it looked like the Queen of Hearts' palace from *Alice in Wonderland*.

The competition was due to start at eight. At seven-thirty, I joined Shelly, Penny and Marguerite by the bar, where we were to be briefed by Marjorie Pine, *Complete Woman International*'s executive editor with responsibility for every issue of the magazine world-wide, as she kept reminding us. Amanda had sent a fax to me that afternoon, saying how sorry she was not to have been able to fly out herself to see my finest hour.

'I want a good clean fight,' Marjorie Pine laughed, showing her long, yellow teeth. 'Remember that what-ever happens here this evening, you are all winners. Each one of you is one half of a fabulous relationship that to you is the best relationship in the world, no matter who takes home the crown tonight.'

We nodded as though she had just revealed some profound truth. Shelly's eyes were glittering madly with the thought of victory regardless.

'Now, if you'd each like to fill out these question-naires,' Marjorie said, handing us each a sheaf of paper and a *Complete Woman* complimentary biro. 'The first round will involve partners matching answers on per-sonal issues. When you've finished those we'll retire to a waiting room so that there can be no communication between you girls and your other halves before the competition begins. We wouldn't want any cheating, would we?'

We sat down at four bar tables and began to fill the questionnaires out. When I looked up at Shelly she was chewing the end of her pencil, poring over some answer as if she were completing a physics A-level. It started out pretty simply. Favourite colours, animals and TV soap. Good job we'd covered all those. Then it went on to the slightly trickier stuff. His mother's maiden name. Good job Hilary Barton-Baxter had been feminist enough to be double-barrelled when they lived next door to us during the seventies.

At the other end of the hotel, the boys were filling out similar forms. I wondered if Jeremy would be able to remember my brand of deodorant and thought strong Natrel Plus thoughts in his direction. Then Marjorie Pine collected our papers together and we retired to the dismal little windowless room where we would have to wait until the hotel audience was assembled. I wondered if Candida would be watching the competition or if her hot-shot director would have whisked her somewhere private for the night. A television crew from Florida was recording the competition for the newly formed 'Romance' satellite channel. When Marjorie mentioned the name of the compere for the evening, Shelly clapped her hands together in delight. The rest of us had never heard of him.

'Perfect,' she gushed. 'Aidan Hobbs is my favourite TV presenter of all time. I think this is a good omen for us.' She meant for her and Luke, of course.

By the time we were finally called out onto the stage, it seemed as if the competition was already over. Certainly there was no doubt in Shelly's mind that she and Luke would come away with the crowns that night. And the money. I was a little irritated by that, since I had already been on a pretty extensive mental shopping spree.

Shelly was first onto the stage. She was wearing her Valentine's Day dress, the one that had more hearts than a sacrifice to that goddess Kali in *Indiana Jones and the Temple of Doom*. Shelly bounced out onto the stage and gave a practised twirl. I stepped out rather more carefully since I couldn't see a thing for the bright lights that glared straight into my face.

'Alison Harris, The Most Romantic Woman in the United Kingdom,' boomed Aidan Hobbs, as I took a shaky bow. There was a polite ripple of applause, punctuated by someone shouting, 'Go girl, go!' I squinted at the front row of the audience and there was Candida, sharing her table with a man who looked like a cross between Cyrano de Bergerac and Mahatma Gandhi. Her Svengali film director, without a doubt. Loretta was sitting on Candida's other side, looking utterly bored as she fanned herself with a menu. But Candida beamed straight at me and gave me a thumbs-up sign. I straightened myself up immediately. Suddenly I was filled with a new confidence. Candida was wishing me luck in a Romantic Couples competition. Why would she do that if she was after my man?

Jeremy was announced next. He too shuffled onto the stage like a deer straight into the glare of car headlights. I made a grab for his hand. 'Candida's here to wish us luck,' I whispered. Jeremy stared into the crowd and focused his attention on Candida's new man.

'He's a complete potato head,' Jeremy hissed to me.

'Who?'

'That director guy.'

'I know he's not exactly Mel Gibson. But look at

the chemistry between them. Sexual attraction often follows when people are impressed by somebody's art. What did you say my mother's maiden name was when you filled in the questionnaire, by the way?' I asked then.

'Smith,' Jeremy whispered. 'That is right, isn't it?'

'No. It's not. But I put Smith too, just in case.' I squeezed his hand hard. The other couples had joined us on the stage and the competition was about to begin. Jeremy still stared ahead into the crowd. I assumed he was just nervous and dug him in the ribs when the first round got under way and it was his turn to take up a bow and shoot an arrow into a papier-mâché cupid's heart.

CHAPTER THIRTY-THREE

I almost fainted with surprise when I discovered that Jeremy and I had actually made it to the final.

'And with just one more round to go, we have two couples head to head with twenty-five points apiece,' shouted Aidan. 'They are Shelly Adamson and Luke Connolly representing the United States of America and David Whitworth and Alison Harris representing the United Kingdom of Grand Bretagne!!!'

The crowd applauded us. I looked across to Shelly with the intention of sharing a friendly smile but she was looking straight ahead at the trophy which stood on a table at the back of the room. No doubt she was visualising holding it aloft. Visualising victory. Visualising herself as one half of the Most Romantic Couple in the World. I tried to visualise myself in her place just as hard.

'What do we get for coming second?' I asked Jeremy defeatistly when the vision refused to take shape.

'We are not going to come second,' he said. He was staring at the trophy as well.

I wondered what on earth the final round of the

competition could be. We had answered just about every possible question on each other's faults and foibles. Been through the mother's maiden name bit. I had even correctly guessed Jeremy's blood group, which was a good job since my attempts at hitting the papier-mâché heart with an arrow had resulted in a nasty nick to Jeremy's ear.

The compere's face twisted into a wicked grin as he contemplated what now awaited us. 'How will we choose between these two lovely couples?' he asked. 'There can be no doubt that there's a lot of love going on here. They've told us how well they work as teams. Now let's see them prove it. Gentlemen . . .'

He waved towards the window.

Outside, the guys who looked after the pool stepped forward and started to roll back the covers. It was always covered over in the evenings, in case someone had one too many pina coladas and decided to go skinny-dipping. Loretta also said that the pool contained that chemical that went purple if you peed in it should such an occasion occur during the day.

'What's going on?' I asked Jeremy.

Shelly too, had lost her concentration while she wondered what was to happen next. A swimming competition? I hoped not. But the pool was no longer full of water. Instead, the surface of whatever it now contained had a distinctly custardy texture.

'Do you think we're going in there?' I asked worriedly.

'Only if we lose,' said Jeremy.

'This round is called,' began Aidan Hobbs triumphantly, 'How Deep is Your Love?'

'Ohmigod,' cursed Shelly. 'We're going in.'

'Out there. Hidden in the depths of our pool of passion is just one golden envelope,' the compere continued. 'A golden envelope which actually contains the prize that these good people have been aiming for all evening. Now all they have to do is find it and, as the saying goes, the finders will be the keepers.'

His assistants were already ushering us out of the restaurant and towards the edge of the pool. I took off my clip-on earrings (a present from Candida – I was itching to get them valued as soon as I got home). Shelly looked down in horror at her hand-sequinned evening dress.

'I'm gonna ruin my outfit,' I heard her hiss to Luke.

'Shelly,' he said manfully. 'We've come this far. I'll buy you a new dress when we get home again, honey. I promise.'

Jeremy held my hand tightly. 'We need to have a strategy,' he whispered. 'We'll take one end each and meet in the middle. You start over there.' He pointed at the deep end.

'Jeremy,' I shrieked. 'That's the deep end. I'll drown!!'

'No you won't. There are loads of people to drag you out if you get into trouble. Just take a deep breath and jump on in. Feel your way along the bottom until you need another breath, then come back up, take another deep breath and start again on the next stretch of pool.'

'You make it all sound so easy,' I said sarcastically.

'It is. We've got just as much chance as them. More even. Shelly won't want to get her hair wet. Let alone covered in that muck.'

I wasn't too keen on the idea myself. The stuff in the

pool looked like custard but heaven only knew what it really was.

By now the audience too had filed out into the hotel garden. As I took off my shoes and looked for somewhere safe to put them, I felt the touch of a hand on my arm.

'I'll look after your shoes for you.' It was Candida. 'Good luck.' She kissed me on the cheek. Then she kissed Jeremy. He stood very stiffly as she brushed her lips against each of his cheeks. 'Good luck to you too.'

Almost shaking Candida off, Jeremy rushed to the shallow end of the pool and took up what he considered to be the optimum position for an effective sweep. I took up my own position at the deep end.

'On your marks,' the compere shouted. 'Get set!'

Shelly wobbled on the edge of the pool, still wearing her high heels. Luke had at least taken off his Stetson.

'Go!'

The shouts of the crowd were suddenly deafening. Jeremy jumped straight in and disappeared below the pink. I hesitated for a moment, making sure that he didn't come up for air horribly disfigured by something caustic in the blancmange before I ran to the other end and gingerly let myself down the steps and into the mire. Shelly was just up to her knees in the shallow end, her face already a picture of desperation as she dabbled in the goo for the envelope like my mother looking for a ring in a sink full of cold washing-up water. No such luxury for me. As soon as I let go of the ladder, I went into the pink stuff right over my head. I struggled back up again and took a deep breath through my custard-filled mouth.

Why had Jeremy taken the shallow end, I cursed. He was at least a foot taller than me.

I struggled back to the ladder and clung to it grimly. Part of me protested that this was incredibly stupid. But ten thousand pounds was at stake. And at the other end of the pool, Shelly was still weeping but industrious.

I closed my eyes and let myself drift to the bottom. I thrashed around with my arms as I fell, after all, who was to say that the envelope was at the bottom. I was feeling pretty weightless myself.

Coming back up for air, I gasped like a grounded fish. My head was spinning and the crowd around the pool merged into a blur of shouting faces. I couldn't see any of my fellow competitors for the blancmange in my eyes. Then Jeremy's head popped up.

'Got it?' he yelled.

'No!' I yelled back.

'Then keep going. Come on. Dive, girl, dive.'

Back down again into the murky pink deep.

Was this what it was like to be in the womb, I wondered? More likely, it was what it felt like to be a dying fly in someone's Angel Delight. I seemed to take ages to sink this time. When my feet hit the bottom, I had to go straight back up again to breathe anyway.

'What are you doing?' Jeremy shouted when he saw me clinging onto the ladder again. It was all right for him, his head never went beneath the surface. But at least he was working his way towards me.

'One more time, Ali,' he yelled to me. 'You know you can do it. One more time.'

I ducked my head under. I was exhausted. So what if I hadn't found the envelope? This dive would definitely be my last. My lungs felt ready to burst. I am going to die down here, I thought. I am going to die in a swimming pool full of synthetic, strawberry gunk for the sake of ten thousand measly pounds. I would almost have been happy if Shelly or Luke had found the envelope then. Anything to get out of this terrible game.

Then, as if by divine intervention, my hand touched the sharp edge of what could only be the envelope. No sooner had I touched it, though, than I had pushed it a little further out of reach. Though I really, really needed to take another breath, I decided to go for it one last time. I thrashed out in the direction of that elusive prize. My fingers closed upon it and I kicked off from the bottom of the pool to get to the surface. But my escape met with some resistance. Mine were not the only fingers clinging on.

I wanted to scream with frustration. I couldn't even see who my opponent was. Perhaps it was Jeremy. But the odds were that it wasn't. I could feel the envelope slipping from my grasp. The only way that I could ensure that Jeremy and I took the money home was for me to fight for it now. I kicked out in the pinkness. My feet made contact with someone soft and suddenly the envelope was all mine.

'I've done it!' I broke through the surface holding the envelope aloft. 'I've done it! I've done it!' Hands appeared from all sides to pull me out of the swamp. I lay at the side of the pool, clutching the envelope to my chest and trying desperately to get the muck out of my lungs and some air in.

Gradually the others surfaced. They looked bewildered as they were pulled out of the pool, and desperate when they realised that the competition was well and truly over.

Shelly exploded with a wail of despair. Luke sat beside her, trying and failing to get her to shut up. Jeremy staggered up the side of the pool to collapse alongside me. He was discreetly clutching his balls.

'I did it!' I said. Lack of oxygen had left me somewhat dazed.

'Yeah, you did it,' he said, licking some pink stuff off my forehead. 'I might even be able to forgive you for kicking me in the balls.'

'Well done, Ali,' Candida gingerly kissed one of my pink cheeks. 'I knew it would be you.'

Jeremy turned away from her and concentrated on rinsing out his hair.

'Well done, Ali,' said Loretta. 'Though I thought I was going to have to do the Heimlich on you at one point.'

'I've got a fine pair of lungs,' I told her. 'My mother always said so.'

Just a brief rub down with a towel, then we took to the podium.

'Congratulations, Alison Harris and David Whitworth!' The compere shouted. 'You are *Complete Woman International*'s Most Romantic Couple in the entire world!!!!'

'Hurrah!!!' screamed the crowd.

Shelly burst into tears again immediately. Jeremy and I just looked at each other. We were still slightly stunned. Marjorie Pine led the applause and soon the whole room rose to give us a standing ovation while the *Complete Woman International* lackeys prodded us towards the stage to pick up our prize.

'I can't understand it,' Shelly was wailing. 'They haven't even set a date to get married to each other. How can that be romantic?'

Even as I looked at the cheque in my hand, I had to agree that it hardly seemed fair. How could romance be measured by the ability to find an envelope in a vat of blancmange? I mean, I'd even managed to kick the supposed love of my life in his family jewels in the process.

'Waaah! It's just not fair!!'

Shelly and Luke didn't pick up their 'World's Second Most Romantic Couple's Prize' that night. Under the circumstances, Marjorie decided that Shelly might prefer to have the consolation prize hamper of fresh fruit and flowers delivered to her room.

But in her haste to get away and lick her wounds, Shelly missed the coup of the holiday. Aidan Hobbs was wrapping the competition up with a few gags about future in-laws when Vadim Caravaggio asked if he might take the stage.

Probably hoping for a film part, Aidan stepped down without a murmur and Vadim took the mike. He was considerably taller than Aidan and had to bend down so that he looked like a nosferatu bending over a virgin's corpse.

'Tonight has been all about romance,' Vadim began. 'And while I don't wish to steal the glory of this wonderful moment from the Most Romantic Couple in the World, I'm sure that in the spirit of true love, they won't mind me taking this opportunity to make a little announcement of my own.'

The crowd was silent with expectation.

'Many of you here will know and love my charming companion Miss Candida Bianca. Candida and I have known each other for several years now, and during that time I have been privileged to come to know her not just as a screen idol, but as a woman. A living, breathing woman with a heart of pure gold.'

I looked across at Loretta in time to see her roll her eyes towards heaven.

'Since the moment we met, Candida has been one of my best friends, and for the past six months, she has also been my lover.'

Gasps all round. *Hello!* had always contested that she had a wild and unassailable crush on Brad Pitt.

'And tonight, I am incredibly thrilled, delighted and ecstatic to announce that Candida Bianca has consented to be my wife . . .'

Ta-daa!

'Wow!'

The spotlight swivelled to catch her in its one-eyed glare. Candida shrugged her shoulders and seemed, oddly for her, to shrink into herself. Vadim bounded down from the stage to sweep her up in his arms. Aidan Hobbs pressed her to take up the mike and say a few words herself.

'Thank you,' she muttered quietly. 'I guess the drinks are on me.'

Despite the fact that the drinks didn't have to be on anyone – this was Antigua's premier all-inclusive resort – the crowd flooded towards the bar, sweeping up Candida and Vadim as it went, until only Jeremy and I were left, all alone, by the pool, with my tiara and an envelope full of dosh.

'My God,' I said. 'I wasn't expecting that.'

'Neither was I,' said Jeremy.

'Shall we go and join them. Toast the other happy couple?'

'Think I'll just wash my hair first,' said Jeremy.

I happily trotted behind him to our hut.

CHAPTER THIRTY-FOUR

And so we had come to our very last night in Antigua. After an hour long shower to get the custard out of our hair, Jeremy and I decided that we would take one last moonlit stroll along the beach that had almost become our own. As we rounded the headland, we stopped and sat down on the soft sand from where we had the best view of the glittering lights in the harbour in front of our hotel.

'This has been such a magical holiday,' I began. 'I can't believe it's nearly over. I've had such a wonderful time.'

'Me too,' Jeremy assured me. 'But not just because we've been here. It's been most magical for me because I have been here with you, Ali.'

'Do you mean that?'

'You know I do. And that part of the holiday doesn't have to end when we get off the plane at Heathrow, you know.'

'But you've got to go back to Warsaw in a week,' I said sadly.

'Yes. But I don't have to go back alone.'

I looked at him disbelievingly. 'Jeremy,' I murmured tentatively. 'What are you suggesting to me?'

'What do you think I'm suggesting? Listen, I know that Warsaw sounds like an awful place but it really isn't as bad as you think. Sure, you can't get a suntan quite like the one we've got here, but we'll be together. And one day soon we'll return to Antigua to start a family.'

I rubbed at my ear. The one that had felt as though it was full of water since that first afternoon in the pool. Something must have been distorting his words.

'Start a family?' I murmured.

'Yes. You and me. I know we're still young, Ali. And I know that you've been hurt in the past. But I feel that this is the right moment for us, don't you? You're the right girl for me. I've never met anyone that I felt so free to be myself with. I just know I've got to be with you for the rest of my life. Ali Harris,' he paused significantly. 'Will you marry me?'

By the time the question had got through my waxy deposits and hit my auditory cortex I was answering Jeremy with a kiss. Simultaneously, the Most Romantic Couple Competition firework display started by the pool and a glittering rocket seared across the sky from the bay. As it burst into a huge green and red carnation of glittering light above our heads it seemed to be blessing us. An omen.

'Yes,' I told him. 'Yes, of course I'll marry you.'

We tumbled back onto the sand, kissing more passionately than we had ever done before. However many lies we had told in the past two weeks, we were definitely not pretending to be the World's Most Romantic Couple that night.

CHAPTER THIRTY-FIVE

For the first time in my life, I didn't feel sad as I packed my case at the end of a holiday. Except that it wasn't just my case any more. It was our case. Jeremy said so. He had started the packing and thrown all our things in together.

'We're not going to be one of those dreadful "his and hers" couples,' he told me. 'What's mine is yours now and vice versa.' I felt like singing with joy when I heard those sweet, sweet words.

As we waited to board our plane back to Heathrow at the tiny airport, I caught sight of Luke and Shelly checking in for their own flight home. Shelly was wearing dark glasses and a big floppy straw hat so that her face was totally obscured, as though she was trying to leave the island incognito. In fact, I only knew for sure that it was her because there simply couldn't have been that many pink gingham luggage sets in the world.

Shelly and Luke stood silently next to the passport control desk. I saw him try to give her an affectionate peck on the cheek but she shrugged him off irritably.

'Not taking the title of the United States Most

Romantic Couple very seriously are they?' Jeremy commented, as he too saw the altercation.

'Oh don't,' I said. 'It's quite sad really. Shelly had her heart set on the world title.'

'Well, I don't think they'll last long enough to fight for it again. They're not really meant for each other.'

'What do you mean?' I asked him. 'What makes you think that?'

'Well, promise me you won't take this the wrong way, but that night, when you were sick and had to go back to our room, Shelly accosted me down on the beach and made me quite a proposition.'

'You're joking?'

''Fraid not. She just kept on and on about how much she had always wanted an Englishman for a lover. How Luke was just an insensitive brute only interested in watching baseball and mending his Chevvy. She wants a real romantic. She even asked me if I knew some poetry.'

'Wow,' I said, remembering my own brush with one half of the USA's Most Romantic Couple. 'So it really was all a facade.'

'Yeah. Not like us.'

'We started out as a facade,' I reminded him.

'But it's the real thing now, isn't it?'

I was so happy, I could have flown home under my own steam.

But our kiss was interrupted by a tap on my shoulder. It was Candida. Loretta hovered in the background, bowed down by the weight of a presidential party's worth of bags.

'Hi. I'm not interrupting anything, am I?' Candida asked.

I smiled magnanimously. She could break up that

one kiss because I knew that I would be kissing Jeremy Baxter for the rest of his life.

Candida rifled through her plush leather Kelly bag, the only thing she was carrying, for something to give us. Finally, she pulled out a little leather-bound notebook and scribbled something with her Mont Blanc propelling pencil.

'Just in case you're ever in Los Angeles,' she said, handing the scrap to Jeremy and looking him deep in the eye.

'Thanks,' he said. 'I'd give you my number in Warsaw but I'm sure you'll have far grander places to stay when you start filming.'

Candida fixed him with a particularly coquettish gaze. 'I'm sure that your place has its charms.'

'Quite,' I said, linking my arm through his. I know it must have looked petty and possessive, but I told myself that I was just eager to make sure we didn't miss our flight.

'You flying home today too?' Jeremy asked Candida, as I started to drag him away.

'Yes,' she said. 'Same flight as Luke and Shelly, I think.'

'Jeremy, they're boarding our flight now,' I told him. They were. Honestly.

'You'd better go,' said Candida. 'I'll see you guys around.'

'Oh, and congratulations on your engagement,' I called after her.

Candida raised her hand in a pretty weak wave.

'Do you think we will see her again?' I asked when Candida finally headed off in the direction of the check-in desk for the flight back to Florida. I couldn't help smiling as I watched Shelly wrap her arm possessively around Luke's back at Candida's approach.

'I doubt it,' Jeremy grunted. 'Real stars like her just play at being friends with people like us.'

'Do you think so? Oh, well. At least I got a real Versace dress out of the whole experience.'

'Yeah,' said Jeremy vaguely. He seemed to be dragging his feet as we got closer to the departure gate.

'Come on,' I chivvied him one more time. 'I don't want to miss our flight. We'd be stuck here for another week before the next one came.'

'Stuck on this beautiful island? What a drag,' said Jeremy sarcastically.

I can't say I was desperate to get back home myself but I had a vague recollection of having things like a cat and a job to go back to, so we finally boarded our shiny jet and left the magical island in the comforts of first class. As I watched Antigua shrinking to a little, blue and green postcard picture while the plane rose higher and higher, our time there had already started to feel like a wonderful dream. At the other end of the flight London loomed like a big, grey splodge of reality. Though a very much better reality than I had left behind now that it had Jeremy in it. For the foreseeable future. Forever.

When we touched down at Heathrow, the weather was typically appalling for the time of year. Determined grey sleet battered the huge picture windows of the terminal as we drifted, still dressed in shorts and sun hats, to pick up our luggage from the baggage carousel.

'Ah well. This is it,' said Jeremy as he manfully pushed our luggage trolley through the green channel in customs. 'The end of our holiday but the start of our new lives. How do you feel?'

'I feel like I'm the luckiest woman in the whole world,' I told him sincerely. 'The only thing that could make me happier would be if Mum and Dad were in the arrivals lounge with a big cheque from our Lottery syndicate.'

'How shallow,' Jeremy laughed.

In fact there was no-one there to greet us. It was odd, since my family are pretty big on airport scenes. But perhaps Mum was still annoyed that I'd got out of Gran's birthday tea. All the better, I thought, as Jeremy and I kissed in the cab back to Brindlesham. I didn't want the rest of the world to intrude on us just yet.

'Back to your place?' Jeremy asked, as the taxi sped us through the city boundary.

'Yes,' I said firmly. 'No, make that my Mum and Dad's. I want to tell them the good news. Tonight.'

'Good idea,' Jeremy squeezed my hand. 'And then we'll go and see my folks. I just know that Mum is going to be over the moon to land a daughter-in-law like you.'

'Do you really think so?'

'Of course. I couldn't have done any better.'

'Charming. My Mum will probably pass out with joy when we tell her. She never really much liked David . . .'

Jeremy put his finger to my lips. 'Sssh,' he said. 'Now that the holiday's over, we've no need to mention that particular name ever again. Agreed?'

'Agreed,' I nodded happily.

'Though I have to say that I'm eternally grateful to him for staying out of your life just long enough so that I could take his place.'

Yes, David, I thought. Thanks for that. Whoever thought that the cloud that marked the end of my relationship with David Whitworth would have such a huge lump of solid silver beneath?

But I should have known that everything had been going just a little too well when I saw the police car parked at the top of Mum and Dad's driveway.

As we paid the taxi driver and unloaded our bags from the boot, I continued to chatter blithely to Jeremy, not thinking for one moment that the patrol car had anything to do with my family. As far as I was concerned, the police were probably staking out the dodgy rabble that had moved into number thirty-three. My mother, who was usually quite tolerant of fraud and other minor misdemeanours amongst her friends and neighbours, had phoned the police to tip them off about the Trustcott family's out-of-date road tax disc after one of their wild-looking children put chewing gum in Berkeley's fur.

'They've come for me,' Jeremy joked as we rang Mum and Dad's doorbell. Then he put his arm around me and nuzzled my ear. We were going to be the perfect picture of togetherness when Mum finally opened the door.

Instead we were met by Jo.

'Deep shit, Ali,' was all she said. 'Deep shit.'

CHAPTER THIRTY-SIX

The police car was indeed something to do with my family. More importantly, the two burly-looking policemen who sat drinking tea at the kitchen table were something to do with me.

'Ali,' said my mother desperately. 'The police are here.'

How could I have missed them? They filled up most of the kitchen in their regulation winter jackets. Seeing me arrive, the younger of the two retrieved his helmet which had been sitting like a tea-cosy on the middle of the kitchen table and put it on. All the better to arrest me in.

'What's going on?' I asked. I was relieved of my holiday bags by one of my sisters and sat down opposite the two strangers to await an explanation.

'Miss Alison Harris?' asked the bigger of the two men. 'Otherwise known as Ali Harris?'

'That's me,' I replied. 'What's happened? Has my cat been run over? Is my flat OK?'

'Miss Alison Harris, you are under arrest under suspicion of a charge of grievous bodily harm. You do not have to say anything . . .' he continued, exactly as they do on TV. 'But it may harm your defence if you do not mention now something which you later rely on in court.' The whole world started to spin sickeningly around me. 'Anything you do say may be given in evidence.'

'Hang on a minute,' interrupted my mother, as she tried to prise the policeman's hand from my arm, while he simultaneously clapped my wrists in a pair of shining handcuffs. 'Grievous bodily harm? Have you gone mad? Look at her, for heaven's sake. She's not a violent criminal. She's not big enough to hurt a fly. Let her go. You've obviously got the wrong girl. Tell him he's got the wrong girl,' she pleaded with my Dad.

'I'm afraid not,' said the policeman. 'Come with us, please, Miss Harris.'

'Where are you taking her?' shrieked my mother as I was led out into the hallway. 'Where are you taking her? Don't worry, Alison,' she called to me. 'This is all a terrible mistake. We'll rescue you as soon as we can. Get the car out, John. Alison, we're going to follow you to the station.'

'This must be a dream,' I murmured to myself, as I was manhandled out of the house and towards the waiting police car. I wondered if the sleeping tablets I had taken to get me through the long flight home were having dodgy side effects. Really dodgy side effects. I mean, me, arrested on a charge of grievous bodily harm? What an insane proposition! Oh, how Jeremy would laugh when I finally woke up and told him about this nightmare.

But right then, in the real world, his handsome tanned face drained of all its colour, as flanked by my hysterical parents, Jeremy watched me being driven away.

I had been dying for a cup of tea since our plane touched down at Heathrow. Never in a million years did I expect that I would get my first cup of PG Tips at the Brindlesham police station. As I sat in a miserable, bare-walled interview room waiting for the duty solicitor to arrive, the over-strong brew congealed in its plastic cup. I knew I wouldn't be able to touch a thing until somebody came into the room with a big smile on his or her face and told me that there had been a serious administrative mistake and that they were really after someone else.

When they did, I told myself, I would sue the bloody Brindlesham Police Force from there until Christmas.

But pretty soon the duty solicitor arrived and I heard the full details of my charge once more, with the in-flight alcohol almost totally worn off and reality slowly dawning. My solicitor, the elderly Mr Wagstaff, looked barely competent enough to tie his own shoelaces as he sat a couple of feet behind me while the officer in charge of the investigation read out the charge. I, Alison Harris, was accused of indecent assault occasioning actual bodily harm, when, on the 2nd February 1998, I did apply a caustic substance to the genitalia of one David Ainsley Devereux Whitworth with the intention of causing him grievous bodily harm.

'But it was only Hot Stuff Heat Rub!' I shrieked. Mr Wagstaff leaned forward and placed a quieting hand on my arm.

'I'd like to request a few moments with my client,' he told the inspector. The tape was switched off while Mr Wagstaff explained my current predicament to me. Best keep quiet, he suggested. And the bottom line?

Never ever cross a man who has a Police Inspector for a big brother.

As you can probably imagine, David's mother, Maureen Whitworth, had hated me from the very start of our relationship, since I was, in her eyes, nothing but an adulterous fast piece who had de-throned the lovely Lisa, queen of cross-stitch and batch baking, future mother of the kind of children that never shouted for sweets at supermarket tills. David's father was fairly ambiguous in his feelings towards me, but erred on the disapproving side for the sake of his marriage.

David's younger sister Marie would bring up the subject of Lisa at every possible opportunity. Every conversation I had with Marie would run along the lines of, 'I've got terrible thrush today, Ali. Lisa never used to get thrush. She always took such good care of her diet . . . and David's.' Even the dog's ear infection provoked a conversation about Lisa's amazing way with little fluffy animals.

Yes, apart from David, his elder brother Barry was the only member of the Whitworth family who seemed to rate me slightly higher than the average serial killer.

If I called round the Whitworths' house to discover that David wasn't home from work yet (he had to go back to live with his folks while Lisa sorted out selling the starter home they had bought together), I would be left standing on the doorstep unless Barry was in. It would always be Barry who invited me over the threshold and made me a cup of tea. Barry was probably the only member of that family apart from David who actually knew what I did for a living. He would always ask about my exciting secretarial life in the engineering industry and in turn he would regale me with long and convoluted stories about Brindlesham's criminal low-life, or at least the ones that I had known at school.

When David and I announced our engagement, I knew that I was resigning myself to life with the mother-in-law from hell, but that realisation was slightly counter-balanced by the fact that I would be getting the brother-in-law of my dreams. Barry Whitworth was funny, warm and generous. He would always make me welcome. And with a bit of luck, he would last far longer than his mum.

That all changed, of course.

One day, while David was still looking for a place of his own, I decided to pay him a surprise visit at his mum's. When I got to the house, it looked as though I had called at the wrong time even though I knew that David had one of his flexi-days off and had said that he would be at home all day. It was winter, four o'clock-ish. Dark already. But there were no lights on in the house. I rang the doorbell anyway, since having come that far, I thought I might as well be sure. The bell rang out in the empty hallway. Nothing. I rang it once more for luck. Then, just as I was about to leave, a light was flicked on in the hallway and Barry lumbered towards the door.

'Who the fuck is it now?' he grumbled as he pulled

back the latch, but when he saw me, his face broke into a generous smile. 'Hello, lovely,' he said. I could tell by the way that his hair was sticking out at all angles that I had dragged him from his bed.

'Is David in?' I asked.

'No,' said Barry. 'But you can come in and wait for him, if you want.'

I had done it so many times before, I agreed without question. Normally, Barry would lumber back to bed to continue sleeping off his hard nightshift, leaving me to help myself with the kettle and the biscuit tin. But this time, he joined me for a cup of tea instead.

'Shouldn't you be in bed?' I asked.

'Nah. I've been asleep for four hours already this afternoon. I want to talk to you.'

'I don't want to keep you up,' I told him.

'Darling,' he said. 'You could keep me up all night.'

From that very first innuendo I knew that something was awry. Barry had never said anything like that to me before. Instead, his comments had always been confined to the brother-in-lawly, if you know what I mean.

Anyway I made the tea and carried Barry's Postman Pat mug through into the sitting room. His parents were away, visiting David's batty grandmother in the north – the only pensioner more loathsome than my own toxic gran. David's sister always went to night-school for a Spanish class on Mondays. I had timed my visit for minimum family contact and I had got it. Barry and I were very much alone.

'Did David say when he was going to be back?' I asked desperately, when Barry squeezed his manly bulk into the chintzy two-seater sofa beside me.

'He didn't say. But I don't suppose it will be anytime soon. He said that if you turned up I should look after you . . .'

I gulped tea nervously as Barry slung his arm along the back of the sofa behind my head. It seemed a matter of mere seconds before that arm was resting along my shoulders. Next thing I knew, Barry was pulling me towards him, his lips puckered up like some dreadful cartoon character waiting for a kiss.

'I've always fancied you,' Barry told me.

'Eeek!' I said. Or words to that effect.

'Come on, Ali, just a little kiss,' he pleaded as I twisted desperately within his manly grasp. 'David won't ever know.'

'No, Barry, I can't,' I protested, as Barry's hot wet lips collided with my burning cheek. 'Please don't kiss me. I don't want to be unfaithful to David.'

'I'm not asking you to be unfaithful,' Barry told me roughly. 'I'm only after a one off shag for heaven's sake.'

He didn't get one, needless to say. By the careful application of a cup of scalding hot tea to his groin, I managed to distract Barry for just long enough to evade his sticky grasp and I was soon on the other side of the room, defending my honour with my Benetton rucksack.

'Aw! Fucking hell,' said Barry. 'What did you do that for?'

'I didn't mean to hurt you,' I lied.

'You got me up for this, you bitch. I could have you done for fucking GBH!'

'Really? And have me tell everyone at the police station exactly why I needed to defend myself?' I retorted. (As if they would have believed me, as I was currently discovering.)

I fled the house just as David arrived home. I didn't even let him get inside, but made him take me to the pub forthwith. I struggled all night long to bring myself to tell him how his brother had tried it on with me but never quite got around to spilling the beans. Fortunately it seemed, neither did Barry. That evening I kept David away from the house until I felt sure that Barry would have left for his nightshift once more.

Barry never mentioned the incident again, but from that day onwards I had one less ally than usual *chez* Whitworth. Now, however, that terrible night in the Whitworths' chintzy sitting room was coming back to haunt me in truly nightmarish style.

'It's most unusual for the Crown Prosecution Services to decide to intervene in this kind of domestic incident,' Mr Wagstaff mused as he flicked through the papers pertaining to my arrest. 'Most unusual.'

Not when the chief witness for the prosecution was related to the local police inspector, I thought wryly. David's brother must have encouraged him to bring a charge against me. Grievous Bodily Harm by way of the severe psychological damage imposed upon him when I Hot Stuff Heat Rubbed his dick all those weeks ago. David couldn't even have spelt the charge on his own.

I couldn't understand it.

'But he got up and walked away,' I told my solicitor. 'Believe me, I didn't do that man any physical damage at all.'

'I'm sure you're right, but we're not talking about physical damage any more. Mr Whitworth is claiming that he has been unable to maintain an erection since the incident. Every time he tries to have sex, he says that he is haunted by an image of your evil face and it quite puts him off the idea of making love to another woman.'

'If only he'd suffered from that before all this happened,' I thought out loud. 'So what's going to happen to me next? And when can I go home?'

'I'm afraid you won't be able to leave the station just yet, Alison. You'll probably be bailed on the condition that you stay well away from Mr Whitworth. And then the matter will be taken to the magistrates' court. With a bit of luck, the magistrates will decide that there is no case to answer and that will be the end of it. The whole matter certainly seems ridiculous to me. But these things can go either way,' he added, sucking his teeth. 'I don't want to get your hopes up.'

'No danger of that,' I told him. 'My hopes are hiding in my boots right now.'

Mr Wagstaff approximated a smile.

'I'll do my very best for you, Alison. Whatever happens, I'm sure I don't need to tell you that if you are bailed tonight, under no circumstances must you bring yourself to the attention of the police in any other way until all this is sorted out.'

'I haven't come to the attention of the police in twenty-five years,' I said indignantly, neglecting to mention the horror of Top Shop or the time when the local bobby came round to tick me off in front of my parents about roller-skating in the school playground during the summer holidays.

'Good. Now you just relax and have another cup of

tea,' said Mr Wagstaff helpfully. 'Meanwhile I'll try to grease the wheels of justice.'

He left me alone again and soon another cup of thick brown stuff masquerading as a tasty beverage was slopped onto the table before me by a spotty police constable who looked as though he was a fifth-former on work experience.

I looked at my watch. I had been at the police station for almost three hours. Twenty-four hours earlier I had been kissing the palm tree outside our beach hut goodbye. As I've said before, what a difference a day makes. This time, just twenty-four hours had taken me from the Caribbean to the clink.

CHAPTER THIRTY-SEVEN

I had thought that I couldn't be held at the police station against my will for longer than a couple of hours. So much for my legal knowledge, gained almost entirely from watching *Murder One* and *Inspector Morse*. After much whispering in the corridor Mr Wagstaff came to tell me that, as far as he was concerned, the worst had happened. I wasn't going to be bailed that night. Instead, because of the seriousness of the charge against me, I was going to be held until the earliest possible opportunity for me to appear before a magistrate. In the eyes of the police, apparently, I was a danger to the public at large.

'You mean, they're not letting me out tonight?' I whimpered.

As Mr Wagstaff nodded I seemed to hear a bell tolling in my mind.

'They can't do this to me!' I wailed. 'I want to see my mum and dad.'

'Just try to get some sleep,' said Mr Wagstaff.

'How can I get some sleep? I'm worried out of my mind.'

Mr Wagstaff just shrugged and asked the officer on duty to let him back out into the corridor. As the metal door of the cell I had been moved into clanged shut behind him, I started to shiver uncontrollably. Partly through cold. (I was still in my shorts, not having been given time to change into something more sensible for February in a bare-walled cell.) But mostly I shivered through fear. I had led a pretty sheltered life up until that point. My years at St Olive's High School for Girls had prepared me for a variety of emergencies that could be averted with a bit of skilful darning, but for nothing so seedy as spending the night in the slammer.

Not that I could sleep at all on that hard bed with its itchy grey blankets. The tales of terrible inmates with which Barry had regaled me all those years ago back when we were still friends, suddenly seemed horribly real. Closing time brought in a bevy of drunken brawlers. A football match held earlier that day had turned out badly for the supporters of Brindlesham FC (not that it ever turned out otherwise), and a fight had broken out on the High Street. Now the protagonists of the warring factions of supporters were being held in cells on opposite sides of the corridor and the fight continued verbally, with insults and tuneless songs hurled backwards and forwards for hours. If I hadn't been a girl, the duty officer said, he would have put some of them in with me. I was quite an inconvenience to them, taking up a whole cell on my own.

'Well, why don't you let me go home?' I asked him.

'What? A dangerous lunatic, like you?' he replied.

Stinging from his insult, I lay down on the hard bed

and pulled a blanket right up to my ears. Where was my knight in shining armour? How long would it take someone – Mum, Dad, Jeremy, anyone – to convince the police that I didn't really need to be locked up? Apart from David Whitworth, I literally had never hurt a fly in my life. In fact I was the kind of girl who constructed elaborate spider ladders to rescue the blighters from the bath rather than flush them straight down the plughole as Emma did.

Finally, exhausted by lack of sleep, jet lag and worry, I started to drift away into a fitful doze. But just as I was dropping off, the little window in the door of my cell was flipped open and someone shone a bright light right onto my face.

'Just checking that you're not killing yourself in there,' someone laughed cruelly.

'Far more likely that I'll die of sleep deprivation,' I snapped back.

Just five hours later, at six o'clock in the morning, I was woken again with my breakfast. Congealed scrambled egg and two pieces of toast that sprang back into shape like rubber if you tried to fold them. I couldn't help thinking back wistfully to that last breakfast on Antigua. Fresh pineapple cut into thick chunky slices. Big smiling slabs of melon, with juice that dribbled down your chin when you bit into it. As I chewed the reconstituted egg, a tear ran down my face and into the corner of my mouth.

'Oh, Mum. Oh, Dad. Oh, Jeremy,' I cried. 'Somebody please come and rescue me.'

Then the door to my cell was thrown open, and for the first time in my life, I was overjoyed to see someone as short and ugly as Mr Wagstaff.

'You're in luck,' he said. 'You can see the magistrates this morning. Right away. Tidy yourself up.'

That was a tall order. I didn't exactly have access to the full range of primping products I need to make myself look even half decent after a good night's sleep, let alone a night on a concrete bench. A female officer accompanied me to the prisoners' bathroom and I had a quick, cold shower with some scratchy soap. After that, I had to put my shorts back on, and my sandals, still itchy with sand. Then I was led the short distance across the road from the police station to the magistrates' court in handcuffs.

Fortunately, the magistrates, as I had hoped, looked a pair of kind women, more inclined to sentence someone to duty on the cake stall at the WI fete than community service. And despite the fact that I looked as though I had just escaped from an amateur dramatics production of *South Pacific* on acid, I was released on bail pending committal for trial.

When I finally was allowed to go, after handing in my passport so that I couldn't flee the country (apparently the fact that I had just come back from Antigua made that highly possible), Dad and Mum were waiting at the police station, together with Jeremy, who had insisted on coming too, to collect me. When I saw Jeremy again, I couldn't help bursting into tears. It was a mixture of relief and joy. The twenty-four hours I had been kept in the cells at the station seemed like the longest twenty-four hours in history. More importantly, it was the longest time Jeremy and I had spent apart since flying to Antigua.

'Thank goodness you're here,' I said, flinging my arms around Jeremy's neck.

'Hmm. Well there's no need to look pleased to see your poor worried parents as well,' said my mother. 'I've been up half the night sick with fear.'

'Oh, I'm sorry, Mum,' I said, flinging my arms around her and my father too.

'What happened?' Jeremy asked urgently. 'We heard you were being charged with attacking someone. They've got it all wrong, of course. Tell me they have. They're letting you off the charge, aren't they?'

I shook my head sadly.

'They didn't get it wrong?'

'Well, they did get it wrong,' I told them all. 'I swear they did. But they're not letting me off yet. I've got to come back again next week. I'm only out on bail.'

'A daughter of mine on bail!' my mother shrieked, as she pressed the back of her hand to her forehead in a dramatic swoon. 'Just like a common criminal.'

'I'm not a criminal, Mum. You know that. It's all just a ridiculous misunderstanding. Mr Wagstaff says he'll sort it out.'

'Who on earth are you charged with attacking?' asked my father.

'David. David Whitworth.'

'David? But he's a grown man. How could you possibly have attacked him?'

'Let's just say I went for his Achilles Heel,' I told them flatly, almost smiling at the euphemism but not quite finding it funny enough to share at that point.

When we got back to the house, my younger sisters

tumbled out to meet us on the driveway. For once, their main concern wasn't what gaudy nick-nacks I had picked up for them in duty free. Instead they had tactfully decided to leave searching my suitcases for pressies for a little while. In fact Jo, who had been doing screen-printing during her obligatory creative arts period at school, had a present for me instead.

'It's still a bit wet,' she explained, as she handed me the voluminous white T-shirt. 'I started it as soon as Mum said what was going on but I really expected you to be in a bit longer to give it a chance to dry out.'

'Thanks,' I said, unfurling the T-shirt so that I could see the full glory of her design. 'Alison Harris is inocent!' it said, in big drippy letters. I wondered if she had missed the extra 'n' out of 'innocent' by mistake or deliberately, so that she could fit the exclamation mark in instead.

'I was going to make them for the whole family,' she continued. 'But they've let you go now so I won't have to bother.'

'I'm only out on bail, Jo,' I explained. 'This fiasco is far from over yet.'

'A daughter of mine on bail,' sighed Mum once more.

'But it will be over soon, my love,' said Jeremy comfortingly. 'We'll get the best lawyers in the land to make sure that this ridiculous farce never even gets as far as court.'

'We can't afford the best lawyers in the land,' I whined. 'I don't think we can even afford Mr Wagstaff for much longer.'

'You're not using Mr Wagstaff of Wagstaff and

Chivers?!' my sister Jane exclaimed. 'Oh, Ali, he's an absolute disaster. When some friends of mine used him to help them move house, he did a search on the wrong property and the whole deal fell through. Not only that, but he charged them for the time he took to make the cock-up in the first place.'

'This gets worse and worse,' I said, sinking into the sofa and accepting a cup of tea thrust at me from one side and a chocolate biscuit from the other.

'We've got to look on the bright side,' Jeremy twittered. 'When we flew back from our holiday yesterday, we were both on cloud nine, weren't we?'

I looked up into his shining eyes and nodded. 'We were. We really were.'

'We had plenty to celebrate then and none of that has changed.'

'You mean?'

'Yes. I think it's time to make the announcement, don't you? Might help everybody sleep just that little bit easier tonight.'

'You say it,' I whispered.

'No, we'll say it together.'

We both took deep breaths and counted to three, then blurted out variously, 'We've got engaged / we're getting married.'

Mum just look confused.

'We've decided to get married,' Jeremy said more slowly, clutching my shaking hand.

'Oh!'

Mum's face crumpled up like a discarded hankie and she burst into tears.

'That wasn't quite the effect we were after.'

'Mum,' I said, wrapping a comforting arm around

her shoulders. 'Mum, it's good news. We're in love. We're getting married. Isn't that fantastic?'

She nodded and blew her nose loudly. 'It's wonderful. Really good news, darling. It's just that it's all come as a bit of a shock. I don't know how much more excitement I can take today. I might have to take one of my pills. John, take me upstairs,' she told my father.

'Dad? Are you pleased?' I asked.

He nodded, but didn't actually say anything. Then he shook Jeremy's hand perfunctorily and helped my mother to her bed.

'Well, that went down like a bacon sarnie at a Jewish wake,' I muttered. 'What do you think, Jo?' She had remained downstairs and was rifling through my suitcases. She pulled out a sarong patterned with gaudy tropical fish and held it against her.

'I think this is lovely.'

'Actually, Jo,' I said, pulling it away from her grubby mitts. 'I wasn't referring to the shopping. Besides, that's for Emma. This is for you.' I pointed out a T-shirt printed with the name of our hotel.

'Great,' she said unenthusiastically.

'Well, if you don't like the design, you could always paint over it.' Jo snatched up the T-shirt and left us alone.

'This is brilliant,' I said sarcastically. 'Wonder if your mother is going to be this pleased as well?'

'She'll be happy enough,' Jeremy assured me.

'When will we tell her?'

'Er, perhaps not just yet. We'll wait until we've found out more about this ridiculous charge you've been landed with, shall we? I think if my mum had to hear as much news as your mother had today, she'd need to take more than a pill to sort her out. She's very highly strung.'

'Aren't all mothers?' I asked.

'It doesn't matter,' said Jeremy soothingly. 'What matters is you and I. That we're happy. And that there are no secrets between us. Ali, I think I need to know exactly what happened between you and David Whitworth now. The whole truth.'

'Sounds like I'm in court already,' I joked.

'You know what I mean. Tell me everything. Not just the bits you told the solicitor. I want to be able to understand what's going on.'

'Well,' I said, bracing myself for disaster. 'It happened like this.'

'I'll stand by you,' Jeremy said determinedly when I had finished telling him the full story. Well, it was almost the full story. In the end, instead of the Hot Stuff Heat Rub aspect, I told him that I had kicked David in the balls, accidentally, while we were having a row. I know it's even more violent, but somehow it sounded less sexual than rubbing something in and I didn't want Jeremy to know that I had been sexual with David so recently.

'I'm so lucky to have you,' I murmured into Jeremy's hair as he gave me the hundredth of many reassuring hugs.

'We'll get you through this, Ali. The man's an idiot. He's obviously overreacting. Thousands of men get kicked in the balls every day. But how many of them go and prosecute?'

'Those with policemen for brothers,' I said sadly. 'Oh, Jeremy, are you serious about standing by me?'

He nodded.

'I don't know what I'd do without you.'

'Well, I'm afraid you'll have to practise for a little while,' said Jeremy then. 'I got a call from the office this afternoon. The place is in a mess. They want me to go back to Poland right away.'

'How right away?' I asked him desperately.

'Right away, like tomorrow morning.'

Waaaah!!! I didn't think I had any tears left in me that day, but I did.

CHAPTER THIRTY-EIGHT

I couldn't even see him to the airport. Next day, while Jeremy was boarding a plane that would take him back to Warsaw, I was waiting to see Mr Wagstaff again, in a room full of men with lots of tattoos and not very much hair who looked as though they could really do some damage to a grown man like David Whitworth. When a chap with the *Titanic* on his tattooed forearm asked me what I had done, I told him I was just delivering some sandwiches to the office.

'You have options,' said Mr Wagstaff, when I finally got to see him.

What a relief.

'At the end of next week,' he continued. 'You will have to appear at the Magistrates' Court again, and this time you will be formally charged. This is the point at which you have to make a choice. You can either be tried at the Magistrates' Court, or ask to go to Crown Court. At the Magistrates' Court you'll be tried by a trio of fuddy-duddy old geezers who will probably convict you because you've never done an exotic hand-job on them.'

I winced. It gave me a very peculiar and unpleasant feeling to hear a man of Mr Wagstaff's age and position say 'hand-job'.

'At Crown Court,' he continued, 'you will appear in front of a jury. There could be lots of people among that jury who will understand exactly how you felt when you administered the Hot Stuff Heat Rub to Mr Whitworth's private parts. On the other hand, the jury could be full of women like your Grandma who won't understand at all.'

'She approves,' I told Mr Wagstaff quickly.

'Well, make it like my Grandma then. She'd have had you locked up for even knowing where a man's genitals were before marriage.'

I managed a small laugh. 'Great. Sounds like a choice between being buried alive or boiled in hot fat. So what's the third option?'

'There isn't one. Crown Court or Magistrates' Court. That's it. Comprendez?'

Nope. I still didn't really understand the difference. 'Well, I guess it has to be the Crown Court,' I said confidently. 'I mean, at least I've got a chance of getting off that way, haven't I? Normal people will be sympathetic towards me when they hear what David is really like.'

'Yes. But if you don't get off . . .' Mr Wagstaff drew in breath in a way that suggested I was about to be horrified. 'We're looking at a charge of indecent assault occasioning actual bodily harm here, Alison. At the very least, we're looking at indecent assault, a very serious charge indeed. A Magistrates' Court can impose a maximum sentence of six months in prison and a maximum fine in the region of five hundred pounds. But if we go to Crown Court?' He made that uncomfortable sucky noise again. 'You could be looking at five years minimum.'

'Five years?' I gasped. 'My God. I'd be in my thirties by the time I got out.'

'You could make it three years with good behaviour. But it is still a long time.'

'This is like a game of Russian roulette,' I wailed. 'What you're telling me is that I could either get off scot-free or go down forever?'

'So what's it to be?' said Mr Wagstaff lightly, as if I had just said 'So it's Harvey Nicks or Harrods'.

I started to chew the fingernails I had always been so precious about again. 'Well, if I go to Magistrates' Court, you reckon I'll definitely be convicted, right?'

'I think so. Unless you're a mason.'

'Then it seems to me that I have to go for trial by jury. Even if the consequences could be worse. I mean, at least that way I've got twelve chances of someone in that jury being sympathetic towards me. Not just two or three. And I am innocent, Mr Wagstaff. I swear I am.'

Mr Wagstaff nodded. 'I'm sure you are. But innocence isn't always the best defence, I'm afraid. We may do OK. After all, you're a very personable girl, Alison. You've never been in trouble before. You're intelligent, smartly dressed, attractive.' He loosened his tie and I gripped the arms of my chair tightly, praying that I wasn't about to be hit upon by my solicitor. But Mr Wagstaff quickly stopped looking at me through his narrowed, shifty eyes and began to make feverish notes again. 'Yes, I think I can groom you into a model citizen, Alison Harris.'

At a cost.

CHAPTER THIRTY-NINE

That afternoon I had to go into work. There was no escaping it. Julie had been calling the flat non-stop for the past fortnight and Emma was running out of patience with her role as my protector. Besides, she warned me, it was just a matter of time before my impending court case came to light. Julie was an avid reader of the court file which appeared in the local newspaper, and she had bedded enough policemen to make it possible that she was, in fact, an official part of the police public relations training programme.

'She'll find out,' was the general consensus.

So I went back to work, clutching the sick note which Emma had written out on a form she had stolen from Ashley's briefcase. He had refused to write the note himself, which Emma said had made her doubt his suitability as a boyfriend. Unsuitability which was quickly forgotten when he gave her another anatomy class, if you know what I mean.

The in-tray on my desk at Hudderston's looked like the lower reaches of the Himalayas. My computer screen was covered with a thick layer of dust into which someone had scrawled the word 'Skiver'. Julie was waiting for me, power-dressed in purple Karen Millen and a pair of surgical-looking boots.

'Back at last,' she trilled. 'Feeling better? I must say you're a terribly funny colour for someone who's been in bed for two weeks.'

'Jaundiced,' I squeaked.

'Mmm. I'd pay good money to get that jaundiced at the Tanning Shop,' she replied. My heart raced with the terror of having been caught out, but Julie was already sorting out the most important pieces of work from my mountainous pile and the discussion seemed to be over.

'You've got a doctor's note, of course,' she said.

I handed her the envelope.

'I don't want it. Give it to Mrs Webber in personnel, when you've got a minute.' Then she left me alone, practically imploding with relief. Mrs Webber in personnel was almost a hundred years old and as blind as a bat. She'd never notice that my note was forged.

I picked up the first report to be typed and switched on my machine. No-one suspected I had been on holiday. I just had to keep my head down and plough on through. And I wouldn't take another minute off work until my magistrates' hearing on the following Friday morning.

Then the phone rang on Julie's desk. She picked it up and her face took on a curious expression. She buzzed through to me. 'It's some woman from a magazine. She says she wants to know how your holiday went.'

'My holiday?' My voice shook like coward yellow jelly. 'It must be Emma having a joke.'

'Funny joke,' said Julie.

'She has a surreal sense of humour.'

'Well, are you going to take this call or what? I haven't got all day.'

'OK,' I squeaked. I watched Julie from the corner of my eye to make sure she put down the phone before talking to my caller. It was Amanda of course.

'How was it?' she shrieked. 'Did you have a fabulous time? Did you swim with dolphins? How did you like the food? And I hear you won the international competition. Darling, I'm so proud of you both. We've decided that we want to do another fashion shoot for our summer holiday issue to celebrate. The World's Most Romantic Couple.' I could almost see her gesticulating with the thrill of it all. 'Want to do it tomorrow, sweetheart? While you've still got a tan?'

'Bleeurgh . . . I . . . er . . . I.' I'd completely forgotten about *Complete Woman*.

'Can't talk eh? I understand. I'm always rushed off my feet first day back at the office after a holiday. Call me when you've got a minute. March issue's out today by the way. You're on pages 14 to 16.'

She rang off. Leaving me clutching the phone as if it might morph into a life belt. The March issue was out already? If anyone saw that magazine I would be finished. Who bought it? I looked around the office, doing a mental head count of the girls and wondering who might trip me up. I thought I was in the clear when I remembered that Irene had a *Complete Woman* pin-up special of the doctors from *ER* blu-tacked to the cupboard above her desk.

So less than an hour back at work, I had to ask Julie if I could have an hour off.

'What for?' she asked, deeply irritated. 'Can't you wait till lunchtime?'

'No. I need painkillers. Now. I need to pick up my prescription.'

Thank God she didn't want to risk having a corpse in the office. She let me go and, rushing straight past the chemist's shop, I headed straight for the nearest newsagent to Hudderston's. And the second nearest. And the third nearest. Within an hour I managed to visit thirteen paper shops, bought 115 copies of *Complete Woman* and spent £230.

I was indeed on pages 14 to 16, five different poses and four big paragraphs about my love life. Jeremy looked fantastic, I thought, as I lovingly fingered his image. I looked scared. But not as scared as I was of anyone at Hudderston's seeing the spread. I allowed myself to keep just one copy, hidden safely at the bottom of my bag. The rest were consigned, in pieces, to a number of skips and bins about town. There was always the possibility that Irene would pick up her copy at Tesco's but I had done all I could do for now. I would have to get Emma to drive me to all the local superstores that night.

'Christ, you look like you've been running a marathon,' said Julie when I fell into the office again, panting desperately for breath. 'Sit down. We don't want you going into hospital again.'

Right then, a week in a mental hospital sounded just fine.

CHAPTER FORTY

That week passed like a sloth with arthritis as my date at the Magistrates' Court drew nearer. Jeremy phoned me nightly. And Irene daily bemoaned the fact that she couldn't get hold of a copy of *Complete Woman* for love nor money in our poxy little town.

Jeremy's calls kept me hanging onto life. Whatever horrors I had to face during a day at Hudderston's evaporated when I heard the telephone ring each night at nine o'clock on the dot. Emma bought herself a mobile phone because she got fed up of me hogging the house line for at least an hour at a time and was convinced that she was missing Ashley's calls. But on the very night Emma bought her new Nokia home, Jeremy told me that he couldn't talk to me for as long as usual.

'I'm going out tonight,' he said.

'Oh?' He usually moaned that there was nothing to do in Warsaw.

'Candida's here.'

'Candida?'

'Yes. She's started to make her film.'

Candida was in Warsaw. In the turmoil that had been my sorry life since returning from Antigua I had almost forgotten that Candida was due to start filming in Poland. But in any case, I certainly hadn't expected her to call Jeremy when she did get there.

'She called you?' I squeaked.

'Not exactly. She got Loretta to give me a buzz.'

That felt slightly better.

'Well, please give her my regards,' I said. Then, 'Things still OK with that fiancé of hers?'

'What? Vadim, I think so.'

I went to bed that night only mildly concerned.

Two days later, I walked into the office to find Irene and Julie bent over a copy of the *Sun*, ooo-ing and aah-ing as though they were seeing the Dead Sea Scrolls for the first time.

'It can't be him,' Irene was saying with wonder in her voice. 'It just can't be. I've known him since he was a little lad. He always had darker hair than that.'

'It is him, Irene,' Julie protested. 'I'd recognise him anywhere. He's obviously just had highlights. Well, who would have thought it. Jeremy Baxter and her.'

I froze. My first thought was that somehow the pictures taken for *Complete Woman* had been syndicated to the *Sun*. My cover had been blown and I was about to get the sack in spectacular style. But that couldn't have been the case. When Julie saw me, she smiled and called me over.

'Alison,' she said. 'You can sort this argument out. Is this or is this not "Boil-face Jeremy Baxter"? The one from junior school.' She jabbed at the paper with a vermilion nail.

I took a deep breath and focused on the picture

which had been the cause of their debate. Was it Jeremy? It certainly looked like him. The guy had his hair. His nose. His sunglasses even. But he was partially obscured by the girl in front of him. The girl who was standing with her back to the camera and her hand on the boy in question's shoulder.

'Who is Candida's mystery man?' the caption beneath the picture asked.

'Candida?' I murmured. 'Is that Candida Bianca?'

'Yeah!' Julie snorted. 'The film star. I couldn't bloody believe it. Can you? Boily Baxter and Candida Bianca? I didn't see that coming when he used to hang around the bus stop waiting for me to come home from school.'

'He waited at the bus stop for you?'

'Yeah. He had a crush on me,' she said in the throw-away manner she seemed to reserve for delivering bombshells. 'But I was too busy with Andy McIntyre. At least he had a motorbike. Jeremy just had O-levels and a bicycle back then. So do you think he's shagging her?' Julie asked, referring once again to the picture.

'I don't know,' I said, as calmly as I could.

'She's kissing him.'

'Yeah,' said Irene, unwittingly coming to my emotional rescue. 'But she could just be kissing him hello, couldn't she? You know how those paparazzi can make a big deal out of something perfectly innocent.'

'Like Fergie sucking that bloke's toes?' Julie shrieked. 'You know what, I almost wish I'd got off with Baxter now. Then I would be able to say that I had him first.'

'Probably not even him,' said Irene, slipping back to her desk at the approach of our boss.

I hoped not. I really hoped not.

I didn't have to tell Emma about the incident. She had bought a copy of the *Sun* on her way to college and knew all about it when she called me at work. She took Irene's view.

'He told you he was seeing her the other night. It's innocent, Ali. You know.'

But Jeremy didn't call on time that night. In fact he didn't call that night at all. I tried to reach him on the numbers that I had for him, but I couldn't make myself understood to the bored-sounding Polish receptionist at his office and no-one answered the telephone at his home. I spent the night in agony. For once, there was something worse on my mind than my impending day in court.

When he finally rang, I was so wound up with waiting that I immediately burst into tears.

'What's wrong?' he asked.

'There's a picture of you in the newspaper,' I sniffed.

As I explained what I'd seen, he just tutted and gave a hollow little laugh. 'Paparazzi,' he sighed, as if they had dogged him his whole life. 'We just went to the opera and then to a restaurant. They'll make a story out of anything.'

'The opera? But you told me you hate all that wailing crap,' I sobbed, testing him with his own words.

'It's not all wailing crap, Ali,' Jeremy protested. 'Candida tells me I've just been listening to the wrong ones. Wagner's *Ring Cycle* was really rather good. If a little long . . .'

'Did Vadim go too?'

'No, he was busy with the crew checking out locations. But he didn't mind that I took Candida out and neither should you.'

'I guess not,' I sniffed.

'No guessing about it. Shit. Listen. There's the doorbell. I've got to go, darling. I'll call you on Thursday night.'

'Thursday!' I protested to no-one. Jeremy had already rung off. Thursday was two days away.

There was no-one to console me but Fattypuss. Emma had gone out with Ashley. Marvin had recently met a rather nice dancer of South American origin and was on his way out to learn how to cha-cha when I caught him. When I rang home, there was no-one in but Jo, and she was dyeing her hair and wouldn't talk in case she got the timing wrong. I sat at the window and looked out into the dark street. Who had been ringing Jeremy's doorbell? Was it the gas man? Or Candida? I needed someone to tell me that even if it was Candida, everything was still all right. Jeremy still loved me. And he would still be flying home in time for my appearance in court, wouldn't he?

My court appearance. I picked up the telephone and my fingers hovered over the digits that made up David's number. I hadn't thought to call him since the whole nightmare began. Perhaps if we just talked he might see his way to dropping the charges. I couldn't believe that he was really psychologically damaged by the whole affair. He had obviously been annoyed about the night before the holiday. Now that he was back in Lisa Brown's arms and seemingly happy there (Emma had seen them picking out curtains in Debenhams), perhaps he could be persuaded that I deserved my happiness too.

Three. Four. Two. I dialled the first three digits slowly. Then punched in the last four digits like a maniac before I could bottle out.

Ring. Ring.

'Hello?'

It was Lisa.

I crashed the receiver back down into its cradle. She wouldn't know who had called.

I had of course forgotten about 1471.

CHAPTER FORTY-ONE

'Darling . . . are you going to tell me what is going on?'

Amanda had caught me on my way out of the door. I clutched the phone tightly and wondered if it was too late to pretend that I was in fact Emma.

'Am I or am I not looking at a picture of David in yesterday's copy of the *Sun*?'

'Eh?'

'Yes! With Candida Bianca. Have you seen a copy? Candida and her mystery man. It really looks like David, but I told myself, he's not in Warsaw. He's hard at work in sunny Brindlesham, busy saving up cash for his impending wedding to the lovely Alison. Tell me I'm imagining things, sweetheart, and I'll let you get on.'

'You're imagining things,' I assured her. 'Someone showed me the picture at work. It's not David. It's just someone who looks very much like him. I guess I'm lucky that Candida Bianca doesn't live in Brindlesham or she'd be after him like a shot,' I added with a very forced laugh.

'Mmm. It is quite a coincidence. You do know that Candida was staying at Santa Bonita all the time that you were there?'

I coughed. 'I had heard that, but, you know, she kept herself pretty much to herself.'

'That's not what I heard,' said Amanda slyly. 'Sugar, if you can let your Auntie Amanda in on a little secret regarding your fiancé and this stella superstar, I might be able to help you get a few little piccies of your own into the paper to help soften the blow of your split. I've got a direct line to Max Clifford . . .'

'There's nothing to say.'

'I know it's embarrassing, being jilted . . .'

Didn't I know it.

'But the sponduliks I'm thinking about could keep you in retail therapy for years. When do you think it happened, darling? Did you know about this while you were on holiday? Did he tell you what was going on before the picture appeared in the *Sun*?'

'There's nothing to talk about. It's perfectly innocent. And I've got to go to court . . . I mean, work.'

'OK. You go to work. I can't force you to make piles of money out of your pain.'

'I'm not in pain,' I said as I slammed the phone down, knocking the phone off the table as I did so to land straight on my toes.

It was just what I needed before my appearance in the Magistrates' Court. The make-up I had so carefully applied to give the impression that I was at once both someone who was feminine and competent was soon running down my face in thick, candy-stripes of mascara, blusher and gloss.

I was still sitting at the bottom of the stairs when

Emma woke up at half-past nine. She needed her sleep, she said. It was hard work being a student. I heard a sharp intake of breath when she saw me slumped by the telephone stand. She rushed down to be with me and didn't bother to hide her disgust at my appearance.

'Christ, you've got Louis Vuitton under your eyes,' she exclaimed. 'Do you know what time it is? Your mother warned me to make sure that you didn't forget about your appearance. Good job I'm skipping lectures again. Do you want some coffee? You ought to eat something before you go out, you know. I'll make some toast.'

I took the toast, slightly overdone, gratefully. Then I let Emma choose a new 'going to see a magistrate' outfit. The one I had put on first thing was now crumpled and covered with tears. Thank God my best friend, like my mother, didn't believe I could stand on my own two feet.

I had to patch up my make-up on the bus to meet Mr Wagstaff. I couldn't have done much of a job, I guessed from his wince when he saw me.

At the Magistrates' Court, I waited to be called with Mr Wagstaff and a selection of the tattooed thugs I had last seen in his office.

'Now you know what you've got to do?' he asked me for the tenth time.

'I'll go in there. They'll ask me my name and describe the offence again and I'll plead not guilty. Then they'll tell me when I have to go to court.'

'Are you sure you're going to plead not guilty? Are you sure you've told me absolutely everything? Are you sure there isn't another side to this story that could get you into very serious trouble indeed when the prosecution calls its witness?'

'I'm innocent,' I told him tearfully. He pulled out his hankie so that I could blow my nose, but he was looking at me in such a way that suggested he had seen this all before. No doubt even the man with 'I love Pit Bull terriers' tattooed across his cheekbone could turn on the waterworks if so required.

'I'm innocent and the jury at the crown court will find me innocent because I'm telling the truth,' I persisted.

'OK,' said Mr Wagstaff. 'But remember what I told you, if we take this to Crown Court, then there is no turning back. If you're found guilty there, you will be looking at a very, very serious sentence indeed.'

'I'm not going to be looking at any sentence,' I sniffed defiantly. 'David Whitworth has blown this out of all proportion. And I've got witnesses to prove it too. There's Emma, my flatmate, she was listening at the door when David came to beg me to go back with him the night before I left for Antigua. She heard him say that I hadn't done him any permanent harm that night. He was prepared to forgive me then if I took him to the Caribbean.'

'And she would be prepared to say all this in court?'

'Emma would do anything for me,' I said triumphantly. Though I knew that I was probably setting myself up for a lifetime's worth of favours in return.

Then I was called. Feeling like Marie Antoinette regretting her comment about the cake, I followed the clerk into the court. The Magistrate I faced this time, an altogether more serious stipendiary magistrate who sat alone, was a portly man who didn't look quite so kind as the old women I had faced before. In fact, he rather looked as though he got off on fining people for letting their dogs foul their own back gardens.

'How do you plead?' the clerk of the court asked me.

'Not guilty,' I whispered.

'What was that?' he asked. 'Guilty?'

'No. Not guilty,' I repeated, making sure there could be no mistake this time.

So I demanded my right to a trial by jury. The Magistrate went quiet for a while and shuffled a huge pile of papers. Mr Wagstaff kept pointing out the opportunities in the process at which the magistrate could decide that I had no case to answer but he didn't and I was duly given the date for my Crown Court trial.

It would take three months to come round. Three whole months. It was a very long time to have such a thing hanging over you. The only consolation was that if my appetite remained affected as it had been for that long, I might be able to wear a bikini if I was free for the summer holidays.

'Keep your chin up,' Mr Wagstaff told me as he slid into the driver's seat of his smart new BMW. 'I'm doing my very best for you.' Then he drove off, leaving me standing alone outside the court house while he went to assure some other poor sucker that everything would be all right. If they liked prison food. I started the long walk back to my house, feeling deeply introspective. I walked extra slowly, figuring that the longer I was away from the phone, the more chance Jeremy would have to ring and make everything better again.

CHAPTER FORTY-TWO

I couldn't believe it when Jeremy called that night to tell me that he would be flying in from Warsaw the very next day, which was Saturday. I must have thanked the Lord about a thousand times for my wonderful boyfriend. He said he had to see me the minute he landed. I said I would be at the airport. No, better than that, he said, he would drive straight to The Aspidistra, which was halfway between my home and the airport and meet me there. Save me the drive, he said. So thoughtful.

I was awake with the birds next morning and spent all day doodling Jeremy's name on the side of the *Radio Times* while I watched all the Open University sociology and politics programmes in the hope that I would see someone whose predicament seemed worse than mine. There was a talk show just before the children's programmes started, where a girl blubbed that her mother had run off with her boyfriend, but I have to say that with her perm it was hardly surprising that she lost out to someone twenty years her senior.

By contrast, I decided that that night I was going to

look a million dollars. I hung Candida's red Versace dress from the shower curtain while I bathed so that the steam would make the creases drop out. I spent an hour on my hair and plastered my lips with seven coats of lipstick, so that I would remain picture perfect no matter how many times he kissed me.

I was ready to go out at half-past five, though Jeremy and I weren't due to meet until eight. I actually sat in the car on the driveway for five minutes at six o'clock and toyed with the idea of driving to the airport to meet him there anyway. It would save him getting a taxi to the restaurant and heaven knows we needed to save all the money we could with the terrifying prospect of my legal costs. But I thought better of it. I didn't know the details of Jeremy's flight for a start, or even which terminal he would be flying into, so it was perfectly possible that I would miss him and end up having to wait even longer to see him for my troubles.

So, I hung on until seven o'clock, then I floated to the restaurant, as light-hearted as a girl with a ball and chain in the back of her mind could possibly be. Trust Jeremy to be thoughtful enough to book a table at my favourite restaurant to cheer me up. We would have a nice long chat about our wedding plans, I told myself, brightening still further at the thought, as I let the Maître d' of The Aspidistra relieve me of my coat.

Jeremy had yet to arrive.

I got myself a drink to steady my butterflies. This would be the first time that Jeremy and I had had a 'reunion' of sorts. I was very much looking forward to it, but I felt I still needed to loosen up a little. Blot out my troubles. A double vodka and tonic arrived at the table forthwith.

By half-past eight I wasn't feeling quite so excited. The waiter kept hovering by the table, trying to get an order from me. I was sure that he even raised his eyebrows disbelievingly when I said for the third time that I was waiting for someone to join me. Perhaps his flight had been delayed, I thought. Half an hour later, I was thinking, perhaps he's had a crash.

But just as I was wondering whether I ought to call the airport, I heard the crunch of car wheels on the gravel driveway of the restaurant and looked out through the window to see a vast limousine swing up to the front entrance. A vast limousine that soon disgorged my boyfriend. I was so astounded that instead of the sweet nothings I had planned, the first thing I said to Jeremy was, 'How on earth did you afford to hire that?'

'Free limo service with the flight,' he said as he squeezed himself into the chair opposite me after barely pecking me on the cheek in greeting.

'What? With economy class Aeroflot? You're kidding. I thought you were lucky if you actually got a seat on the plane, let alone a lift home in a stretch limo.'

'Look, don't worry about it, OK. It wasn't your money.'

That ruffled my feathers a bit.

'Mineral water,' Jeremy barked at the waiter.

'Aren't you going to have something a bit stronger? It is a celebration of sorts, isn't it? Seeing each other again after all those horrible weeks apart.'

'I need to keep a clear head.'

'How long are you here for?'

'Just until tomorrow.'

'Is that all?' I started to miss him in anticipation already.

'It's long enough.'

'Remember this dress?' I asked him, fishing for a compliment to lighten things up.

'Yes, it's Candida's. Have you ordered yet?' he asked, changing the subject straightaway.

'No,' I told him. 'I was waiting for you.'

'I'll have the chicken salad. No dressing.'

I almost laughed. 'Chicken salad with no dressing. Isn't that a bit dull? Why don't you have a steak?'

'I'm watching my health,' he replied. 'You should think about doing the same too, you know.'

'Well, my diet's been the least of my worries lately,' I muttered. 'I can barely hold down water. Oh, Jeremy, I can't tell you how much I've been looking forward to seeing you again. Hearing your voice last night, after that awful morning in court, made me remember that it's all going to be all right in the end. Just seeing your face makes me feel so much happier. Only you can make me feel better these days.'

And after that little outburst, I could resist no longer. I got up from my seat and flung my arms around him, plastering kisses all over his face and head like a deranged puppy dog.

But when I pulled away from him to take my seat, I had an awful feeling that that night, Jeremy wouldn't be making me feel better at all. He had that look in his eyes. The one that I had seen in David's eyes on that terrible Christmas Day in the hospital. Jeremy was distracted. Desperate. Needing to say something that I really wouldn't want to hear.

Though he never got round to saying it that night.

He ate his salad. He refused dessert. He ordered coffee. No milk or sugar. Decaffeinated. And then he excused himself to the little boys' room. I drank my coffee. Milk and two sugars. Extra strong. I drank his coffee. He didn't come back.

At first I gave him the benefit of the doubt. I mean, maybe he had constipation. I had heard all the horror stories about Polish food. Then darker thoughts started to gather at the back of my mind. I had recently developed the imagination of a Stephen King. What if he had slipped in a puddle of something unspeakable on the bathroom floor and knocked himself out on a urinal? What if, even as I unwrapped the foil-covered chocolate mints that came with the bill, he was drowning, face-down in a lavatory pan?

The restaurant started to empty, as two by two the guests gathered up their coats and left in a flurry of air kisses. The waiters hovered by the till, shining up wine glasses and cutlery in readiness for the next day's diners. The bill for our meal lay folded in front of me. The Maître d' wandered past and looked pointedly at the slip of paper that I hadn't even bothered to look at. Jeremy had told me the night before that this would be his treat.

'Ahem,' a waiter coughed discreetly. 'I'm afraid that the restaurant will be closing for the night in ten minutes time, madam.'

'Er, yes,' I squeaked. 'I know that. It's just that I'm waiting for my boyfriend to come back from the bathroom. I don't suppose you could pop and see what's become of him, could you? He doesn't usually spend such a long time in the loos.'

One of the waiters standing by the till, covered his smile and gave a cough to choke a giggle.

'But monsieur has already left,' said the man who was talking to me. 'He left almost an hour ago, madam. He said that he had received a bleeper message calling him into work and that you would be staying for coffee alone.'

'He what?' I didn't even know he had a bleeper.

'You mean, he didn't tell you?'

The look on my face must have told the waiter all he needed to know.

'Oh, madam. I am so sorry.'

'You're talking rubbish.'

I got to my feet and ran to the men's room. I had to pass the exit on my way there, but I still wouldn't believe that Jeremy could possibly have slipped out without telling me. I wouldn't even start to entertain the idea until I had banged open every cubicle door in that room and left one elderly gentleman in particular feeling rather embarrassed.

'He can't have left me!' I wailed.

'Er, would you mind closing the door on your way out,' said the gentleman I had interrupted while evacuating his bowels.

I stumbled back out into the restaurant, where the Maître d' was still waiting for me with the bill.

'Madam, if I could beg your kind attention . . .'

'Wait,' I pleaded. 'He's got to be round here somewhere. Perhaps he stumbled into the ladies' room by mistake. He wouldn't have gone home without me. I know he wouldn't. And he certainly wouldn't have left this jacket,' I added, pointing triumphantly at the Giorgio Armani creation which was still hanging from the back of Jeremy's chair. That jacket was Jeremy's pride and joy. If he could have got away with it, I'm sure he would have worn it inside out just so that everyone could see the label.

I was just about to wreak havoc in the ladies' room when the telephone rang. It was a mobile phone. Jeremy's mobile phone, ringing from the pocket of Jeremy's jacket.

'And he wouldn't have left his phone,' I said with something bordering on hysterical relief. The phone continued to ring out accusingly, its ugly tone disrupting the calm ambience of the restaurant almost as much as I had been.

'If you wouldn't mind answering it, madam.'

'But . . . I don't know if I should. I mean, it's his phone.'

'Then turn it off. This is a mobile phone-free zone, I'm afraid.'

'All right. I'll answer it.'

I pulled the damn thing out of Jeremy's pocket and looked at it in confusion for a clue as to how it might actually open. After another five rings, the waiter took the phone from my hand and opened it himself.

'Hello,' I said tentatively, when he handed the phone back to me. 'Jeremy Baxter's phone.'

'I know,' said the voice at the other end of the line. 'I am Jeremy.'

'Jeremy,' I giggled hysterically. 'Where on earth are you? I was beginning to worry. I bet you're calling me from the lobby, aren't you? Well, the joke's wearing a bit thin on the waiter, so you'd better come back in here and rescue me right now. Where are you?' I scanned the restaurant to see if I could see him hiding behind a potted plant, à la his namesake, Sir Jeremy Beadle.

'I'm on my way back to the airport.'

'What?'

'I'm about a mile from Gatwick,' he sighed. And thirty miles from me! 'I'm sorry to do this to you, Ali, but I'm not coming back. Not tonight.'

I must have gone very pale indeed. The waiter stepped forward to support me, then pulled out a seat and made me sit down. 'Jeremy,' I said, regaining just a little composure. 'What's going on? Have you got to get back to Poland for work or something?'

'No. It's just that I could see how the evening was panning out and I thought that this would be the best way to end things.'

'The evening?'

'No. Things. Us. To end us.'

'Aaaagh!' I shrieked. 'Please tell me you're joking.'

'Alison, I'm afraid that I've never been more serious in my life.'

'Jeremy, please stop messing about. The last thing I need right now is for you to start acting the silly bugger.'

'Alison, I'm telling you that our relationship is over.'

'But we're engaged!'

'That's over too.'

'No,' I whined. 'You can't end things. Not like this. Not over the telephone. It's so cowardly. It's so mean. Come back here at once.'

'I could have sent you a fax instead,' he protested. 'Look, I've got to go. The phone in this limo starts to cut out as soon as we get under the flight paths. Look after yourself, Ali. Oh, and you can keep that mobile if you like.'

'No. No. Noooo!!' I wailed with anguish but he was already gone. I tried to call him back at once. I punched 1471 into the mobile until I was blue in the face but it wouldn't give me a number. It had to be a joke. It just had to be a joke. I dialled 192 and tried to get a number for the airport so that I could demand that the next plane to Warsaw didn't take off until Jeremy and I had sorted this out.

'A-hem,' the waiter interrupted me. 'Since we've established that sir won't be coming back to the restaurant this evening, I wonder if perhaps you could spare just a moment to consider our unfinished business?' He fluttered the bill like a little fan.

'Christ! I don't think I've got enough money,' I warned him, when I clocked the ridiculous amount. I rummaged deep in my handbag and came up with a furry cough sweet and two tenners. I was at least thirty pounds shy of the total.

'How could he do this to me?' I asked nobody in particular. 'How could he do this to me? He was supposed to be supporting me in my hour of need. Cheering me up. Not pushing me to the brink of bloody suicide.'

'Madam, if you would like to step into my office.' The Maître d' shuffled me out of the way of his other guests. 'I am sure that we can come to some sort of arrangement. Perhaps you have something that you could leave with us as security while you go to find the rest of the money. Your passport, perhaps?'

'My passport? You must be joking. I'm on bail. My passport's with the police.'

That didn't exactly inspire his confidence in my ability to find the rest of the dosh.

'Then your driving licence, perhaps.'

'I haven't got that with me either.'

I was almost blind from crying. Now I flung myself at the Maître d's feet and begged him to let me wash up or something.

'That won't be necessary,' he said, prising me from his knees. 'We do have a dishwasher. Perhaps, under the circumstances, we might be able to waive some of madam's bill this evening. You've obviously had a bit of a shock. I'll tell you what. I'll take the mobile phone and we'll say no more about it. Oh, and the money that you do have.'

But he had to prise that phone from my stiffly-gripped hand, as though he was prising a lock of Jeremy's hair from me. Apart from the Armani jacket he had left behind which I had no intention of letting go, it was my last point of contact with him. What if he tried to call me back, to tell me that it was all just a horrible dream?

'He can call you at home,' said the waiter, as he parted me from the phone with a final, determined yank.

He summoned me a taxi then, obviously keen to get me off the premises before I put the last remaining diners off their food. He wouldn't let me drive my own car for fear I'd scratch the gateposts on my way out. So, bodily bundled into the back of the taxi with my coat still only half on, I curled up on the seat and cried out my heart. I couldn't believe that Jeremy was deserting me. Why? Why? Why? Was it because he was concerned for his bloody reputation as the chief of

Eastern Europe in the face of my impending court case? What about the conversation we had had at the airport in which he had the cheek to accuse me of worrying too much about what other people thought when I refused to join the Mile High Club? Thinking about how happy I had been too, as we set off for Antigua, made me feel so much worse right then.

The taxi driver let me bawl for a good ten minutes before he asked me where I wanted to go. Sweet man. He didn't even run the meter while I cried.

'I've got to stand on my own two feet,' I whispered to myself like a mantra as the taxi sped me home. Unfortunately, my legs felt like jelly and I collapsed in a soggy heap at the bottom of the hallway as soon as I got into the house, and there I stayed with only Fattypuss to warm me, until Emma came back from Ashley's house to get a fresh pair of knickers the next day.

CHAPTER FORTY-THREE

'You have got to pull yourself together,' Emma said as she manhandled me out of my coat and into my dressing-gown. 'And you've got to start right away.'

Thank God it was Sunday and I didn't have to go to work. I installed myself on the sofa and refused to move while I listened to Emma's pep-talk.

'My life is falling apart,' I wailed periodically.

'It is not,' said Emma flatly. 'You've still got your family. And your health.'

I was rapidly losing my mental health.

'Jeremy has left me,' I wailed.

'Jeremy is just running scared. He'll probably call and apologise when he realises what an idiot he's been.'

'Do you think so?'

'Yeah. And then you'll have to decide whether you want to take such a schmuck-head back or not.'

I sniffed and took a handful of the Pringles that Emma had dug out of her emergency supplies.

'There's still the court case to get through.'

'I know. But I was talking to Lorna in Boots yesterday,' Emma said through a mouthful of crumbs. 'She says that she wishes you luck.'

'What? Lorna?'

'Yeah. And she's well in with David's gang so I think that should give you some idea of how a jury is going to react. You'll get off, Ali. You only have to tell them how he dumped you on Christmas Day and they'll be queuing up to Hot Stuff Heat Rub him themselves. In the meantime, just chill out. Live a normal life. Get up. Go to work. Come home. Eat Pringles. Three months will pass before you know it.'

We polished off two tubes of Pringles that night. One original and one cheese and chive. And two bottles of wine to go with them. One red. One white. I slept like a plank and would have slept right through my alarm if Fattypuss hadn't woken me up with a present.

'See,' said Emma as I scraped the remains of a vole into the pedal bin. 'Fattypuss loves you. Everybody is on your side. When you get to court, they'll turn out in their hundreds to support you.'

I didn't expect to see a party of people gathered in my honour quite so soon as that morning however. When I got to work – it took me three attempts on the bus because I kept having to get off to throw up – it seemed as though everyone who had ever worked at Hudderston Heavy Engineering Co. was squashed into the admin office where I whiled away my days dreaming of death's sweet release.

When I walked in, the room suddenly went silent.

Even the big ugly grinding machines that provided a constant background growl and whine to the working day were quiet. People parted as I passed them by on the way to my desk. A desk which I hardly recognised since someone had kindly removed every last piece of paper from my in-tray and piled the extra work into Bridget's.

'All right, everybody?' I asked.

I was met with silence. Even Julie just looked down at her desk diary and said nothing. Then Mr Chivers, the factory foreman, poked his head around his office door and summoned me straight to him before I even had a chance to take my coat off.

'What's up?' I asked innocently. 'Sorry I'm a bit late. I was feeling sick. I had to get off the bus a couple of times.'

'That's OK,' he said to my surprise. 'Er, Alison. I wonder if you might sit down.' He pulled my seat out for me.

In front of him on his desk, I could see my personnel file. Mr Chivers picked up the flap and studied something on top of the pile of papers I had accumulated during my years at Hudderston's. He took a deep breath. 'Well, Alison,' he exhaled. 'I have to say I really don't know where to begin.'

'Try the beginning,' I said facetiously.

'Yes, I suppose that would be a start.' He reached into my file to pull something out. It was a copy of the *Sun*. He turned to page six. It was a copy of the *Sun* containing a picture of me!

He linked his fingers in front of him and leaned forward on his desk earnestly while I studied the open paper in horror. For a second, he was distracted by something outside his office, and when I glanced round, I could see that a crowd had gathered outside the frosted glass panels that served as walls to cut him, the boss, off from the hoi-polloi. Suddenly, I knew how it felt to be a goldfish.

'What is this about?' I squeaked.

'Exactly. What is this about?' echoed Mr Chivers. 'Perhaps you should read the caption.'

The photograph was an out-take from the *Complete Woman* shoot. I was wearing the blue shift dress that I had liked so much. Jeremy had his arms around me and he was looking into my eyes with great bucketfuls of love.

'The look of love,' the caption said. 'As Alison Harris and David Whitworth are pronounced the United Kingdom's Most Romantic Couple. But just two weeks later, lovely secretary Alison lost her fiancé David to Candida Bianca when the couple met Hollywood's brightest star at Antigua's Santa Bonita resort.'

'It's not jaundice, you've got, is it?' said Mr Chivers. 'It's a suntan.'

'I . . . I . . .' I couldn't begin to protest.

'You told Julie that you had complications as a result of your appendectomy. You told her that you had septicaemia and wouldn't even be able to get out of bed for two weeks. Next thing we know we're reading about your Caribbean holiday in the *Sun*. And I don't like to be made a fool of.'

I just stared at the photograph of me and Jeremy looking so happy. Then I stared at the picture beside it. Jeremy and Candida Bianca, looking even happier. The caption to that picture said that it had been taken on Sunday morning, as the couple shared a romantic breakfast in a Warsaw cafe. No wonder he had been in such a hurry to get back.

'What do you have to say for yourself?' asked Mr Chivers.

'I just can't believe it. It says here that she's not going to marry Vadim any more.'

Mr Chivers shook his head in frustration. 'What are you talking about? Aren't you even going to say you're sorry? Pretending to be sick so that you can take extra holiday is a very serious matter, you know. And as for your sick note? Don't you realise that forging a doctor's signature could see you ending up in court?'

I pushed the paper away from me and sank back into my seat, my eyes filled with hot, stinging tears.

'Alison? Alison? What have you got to say in your defence?'

What did I have to say in my defence? Suddenly it hit me that I was about to lose my job. I got to my feet and glared down on Chivers with what I hoped was a look of withering disdain. 'I was in love, that's my defence,' I cried. 'Haven't you ever done something stupid for the love of the person you want most in the whole world? I needed that holiday with Jeremy. I don't care what you think about my methods for getting the time. I'm handing in my resignation right now.'

'Alison!'

'Don't try and change my mind. I know when I'm not wanted. It's clear that you aren't a kind enough man to understand, Mr Chivers, and I don't want to work for a heartless worm. You can stuff your rotten job. I never liked working here anyway. I hate this factory and I especially hate you, Mr Chivers, thinking you're trendy with that disgusting shiny suit of yours and your bloody Mickey Mouse tie. You like to think you're one of the lads, don't you? But all the girls call you Mr Shivers behind your back because that's what you send down their spines. I've waited four long years to tell you that you ought to buy a wig that fits, and you should see a dental hygienist before you kill any more of the office plants.'

With that, I stormed out dramatically, leaving Mr Chivers gulping pathetically for air as if I had just punched him. As I passed her, even Julie was gasping with surprise at the ferocity of my attack.

'You can keep my desk tidy if you like,' I told her.

It was only when I got outside the building that the magnitude of what had just passed became clear.

I had just given up my job. The job I had held down for four years. If I had managed to limp on to five I would have been given a free Marks and Spencers gift voucher. I had thought that I was calling Chivers' bluff but standing outside the factory gates, it became horribly clear that in actual fact I had played straight into his sweaty hands.

If I'd grovelled, perhaps he would have felt obliged to give me another chance. I could imagine the uproar I had left behind. The gossip would keep Irene and Julie fuelled up for a fortnight. Perhaps Bridget would have a quiet week or two until the scandal surrounding me died down.

Perhaps I should have grovelled, I thought as I sank down onto a filthy bench covered with pigeon shit. It would have been painful but the fact was, I needed a job to pay my solicitor's fees, and how was I going to get another one with a possible conviction hanging over my head like the sword of Damocles?

* * *

Shock swept through my body like waves, reminding me of the nausea I had felt moments before my appendix burst. In the dustbin beside the bench, I saw a recently-dumped copy of that morning's *Sun*. I pulled it out and flicked to the photo that had been my Nemesis. Amanda must have called the *Sun* and told them the story. I could have strangled her with my bare hands.

But in a moment of rare lucidity I remembered the conversation we had had the previous week and the fact that she had promised she could get me money for a story like this. I'd just lost my job. And I needed money. I dug my last fifty pence piece out of my tattered purse and made for a pay phone.

'*Complete Woman,*' she trilled. 'How may I help you?'

'Amanda,' I sobbed. 'It's Ali. You've got to help me. I think you were right. I want to tell the whole story now.'

'Oh. And which story would that be?' she asked me frostily. 'Seems you've been telling quite a lot of stories lately.'

'What do you mean?'

'I just had a call from my contact at the *Sun* telling me to get my facts straight before I ring him with a lead. Then I get a call from the *Brindlesham Herald* asking for more pictures of Jeremy Baxter. Jeremy Baxter, I said. Who the hell is he? What on earth is that about, Alison?'

'I can explain.'

'You don't need to. I know now. I've been on the phone to Candida's agent for the last half hour. That wasn't your fiancé that you took to Antigua at all, was it? You were dumped by the real David Whitworth and so you bribed Jeremy Baxter to pretend to be your man.'

'So? I was in love with Jeremy and now I find out that he's gone off with her. There's still a story to be told, isn't there? What about the money you got for talking to the *Sun*? You owe me half of that.'

'Au contraire, Alison. I'm afraid that you owe *Complete Woman* ten thousand pounds for attempting to defraud the judges of a major international competition.'

She slammed the phone down. Ten thousand pounds. Was she serious? I hoped not. I had given the money to Jeremy to invest and I could hardly call him up right then.

CHAPTER FORTY-FOUR

'Woe is me,' I wailed as I tumbled in through the front door.

'Alison!' Emma careered down the hall towards me. 'What on earth is going on? The phone's been ringing non-stop. I've been talking to the *Sun*, *The Times*, even the *Brindlesham Herald*. They all want to know about you and David. I told them that the case doesn't come to court until the end of the month.'

'You mentioned the case.'

'Yeah, and the bizarre thing was that even though they were ringing up about David, the whole indecent assault case thing seemed to be news to them. I couldn't understand that. What's going on, Ali? I'm worried that I've told them something I shouldn't have done.'

She had indeed. It was just a matter of hours before the first copies of the *Brindlesham Herald* hit the newsstands with the damning headline – 'Brindlesham Bobbitt!'.

What a scoop for a local rag that had carried three front page stories about lost cats in the first two months of the year alone! Brindlesham Boy dumps psycho for a film star, and what a film star! What a psycho! If the story hadn't been about me, I might have enjoyed counting up the number of words they had found to avoid the use of 'penis'.

At least the *Brindlesham Herald* couldn't taunt me with pictures of Jeremy or Candida. The photograph they had of me had been taken when I won the art prize at secondary school. I was wearing my tie in the trendy narrow knot I had sported the year before I took my GCSEs.

'Britain's own Lorena!!' proclaimed the headlines inside. 'Pretty young secretary Alison Harris (26) looks the picture of innocence in this picture of her as a schoolgirl at Brindlesham's own St Olive's High School for Girls. But while the wicked young woman was enjoying a steamy holiday romance in the Caribbean, her fiancé David Whitworth was piecing together the tatters of his life after the love affair that has left him permanently disabled!'

Where do newspapers get their facts from? I wondered angrily. For a start I was still only 25 and David Whitworth was most definitely not my fiancé. I could only read the report a sentence at a time, because my blood was so close to boiling.

So David had been heartbroken, had he? According to the *Brindlesham Herald*, I had left him for a third party in our relationship, then bitterly launched my attack on him, because, while I didn't want him for myself, I didn't want him to have anyone else.

'Lies, lies, lies,' I protested out loud.

My anger grew around me like an impenetrable shell of fury. Up until then I had been simply dazed by the things that were happening around me. Now I was ready to lash out at the next unfortunate to cross me.

'What can I do about this?' I asked Emma, slapping the paper onto the coffee table in front of her.

'Ignore it,' she said helpfully.

'It was you who put them onto the court case story.'

'When they rang up asking about David I assumed they already knew.'

'Couldn't you have guessed that they really wanted to know about Jeremy after all that Candida stuff in the *Sun*?'

'Well, I'm sorry if I'm not quick enough to keep up with the web of lies that you've been spinning round yourself for the last month,' she shouted back. 'I was trying to help you. I defended you on the phone. I told everyone who called that you acted out of self-defence.'

'Fat lot of good that did me. I've been made out to be like some kind of Hannibal Lecter.'

'I was really trying to help you, Ali,' said Emma, slipping her arm around my shoulders.

I shrugged her off. 'I'm not talking to you any more.'

Emma sprang away, looking hurt.

Then the doorbell rang and I used the excuse to escape her kicked puppy dog gaze.

Marvin stood on the doorstep, flanked by his new dancing partner Chico. In his hand he carried a copy of that despicable *Brindlesham Herald*.

'Not very nice, is it?' he said insightfully. 'And where did they get that photograph? You look like you're auditioning for Bananarama.'

'Aaaagh.' I slammed the door in his face. 'Go away, you evil queen,' I shouted. 'It's not funny. None of this is funny. You're reading about my life.'

Marvin shouted through the letter box. 'Does that mean we can't come in?'

'There must be someone I can sue?' I continued to rant. 'All this stuff is libel, surely.'

'If you want to bring a libel case you have to able to prove that what they're saying isn't true,' said Marvin, still through the letter box. He was also a big fan of *Murder One*.

'It's so unfair,' I wailed.

'Let us in, Ali. Chico here did a law degree. Maybe he can give you some advice.'

'I don't want you to come in,' I sniffed. 'You're only here to make fun of me.'

'We're here to be your friends.' For a moment the letter box was shut, then it opened again as Marvin pushed through a tissue. I took it without thanking him and blew my nose hard.

'Attagirl,' said Marvin. 'Feeling better already, I'll bet. Now let us come inside.'

I opened the door reluctantly.

'Phew,' said Marvin. 'You don't look much cop tonight.' Chico nodded in agreement, though I can't say I thought much of his fun-fur salopettes either. 'Ali love, this is Chico.'

'I recognised him from your description.'

'Yeah? Well, why don't you go and make him a nice cup of tea,' he suggested, as he craned his neck towards the front room. 'Is Emma in?'

'She's through there.'

'Both of us want milk but no sugar. Run along.'

I trudged into the kitchen and put the kettle on. I shouldn't be so hard on my friends, I told myself. They really did want to support me. They weren't the type of people who would just turn up to gloat.

Then I heard a piercing shriek of laughter from the sitting room.

'What is it now?' I asked suspiciously, as I stood in the doorway with an empty teapot in my hand.

Marvin stuffed something down the side of the sofa guiltily. Emma stifled a giggle and Chico looked at the ground.

'What is it?' I demanded, marching over to the sofa and pulling the swiftly-hidden paper out.

It was a copy of the next morning's *Sun*.

'Where did you get this?'

'I was in London tonight. You can get the next day's papers from a stall outside Charing Cross.'

'And what was so funny about this one?'

I flicked open to page three and knew. There I was. In all my glory. It was a picture taken during my fortnight in Antigua. I was wearing a sunny smile and no top.

Suddenly the *Brindlesham Herald*'s account of my misspent life was about to seem like Enid Blyton. I held that copy of the *Sun* with shaking hands.

'Is this the face of Britain's Most Dangerous Woman?' the headline asked. 'Alison Harris shows the form that helped her exert such a fatal attraction on insurance salesman David Whitworth and Candida Bianca's new man, model Jeremy Baxter.'

Where on earth had that picture of me come from?

'Ali Harris, page three girl,' said Marvin admiringly. 'You've got to be pleased with that.'

'Pleased? I'd be more pleased if my tits just dropped off,' I shouted. 'This is libel. This is slander. It's going to ruin my image in front of a jury. If this doesn't stop, I'm going to have been found guilty before I even get to court. It must be illegal.' I picked up the phone and began to dial Mr Wagstaff.

But Mr Wagstaff was in a meeting. His secretary promised that he would call me back straightaway. That would be the next day, since Mr Wagstaff was the kind of provincial solicitor who would have knocked off at five on the dot, even if he was representing the Kray twins.

Emma took the *Sun* from me and flicked to page three again. 'This is so hilarious. My flatmate on page three. Whoever would have thought she had it in her?'

CHAPTER FORTY-FIVE

I was glad that my misfortunes were making everybody else so happy. When I was telling people the story of my disaster, I could almost believe that it was funny myself, but the fact was, I was in deep trouble. I lay awake, staring at the ceiling, occasionally willing it to turn into the thatched roof of that distantly-remembered beach hut in Antigua. A wish which would never be granted.

I tried not to think about the case. I tried to keep my spirits up by promising that when this whole shambles was over, I would take a trip around the world. Then I would plan my imaginary itinerary, complete with prospective dates and that would start me off on the downward spiral again. How could I possibly set a date for a holiday when I didn't know how long I might have to spend in prison?

Prison. What a horrible word. What a terrible place. All I knew of women's prisons I had gleaned from *Prisoner Cell Block H*. In real life, the only person I knew who had actually been inside was a boy from the year above me at junior school who had done three months for persistently having no car insurance. But he was hard. He had tattoos on his eyelids before he went down. What would become of sweet, little, innocent me?

Pretty soon, my imaginary walk down a sandy beach was interrupted by a vision of me on a very different walk. This time, I was walking in through the gates of Holloway prison. I could see the women who were already there checking out me and the other new arrivals who tumbled out of the police van onto the tarmac behind me. The old-timers were no doubt planning hideous ways to make my acquaintance.

Would I be allowed to live out my sentence quietly, I wondered? Would I be able to spend time alone in my cell learning how to knit and catching up on the classics I had always meant to read? Or would I be picked on in the showers, forced to become the slave of a bigger and far butcher woman in return for her protection?

Would my protector make me kiss her? That was probably the least of my worries, I decided with a shudder.

At breakfast, Emma noticed that I was looking even less optimistic than I had done the night before and asked me what was wrong.

'No point dwelling on it,' she assured me. 'You've not been sentenced yet and you'll probably get off. Best to get on with life as normal,' she added flippantly.

But what was normal now? I dreaded the thud of the newspaper on the doormat.

* * *

The papers were late but a letter from *Complete Woman* came by registered post. Having taken receipt of it, Emma propped the letter against the toaster so that I wouldn't miss it when I had finished chucking up in the bathroom. I was surviving on the traditional 'Just been dumped, tea and toast diet'.

'Dear Ms Harris,' the letter began. It seemed like no-one was using my Christian name anymore. 'It is with great regret that we have to write to you regarding your disqualification from *Complete Woman International*'s Most Romantic Couple Competition on the grounds that your companion on the prize holiday, one Mr Jeremy Baxter, was not the man you described in your original winning competition entry. Additionally, in view of the adverse publicity generated by your impending court case and with regard to your former fiancé, we find that we have no choice but to strip you of your "Most Romantic" title and ask that you return your winner's sash to this office by registered post. We shall be writing to you shortly detailing the further action which will have to be taken regarding the grand prize . . .'

'They're going to ask me to pay for the holiday, aren't they?' I said worriedly.

Emma placed a sympathetic hand on my shoulder. 'I'm sure they can't do that,' she replied. But I could tell by her voice that she was about as convinced as I was. 'OK,' she admitted. 'So you might have to cough up, but you'll only have to cough up for half the trip. Jeremy owes the rest. How much can it possibly be, anyway?'

'Try five thousand pounds.'

'For two weeks in a beach hut.'

'A beach hut frequented by some of the most glittering stars of stage and screen. It had air-conditioning.'

'Five thousand pounds,' Emma murmured. 'I don't think I've ever seen that much money in my life.'

'Fifteen thousand pounds with the prize money as well. What am I going to do?' I whined again.

'We'll think of something,' she said, picking up the paper, which the paperboy just poked through the door. 'Let's see what Justin Toper has to say in his horoscope column.'

'Good news?' I asked, when she seemed to have had enough time to read the whole paper, let alone what Justin had to say about the week ahead for Libra.

'Do you want me to read what your stars say? Or do you want me to tell you the truth?'

Emma pushed the tabloid across the table towards me. It was folded open at a picture of David, looking pained.

'Britain's Bobbitt even taunted me from the other side of the world,' said the caption. Underneath the picture, I discovered that they had reproduced the postcard I sent to David from Antigua, with careful highlighting over the words 'hot stuff' and a nice bit of editing so that the next sentence read 'The only thing I have to worry about is where my next cock is coming from!'.

As if that wasn't bad enough, the unravelling of my disastrous so-called love life continued overleaf. But this time, the narrator of the gossip was someone I didn't know at all. At least, I didn't recognise Shelly without the Waltons' dress she habitually wore to dinner. The *Sun* had her pictured in a fringed Western bikini.

'British Bobbitt's love slave begged me to help him

escape!' screeched the headline. I skimmed quickly through the story as though that might make it hurt less. 'Charming computer expert Baxter made love to me beneath the Caribbean moon while psycho Harris slept off massive booze binge.'

'Where do they drag them up from?' Emma asked. She had been reading over my shoulder. 'I mean, who are they kidding? When did Jeremy have time to get it on with her? You told me you were holed up in your love nest all week.'

'If only,' I sighed. 'There was just one night. One night when I had too many margaritas and had to be put to bed by eleven. Jeremy told me that he went for a moonlit walk on the sand, but he said that he went all alone.'

Emma's face grew serious for a moment but then she forced a smile back onto her lips. 'In which case he probably was on his own. This is made up, obviously.'

'I wish I was so sure.' I remembered how frosty Shelly had become towards me after that drunken night. I had assumed that it was just because of her inherent prudishness and dislike of puke, but now I knew differently. And as I read on, I knew for sure that she was telling the truth.

'He told me that he loved me in Polish,' the girl wrote. 'Many men on holiday try to seduce the girls they meet, but this time I thought it was different. This time I thought it was true love. If only we could get rid of his evil girlfriend.'

'He told me that he loved me in Polish too!' I whined.

'Oh, Ali,' Emma wrapped her arms around me and

stroked my hair. 'Oh, Ali, I should never have shown you this. I thought we could have a laugh about it. I thought that it would be a pack of press lies that we could tear to pieces to make you feel better.'

'How could Jeremy do this to me?'

'I don't know,' said Emma. 'I mean, normally I'd say it's just the way men are, but I still can't quite get my head around it. When you came back from Antigua, I thought I had never seen a man so much in love as Jeremy appeared to be with you.'

'It wasn't me,' I said sadly. 'It was the freebie holiday and the nice big cheque.'

'Don't think like that.'

'What did I do to deserve this? It's bad enough that he's been running around with Candida, but Shelly too?'

'Oh, Ali,' Emma sighed.

'I can't stand this,' I told her suddenly. 'I'm going out for a walk.'

I got up and shrugged on my coat. 'Don't wait up.'

'Ali!' Emma chased me to the front door. 'Ali, where are you going? Don't you dare go anywhere near the canal. He isn't worth it, you know. Nobody's worth throwing away your life for.'

'I'm not going to top myself,' I shouted back cheerily. 'I'm just going to buy some fags.'

Out of town shopping had done for the corner shop in our town so I had quite a walk ahead of me. The only place open within half a mile of our house was the all night garage by the end of the dual carriageway. As each of the little local businesses folded, they seemed to have been incorporated into the nasty neon warehouse of a shop behind the petrol pumps. At least at the twenty-four-hour garage you could get just about everything except the kitchen sink. But you could send a fax to order one of those if you needed to.

'Twenty Marlboros,' I muttered to the girl behind the desk.

The girl didn't even look up from her copy of the *Sun*, which, to my distress, was open at that page. She reached down the fags from the shelf behind her and placed them in front of me.

'How much?' I asked.

'Two sixty nine,' she muttered gracelessly.

I reached into my pocket and pulled out my change. Not very impressive. I figured that I had about three pounds, but when I actually counted it out, I discovered that I actually had only two pounds fifty and an assortment of Antiguan small coins. The girl was still reading her paper, tracing the lines with her finger so that she didn't lose her place while she mouthed the words. I shoved all the coins I had down in front of her, said thanks and turned to leave.

I was almost off the forecourt when the commotion started.

'It's her! It's that psycho out the paper!' someone was shrieking. 'She's trying to run off without paying.'

Next thing I knew, the air was filled with a fair old cacophony of sirens. The cashier had set off the emergency bell and I was being bodily lifted from my feet by two men that I would far rather have had protecting my body than apprehending it.

'Hey, what do you think you're doing?' I shouted, as they marched me back to the garage, across a forecourt full of gawpers, with my feet kicking the air as if I was some kind of cartoon baddie who had just tried to rob a Wild West bank in Toon Town.

'I've called the police,' the cashier told the men breathlessly. 'They say they'll be here any minute. They said we shouldn't try to approach her in case she's armed.'

'Armed? What on earth are you talking about?' I protested. 'I'm not armed, you idiots. I just came out for a packet of fags, not a fight. When the police get here I'll have them arrest the pair of you for GBH,' I warned my burly captors. 'You're hurting my wrists.'

The men laughed. ''Fraid you'll have to put up with it, darlin',' the bigger one said. 'I think the police will agree that we're only using the kind of force necessary to apprehend the likes of you. You psycho.'

'Yeah,' said the smaller one. Though he was a good foot shorter than his mate, he had a meaner look, like a Pit Bull fresh from a fight with a badger. 'Women like you give my missus ideas.'

'Good ones by the look of you,' I told him.

''Ere, you shut your mouth,' said Mr Pit-Bull. 'Or I'll shut it for you.'

Thank God the police arrived just then.

'What's all this about?'

It was Inspector Heath, one of the men who had arrested me when I got back from holiday, flanked by two other policemen in the full riot gear get-up. I wondered if that was because they had got the call from a garage, or because they were coming for me.

'Alison Harris,' Inspector Heath said in his schoolteacher's voice. 'What on earth have you been getting up to now?'

'Nothing!' I protested.

'Yeah, right,' said the cashier sarcastically. 'She tried to rob me, she did. These kind gentlemen stepped in to prevent any violence.'

'I did not try to rob her!'

'Alison, you'll have a chance to speak down at the station,' Inspector Heath warned me. Then he turned to the cashier, 'Ms . . . Adams,' he read her badge. 'I'll have to take a statement.'

Meanwhile, I was bundled roughly into a police car for the second time that month.

'You again!' said the driver.

'Watch it,' I warned him. 'I'm armed.'

Immediately, the two officers flanking me prepared to attack.

'Don't worry,' I told them. 'It's only a tube of Bonjela. I've got an ulcer from all this stress.'

'Don't joke with us, Alison,' the driver said seriously. 'These men are highly trained weapons in themselves.'

I took a good look at them. Both thirty-something. Both with the kind of paunches that would give a woman in the seventh month of pregnancy cause for concern. And I thought that the coffee and donuts thing only happened in New York.

Mr Wagstaff was waiting for me when we arrived at the station. Not because he'd hurried there to be with me, you understand. He was visiting the bloke with the *Titanic* tattoo who had just been caught in the Mayor's flowerbeds with an armful of rare Royal Worcester.

Mr Wagstaff shook his head pitifully when he saw me. 'What did I tell you about keeping out of trouble?'

'I am not in trouble. I got some Antiguan and English coins mixed up, that's all.'

'You need a good spanking you do,' said my solicitor. I made a mental note to ask for legal aid and another duty solicitor as soon as I got the chance. 'Alison, I can't defend you if you don't try to defend yourself. I've heard reports that you've been calling the chief witness for the prosecution.'

'Who?'

'Mr Whitworth.'

'I never did.'

'Next time, before you dial his number, remember to dial 141.'

This time it was Emma who came to fetch me from the police station. I had made Inspector Heath swear that he wouldn't tell my Mum that I had been in again, even though the situation had been rectified quite calmly. Inspector Heath told the cashier that she should have given me the opportunity to rectify my mistake with the foreign coins. Apparently she hadn't dared ask me because of the hard-drinking, violent image of me she had got from the tabloids.

I was allowed to exit the station from a back door since a hack from the local paper was hanging around in reception, tipped off by one of the cashier's lardy heroes, no doubt. I had been lucky so far that the press hadn't been camping outside my door, since they seemed far more concerned with getting a quote about Candida from the Baxters. Anyway, I ducked down in the back seat while Emma drove past the front of the station like a bat out of hell, so fast in fact, that I half expected a dozen bobbies to pile out of the station door and arrest us for speeding. What a great way to round off the evening that could have been.

'Perhaps you should get out of town for a while?' Emma suggested that evening. 'Go to Wales or somewhere like that. Somewhere where no-one will recognise your face.'

'Too late for that,' I told her sadly. 'Hiding myself away is what I should have done the first time David chucked me. That way I wouldn't have been here and vulnerable when Lisa went on her bloody self-assertiveness course in Hastings and I'd never even have met flaming Jeremy Baxter.'

'No good wishing you could turn the clock back,' said Emma helpfully.

'Didn't anyone ever tell you not to say things like that to dangerous criminals?'

'Anyway, since you've been out,' Emma continued blithely, 'I've been thinking about ways you can earn money to pay off the money you owe *Complete Woman*. The papers are interested in this case, right? So you should tell your side of the story to one of them, in return for some nice hard cash.'

'Nice idea, but I'm kind of under a court order at the moment, darling.'

'Does that stop you from selling your story?'

'Since I'm doing my very best not to get banged up for the next five years, I guess it probably does.'

'What about close friends of yours? What if someone told your story for you?'

'Like who?'

Emma shrugged.

'I don't know. But I wasn't thinking of volunteering myself,' she added quickly. 'Ashley would just die with embarrassment. Someone in your family perhaps?'

'What? Like one of my sisters? They wouldn't piss on me if I was on fire.'

'There's got to be someone who can help tell your side of the story.'

'No-one I can think of,' I muttered. 'Just forget about it.'

Though in fact, at that very moment, someone very closely related to me indeed was telling all.

CHAPTER FORTY-SIX

'That's it. I don't care if she does write us out of the will. She's betrayed our family!' screamed my Mum. 'My own mother. Seventy-two years old and just look at her, lying on that chaise lounge thingy in a see-through negligee like she's bloody well got something to show off about.'

'I dunno. Hope I've inherited her legs,' said Jo, treading on very thin ice.

'I can't believe she said all this rubbish,' Mum continued as I stared in horror at my half-dressed grandmother and Jo scanned through the text.

'My hot-headed granddaughter gets it all from me,' said glamorous granny Renee Marlene.

'I didn't know Marlene was her surname,' Jane chipped in.

'It bloody isn't,' said Mum. 'That was the name she used when she thought she had a chance of making it big as a cabaret singer in the working men's clubs. I've never been so humiliated in all my life,' she continued.

'Join the club,' said I.

'Well if she thinks she's keeping the money she

earned from this filth, she's got another think coming. Get your coat, Ali. We're going round that home right now to sort this out.'

When we got to Daisy Knoll retirement home, it was pretty easy to find out where Gran was. She hadn't exactly gone into hiding since her tabloid debut. No, far from it. She was sitting in the best chair in the day room, surrounded by dribbling admirers. I know, the men in there were always dribbling, but this time they appeared to be dribbling with intent.

'A word, please, Mother,' said Mum, making sure that all Gran's admirers were reminded that she still was a grandma as well as Renee Marlene, star of stage and . . . well, star of the stage at the Royal British Legion club. Once. When the comedian they'd actually booked had to go home with food poisoning. 'Where's the money?'

'See? Didn't I tell you,' Gran said sadly to one of her companions. 'They don't care about me. It's all about money. They just want me out of the way so they can spend their inheritance.'

'I'm not talking about our bloody inheritance,' Mum snapped. 'You've sold just about everything you ever had anyway. I'm talking about the newspapers, Mother. Where's the money from that?'

'I didn't get any,' Gran replied indignantly.

'You liar, they must have paid you something for betraying your own flesh and blood.'

'They didn't. I said I didn't want anything. I wasn't going to do it at all, but the young man said I might have a career ahead of me as a model. He said I could keep the photos he took, for my portfolio.'

'A model,' Mum sneered. 'For what, for heaven's sake? For the dinosaur models in the sequel to *The Lost World*.'

'He said that there's a growing demand for women of a certain age.'

'By that they mean girls who are twenty-seven or twenty-eight,' I explained patiently. 'Not seventy-two, Gran.'

'You're just jealous, both of you,' Gran spat. 'You wish it had been you on them pages.'

'But it was me, Gran, don't you see?' I protested. 'You talked about my love life to the press.'

'Love life, pah! That's a laugh. I had to make most of it up.'

'Well, I wish you hadn't bothered. I'm awaiting trial for indecent assault, Gran. This kind of publicity is the last thing I need.'

One of the residents, who had been dragging himself nearer the fracas on his Zimmer frame, got one of his legs tangled up in a knitting bag then and went arse over tit into someone else's thousand-piece jigsaw.

'Look what you've done,' said Gran, to distract me from my argument.

'I wasn't anywhere near him.'

'So? He was trying to leave the room because you were shouting at me.'

'I wasn't shouting,' I said, trying to keep my voice down.

'It was peaceful in here before you two came in shouting the odds. Can't you see we're all old people here? We need our peace and quiet.'

'Don't try and change the subject,' my mother interrupted. 'You've betrayed the family.'

'The family! Ha! You only bother with me because you want to know what's in my will. Well, I'll put you out of your misery, Josephine. I've left it all to your sister. Every last penny. Because when she comes round here she acts like she's pleased to see me. The only person in your family who's ever pleased to see me is the dog.'

A murmur of agreement rustled around the room.

'That's probably because the dog likes to sniff things that are decaying, you rotten old bag,' said Mum.

My mouth dropped open.

'I'll tell you why my sister always looks so happy to see you – it's because she only has to see you twice a year. She doesn't get you every single bloody day of the week, week in week out, moaning on about your varicose veins and your itchy piles . . .'

'I do not have piles,' said Gran, going crimson in front of her admirers.

'You certainly do. And then there's your bloody bedsores and your uncontrollable wind . . . Do you want me to go on? Embarrassing, isn't it? Having all your secrets revealed in public. And that's what it was like this morning when our Ali opened the newspaper to find two whole pages of you going on about her love life. You can keep your fucking inheritance, because as far as I'm concerned, that's not the kind of behaviour I want associated with my family at all.'

With that, Mum turned and stalked out of the day room, leaving the entire collection of Daisy Knoll residents on the verge of a communal coronary.

'She doesn't mean it, Gran,' I said comfortingly, patting the old woman on her Frank Usher clad arm. 'She'll probably run back in and apologise in a minute.' But there was no sign of that. Through the huge windows of the day room I could see Mum getting into her car and firing up the engine. Then, with a face like thunder, she sat and waited for me to join her.

Let me explain my latest predicament. Even though Gran had betrayed me to the press, choosing sides at this point was like having to choose between Genghis Khan and Vlad the Impaler. I knew that when Gran and Mum made it up again, which they would do soon enough, I would come off badly, whatever, as the cause of their row.

So I flipped a mental coin and decided to go with Mum. Besides, I actually still had to tell her that the rumours she had heard about Candida and Jeremy were true and that the wedding was off.

'I'm writing you out of the will too!' Gran shouted from the day-room patio as I legged it to the car park.

'Great,' I said, slipping into the car beside Mum. 'At this rate, there'll be no-one left on my side. Even Jeremy's deserted me . . .'

'What?'

Never tell your mother that a wedding's off when she's pulling out onto a dual carriageway.

'The swine!' my mother was still shrieking uncontrollably as she pulled the car into a handbrake turn in the driveway of our family home, having narrowly avoided a twenty-car pile-up while she cursed the Baxter family name in seven different languages. 'How could he do this to you?'

'I've been asking myself exactly the same question.'

'You were supposed to be getting married.'

'That doesn't seem to mean anything much these days,' I said ruefully.

'I didn't ever like him,' said my father later from behind the shield of his newspaper.

'What?' asked my mother and I.

'I didn't ever like him. Always poncing about talking about how he's head of Eastern Europe and all that and showing off about his fancy car. I could see straight through him the first time he came round.'

Now this was unusual. My father rarely spoke when we girls were in full assassinatory swing, let alone to pass a judgement.

'Well fan-bloody-tastic. Why didn't you say this before?' I asked.

'Didn't think it was my place to. I don't want to interfere.'

'Well I bloody well wish you guys would interfere from time to time,' I said in exasperation. 'You know, before I get engaged to these losers, rather than waiting until I've been dumped to tell me that his eyes were too close together or that he just had a funny way about him that made you know it would all end in tears. Isn't that what parents are for? To stop you from making these ruinous mistakes?'

Dad retreated behind his paper again.

My mother, for once, leapt to his defence. 'Your father's right. We don't want to interfere with these things. When I have told you that I don't like your boyfriends in the past, it only seems to have made you all the more determined to throw yourself after them. What if we'd turned against Jeremy and he had gone and married you after all . . . He might not have let us see the grandchildren.'

'You mean you would have let me marry the wrong man?'

'If that was what you wanted, dear. Cup of tea?'

'I don't think a cup of tea is going to make things seem any better right now, Mum,' I told her.

'You're right. After the day I've had, I need half a bottle of whisky and a good punch up. That'd release some pent-up frustration.'

'I think I'd better go home,' I said.

'No, Ali. Not yet. Your father and I have got something important to tell you,' Mum announced.

'I think I'll just check on the shed,' said Dad. Strangely Mum nodded her consent.

'What is it? I thought you said that you and Dad had something important to tell me.'

'I think I can speak for your father.'

I waited to hear the latest piece of terrible news that would push me over the edge from purgatory into oblivion. But it didn't come. 'Your father and I have been trying it out. And it doesn't hurt at all.'

'Well, great,' I said, just a little confused. 'That's means you must have been doing it right.'

'No. You don't understand, darling. We've been trying it out with the Hot Stuff Heat Rub. It doesn't hurt at all. Just tingles. Your father and I are respectable people, pillars of the community. And we're prepared to stand up in court and tell the world that Hot Stuff Heat Rub can be part of a healthy and normal sex life.'

I choked on my chocolate hobnob. The idea of my parents having a sex life at all was bad enough. But a healthy and normal one? They had three daughters for heaven's sake!

'What do you say? We want to support you in your time of need, darling.'

'Yes. But Mum . . . I mean, what would the neighbours think.'

'The neighbours? Pah! I've learned a thing or two about neighbours today. And I happen to know for a fact that Mrs Baxter has more than one pair of suspenders in her closet. We're all adults, Alison. People don't just stop having sexual lives once they're married, you know.'

'I thought that was the whole point.'

I prayed that my solicitor would think it was as bad an idea as I did.

'Just stay out of this, Mum,' I said firmly. 'I don't want you or Dad anywhere near the witness stand. I know you're trying to help, but the best thing you can do now is make me a cup of tea and keep clear of the whole situation.'

CHAPTER FORTY-SEVEN

Fat chance.

Later that night, I got a rather distressed phone call from Dad. Turned out that when he got back from the shed, for the first time in his married life he discovered that Mum wasn't waiting in the kitchen to berate him . . . And the reason? It was because his wife was being held in the police cells.

'And your sisters too,' he said forlornly. 'They didn't know I was still in the shed . . . Your sister says that she tried to phone you but you had that silly machine on.'

I played back my answer-machine messages while I got ready to meet Dad at the station to try to bail my family out.

'We're in the clink,' it was my sister Jo. 'And it was all in aid of you, Alison, so you had better get down here pronto and bail us out.'

'What on earth happened?' I asked Dad when I met him on the forecourt of the station.

'Something about a fight. Mrs Baxter and her daughter came round to the house for some reason. I think it was to ask if you could return Jeremy's Giorgio Armani swimming trunks. Well, your mum just saw red and went for her. Pulling her hair out. Scratching and kicking. Jennifer Baxter joined in on her mum's side and after that your sisters had to get involved.'

'But why?'

'To defend your honour,' said Jo proudly, after they had been released with a warning. 'She came round our house accusing you of being a Jezebel, tempting her precious son into marriage with your skimpy bikinis and fancy holidays. She said you wanted to turn him into a sex slave. She read that in the papers. I told her that if you wanted a sex slave you wouldn't have gone for someone with boils on his knob.'

'Thanks, Jo. I'm sure that went down really well.'

'That woman's got a nerve,' said Mum. 'Anyway, as soon as I saw her I knew I was going to hit her, no matter what she said. Always acted like she's too good for the likes of us, she has. She didn't know that I saw her, at my own anniversary party, running her finger along the mantelpiece to check for dust. Well, I told her today, that it's a bit rich her checking my house for dust when she's got a whole built-in wardrobe complex full of skeletons. That daughter of hers was done for shoplifting once, you know.'

Jo smirked. 'Wasn't Ali . . .'

Mum slapped her. Jane sat silently in the back of the car, between my mother and Jo, the hard-nuts.

'I'm not happy about all this violence,' she said solemnly.

'Oh, Jane,' Jo exclaimed. 'But you were the best of us all. When it looked like Mum and I were going to lose the fight, Jane leapt in with one of those fancy martial arts kicks of hers and took the pair of them out in one move.' Jo did a little demonstration with her hands. 'I always knew that prancing about in the garden every morning would come in handy one day.'

'It's meant to be a peaceful art,' Jane explained. 'It's supposed to be a form of meditation, not used like boxing.'

'Whatever,' said Jo.

'Listen,' I said, turning round to the three of them in the back seat. 'I'm very grateful for what you did today, standing up for me and all that but, in future, I think that you guys had better keep your noses clean. Don't rise to provocation. This kind of behaviour isn't going to do my court appearance much good. Do you want David's barrister to be able to say that I come from an unruly and dangerous family?'

'Yeah,' said Jo.

'Button it,' said my mother. 'Ali's right. There's to be no more fighting, girls. Though I have to say that I'm very proud of you both and if any woman deserved to lose a handful of hair this afternoon it's that Baxter woman. I'll give her dust on the mantelpiece.'

'Wild Women in Worcester Street' was the headline in the local paper. And most of the nationals.

I warned my family that I didn't ever want to hear the name Baxter again.

Emma, unfortunately, didn't seem to think that the embargo extended to her. I was reading the report of my family's disgrace in the street outside their house when Emma came home, looking breathless and excited.

'I've got something to tell you,' she panted as she unpacked her shopping bags. 'How are you feeling today?'

'Terrible. Devastated.'

'Oh, well perhaps I shouldn't say.'

'Say what?'

'Doesn't matter.'

'No, Emma, you can't do this to me. You can't come home and say you've got something to tell me and then not tell me anything.'

'OK. Sit down.'

'I am sitting down,' I said irritably.

'OK. I'll sit down.' She took a chair opposite me. 'No. I can't say.'

'You've got to say, or I'll kill you.'

'I think I've worked out how that photo of you with no top on got into the papers.'

I leaned forward on the table, to better hear what she was about to come out with next.

'Jeremy is back in town.'

'What? He's supposed to be in Poland.'

'He must be on holiday.'

I felt suddenly boiling hot, then freezing cold. I put my hand to my mouth to pre-empt a wave of nausea. 'He's back. Do you think he's heard about my trial date? Do you think he's left Candida and come back to support me through it?' The clouds in my mind parted for just a second.

Emma reached across the table to take my hand. I knew then that the news was bad.

'Er . . . He wasn't on his own, Ali. That's the whole point. He was with someone else. A woman.'

'His mum? His sister?'

'Uh-uh,' she shook her head. 'Remember that skinny posh tart from the magazine?'

'Amanda?'

'That's the one. It was her. Hanging on his arm like a handbag she was.'

'You're pulling my leg. You don't even know what she looks like.'

'Unfortunately, I do. I read *Complete Woman* once. Under duress. It was definitely her. I followed them into Betty's.'

'Emma, tell me you didn't?'

'Well, it's a free country and I wanted a cup of tea. I sat right behind them. Jeremy didn't notice me, or if he did, he pretended not to. Though I guess I have changed a bit since February.'

Emma had recently dyed her hair pale blue to mark the beginning of summer.

'Anyway, I couldn't help overhearing their conversation. Jeremy was talking so loud, seemed like he wanted the whole place to hear. So, she said to him, "I've got you two weeks in Florida lined up for next month. They loved the pictures. And I'm going to be the stylist." Then he said, "Oh darling, how clever of you. Who's the photographer? I don't want any old snapper now that I'm going to be the new Boss boy."'

'Boss boy?'

'Model. For the Boss campaign. God, Ali, it made me sick. They went on for half an hour about how good his portfolio was and how he would soon be putting the wind up that bloke who posed in nothing but a tie for Versace. Jeremy Baxter, a model. Can you imagine it?'

'Unfortunately, yes.'

'Anyway, don't you see what I'm getting at?'

'You're breaking my heart again.'

'It's obvious that Jeremy and Amanda are swapping favours. He got the fashion shoot. She got . . .'

'Him?'

'No. She probably wants him, sure. But he's shacked up with Candida and what Amanda got instead was an exclusive on Britain's Lorena Bobbitt. You wanted to know how they got pictures of you in your bikini? It's simple. Jeremy supplied them.'

'No.'

'Makes perfect sense to me, Ali.'

'But he was so upset about that. Apparently he told his mother that the newspaper coverage was the reason why he couldn't marry me.'

'A great excuse. But now you know the source of the press leak, you can get him into some real trouble. I think it's contempt of court, or something. Aren't you happy?'

'He wouldn't have done that to me,' I murmured, shaking my head.

'Ali, I could tell from the very first time I met him that he was the kind of bloke who would do anything to anybody. I mean, even while I was watching him with Amanda in Betty's. She was gazing at him like a sodding puppy but he didn't even look at her. He kept looking at his reflection in the mirror, like he can't believe his luck that he's grown out of those boils. Then, when Amanda went to the ladies, Jeremy slipped the waitress his phone number. He is pond scum. A pimple on the face of humanity.' Emma was enjoying herself.

'I wish you hadn't told me about all this,' I said sadly.

'He deserves to be punished.'

'I don't know if I can face even seeing him again.'

'He hated Fattypuss.'

I needed no better reason to blow the whistle.

'I'll call Mr Wagstaff in the morning.'

I had another prison dream that night. This time was worse than ever. As I was led from the van to the heavy, iron-studded oak gates that would separate me from the folks that I loved for eternity, with no time off for good behaviour, I couldn't help noticing that the prison warden awaiting me had a familiar pink gingham handbag hanging incongruously from her uniform-clad shoulder.

'Well, well, well. Miss Alison Harris,' she said, in an oddly un-English drawl. 'I've been waiting for you.'

She tilted back the brim of her prison officer's hat and grinned at me through horrible cerise-painted lips.

'Take her to the blancmange room!' ordered Shelly, America's Most Romantic Woman and Holloway prison's newest and most terrifying guard. I was led away, screaming like a stuck pig, to a fate far worse than lesbian frottage in the showers.

The guards took off my handcuffs when we arrived at the pink-painted door. They pushed me against it so that I could look through the tiny barred window and see what lay ahead.

'But I'll drown,' I pleaded. The room was six feet deep in strawberry whip.

'Ha ha ha. Do you think I care?' asked Shelly. 'After what you did to me?'

'But I didn't mean to do anything to you, Shelly. I liked you. I thought you'd win the competition. Honest I did.'

'Silence, bitch. You stole what was rightfully mine.'

She bound my mouth shut with a heart-patterned bandanna.

'Now, I'm willing to give you just one more chance. Somewhere inside that room is a golden envelope. And inside that golden envelope is a golden key. The golden key that opens this door, Alison. Find that key and you're outta here. Don't find it and you'll rot in jelly!!! Ha ha ha!!'

Then she opened the door to the cell and pushed me inside, with barely time to take a deep breath before I was plunged into the gunk.

Blindly, I thrashed about me. I had done it before, I told myself. I could do it again. I could find the envelope. I could escape from this hell. I just had to be methodical. Only methodical ain't easy when you're blinded by pink goo.

My hands grabbed at nothing. My ears and throat were filling with strawberry gunk. My nose was plugged shut with blancmange. I was never going to find it. I was going to die there. At least my sentence wouldn't be long. I would soon be with the angels in heaven . . .

'For God's sake, Ali. Wake up!!'

Emma shook me awake. I was strangling myself in my own duvet.

'I heard you knock the lamp off your bedside table,' she explained. 'You were holding your breath or something. Your face was going blue.'

I sat up in bed, panting and clutching at my throat. Emma passed me a glass of water.

'I was going to throw this over your face if you didn't come round,' she explained.

I took the drink gratefully and swallowed it in three greedy gulps. 'I'm finished, Emma,' I told her when I was able to speak again. 'If I have to go to prison I'll die of fear. If the nightmares I'm having already don't do for me first, that is.'

'I don't know what to say,' said Emma, unusually lost for words. 'I told you things couldn't get any worse last week, but they did.'

'Yeah. Thanks.'

Fattypuss, who was never the type of cat who actually went out hunting at nights, slinked out from behind the curtain and insinuated herself onto my knees.

'How did I get into this much trouble just by loving someone? Loving someone shouldn't be so very hard.'

'Yeah, but you didn't just love a someone,' Emma pointed out. 'You loved a man.'

'I'll never make that mistake again. Next time, I'll fall for a woman. I'll meet a lovely girl and become a lesbian. That'll be much better.'

Emma took her arm from around my shoulders again and began to fiddle with the tassels on the edge of one of my cushions.

'I don't think you can become a lesbian just like that,' she told me.

It would be a matter of hours before I got my chance to ask.

CHAPTER FORTY-EIGHT

A phone call in the middle of the night. Emma answered, thankfully. But it was for me. I knocked Mickey Mouse off the bedside table when I went to pick up the receiver, and it took another two minutes of fumbling about in the dark to find him again. I wondered who on earth it could be. Perhaps it was Jeremy, calling to tell me that he had made a terrible mistake. It was usually calls from abroad that came at such ridiculous times. Well, I was right on that count.

'Ali?' asked an unfamiliar voice.

'Who is this?'

'It's me. It's Loretta. Remember?'

'Loretta?' For a moment I didn't remember her at all. Then her bleached blonde crop and dungarees came into my mind's eye and I felt a stab of pain. After all, it was her boss who had marked the beginning of the end for me and Jeremy.

'Alison? Are you OK over there? I've been hearing terrible things. I hear you might be going to prison. I want to help you, Alison. You saved my life in Antigua. Now I want to do anything I can to put things right.'

'It's too late. How can I get Jeremy back? He's fallen for the most beautiful woman in the world, and to make things worse, she reciprocates the way he's feeling. I've lost him forever.'

'I'm not talking about Jeremy any more.'

'Well, what else could you help me with?'

'With your court case.'

'How do you know about that?' I asked in surprise.

'It's in just about every newspaper I pick up. Besides Jeremy tells Candida everything and Candida sometimes tells me. Indecent assault on a member of the oppressive sex, eh?'

'I didn't do it. Well, I did do it, but I certainly didn't mean to hurt him as much as he claims I did.'

'I know. And the chances are, you didn't. Listen, I want you to meet a friend of mine. She's in London this week, at the feminist film festival.'

'Is she a lawyer?' I asked.

'No, she's a film producer.'

'What help will that be to me?'

'I don't know yet. But she's usually pretty good at finding solutions to this kind of shit.'

'In America maybe. But I'm going to be tried by a British jury, Loretta. A life sentence is pretty much a forgone conclusion for what they think I've done.'

'Just see what you think of her. I'll get her to call you tomorrow. Look, I can't tell you how sad I am for you, Alison. You're a truly decent person. If Candida hadn't crossed your path, perhaps Jeremy would still be there to support you. Not that the support of a man is worth anything. Anything at all.'

I was almost ready to agree with her.

'We sisters have got to stick together. I'll try and make it over for your case, if it gets as far as court.'

'Oh, it will.'

'We'll see. Candida gave me my marching orders again this morning, and with a bit of luck, she'll have meant it. And if it's any consolation, I don't think that Jeremy is going to last too long with her either.'

'You mean that?'

'He made some kind of comment about her ingrowing toenail. And if there's one thing I've learned, it's that goddesses don't like to learn about their own imperfections. Listen, I've got to go. Sounds like she's on thc warpath.'

In the background I could just about make out Candida shouting, 'Where's my fucking conditioner?'

'Listen, you'll love my friend,' Loretta whispered. 'She'll be with you tomorrow morning.'

'Loretta, I . . .'

But she was gone. She hadn't even told me the name of the woman I was expecting.

'What was that about?' Emma asked.

'Someone I met on holiday. Wants to offer her services.'

'In what way?'

'Exactly.'

CHAPTER FORTY-NINE

'Hi. I'm Marcie Guttenberg, feminist film producer,' said the woman who had muscled her way into our kitchen, pushing her specs a little further up her nose as she settled into a chair with Fattypuss on her lap. She was Loretta's friend, she told me, then she announced, 'I'm here on behalf of the Sapphire Society.'

'Sapphire Society?'

'Yeah. It was meant to be Sapphic but the totally phallocentric guy at the printers thought that we'd made a spelling mistake. Anyway, I'm here to shake you warmly by the hand on behalf of all my sisters in the worldwide feminist and lesbian communities.'

She took my hand in both of hers and made like she was making a margarita.

'What you have done, Alison, is strike a blow for womankind. You have triumphed over the oppressor.'

'Not yet I haven't,' I said grimly. 'Court case starts in two days.'

'Ah, yes. Your sisters send their best wishes for that. But in our hearts, whatever the outcome, we want you to know that as far as womankind is concerned you have already won. You have shown the women of this misogynistic world that passivity is not the only way forward. That closing your eyes and putting up with male oppression is not the only way to get through this patriarchal life.'

'I have?'

'You have. And we salute you.'

She started searching in her Prada rucksack for something.

'We'd like you to have this,' she said. 'To bring you luck in court. And to remind you of what it is we are fighting for.'

I accepted the little package with a weak smile.

'What is it?'

'You'll see.'

I opened the box up and there before me was a little golden penis on a stick-pin. It looked pretty floppy.

'It's for your lapel. Like a shrivelled head,' Marcie explained. 'A trophy.'

'Uh, thanks.'

'Here's to the next one.' She tapped her clenched fist against my own in a gesture of solidarity.

'I don't think there will be an opportunity for a next one.'

'That's the spirit,' Marcie laughed. 'You know, you have a beautiful cat.'

Marcie Guttenberg was difficult to get rid of. Fattypuss adored her. And Emma didn't help things by bringing cup after cup of camomile tea to slake the woman's thirst. She must have needed it, talking nineteen to the dozen as she regaled us with stories of revenge and mutilation that even Emma's bloodthirsty doctor Ashley might have found hard to stomach.

'You mean she tied it to a helium balloon,' said Emma. 'That's fantastic. I would have loved to have seen his face.'

'Yeah. And he didn't ever get it back. Lorena Bobbitt should never have told those policemen where she threw that dick she cut off. I mean, the man's now making a living as a porn star, for heaven's sake! If that doesn't defeat the object of the whole damn exercise, I really don't know what does.'

'Do you think David will become a porn star?' Emma asked me mischievously.

'Don't be ridiculous,' I said. 'He can't act.'

'Honey,' said Marcie. 'For a feminist icon, you've sure led a sheltered life. I bet he's already getting himself an agent. We have to stop this rot, Alison. We've got to help you win this case.'

'I have a solicitor for that,' I said.

'I think I can come up with something a little more effective,' Marcie assured me.

After Marcie left, Emma ticked me off for being a little less than positive about her visit.

'She wants to help you. She's a nice woman.'

'She a nutter. And her patchouli oil perfume gave Fattypuss a sneezing fit.'

'I liked her.'

'You would.'

'You could do worse than have her as an ally.'

'Emma, what's she going to do? You know as well as I do, that for all her pontificating today she will probably just stand outside the courthouse with an obscene banner and make the jury think that I'm not just a jilted lover but an insane anti-man terrorist. I think it's best that I stay as far out of her way as possible. If she calls again, you'll have to pretend that we've had the number changed or something. I don't know why Loretta put her in touch with me. I mean, with respect, what use are all the good wishes in the world to me right now?'

'It's nice to know you've touched someone's heart. And don't you like the brooch she gave you?'

'Put it this way, I'm not going to be wearing it in court.'

But what does one wear when one has to appear in court on a charge of indecent assault occasioning actual bodily harm? As I stood in front of my wardrobe, the night before my case was due to begin, I wished that I still had the services of Amanda from *Complete Woman* to call upon, but no doubt it was against *Complete Woman* policy to dress the accused.

'Emma, what do you think?'

'Wear that little black number you got for your twenty-first birthday party,' she suggested. 'After all, it could be those nasty blue trouser suits for you from here on.'

'Thanks very much. That's just what I need. My own best friend doesn't think I'm going to get off.'

Emma jumped up from the bed to hug me. 'Oh, Ali! I do think you're going to get off. Honest I do. I wouldn't joke about the blue trouser suits if I thought that you were actually going to have to wear them.'

'Right.'

'Wear your navy blue suit,' she said more helpfully.

'Your job interview one. That looks smart and respectable. No one would ever believe you were capable of atrocities against mankind in that outfit.'

I pulled the suit out of my wardrobe and hung it from the door.

'And the pale green shirt,' Emma continued. 'Bit of colour but not too much. Stylish yet serious. And what are you going to do with your hair?'

'Hadn't even thought about it.' It was true, I hadn't thought about my hair for a very long time. The ends of my grown out layers were still bleached and frayed from those distant calm-before-the-storm weeks in Antigua.

'You need to wear it up,' Emma decided. 'I'll do it for you. French plait, I think. Not as severe as a bun but still very neat and tidy. I'll try it now.'

She began to fiddle about with my hair and suddenly I couldn't stop myself from crying. Big fat tears rolled down my cheeks and plopped onto the green shirt which I still held in my hands.

'Hey,' Emma said. 'Watch the shirt, you've got to wear that tomorrow.' Then, with slightly more concern, she asked, 'What is it, Ali? Can I help?'

I shook my head and sniffed violently. 'No. No-one can help. Oh, Emma, I feel like I'm Mary Queen of Scots. I feel like it's my last night on earth and I'm preparing to have my head chopped off in the morning.'

'Ali,' said Emma seriously. 'You mustn't think like that. Tomorrow will be fine. You will be magnificent. No jury in the world will convict you of assaulting David once they've actually met the swine. I give you my guarantee that you will get off. Once you tell them how David dumped you on Christmas Day, while you were languishing in hospital, and then tried to worm his way back into your life for a freebie holiday, they'll be lining up to stone him to death.'

'It was like that, wasn't it? I mean, he did deserve it, didn't he? I didn't really just overreact, did I?'

'Of course you didn't. And everyone will see that. Look, you're the one who's been wronged around here, darling. Besides, David looks far shiftier than you do.'

CHAPTER FIFTY

But we hadn't reckoned on David having access to the style gurus of the world. According to the grapevine, all the top men's magazines were falling over themselves to dress him for the trial and when I was brought into the court, in handcuffs, I was almost confused by how fabulous he looked. I got the kind of feeling that I thought I would have walking down the aisle to marry him. Only this time, he definitely wasn't setting out to make an honest woman of me.

The case was called Regina v. Harris

'All rise!'

Now this was the bit I remembered from the movies. The judge swept in, swathed in robes and topped off with a spectacular wig. I was so taken in by the outfit that it took me a moment to register that my judge, Judge Olivia Maxwell-Harris, was a woman. When she took her seat, she was so short that her head and shoulders were barely visible over the top of the bench.

The clerk of the court, a little man whose robes had obviously been made for his big brother then called me into the dock.

'You're going to be arraigned,' my barrister warned me. It sounded painful and I was shaking like a leaf as I took the stand.

'Alison Harris,' the clerk began. 'It is charged that on the 2nd February 1998, you did indecently assault Mr David Whitworth with the intention of causing him Actual Bodily Harm. How say you, are you guilty, or not guilty?'

'Not guilty,' I squeaked. I heard a stifled whoop from my sister Jo in the public gallery. The clerk nodded and I was allowed to stand down again.

Then the jury was sworn in, one by one. I tried to gauge their mood and moral preferences while Mr Tailforth, my barrister (Mr Wagstaff would have been way out of his depth – no kidding) briefed me on how I should behave. There were seven men and five women. That was bad news for a start, since I figured that any red-blooded man would almost certainly find himself on David's side of the fence. Of the women, only two looked like the kind of girls I could be friends with. One of them, an older lady with thick bi-focal lenses in her glasses, was staring at me as if she needed to remember every line on my face for a neighbourhood watch drawing she would produce when she got home. Of course, it might just have been her bi-focals that were giving me that impression.

'I think we have a sympathetic jury,' said Mr Tailforth.

'You're kidding,' I snorted. 'At least ten of them look as though they agree with hanging for bicycle theft.'

'Alison. Try not to let your opinions be reflected in your behaviour today. I don't want to see a sulky schoolgirl up there when you take the stand. I want to see a confident, mature young woman who played a practical joke that went just a tiny bit too far.'

'When will I have to get up there and say what really happened?' I asked him.

'We may not even get our chance today,' Mr Tailforth warned me. 'The prosecution goes first. And they're calling four witnesses.'

'Four? I don't get it. Who?'

My barrister shushed me as David's man stood up to present the case.

'Ladies and Gentlemen of the jury, what we have here is a clear case of indecent assault with intent to cause malicious wounding. We will be calling four witnesses.'

'Four,' I said again. 'I don't understand. There were only two of us in the room that day. Where has he got four witnesses from?'

Mr Tailforth flicked through the details of the prosecution's case in the notes before him. 'Medical opinion, character witnesses.'

I scanned the rows of seats behind the prosecution to see who they might be calling. There was a shuffly looking bloke in an ill-fitting suit. Probably the medical expert, I thought hopefully. I wouldn't have trusted him with Fattypuss.

But there, in the row behind him, my eyes met with someone I hadn't expected to see. Andrew. Andrew from Marvin's dinner party. Andrew, the one who got 'stung'.

'Oh my God,' I murmured. 'They can't be calling him. This is the end.'

'The defence calls upon David Whitworth to take the stand.'

David swaggered – no, make that limped – up to the stand and took the oath. As he envoked Almighty God, I waited for the thunderbolt, but none came. Then his lawyer started the ball rolling in David's favour by asking him if he felt comfortable standing up in the stand – in view of his physical condition.

My brief rolled his eyes.

'So, Mr Whitworth, perhaps you would like to begin by describing your relationship with the defendant, Ms Harris. How you met, perhaps? The early days of your relationship. And its subsequent deterioration to the sorry position we find ourselves in today.'

'Well,' David cleared his throat. 'When I met Miss Harris, I was actually already engaged to someone else, Miss Brown. I didn't want to get involved with someone else, but Alison, I mean Miss Harris, had a powerful personality even then and I felt that I was being coerced into something that I didn't really want to do.'

Then followed the story of our first blissful months together. Only I barely recognised them. I had pursued him rabidly, according to this tale. There was no mention of the fact that I had refused to see David for a week, to give him a chance to sort out his feelings for Lisa. Instead I was portrayed as horribly jealous, waiting for him every lunchtime outside his place of work. No mention of the fact that he wanted me to be there. That he said I made the best sandwiches . . .

And our engagement? I had asked him to marry me of course. No mention of the night that he went down on one knee in the middle of the park and shoved a ring-pull onto my finger in lieu of the real thing. David made himself sound like a man truly beleaguered. Hounded by a girl with only one thing on her mind.

'And the first hint that Miss Harris might have a dangerously violent temper?' asked David's barrister.

'Leading question,' shouted Mr Tailforth, jumping to his feet but the judge simply waved him back down.

'That came late last year,' said David solemnly, 'when Miss Harris visited my family home while I was out for the evening. My elder brother, Police Inspector Barry Whitworth, was at home on his own. Miss Harris forced herself upon him and, when she was spurned, she tried to use violence to get her own way.'

'You didn't tell me about this,' whispered my brief urgently.

'Well, I'm sorry if I didn't manage to pre-empt all of David's lies,' I hissed back.

'We'll hear more about that from Police Inspector Whitworth himself later on,' said David's brief, smugly. 'And finally, if you could describe, in your own words, the morning in question. Saturday, the second of February . . .'

Now this was a work of pure fiction.

I had begged David to go to Antigua with me, he claimed. He had refused. He didn't want to be unfaithful to Lisa. I had accosted him in the hallway, where he stood fully clothed, and shoved my hand down his trousers to rub on the Hot Stuff Heat Rub.

'That's rubbish!' I cried.

Judge Maxwell-Harris told me to be silent.

'That's rubbish,' I said, more quietly this time. 'He didn't even say that he was in bed with me at the time.'

'We'll get our chance in a minute,' Mr Tailforth promised me.

But it wasn't to be. When David's brief had finished with him, Mr Tailforth got up again and rearranged his gown, in readiness to begin his questioning. At which point, David decided to have an asthma attack, which quite clearly wouldn't pass until all danger of cross-examination was over.

David was led away and Mr Tailforth returned to me, sighing with exasperation.

'History of asthma, your ex-fiancé?'

I shrugged.

'I didn't think so.'

Inspector Barry Whitworth came next.

I had never seen him looking so smart. When I had seen Barry in his uniform in the past, it was usually after a hard night playing darts at the station while on cell duty. Then he would be sweaty and his special unthrottleable tie would hang loose. Now, taking the stand with his official hat tucked under his arm, he looked like Tom Cruise playing the good naval officer in that movie about a court marshal. Mr Tailforth looked at me and winced.

Barry took the oath like a pro, and under the prosecution brief's careful guidance, he poured forth a story of that night at his house, which even almost convinced me, though it was quite unlike the truth.

'Unusually for me,' Barry continued. 'I made a very poor judgement of character when I met Miss Alison Harris for the first time. That night, I faced a battle for my virtue far worse than any fight I have ever had with one of the more traditional criminal fraternity.'

'Thank you Detective Constable Whitworth,' said his brief, turning to the jury and smiling as he did so. 'That will be all.'

Mr Tailforth got to his feet and cleared his throat dramatically.

'I'll tear this one to pieces,' he promised.

'Detective Constable Whitworth,' Mr Tailforth began. 'You are six feet tall are you not?'

Barry straightened himself up, 'Six foot one as a matter of fact.'

'And looking at you from here, I'd say that you must weigh in the region of fifteen stones.'

Barry sucked in his stomach.

'Fourteen and a half.'

'While my client here is only five feet two inches in height and weighs, at most, nine and a half stone.'

I sucked in my stomach but managed to resist the urge to inform the members of the jury that I was nine stone max on a bad day.

Mr Tailforth stepped from the box and put his fingers to his chin in a gesture of thought. 'A grown man,' he thought aloud, 'of six feet in height, who arrests dangerous and often armed criminals for a living, scared of a girl almost a foot shorter than him and just about half his weight?'

A couple of the girls in the jury shook their heads.

'I didn't think so. I rest my case.'

'Is that all you're going to say to him?' I asked, when Mr Tailforth swaggered back to me again.

'Trust me. It was enough to get them thinking.'

I wasn't so sure.

CHAPTER FIFTY-ONE

Up in the public gallery, Marvin, Emma and Ashley shared Marks and Spencers' salmon sarnies as they watched the events unfold. When I looked up at Emma she had an expression on her face which reflected the way I thought the case was going. That is to say badly. When she caught sight of me looking at her, however, she gave me a cheery thumbs-up.

I was sure that David and his brother had charmed the jury. After all they had shown all the traits that attracted me to the Whitworth brothers in the first place. They had been quiet-spoken, charming, eloquent. They looked like the kind of boys you wanted to take home to your mum. And Tailforth had done little to squash the image they created.

Who was on next?

'The prosecution calls Miss Lisa Brown.'

My nemesis.

Lisa looked different from usual. She was wearing a pretty little pink number with huge gilt buttons which made her look almost fragile. Her hair, usually scraped back so severely before, was in a looser style now, with little tendrils that hung down upon her cheeks. It was clear that someone had been advising her to be a little less *Dynasty* when she took the stand.

And she very nearly didn't, tripping over the step into the box in her new high heels.

'Lisa Brown,' the witness squeaked when the clerk of the court asked her name.

'Do you promise to swear by Almighty God to tell the truth, the whole truth and nothing but the truth, so help you God?'

'I do,' Lisa squeaked again.

'Tell me about your relationship with Mr Whitworth, Miss Brown. From the beginning, when you first met each other.'

Lisa beamed stiffly. 'We met at a Deacon Blue concert,' she began. 'My brother introduced David to me because he had known him since school. My brother was very careful about introducing me to people,' she added for good measure. 'He was always looking out for me. Making sure that I didn't get mixed up with the wrong kind of people. I knew straightaway that David wasn't from the wrong sort of people though.'

'And what are the wrong sort of people.'

'Oh, you know. The kind of people who use violence against someone else when they don't get their own way.'

'And David wasn't like that.'

'Oh no. David was the gentlest man I had ever met. He loves children and animals,' she added. 'We had the perfect relationship. We liked the same things. We shared the same values. We had the same vision of our future lives.'

We had the same script-writer, I added mentally to her list.

'I thought that we would be happy forever,' she continued. 'We were going to get married and start a family,' Lisa suddenly dabbed at her eyes.

I glanced over to the jury and noticed to my horror that the three women in the front row were sniffing discreetly too. The men were just transfixed by Lisa's tragically heaving bosom.

'I had chosen the dress and booked the reception. Everything was in place. Then I had to go to Bosnia. On a mercy mission. For the orphaned children. It was part of my civilian police worker training.'

Mr Tailforth groaned.

'I was going to be away for a long time. Two weeks. David gets lonely. I rang home every day, but you know, it's just not the same as being together. That's when she made her move. She saw that David was lonely with me away and made advances to him while I was helping the poor orphans of the former Yugoslavia.'

'She being?'

'Alison Harris.'

'And would Miss Harris have known that you were away from Brindlesham?'

'Oh, yes. My mission was well-documented in the local press.'

I couldn't help wondering where Lisa picked up a word like documented. Crown Court seemed to bring out the verbosity in everyone.

'When I got back, it was as if David had been replaced by someone else. As if someone had sucked out the soul that I had been in love with and put another, less loving soul in its place.'

How tragically familiar this sounded.

'It was as if she had put a spell on him. But since then, I realise that it was probably just that he was afraid of her violent temper.'

'Objection, your honour!' shouted Mr Tailforth.

'Overruled,' said Maxwell-Harris.

'It took him two whole years to find the strength to come back to me,' Lisa concluded. 'And that was when she decided to maim him for life.'

'Your witness,' said David's brief. But before Tailforth had even made it to the stand, Lisa was having a funny turn.

'I think I'm going to faint,' she murmured. 'It's ever so hot in here.'

'This is ridiculous!' Tailforth shouted.

'I think my witness needs medical attention,' David's brief replied.

The clerk of the court rushed forward to help Lisa down from the stand. She smiled bravely at him for the benefit of the jury, then rushed to the back of the court, where she was congratulated by my one-time future mother-in-law.

And the case was adjourned for the night.

'This is terrible,' I groaned when Tailforth and I were alone in the hallway. 'You haven't even had a chance to talk to any of his witnesses properly.'

'No,' said Mr Tailforth. 'It's not all lost. We've still got our turn to come. Now that he's started to bring your good character into disrepute, we can let all hell loose against him. Who do you know who can dish the dirt? Ex-girlfriends?'

'The only girlfriend he ever had before me as far as I know is Lisa, and as you saw this afternoon, she's very much on the prosecution side of this case.'

Mr Tailforth scratched his moustache. 'Mmm. And you're sure he's never made a pass at any of your friends?'

'They haven't told me if he did.'

'Harder than I thought. Looks like we're just going to have to go on what you say. Were there ever any incidents when Mr Whitworth was violent towards you?'

'Well, he once threw a golf club in my direction when he lost a game of crazy golf at Brighton, but I don't think there was any malicious intent.'

'What do you mean?' said Tailforth, eyes brightening. 'The man sounds like a nutter.'

'And he once threw my cat down the stairs . . . after she'd peed on his new suede jacket.'

'Perfect. Animal abuse. It's well-known that that kind of behaviour leads to worse things later on.'

'What could be worse than throwing a cat down the stairs?' I asked. Though in fact David had only thrown Fattypuss from the second stair of the flight, and she had landed perfectly and hissed at him for good measure upon doing so.

'Will that do it?'

'It might help. English juries are terribly uptight about animals.'

'But apart from that?'

'I don't know. But I should get a chance to question both David and Lisa Brown properly tomorrow. I'll find the hole in their story if there is one and pick the case to pieces.'

'You sound optimistic.'

'Never say die.'

I gave him a weak thumbs-up sign as he left me to go home.

CHAPTER FIFTY-TWO

But behind the brave face I was about as optimistic as Eeyore. 'I'm finished,' I told my family that night. 'I know I am. This is my last night of freedom.'

My Mum threw a comforting arm around my shoulder but I could tell that she was feeling the same way. By the time David had finished giving his evidence he had had a halo floating over his head. I, by contrast, was fast becoming a Jezebel. A sluttish whore with unnatural physical urges that manifested themselves in violence if I didn't get enough sex. When I took the stand the next day I knew I would have a very long and difficult task ahead of me. It would be like having to crawl back into the jury's good books over the Sahara desert.

'They'll know that he was lying,' said Mum. 'When they hear your side of the story, they'll soon realise that he was exaggerating. Ooh, I'd like to get up there myself and give evidence about all the times he made my favourite daughter cry.'

Jo and Jane looked up in surprise.

'Oh, you're all my favourite daughters,' Mum back-pedalled. 'But Alison needs all our support now. What did you think of the trial today, Jo?'

'I thought that David came out of it looking like a saint and smelling of Chanel number five. That's made of roses,' she added, in case we didn't get the reference.

'Thank you,' said Mum, before Jo could do any more damage. 'Jane?'

'Well, he did give a pretty good show,' Jane said carefully. 'But I think that the women in the jury will have seen through the facade. Especially that asthma attack . . . And Lisa's fainting fit. I mean . . .'

'Great,' I said forlornly. 'But that still leaves me with a minority on my side. I'm going down. You guys had better be prepared to smuggle loads of cigarettes in when you come to visit me at Holloway.'

'Cool,' said Jo. 'I've always wanted to go inside there and have a good look round. Who do they keep locked up there, Ali? Anyone famous?'

'No-one I want to mix with. Oh, Jo, I should have listened to you when you said that his eyes were too small. You were right. David Whitworth is mean. Why does he want to put me through all this? He's got someone new. I'm left with nothing.'

'Yeah,' said Jo. 'But he has lost the use of his dick.'

'So he says. And if he hadn't already lost the use of it, I would be first in line to chop it off,' said Mum.

My father, who had been attempting to read a newspaper throughout this conversation winced.

I went to bed early. Fattypuss padded across the room and lay on my chest in a gesture of solidarity. I had made

Emma promise that she would look after the cat well while I was inside and not try to put her on a diet in an attempt to make her look less like Bagpuss and more like the Siamese cross she was supposed to be.

'I wish I could take you with me,' I told the purring flea-bag.

But since the British prison system doesn't even allow babies to stay with their mothers after the age of six months or so, I figured that being allowed to take my geriatric cat with me was probably out of the question.

The only thing that could save me now was for someone on the prosecution's team of witnesses to drive home via Damascus.

CHAPTER FIFTY-THREE

After a frugal last breakfast of Marmite on toast, I hugged Fattypuss almost to death while I waited for the taxi to take me to court.

I wore my sentencing outfit. The little black dress that had last seen an airing at my twenty-first birthday. It was probably a bit over the top, with its diamante straps, but I wanted everyone to remember me looking my best. Needless to say, by the time I got to the door, I had rather spoiled the effect by getting myself covered in cat hairs.

Emma was unusually quiet as we were driven into town. My parents, who were already waiting for me in the court lobby, looked as if they hadn't slept too well themselves. My sisters hugged me and I was sure that even Jo had a tear in her eye.

'Don't kiss me,' said my mother. 'It makes me think you're not coming back.'

'We've got to say goodbye properly,' I insisted. 'Just in case I don't.'

'Can nothing persuade that wicked man to drop this case against you?' said my mother loudly as David's brief shuffled into court. 'He's depriving a mother of her eldest daughter. Her comfort and joy. Her grandmother may not even live to see the day when she's released.'

'Sssh,' I hissed. 'How is Gran anyway?'

'She's talking to us again,' said Jo. 'She rang up to say she's got a photo shoot for *Golden World* today. That's that old biddies' magazine they give away free at the post office. Otherwise she'd be here.'

'She wishes you luck,' Jane added.

We were interrupted by Mr Tailforth then. 'Feeling ready to win?' he asked me. My whole family looked at him in disgust. This was no time for jokes. The only possible positive outcome as far as we could see was that I would be sent to an open prison.

Mr Tailforth motioned me forward. As he did, my mother threw me her jacket. 'Put that on,' she said. 'If you've got any chance at all, you don't want to blow it with those stupid diamante straps.'

Inside the courtroom, David's brief lolled in his chair as though he had already won. Barry and Lisa sat behind him. Lisa was dressed in another Jackie O-style suit. In tangerine this time. She was wringing a paper handkerchief into shreds between her hands. She looked nervous. Her cheeks were surprisingly white instead of their usual Lancome pink. I suppose she was concerned about her cross-examination which should be the first task of the morning. She couldn't exactly fake another fainting fit.

'Are you going to be especially cruel to her?' I asked Mr Tailforth hopefully.

Soon the room was silenced again as Judge Maxwell-Harris swept majestically to her chair. She addressed the room briefly, recapping the previous day's events and reminding the jury what was expected of them. We were to pick up where we had left off. That is, Lisa was to go back on the stand.

When she was called, she got to her feet about as steadily as a new-born giraffe. For a moment, she seemed utterly unable to take a step forward. I saw David's mother give her a smile of encouragement. She looked at her as if she had never seen her before in her life. Then she made a terrible snorting sound as she held back a sob.

'What on earth is the matter with her?' I asked Mr Tailforth as Lisa had to be helped back into the stand by a pair of ushers.

'I have a reputation for harshness,' said Tailforth slightly proudly.

'I can't do it,' Lisa squeaked in the direction of David's barrister. 'I don't want to take the stand again. You've got to let me go.'

David's barrister seemed to be considering the possibility of asking whether Lisa could stand back down, but Judge Maxwell-Harris was determined that no more time should be wasted by sickly prosecution witnesses.

I looked up at the gallery. Emma and Marvin were leaning forward over the barrier to get the best view. Ashley was there too. Perhaps David's barrister would call for a doctor and Ashley would be able to prove that Lisa was just pretending to be sick so that she didn't have to tell the truth about me and her boyfriend.

'Miss Brown,' said Judge Maxwell-Harris impatiently. 'Do you think you might be ready in a moment?'

Lisa put her hand to her mouth as if she was about to be sick.

'Please don't let her get away with this,' I begged God. 'Please make her be well enough to be cross-examined.'

The clerk stepped forward with the bible.

'I can't do it!' Lisa pleaded.

'Miss Brown,' said Judge Maxwell-Harris, 'you will do it or I will have you charged with contempt of court.'

Talking of which, I spotted another familiar face in the gallery. Amanda from *Complete Woman* was there with her reporter's notebook, unaware that the wheels of justice would soon be rolling in her direction, even if I had to put them in motion from behind a locked door.

With a sob in her voice, Lisa finally took the oath. She was allowed to sit, but she certainly wasn't going to be allowed to stand down until some questions had been answered.

Tailforth drew himself to his full height and cleared his throat like a man who meant business. As he walked up to the stand, Lisa's eyes widened in fear. But I wanted her to suffer, because it seemed certain that I soon would be.

'Miss Brown,' Tailforth began. 'Yesterday, we all heard the heart-warming story of your relationship with Mr Whitworth up until the night of February 2nd 1998. Today, I would like to ask you about more recent aspects of your relationship with the prosecution's chief witness. And much as I hate to dwell on the sordid, I'd like to start with the last time you had sexual relations . . .'

'What?'

'The last time you had sex,' Mr Tailforth repeated. 'Or would you prefer, the last time you "made love"?'

Trembling so much that it was making her dangly earrings shake, Lisa started to speak.

'We had a wonderful love life,' she began, barely audibly.

'Speak up, Miss Brown,' said the Judge.

'I wanted to save myself for marriage, you understand, but once David and I became engaged, I decided that it wasn't worth waiting any longer.'

'You say that you "had" a wonderful love life. When did things change, Miss Brown?'

When I came into the equation of course.

'But when you got back together following the end of Mr Whitworth's engagement to Miss Harris, things were as they once had been again?'

Lisa nodded.

'Until?'

'The 2nd of February,' she whispered.

'And ever since that morning, when he claims that he was assaulted by Miss Harris, would you confirm that Mr Whitworth has been unable to maintain a satisfactory erection?'

Lisa's face contorted at the question. The 64 million dollar question. Had he, or had he not, been able to function 'as a man' since that terrible night, Tailforth repeated.

'Er . . .' said Lisa.

'Perhaps you don't understand the question,' said Mr Tailforth cruelly. 'Has Mr Whitworth been able to make love to you, as a man?'

I held my breath as I waited for her to speak. Time seemed to expand like a rubber band. Up in the gallery, my family and friends were in danger of tumbling into the courtroom as they craned to hear Lisa answer.

'He has,' Lisa blurted suddenly.

David's brief's face registered a look of surprise. So did mine.

Mr Tailforth continued calmly, sensing that Lisa was about to crack. 'You mean that he has been unable to maintain an erection?'

'No,' Lisa squeaked. 'I mean that he has been able to function as a man since February the 2nd.'

David's brief shook his head and groaned, 'No!'

'But surely you mean in a day to day, "going about his business" sense,' Mr Tailforth persisted. 'And not in the bedroom.'

'No. I mean in the bedroom. David Whitworth made love to me the very night after he last saw Ali Harris.'

'With penetration.'

'With everything.'

A snigger went around the public gallery.

'He's been lying to you,' she blubbed. 'He wasn't hurt by what Alison did to him at all. It didn't affect his performance one little bit. In fact, when David's brother told him that he might be able to sue Alison and get some money out of the whole fiasco, David's performance in the bedroom went through the roof, if you know what I mean. And not just with me.'

David's brief's eyes pleaded with her to shut up. Beside him, David's solicitor was scribbling frantically, a smile he couldn't suppress stretching across his face like a slice of melon despite the fact that their case was crumbling like year-old Parmesan.

'We're home and dry,' Tailforth's assistant scribbled on a note to me. And though the jury still had to make its mind up, I felt the muscles in the back of my neck begin to unknot themselves as Lisa continued to spill the beans all across the courtroom floor.

'A week after Alison put Hot Stuff Heat Rub on David Whitworth's penis, we were still having it away up to three times a night.' She allowed herself a small, proud smile. 'All that stuff about him not being able to get an erection because of the psychological damage she had inflicted on him was a lie. There was no damage at all. In fact, when he went to the doctor for an examination to be used in the evidence against her, he got me to rub some Hot Stuff Heat Rub on him in the car just before we got to the surgery. So that he would be walking funny when he went in.'

David's mother gasped and I heard a thud as she fell off her chair in shock. But Lisa hadn't finished.

'When I got home from work last night there was a strange car parked outside our house. It was a flash car. A big Mercedes or something. Now I don't know anyone with a car like that, so I assumed it belonged to David's solicitor. I let myself into the house, but David wasn't in the kitchen, or in the living room. He was upstairs. And when I walked in on him, there was a woman between his knees on the bedroom floor. She was giving him a blow-job!'

I clapped my hand to my mouth to stifle a laugh.

David's mother screamed.

'I pulled her away by the hair. She didn't half scream. And then I slapped her around the face. Who the fuck are you? I asked her. David told me to let go of her hair but half of it had just come off in my hand anyway. It was one of those false bits. A hair-piece. The whole of her plait. Well, as you can imagine, I chased her out of my house and back into her car, which was the Merc of course. When I got back in, I expected David to at least say that he was sorry or something, but he didn't. He was in a complete rage.'

'A complete rage?' mused Tailforth. 'And why was that?'

'He said I'd probably just ruined his career.'

'His career? What? His career in insurance?' asked Tailforth in mock innocence.

'No, his career as a film star. In pornography.'

There was a moment's silence while it sank in.

Then David's mother had to be carried out of the court.

'As a porn star?' Tailforth asked once more.

'Yes,' Lisa sobbed. 'That woman. That false-haired tart giving my boyfriend a blow-job, was the owner of this country's biggest porn production company. Stiff Upper Lip Films, David said it was called. She said she wanted to make a film about David's life story. She was giving him a blow-job to make sure his performance on celluloid wouldn't be a flop!'

There was an explosion of laughter from the gallery. And soon the whole courtroom had erupted in a fit of the giggles.

'What's so funny?' asked Lisa innocently.

Judge Maxwell-Harris restored order at once.

'Hardly the actions of a man who has been living in fear of what a jealous woman might do to his nether regions, don't you think?' asked Mr Tailforth.

'That's right,' Lisa sniffed. 'So much for him being too frightened to let anyone touch him. David Whitworth asked me to lie for him, your honour. But I can't lie when the good name of my fellow woman is at stake.'

A huge cheer went up from the gallery then. It was the Sapphire Society of course. And all around them, the crowd began a hesitant round of applause. Lisa looked towards me for reassurance that she had done the right thing. I managed just a tiny thumbs-up. David's sister was on her feet.

'She's lying. She's not telling the truth,' David's sister protested.

Judge Maxwell-Harris made her sit back down.

'It's the real story,' Lisa concluded. 'David Whitworth is a lying bastard and you can tell him from me,' she addressed Judge Maxwell-Harris, as she ripped off her diamond ring, 'that our impending engagement is off.'

With that, Lisa left the witness box without being dismissed, and ran out of the courtroom as fast as her orange kitten-heeled shoes would carry her.

'It's all right,' said Mr Tailforth, when someone made a move to retrieve her. 'I don't think there's any need for further questioning.'

I looked up at the gallery. A row of friendly faces giving me the thumbs-up. Even Amanda looked faintly pleased with the way things were turning out. Though I was far from through ruining her life.

'We would like to request a recess,' said David's brief.

I bet they would, I thought.

CHAPTER FIFTY-FOUR

So, our destruction of David's case was pretty straightforward after that. The golden boy, seduced by an evil ex-girlfriend, tragically injured while trying to escape her wicked clutches, was all but forgotten. Here was the truth. A hopeless womaniser, driven by the promise of a free holiday, drove his shy, insecure ex-fiancée to try to salvage the last vestiges of her self-esteem by an action she did not for one moment think would have a permanent effect. And the fact was that it quite obviously hadn't.

As great moments go, I don't think I'll ever have such a great moment in my life again as the moment when David Whitworth realised that he had been rumbled. My heart soared when Judge Maxwell-Harris agreed with Mr Tailforth's submission that there simply was no case to answer and, giving David a hard stare, told him that he was guilty of a very serious crime indeed, blackening the good name and reputation of a fine, upstanding young pillar of the community like me. I could have punched the air when she warned him that further action might be forthcoming. The case was dismissed and I stepped out into the sunshine feeling elated in a subdued kind of way, as though I had spent the past few months behind bars anyway.

Marcie Guttenberg and her Sapphire gang were waiting on the step, carrying banners which proclaimed me to be a heroine for womankind. Champagne corks popped and I was drenched in the froth that was sprayed all over my head. Flowers were pressed into my hands from all sides and into Lisa's hands too. After all, it was her brave testimony that had really saved the day.

As it turned out, my real knight in shining armour was Marcie Guttenberg. As the Sapphire Sisters bore me aloft to the car park, Marcie explained that not every lesbian fitted in with my narrow stereotype and that the glamorous owner of Stiff Upper Lip Films was one of them. It was Marcie who had arranged for David to be in the throes of that kind sister's enticement just at the moment when Lisa walked through the door. At Loretta's prompting, of course. I shouldn't forget her.

'Who are these strange women?' Lisa asked me, as she wiped a smudge of Marcie's militant red lipstick from her cheek.

'They're the Sapphire Sisters,' I told her. 'And I think that kiss means you're an honorary member.'

'I don't know if I want to be,' she said. Same old Lisa creeping through.

'Make the most of the adoration, I say,' I told her. 'Don't think either of us are going to be getting much action from the opposite sex for a while.'

'Oh, why did this have to happen to me?' Lisa suddenly broke down. 'I loved him. He loved me. We were going to get married. What am I going to do now?'

'Join my club,' I told her. 'We'll get over this together, Lisa. I promise you we will.'

My parents were throwing a party in my honour that night. The outside of their house was decorated with a huge banner proclaiming, 'Ali Harris is innocent'. Spelt properly this time. The neighbours were all crammed into the sitting room in the dark, pretending not to be there when Dad brought me to the house. Unfortunately, I'd seen the lights go out as we pulled into the drive so I wasn't able to act too surprised.

'Everybody's here,' said Mum, as she ushered me into the party. The neighbours (minus the Baxters, of course) and all the maiden aunts. Gran had her place of honour in Mum's usual seat and they were wearing matching dresses. Yellow meringues this time.

'Do you get it?' Mum asked, as she stood beside her own mother and they were joined by my sisters in a pair of sunshine coloured lycra inner tubes. 'It's yellow. For "tie a yellow ribbon round the old oak tree". It was in case you went down. To let you know that we wouldn't forget you whatever.'

I couldn't help crying then. Big tears of relief rolled down my cheeks and plopped into the gin and tonic which had been helpfully placed in my hand.

'We knew you didn't do it, Alison,' said Mr Griffiths slapping me heartily between the shoulders. 'I mean, you always acted like a lady whenever you took me home. Even when I was drunk enough to be taken advantage of. I would have given evidence in support of your honour you know . . .'

'Thank you,' I told him. 'Thank you all.'

What a laugh it was, though. The room was full of people who might never have spoken to my mother again if I hadn't got off that charge.

'Let's have a sing-song,' piped up Gran. 'What about Jailhouse Rock?'

I had hoped that my notoriety would start to fade as soon as the court case was over, but during the rest of that week I had calls from publicity agents all over the country. Did I want to speak to the nation on *Radio Middle of Nowhere*? Would I give an interview to the *Out in the Sticks Somewhere Times*? There were bigger things too, though. I got one call from an American film producer. For a moment I could see myself as the next Sandra Bullock, then he explained the plot of his film. It was a recreation of my last night with David of course, and the film, which would go straight to video, would never be seen in our local Blockbuster.

I turned everything down. Celebrity is one thing, but notoriety is another and I didn't need it. Besides, I had another court case coming up. And if I jumped on the publicity bandwagon, it might seem a bit odd that I was pressing charges against Jeremy Baxter and the assistant editor of *Complete Woman* for libel, defamation and slander.

Yes, I'm afraid poor old Jeremy's luck was going from bad to worse. I was staying out of his way, pending the libel hearing, but Emma did see him once more. In the accident unit of the hospital where this sorry saga started.

Emma was waiting for Ashley to stitch up some drunken Saturday night fighter so that they could catch the last showing of *Blade Runner: Director's Cut*. (Yep, Ashley and Emma have passed the six month mark though she still doesn't understand blood pressure.) Jeremy was waiting to be seen by someone like Ashley.

He wasn't alone. He was with Amanda. The *Complete Woman* herself. He had a tablecloth wrapped around his head like a makeshift turban. Emma didn't like to walk straight up to them to find out what was wrong, but the nurse on reception had no qualms about informing her that the chap in the tablecloth turban had had a terrible accident with his hair. Turned out that, while having a romantic dinner with the queen of twee, Jeremy had leaned too close to the candles on the centre of the table and set his heavily lacquered fringe on fire. Went up like a nylon nightie apparently and things only got worse when Amanda reached for her brandy to put the conflagration out. Heaven only knew if Jeremy's luscious locks would ever grow back again. Whatever, it seems like Jeremy's catwalk career is going to be on hold for a while, unless Jean Paul Gaultier decides that the singed look is in. And Candida went straight back to Vadim.

Meanwhile, David has gone underground. His brother Barry is awaiting disciplinary action for inciting a sibling to waste police time. Lisa got a transfer to the switchboard of another police station and has started to go out with a fireman. She didn't reply to the Sapphire Sisters' request that she be the cover girl of their summer newsletter.

And me? Well, you'll be amused to learn that I got an interesting letter through the post this morning. It was from *You and Your Kitty*. Don't ask me why I did it, but I entered their Christmas anagram competition while I was languishing in hospital all those months ago and this morning I discovered that I've won a lifetime's supply of cat food.

Not much use to me anymore. You see, Fattypuss upped and died last week. One minute she was hissing at Berkeley from the safety of my bedroom windowsill, the next she was the wrong way up in the flowerbed. First time ever she hadn't managed to land on her feet.

So, all tears and sniffles, I called the editorial assistant at *You and Your Kitty* and told her the sorry news. The whole office was distraught, as you can probably imagine.

'I don't think I can bring myself to get another cat just yet,' I sniffled. 'Any chance I could just have the money?'

There wasn't of course. Three hundred and sixty five tins of gourmet guppy goulash were already cluttering up the *You and Your Kitty* office as they waited to be collected. And that's how I ended up spending the afternoon at the local cat sanctuary. I thought I would donate the food to them, you see.

I had to wait a long time to be attended to. There was a kitty emergency going on in the back. Apparently, some cat that had been dumped on the doorstep only two days before, was suddenly having kittens. It happens quite a lot, explained the receptionist. People dumping cats that are just about to give birth.

'What will happen to them?' I asked.

'Well, if they're cute they'll be homed. If they're not,' she made a slashing motion across her throat.

'You won't really have them put down?' I said in horror.

'More mouths to feed,' she said.

Anyway, while I was waiting to be attended to, a rather wonderful looking man walked into the waiting room. He was handsome in a gentleman farmer kind of way, all strong curly hair and great thick forearms. He marched up to the desk and attracted the receptionist's full attention straightaway. I'm afraid I just couldn't help straining to hear what he was about.

'I've given her 50 mils,' he said. 'She should sleep for another three hours or so.'

'Oh, thank you Doctor Farringdon. Mrs Smith will be ever so relieved that you managed to save her Miffy.'

Mr Gorgeous got ten extra lushness points instantly when I discovered that he was a vet! As Julie had once pointed out, even more money than a doctor and no scantily-clad female patients to catch his eye. Unless he had a thing about sheep, of course.

'Right, I'm off,' he told the receptionist. 'If you need me, give me a call.'

Then he turned to leave. But on the way out he caught my eye and hesitated by the door.

'Do I know you?' he asked.

I straightened myself up automatically.

'Me? Are you talking to me?' I squeaked.

'Yes. I'm sure I know you from somewhere.'

I shrugged. 'Well, I guess I have been pretty prominent in the local paper of late.'

'No. That's not it. I never read that rag. I'm sure we

met at a party. Or a club? Yes, a club! Now it's all coming back to me.'

And it was coming back to me too. The girls' night out I couldn't escape from. The gorilla. The epileptic fit. The handsome vet who sorted everything out.

'You ran off.'

'I didn't mean to.'

'I was worried about you. You looked like you were in shock.'

'I was embarrassed. But I've learned first aid since, as a result,' I added in an attempt to save face. It was almost true.

'That's good. I thought you looked kind.'

'Oh, she's very kind,' interrupted the receptionist. 'Look what she just brought in.' She showed Dr Farringdon the cat food.

'I won a competition, but my cat just died,' I explained.

'What a coincidence. One of my patients has just had five kittens. Want to take one home?'

'Oh no,' I said. 'I mean what about the vet's bill.'

Dr Farringdon smiled. 'We could come to some arrangement. In The Rotunda? Over a beer.'

I'm going to wear that red Versace dress . . .

Well, you didn't expect me to end up with Black Beauty?